Warrior's
Lady

Also by Madeline Baker
in Large Print:

Lakota Love Song
Reckless Embrace

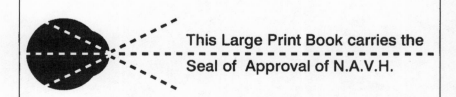

Warrior's
Lady

Madeline Baker

WHEELER PUBLISHING

Copyright © 1993 by Madeline Baker

Published in 2003 by arrangement with Leisure Books,
a division of Dorchester Publishing Co., Inc.

Wheeler Large Print Romance.

The text of this Large Print edition is unabridged.
Other aspects of the book may vary from the original edition.

Set in 16 pt. Plantin by Al Chase.

Printed in the United States on permanent paper.

Library of Congress Cataloging-in-Publication Data

Baker, Madeline.
    Warrior's lady / Madeline Baker.
      p. cm.
    ISBN 1-58724-507-8 (lg. print : hc : alk. paper)
    1. Indians of North America — Fiction. 2. Women pioneers
— Fiction. 3. Large type books. I. Title.
PS3552.A4318W37 2003
   813'.54—dc22   2003053792

To Bronwyn Wolfe,
Candis Terry, and Heather Cullman —
Three new friends
who share my love for writing,
The Last of the Mohicans,
and *The Phantom of the Opera*.

Thanks for your friendship and laughter.

As the Founder/CEO of NAVH, the only national health agency solely devoted to those who, although not totally blind, have an eye disease which could lead to serious visual impairment, I am pleased to recognize Thorndike Press* as one of the leading publishers in the large print field.

Founded in 1954 in San Francisco to prepare large print textbooks for partially seeing children, NAVH became the pioneer and standard setting agency in the preparation of large type.

Today, those publishers who meet our standards carry the prestigious "Seal of Approval" indicating high quality large print. We are delighted that Thorndike Press is one of the publishers whose titles meet these standards. We are also pleased to recognize the significant contribution Thorndike Press is making in this important and growing field.

Lorraine H. Marchi, L.H.D.
Founder/CEO
NAVH

* Thorndike Press encompasses the following imprints: Thorndike, Wheeler, Walker and Large Pr int Press.

Chapter One

Spread-eagled on the iron-bound table, he tugged against the thick leather straps that bound his wrists and ankles, writhing helplessly in an agony of blood and bruised flesh.

Weeping, cursing, he fell back, his eyes closing beneath the heavy black hood that covered his head and neck like a shroud. The material, created by an ancient Fen wizard, seemed to breathe with a life of its own, allowing air to circulate while completely shutting out the light.

Where was she?

He clenched his fists against the pain splintering through him, praying that he would bleed to death before she came, praying that she would hurry. He could feel the blood dripping from his wounds. Worse than the pain was the weakness, the weariness that engulfed him after defying the Gamesmen for hours at a time.

He yearned toward the mists of darkness that swirled just out of reach, knowing that death was the only escape from the hell in which he lived, knowing that, as much as he desired it, death would not find him this day.

His tormentors were skilled at the Games, carefully inflicting wounds that were at times exquisitely painful but never fatal.

Once, he had tried to starve himself, but the giants who guarded the dungeon had forced the bitter yellow gruel down his throat by means of a thin hollow tube. It had been a most disagreeable experience, one he had no wish to repeat.

On those days when he was left alone in his cell, imprisoned in the darkness of his cell rather than the eternal darkness of the hood, he longed for the Maje's presence, the sound of her voice. He ached for the touch of her hands, wondering what it would be like to feel her touch, not in healing, but in love.

He was on the brink of oblivion when he heard the door open, and she was there. He could feel her presence beside him, the empathy radiating from her in golden waves of tranquility that were almost tangible.

He felt the warmth of her hands moving toward him and he shook his head violently from side to side. "Don't." His voice was weak, uneven, muffled by the hood.

"I must." Her voice was low and soft.

"No." He opened his eyes, wishing he could see her face just once. "Let me die," he begged. But it was a foolish hope, for his wounds, while painful, were not life-threatening. Still, there was always a possibility that he might bleed to death if she withheld her gift.

"I cannot."

"Please . . ." He forced the word through clenched teeth, hating the weakness that made him plead, the misery and exhaustion that stripped him of his courage, his pride.

"I cannot," she said again, and he seemed to wither before her, as if he'd lost all hope.

And perhaps he had, she thought sadly, but she could not let him die. She was a Maje, a healer. She could not see him suffer and refuse to help.

Slowly, she laid her hands over the bloody wounds in his chest.

The heat suffused him immediately. Wanting only to die, he tried to fight it, to turn it back, but he was defenseless against the strength of her touch. He felt the healing power flow from her hands, heard the harsh rasp of her breath as she absorbed his pain into her own body, amazed that she would willingly do such a thing. And then he remembered she was a prisoner, as he was, compelled to obey or suffer the consequences.

The heat of her touch increased, seeping down through layers of skin and muscle and tissue, filling him with a strange lassitude. His eyes closed. His body relaxed as she placed her hands on his naked flesh, moving slowly, deliberately, from the most serious injury to the least.

Her warmth and vitality flowed into him, healing, revitalizing, and then the pain was gone, and he was whole again.

Whole — to spend another night chained in the darkness, alone.

Whole — to face them again in the morning. He was their toy, an amusement to help wile away the long hours of the dark Hovis winter.

The ancient Games of Skill, originally intended to test the mettle of warriors, had been corrupted, until the Games were no longer a contest of strength and courage, man to man, but a sadistic ritual to see how much a condemned man could endure without breaking. The Games had been outlawed in every province, until the Minister of War and his cronies had decided to reestablish them in the Pavilion, which was located in an abandoned walled city located a league and a half from the king's palace at Heth.

How long had he been here? How long since he'd seen the sun, a friendly face, heard anything but the song of the lash and the sound of his own screams? A month? A year? It seemed a lifetime. The only bright spot in his dismal existence was the fact that they didn't play the Games every day.

And yet, it wasn't the pain of the Games that made him long for the escape of death, it was the loss of his freedom, the constant darkness of the hood, the awful fear that he was gradually losing his identity.

Time and again he repeated his name as he endured the long lonely hours.

He summoned the image of his ancestral home to mind, mentally walking down each long corridor, through each room. He imagined he was riding his war horse across the sun-kissed fields. He recalled the smell of freshly turned earth, the light and heat of a summer day, so different from the constant darkness of the dungeon. . . .

He felt her presence withdraw, felt the coldness that always encompassed him when she left the chamber, leaving him there, alone, in the darkness.

Chapter Two

He was trembling with pain and fatigue when next she went to him.

He wasn't on the table this time, but manacled to the cold stone wall, his arms and legs stretched to the limits of endurance, naked, as always, save for the scant scrap of black cloth carelessly knotted around his loins.

She felt her heart constrict as her gaze moved over him. Even in the darkness, she could see him clearly: his head completely covered by the hood, his lean muscular body covered with burns and welts. Bad as they looked, none of the wounds was fatal, but the Gamesmen were skilled at inflicting pain.

It went against everything she believed in to heal this man, knowing he would have to endure more of the same on the morrow. In any other circumstance, she would have died rather than allow her powers to be used for such a purpose, but her death would not bring an end to his suffering. Indeed, it would only prolong it, for without her gift, he would be left to heal on his own, his body forced to suffer its aches and pains for days instead of hours.

12

She felt his distress even before she touched him. It was not the pain of the flesh that tormented him the most; rather it was the loss of his freedom, the sense of helplessness, of utter hopelessness, that festered in his soul.

She wished she could free him, but she was a prisoner in the Pavilion just as he was, compelled to obey or face the consequences. And she didn't have the courage to defy her captors, to face the awful tortures of which the Gamesmen were masters.

She moved toward him, trying not to care that he was suffering, trying not to think of the pain that would come to her when she placed her hands upon him.

His head jerked up as he sensed her presence. She was here. He blinked back the tears of relief that welled in his eyes, hating himself for his weakness, for craving her touch. But tonight the pain was worse than usual. Tonight they had been unusually creative. Wielding their finely honed knives with infinite skill and care, they had carved pictures on his chest and legs and arms — a war horse here, a two-headed redsnake there, the sharp blades of the Gamesmen piercing his flesh with restraint so that they did little more than break the skin. One had drawn a fair representation of a fire-breathing dragon across his right thigh, and then pressed a glowing chunk of coal against his skin, burning the outer layer of flesh so that smoke seemed to billow from the dragon's mouth.

It had been the searing of his skin, the smell of his own singed flesh, that had provoked his first anguished scream, the threat of being burned again that had made him cry for mercy.

It was what they had been waiting for, the screams, the pleading, that made the Games worthwhile. He had heard one of the Gamesmen howl with victory as he collected his winnings from the other two.

They delighted in his cries. A new Game Piece was drawn at each session to see what response would signal the end of the Game, and then they wagered to see who could first produce the required response, betting large sums of lucre to see who could force him to cry out first, who could make him scream the loudest, the longest. Who could make him beg for mercy. He never knew what reaction they were looking for, which response would bring an end to the Game.

In the beginning, he had screamed at the first cut or the first stroke of the lash, hoping to bring a quick end to the torment, but they had soon cured him of that.

In punishment, they had flogged him unmercifully, then left him to hang by his bound wrists while the blood and the sweat poured from his body. The minutes had gone by, slowly stretching into hours, each hour seeming longer than the last. Pain had wracked him from neck to heel. He had shivered uncontrollably as his tortured muscles screamed for relief.

Hooded, he had waited in the dark, wondering if they would come back, or if they intended to leave him there to die. And while he waited, he recalled every gruesome tale he had ever heard about what went on in the Pavilion.

Even now, he hated himself for his weakness, for submitting to their will, for not dying when he had the chance and thereby putting an end to the misery in which he lived.

But, in the beginning, he hadn't fully realized what kind of life awaited him at their hands. In the beginning, he had wanted only to live, to put an end to the agony that burned through every inch of his flesh. Desperate to end the pain, he would have promised them anything. Only when they had obtained his oath to play the Games their way, his promise to stifle his cries until he could no longer endure whatever torture they saw fit to inflict on him, had they let the Maje come to him. . . .

And now she was here again. Relief washed through him as he felt her nearness, and then her hands were touching him, drawing out the pain, restoring his mutilated flesh. He heard her gasp, felt her hands tremble as his suffering became hers.

He regretted causing her pain.

He hated her for healing him.

He loved her for healing him.

Weary and confused, he closed his eyes, surrendering to her touch, his thoughts wandering toward home. He could see it all so clearly: the rolling green hills, the towering Iswan trees with their brilliant gold and green leaves, the black and white gentlesheep grazing on the flowering hillsides, his war horse, Gabault, racing across the pasture, the sun shining down on the delicate stained glass windows of Greyebridge Castle. . . .

"It is beautiful."

Her voice drew him back to the present. Reluctantly, he opened his eyes to the eternal darkness inside the stifling black hood. "What?"

"It is beautiful. Thy home."

"You've been there?" he asked, and then wondered how she could possibly know where he had been born.

"No."

She gazed at him in astonishment, aware for the first time that she could read his thoughts. It was a talent given to others of her kind, to be able to probe the minds of other people, but she had never been able to discern the thoughts of any but those of her own race. Until now.

16

"I saw it in thy mind," she said, still amazed at her ability to do so. "Rolling hills and a castle of grey stone."

He grunted softly, his heart wrenching with the knowledge that he would never see Greyebridge Castle again.

"Maje," he implored. "Let me die. Can you not see that I yearn for death? Please, let me die."

She wept silent tears at the bitter anguish in his voice. "I cannot. To do as thee asks would cost me my life, and though it is not worth much, I am in no hurry to lose it."

"Forgive me."

For a moment only, she laid her hand over his cloth-covered cheek, wondering what he looked like beneath the hood, wondering if he was dark or fair, old or young, handsome or plain.

For a moment, she thought of lifting the hood so she could see his face, but to do so would only make it harder to remain detached. For now, he was only an entity burdened with pain that she could heal. But if she knew him, his hopes and dreams, the shape of his mouth, the color of his eyes, he would no longer be just a faceless body, but a man, a life.

He let out a sigh as he felt the warmth of her touch through the heavy cloth, felt his throat constrict with unshed tears at her gentleness. Except for those times when she

17

came to heal him, he had not experienced kindness since he had been declared a rebel and sent to the Pavilion. It left him feeling weak and hungry for more.

"She . . ." He did not know her name; always, in his mind, he called her she.

At the sound of his voice, her hand fell away from his cloth-covered cheek and she took a step back. "I must go. I pray they will soon tire of thee and give thee rest."

He shuddered convulsively, not wanting to think about the three who had been there that afternoon, who would come again in a day or two.

Thal, who was so skilled with the longboar knife.

Siid, who loved to play with fire.

Gar, who preferred the long whip made of braided chain and hemp.

Of the nine warriors who came to take a turn at him, these three were the ones he feared most, the ones who stayed the longest, and played the hardest.

"She!" He called for her, but she was already gone, leaving him alone in the long narrow chamber that was always colder and darker without her presence.

Early morning was his only respite from the chains that bound his hands and feet.

Shortly after dawn, one of the Giants who worked at the Pavilion entered his cell and removed the shackles. For two hours, he was left alone, free of any restraint, to eat the tasteless slop that passed for food, to relieve himself in the crude chamber pot in the corner, to prowl the dismal confines of his dark prison, wondering which of the Games his captors would choose to play that day.

Now, sitting on the cold stone floor, he wondered if the King had returned to Heth, if anyone but Rorke knew of his imprisonment in the Pavilion.

Jarrett swore under his breath. His whole trial had been a farce. It was unlawful for a warrior of Jarrett's station to be tried by any but the King, but Tyrell had been away from the palace, visiting his allies to ascertain their loyalty in case of war with Aldane.

Alone and by night, Jarrett had been taken to the Great Hall to be judged by Lord Rorke, who was not only the king's son-in-law, but the Minister of War as well. Rorke, who had once been his friend.

Jarrett swore under his breath as the memories pressed in on him. Bound and gagged, he had been given no opportunity to speak in his own behalf. Instead, Rorke had found him guilty of treason, decreeing that he would be sent to the Pavilion, to be a pawn in the ancient Games for as long as he lived.

Rorke himself had delivered Jarrett to the Pavilion, where all who took part in the Games had sworn a blood oath never to re-

19

veal his whereabouts, just as they had sworn
never to reveal that the Games were again
being played. Rorke had lamented the fact
that he would have to delay his own partici-
pation in the Games, but in the King's absence, Rorke's duties as Minister of War had
to take precedence over his own pleasure. He
had business to attend to in Heth, and then
in Cornith. But he would be back, he had
promised with a malicious grin, just as soon
as possible.

Jarrett stared at the floor, wondering if
Tyrell had returned to Heth, wondering if
war had been declared, wondering what
Rorke hoped to gain by keeping him imprisoned in the Pavilion. He thought of his
mother, wondering what she thought of his
sudden disappearance. Did she think him
dead?

Questions, he thought. So many questions,
and he had no answers for any of them.

They came at the usual time, the three he
feared above the others. Siid picked up the
hood, twirling it between his fat stubby fingers, while Thal and Gar dragged him to the
wall, reaching for the heavy iron shackles,
talking about him as if he could not understand their words, as if he were an inanimate
object lacking the powers of thought and
speech.

He felt the anger rising within him, the
fear. Once, he had been a warrior without

equal. Men had respected him, deferring to his wisdom and judgment. Women had openly admired him, vying for his attention. Here, he was treated like an animal. Nay, less than an animal, for no self-respecting man would abuse a dog or a horse as he had been abused.

With a cry of despair, he jerked from their grasp, darting behind the heavy metal table, his eyes wild as he sought a weapon, his blood singing with the need to be free.

"No more!" He shrieked the words. "No more!"

His tormentors looked startled, as if a favorite pet had suddenly turned vicious.

And then they looked pleased. He had not defied them for so long, they had thought him completely cowed.

"Ah," Gar said with a malicious grin. "It would seem that our noble Jarrett desires to play a new Game."

"Then let us oblige him," Siid remarked. He moved to stand in front of the thick wooden door, drawing his heavy sword as he did so.

Gar and Thal grinned at each other, and then started toward the table, one going to the left, the other to the right.

With a deep-throated growl of resignation, Jarrett realized he was trapped between them. There was nowhere to go, no way to avoid the Gamesmen who were advancing toward him, their swords drawn and ready.

Thal drew first blood, opening a shallow, six-inch gash along Jarrett's left thigh.

Gar matched it by piercing Jarrett's right thigh.

Thal lifted one bushy white brow, then, with a sharp thrust, he plunged the tip of his blade into Jarrett's left shoulder.

Gar did likewise on the right, and then, taking the lead, he raked the point of his blade down the length of Jarrett's right arm.

For the next hour, they played their game, Thal targeting the left side of Jarrett's body, Gar the right.

Jarrett watched their faces, sickened by the cruel delight that glowed in their red-rimmed eyes as they tormented him, never inflicting a wound that could be fatal or crippling. They did not want him helpless or unconscious. They wanted to challenge his stamina, to drive him to the very brink, to see if they could provoke him into fighting back even though he knew he could not win.

By mid-day, the smell of blood and sweat was strong in the room. Shortly thereafter, one of the Giants arrived with a tray of food. Jarrett was left to lie on the rough-hewn wooden floor while his captors sat down to eat Second Meal.

After serving the Gamesmen, the giant smeared a sticky green salve over Jarrett's wounds to stem the bleeding, and then left the room.

Over a glass of yellow Freywine, Siid complained that his companions were not playing fair.

"Surely it is my turn now," he said, and Gar and Thal willingly agreed.

For another hour, they sat at the table, speaking of distant battles as they stuffed themselves with bread and cheese and sweet Freywine.

Gar mentioned there was word of discontent among the Giants who worked in the lower dungeons, keeping the cells clean, keeping the prisoners in line.

Thal shrugged. The Giants were always disgruntled, but too lazy to do anything about it other than complain from time to time.

Jarrett lay where they had left him, his eyes closed as he gathered his strength to face the afternoon Games. It was hard to breathe, hard to think of anything but the steady, monotonous pain that pulsed through him.

Too soon, they were ready for him again. Gar and Thal forced him to his feet. Shoving him against the wall, they stretched his arms to their limits, holding him immobile while Siid locked the heavy shackles in place.

Jarrett pressed his cheek against the cold stone, his heart pounding in dreadful anticipation of what was to come. He was tired, so tired.

"What about the hood?" Thal asked.

Gar shrugged. "It won't hurt to leave it off this time," he remarked, and Siid agreed.

Jarrett drew a deep breath as he heard Gar shake out the deadly whip. He stifled a gasp as the lash bit into his flesh, the weighted leather tip dancing across his bared skin in an endless nightmare as Gar displayed his skill. A one-inch cut here, a narrow incision there. Here only an angry red welt, there a shallow gash.

Jarrett's heart beat in time to the crack of the lash. He pressed his forehead to the damp stone, stared in horrified fascination at the crimson pool gathering at his feet. So much blood, he thought dully. Surely even she could not heal him this time.

He opened his mouth to cry out. Surely he had given them enough entertainment for one day. Surely it would be permissible to give utterance to the first cry now and thereby signal that he was near the end of his endurance.

And then he saw Siid standing beside him, his red-rimmed eyes filled with warning.

Scream now, Siid seemed to say, *and I will leave you to hang there, as you are, until morning.*

Jarrett understood. Today, whoever had drawn First Cry would be the winner. Gar had won the Games the day before when he had drawn Longest Cry, and Thal, the day before that, when he had drawn the Beg card. Siid did not wish to lose again.

Jarrett bit down on his lower lip, choking back the cry in his throat.

Only when Siid rubbed a handful of raw salt into his torn flesh did he give voice to the awful agony that engulfed him.

"I couldn't let you two have *all* the fun," Siid remarked, slapping Gar on the back. "I declare myself the winner and the Games over."

The darkness came then, hovering at the edge of Jarrett's vision, promising peace, promising oblivion.

With a hoarse cry of surrender, he plunged into the abyss, falling, falling, into nothingness.

Chapter Three

"Jarrett. Jarrett? Jarrett!"

The voice called to him, softly pleading for his return, beckoning him to come back from the Dark Beyond. It was her voice, and he could not deny her.

"She?"

He mouthed the word, but no sound emerged from his throat.

"I am here."

He choked back the bile in his throat, moistened his lips with the tip of his tongue. "Let me die." He opened his eyes to the eternal darkness of the hood. "For the love of the All Father," he rasped, "let me die."

"I cannot."

She was weeping, he thought, dazed. Weeping for him. He could feel her silent tears as they fell on his mutilated back, as soft as the raindrops of First Month. It was incredible, he thought. Women had desired him, they had fought for his favors, they had cheered for him in tournaments, but they had never wept for him.

He tried to lift his arm, wanting to touch her, but his hands were cuffed together, fastened by a short length of chain to an iron ring set in the floor.

"Please," he begged. "Let me die."

She shook her head in helpless frustration. Even if she could, she would not let him die, not now, not when she had seen his face.

He had been lying on the floor, unconscious, when Thal had sent for her. His head had not yet been covered with the hood, and she had seen him for the first time: the fine straight nose, the shape of his mouth, the faintly arched black brows, the straight black hair that reached his shoulders. He was beautiful, like the marble statue of a young Gweneth warrior she had seen long ago.

Swallowing the nausea that rose in her throat, she placed her hands on the torn flesh of his back. His skin was hot and damp beneath her palms. A tremor raced up her arms as she drew his pain into herself, feeling each stroke of the lash, each drop of blood.

"Thee must turn over," she said when his back was healed.

With an effort, he did as bidden, exposing the shallow cuts that covered his chest and shoulders.

As always, there were many wounds, inflicted with great care and great skill. She placed her hand over the worst of the lot.

"She . . . tell me . . . your name." It was an effort to breathe, to speak.

27

"No." She shook her head.

"Can you not . . . give me . . . that much of yourself?"

"I give thee life."

"I do not ask for my life," he said bitterly. Months of anger and frustration boiled up inside him. "If you had the compassion of an Orvan Redsnake, you would let me die!"

"Thee does not mean that."

"No," he admitted contritely. He didn't want to die. He could stand the pain. But the constant weight of the heavy chains shriveled his spirit; the eternal darkness dragged him deeper and deeper into despair. He was vulnerable, helpless to fight back, and he was tired. So tired of it all.

"How can I explain it to thee?" she asked, her hands moving soft as a shadow to the wound on his right shoulder. "I do not want to know thee. I do not want thee to know me." She drew a harsh, sobbing breath. "When they tire of thee, they will kill thee and move on to another. I do not want to know thee! Can thee not understand? I do not want to grieve for thee. I do not want to remember thee when thou art gone."

He stared into the blackness of the hood, his own grief and pain forgotten as he heard the anguish in her voice.

He understood then, understood clearly for the first time that she felt more than his pain. She felt his fear and his despair; she would feel his death. It would hurt her all the more if they became friends instead of strangers trapped in a nightmare.

"Forgive me, Maje. I was wrong to ask it of thee." Unconsciously, he used her quaint form of speech.

"There is nothing to forgive." She stood back from the table, her gaze moving over him. His body was whole once more, hard and well-muscled, perfectly formed, without scar or blemish.

The weariness overcame her then and she left the room, her steps slow and heavy, her heart aching for Jarrett. She would not forget him when he was gone, she thought. She would never forget him, for she had seen his face. But, more than that, she had seen his heart, and his soul.

Week after week, the Games went on. Sometimes they used him for target practice, making him run the length of the long, narrow corridor outside his chamber while they hurled rocks at him. Sometimes, when they had no wish to play, they let Gar whip him a few times, then they tied him by his wrists and left him hanging from the rafters like the carcass of some dead animal while they played cards in a corner of the room, not caring that the shallow cuts ached unceasingly, that great horned flies came to bite him, gorging themselves on his blood, not caring that the quivering muscles in his arms and shoulders screamed for relief.

Sometimes they tied a cord around his neck, securing the hood in place, and then they bound his hands behind his back, lashed his feet together, and lowered him into a deep pool of dark water. Up and down, they played him like a fish, leaving him under the water for longer and longer periods of time so that he barely had time to draw a breath from one submerging to the next.

It was that Game that terrified him the most. Though he was always helpless against them, always at their mercy, there was something about being bound and lowered into the pool — weightless, sightless, with nothing but the pounding of his blood in his ears — that reached into the very depths of his fears.

There were always nightmares after a trip to the pool, nightmares more frightening than the hell in which he lived, more terrifying than the thought of being denied the healing powers of the Maje, of being left alone to die slowly immersed in never-ending darkness and pain.

Fortunately, they did not play the Water Game often, for there was no way to hear his silent screams, and it was his screams that drove them on, that made the Games worthwhile.

On this day, they had been even more enthusiastic than usual, their spirits high as they discussed the possibility of war with Aldane.

The talk of war overrode their fascination with the sound of his cries and some of their blows were careless, striking places that were taboo, sometimes cutting deeper than usual, the sight of his blood less interesting than the prospect of shedding the blood of the Aldanites.

Jarrett closed his eyes and prayed for war, knowing only something as urgent as war could bring an end to the Games, for the Gamesmen would all be called to fight. Strange, he thought, that only something as awful as war between Aldane and Fenduzia could deliver him from the horror in which he lived.

They left him early that night, eager to go to the Hall and hear the latest news.

Spread-eagled on the table, hooded and alone, he closed his eyes, waiting. Waiting for she who had no name.

Hours passed. His wounds ached, throbbing to the beat of his heart. Had they forgotten to send for her? He tried to think of home, of his life before the Pavilion, but the pain was constant, robbing him of coherent thought.

Where was she?

When he had given up hope of her coming, he heard the heavy door slide open.

"She?"

"I am here."

His relief was almost painful. A sigh of gratitude whispered past his lips as she laid her hands upon him, healing his hurts, quelling his pain.

"Something troubles you," he remarked as she lifted her hand for the last time.

She did not want to tell him the truth, but it was beyond her power to lie. "Yes."

"What is it?"

"It is said that war with Aldane is imminent. Preparations are already being made."

Jarrett nodded. "Go on."

"The prisoners . . ."

He felt the hard cold hand of fear curl around his insides. "What about the prisoners?"

"They are to be executed."

Of course, he thought, the Games had been outlawed eons ago. The Gamesmen couldn't take a chance on having it known that they were still playing the Games, that prisoners were being held captive without the King's knowledge for the entertainment of a small group of Rorke's friends.

"How many other prisoners are there?"

"Eleven, as of last night."

Eleven other men, men he'd never seen, all living in the same hell. They had been culled from prisons in other provinces, men convicted of murder or treason, men without families, who would not be missed.

"Do you heal them all?"

"No. Only you. The others are left to die of their wounds if they are not strong enough to survive."

He pondered that for a moment, wondering why they had kept him alive so long. "How much longer . . . when will they end it?"

"I do not know."

"What month is it?"

"Fifth month."

Fifth month. The first month of spring.

"There is to be one last Game," she went on, unable to stay the words. "It will be held in the Great Arena. Lots have already been drawn."

"Who . . ."

"Siid. Gar. Thal." She hesitated. "It is said the Minister of War himself will participate in the final Game."

Rorke. It was his worst nightmare come true. Freed from the need to be cautious or to give heed to the basic Rules of the Game, Rorke and the others would be able to use their knives and torches and whips in ways and places they had previously avoided in order to keep him alive.

He fought down the terror that rose within him, threatening to send him over the brink into madness. The aloneness was heavy within him then, and he wished he could hold her hand for just a moment, feel the smoothness of her skin, the gentle warmth of

33

her touch, not in healing, but in friendship.

The thought had no sooner crossed his mind than he felt her fingers entwine with his, felt the gentle squeeze of her hand.

"She." The word whispered past his lips, a sigh and a prayer.

"I am here."

He looked into his soul and faced the truth. "I'm afraid." The words slipped past his lips in a barely audible whisper. *Coward,* he thought, and despised himself for his weakness.

She squeezed his hand a little tighter. "Thee is not a coward," she remarked quietly. "A coward would have gone mad long since. Thee is a brave man, my Lord Jarrett of Gweneth."

Lord Jarrett. How long since he had been called by the title of his birth? Once, it had seemed important, but no longer. "You know who I am?"

"It has come to me, a little at a time."

"I would know your name and see your face before I die."

"No. Do not ask it of me."

"They will have my life. Never again will I feel thy touch, or hear thy voice." How readily her quaint speech came to him, he thought, bemused.

"I cannot . . ." She shook her head, not wanting to deny him anything that was in her power to give, and yet reluctant to give him any more of herself than her power to heal.

"Please." How easily he had grown used to begging, he thought. Please don't hit me again. Please don't burn me again. Please don't cut me again. Please, please, please. It was ironic that he should have to beg to know a lady's name, to see a lady's face, he who had once had women of all ages at his beck and call, vying for his favors.

He felt her fingers slide over his shoulders to rest at the lower edge of the hood.

"Please." He sensed her wakening and wondered if she could fathom how much he hated the hood that covered his face like a death shroud. It made him feel vulnerable, degraded, to be forever in darkness, to be robbed of his sight for no reason other than that the Gamesmen desired it.

He held his breath as her fingers curled around the heavy black cloth. He raised his head from the table, waiting, hoping, and suddenly, with a sharp jerk, she yanked the hood from his head and tossed it to the floor.

There was only a single candle in the room, but it was enough.

She stared at him for a long moment, knowing it had been a mistake to remove the hood. If the eyes were indeed the mirror of the soul, then Jarrett's soul was filled with pain. His eyes were green and dark and tur-bulent — haunting eyes that were filled with the pain he'd endured in the past, the knowledge of the pain that was to come. Eyes filled with weariness and frustration and silent rage.

She wished she had never seen his eyes. She would never be free of them now.

Jarrett blinked against the light, felt the breath rush from his body as his gaze focused on her face. For months, he had been mesmerized by the soft sweetness of her voice, imagining that the beautiful voice resided in an equally beautiful body. Now he saw that his dreams had not even come close to the vision that stood beside him.

She wore a blue gown that should have been ugly, but it caressed her body lovingly, clearly outlining the feminine shape the All Father had given her: the narrow waist, the slim hips, the curve of her breasts. Her hands were small and delicate. Her eyes, wide-set and slanted, were the color of the wildflowers that grew near Greyebridge Castle on the isle of Gweneth, a deep dark blue that was almost purple. Her brows were delicately arched, her lashes long and thick.

"Thee is beautiful," he murmured.

A faint blush tinged her cheeks. "Thee thinks so?"

"Indeed." Her skin was the color of rich cream, her hair like fine strands of twined silver, bright, luminous. Unbound, it cascaded down her back, a glorious shimmering mass of waves that fell past her hips. Her lips were as pink as the sky at dawn.

"Do not look at me so," she murmured.

"I cannot help myself. You are more lovely than I had imagined. Will you tell me your name?"

It was hard to resist the gentle urging of his voice, the pleading in his eyes, but she shook her head. "Please, do not ask it of me."

Jarrett nodded, understanding her need to hold something back, to hang on to some small part of herself that was hers and hers alone.

"Jarrett . . ."

"More bad news?"

"I hesitate to tell thee, yet I feel thee should know all."

"Go on."

"The last Game will be . . . different."

Jarrett frowned. "What do you mean?"

"They wish to experiment with thee. And with me."

"Experiment? How?"

He was watching her intently, his eyes dark. She saw the muscles tense in his arms as his hands curled into tight fists.

"They wish to know the full extent of my powers."

He shook his head. "I don't understand."

"They want to know if I can restore . . . if I can revitalize . . ."

It was harder to say than she had imagined. Instinctively feeling the need to comfort him, she took his hand in hers, felt the slight tremor that pulsed through him as he waited for her to tell him the rest.

"On the battlefield . . . if a man should lose an arm or a leg . . . they want to find out if I can restore a severed limb, or cause a new one to grow in its place."

He was going to be sick. He felt the bile rise in his throat as he realized what she was saying. They were going to amputate an arm or a leg and see if she had the power to make him whole again. Fear twisted in his gut, writhing like a snake biting its own tail.

He fought down the urge to vomit, his gaze intent upon her face. "Can you do it?"

"I do not know. I have never had the opportunity to try."

"But it can be done?"

"Yes, if a Maje can be found before the victim bleeds to death."

"You mean you can't raise the dead, too?"

Her face went white.

"She?" He squeezed her hand, his breath trapped in his throat as he waited for her answer.

She turned away, unable to face him. "I will be given the opportunity to find out."

He stared at her for a long while, his mind refusing to believe what he'd heard. He didn't fear death so much. He had been a warrior. Death had ridden beside him at every battle. But dismemberment . . . to be deliberately cut apart . . . to discover if she could make him whole again. And then, if she were capable of restoring or replacing whatever limb they chose to amputate, they would hack it off again and he would be left to bleed to death so they could discover if she could restore life. And in the end, no matter what pain he endured, what miracles she worked upon his unwilling flesh, he was still fated to die at the hands of a man he had once called friend.

"I will not do it." She gazed down at the table to where their two hands were still joined together. "I promise thee that I will not."

"You must," he retorted, his voice filled with bitterness. "The Maje cannot refuse to heal."

She looked up, meeting his gaze. "Have you never wondered why my people are so few in number?"

Slowly, he shook his head.

"It is our fate to heal, though my People have many other gifts besides healing. My mother has the power to control the elements. My father has power over fire and water. Many of my people have been captured because of these gifts, but if our power is to be abused, as the Fen wish to abuse my power, then my people chose to die rather than be the instrument of causing destruction or prolonging pain. As I will die."

"No!"

"It is our way."

"She, you must not! Promise me."

"Does thee understand fully what thee is asking? They will not be content to try it once. If they cut off thy hand and I heal thee, they will cut off thy arm, and then thy leg, until they have tested my powers to the fullest." She took a deep breath. "It is not only thy pain I fear, but my own, as well."

Selfish swine, he thought, to think only of the suffering that waited for him, completely forgetting that, in healing him, she would suffer the same anguish.

He glanced at their joined hands — his large and dark, the fingers long and blunt, capable of wielding a sword or a knife with ease; hers, small and pale in comparison, the fingers dainty, tapered, filled with the power to soothe, to heal.

There was only one answer for both of them, and it was there, in their joined hands.

Escape.

Chapter Four

"It's the only way out for either of us," Jarrett argued.

"No." She shook her head, afraid of what he was suggesting, afraid even to think of it.

"She, listen to me. I'll protect you once we get out of here, I swear it."

"No."

"Do you want to die?"

"No."

"Then help me. I'll take you back to Gweneth with me, or I'll take you home, to Majeulla."

She tried to wrest her hand from his. "Please, let me go."

His hand tightened on hers. "She, it's the only way. What other choice do you have?" He looked deep into her eyes and saw the fear there. "What if you can't find the courage to take your own life?" he asked ruthlessly. "What then? Will you be able to endure the pain of watching them cut me up a hundred times, of healing me a hundred times? Would you rather endure that than risk freedom?"

"No, no. I just want to go home." She

tried again to wrest her hand from his, but she was no match for his strength. She stared into his eyes, eyes that were as green as the leaves of a midnight flower. She saw the fear that lurked within their depths, and mingled with that fear she saw desperation, and a bright glimmer of hope.

She lowered her head, unable to meet his searching gaze any longer. What if she helped him escape? What if she were caught?

She shuddered to think of what would happen to her if the Fen decided they no longer needed her healing powers. It was her ability to ease pain and suffering that made her valuable in their eyes; it was the fear of destroying her powers that had kept her safe from their lust, for it was well known that to defile a Maje was to destroy her powers. It was a myth that had been spread for countless generations, a myth that had been perpetrated in hopes of protecting the women of Majeulla from the lust of outsiders. It had worked so far, but what if they caught her helping Jarrett to escape? What if, in their anger, they decided to humble her in the most elemental way? What if they defiled her?

She would rather die than be subjected to such a fate.

And what of Jarrett? Had she the courage, she would take her own life rather than cause him a single moment of needless suffering.

She felt Jarrett's fingers tighten over her

own, felt the tremor that shook his body.

How could she bear to see him hacked to pieces? How would she bear the agony of watching him suffer, of making him whole over and over again?

The pain she had endured in healing him in the past would be as nothing compared to what lay ahead. She would have to be in the room while they used their knives on him to ensure that he did not bleed to death while they summoned her.

She would hear his screams, feel the knife cut into his flesh as if it were her own. . . .

Slowly, she raised her head and looked into his eyes. "Thee promises to take me home?"

"I promise."

"How soon does thee wish to leave?"

The sense of relief, the promise of freedom, left him weak. "As soon as possible. Can you find your way out of the dungeons?"

"Yes."

He nodded, his thoughts racing. "The Giant?"

"I can subdue him."

Assured by the confidence in her voice, he didn't waste time asking how. "You must bring me his weapons."

"Yes." Her gaze moved over Jarrett's body. "And raiment."

Clothes, he thought. How long since he'd worn anything but a death shroud and a scrap of black cloth?

"Don't wait too long," he said. "Promise me?"

Her heart was pounding like a wild thing caught in the jaws of a trap. She wanted to say she'd changed her mind, that there had to be another way, but in the end she only nodded. "I promise."

He smiled at her then, and she felt the force of it radiate through every fiber of her being, filling her with warmth and light and the promise of a rainbow when the storm was over.

"I must go." She felt a sharp stab of regret as she dropped the hood in place. She saw him shudder, sensed the revulsion that swept through him as the cloth settled over his face.

"She?"

"I must go," she said again, but she made no move to leave the cell.

It was growing more and more difficult to leave him, and so she lingered at his side, holding his hand in hers.

It still amazed her, that she could so easily read his thoughts. She knew how he hated the hood, how he loathed the long hours of being alone in the silent darkness. His emotions were so strong, she felt them as keenly as her own: his rage, his turmoil, his driving need to be free, his desire for vengeance.

She gazed at his fingers, entwined with her

own, and knew she had no right to care for him as she did.

"I must go," she said hoarsely, and giving his hand a squeeze, she hurried from the cell, fleeing from thoughts and feelings she was afraid to acknowledge.

That night, she lay in her narrow bed, staring up at the curved ceiling. Tomorrow. She would act tomorrow. A bit of noxious gimweed in the giant's evening ale would render him unconscious. She would take his clothes and his weapons, the keys to the manacles that bound Jarrett's hands and feet. In the dark of tenth hour, when the dungeon was quiet, she would free Jarrett. They would climb the winding staircase that led to the kitchens and escape through the back door into the huge yard that housed the stables.

If luck went with them, if the herdboys did not hear them, if the helldogs did not raise an alarm, if the horses did not shy from strangers, they might make it safely out of the Pavilion.

If, she thought, and prayed that the gods of the Maje and the Fen would be with them.

She felt his pain even before she opened the door, and all her doubts fled. It was time to go, now. Knowing that the Games were soon to be ended, the Gamesmen were being less careful with their weapons. Even though the Games were played in secret, the players had always held to the Rules of the Games: no wounds above the neck, no wounds that were fatal, or crippling, or emasculating. But now the Games were coming to an end, and they were no longer obeying the Rules. Prisoners were being allowed to die horrible deaths each night since only one participant was needed for the Final Game.

And that one was here, waiting for her.

"She?"

"I am here. Do not try to speak. All is arranged."

His breathing was shallow, labored, painful to hear. With gentle hands, she removed the hood. His face, she thought in despair. His beautiful face, swollen and discolored. She wept as she placed her hands upon him, infusing him with her warmth, letting the gift flow from her hands to his, her spirit to his. She choked back a groan, not wanting him to know the pain she felt.

There seemed not an inch of flesh that was untouched. How had he endured so many months of abuse? She had seen some of the other prisoners — prisoners who had gone mad from the pain, from the constant fear and abuse, their spirits crushed so completely that even her powers could not call their minds out of darkness.

His skin was flushed, hot beneath her fingertips, his muscles rigid. Slowly, her hands moved over him, withdrawing the fever, soothing the pain. The blood returned to his veins, the torn flesh meshed, leaving neither scar nor blemish.

Exhausted, her own body quivering with the pain that had been his, she dropped her hands to her sides. For a moment, she stood there with her eyes closed, willing her limbs to stop their trembling. Usually, she sought sleep after such an extensive healing, but there was no time to rest now, no time to waste.

She had not removed the manacles earlier in case someone should enter the chamber unexpectedly. Now, taking the key from her pocket, she unlocked the manacles from his wrists and ankles, then offered him the shirt and breeches she had taken from the Giant. The shirt covered Jarrett like a shroud, falling to his knees. A faint smile curved her lips as she handed him the Giant's sword, his bow, and a quiver of arrows.

Jarrett took the weapons. Slinging the bow and the quiver over his left shoulder, he made a pass with the sword. It was a powerful weapon, longer and heavier than he was accustomed to.

"Ready?" he asked, and she nodded in reply, too frightened to speak now that the hour of their escape had come.

He took her hand and they left the chamber on silent feet. Outside, she led the way down the dimly lit corridor to the winding staircase. Slowly, step by step, they made their way up from the dungeon to the kitchens. They paused in the doorway, listening, but it was still too early for the cooks to be about. Their footsteps echoed as they crossed the plank floor to the door that opened onto the stable yard.

Her heart was pounding so loudly, it drowned out every other sound as Jarrett stepped into the yard. A helldog rose from the dirt, hackles bristling as it walked, stiff-legged, toward them.

Jarrett froze in mid-stride, but she went forward, unafraid. She spoke a single quiet word, and the helldog returned to its place.

They entered the first barn. Jarrett drew a deep breath, filling his lungs with the scent of horses and hay, of freedom. In moments, he had two horses saddled.

He had just lifted her onto the back of a long-legged bay mare when a herdboy rose from behind a pile of straw where he'd been sleeping.

For a moment, Jarrett and the boy stared at each other. "Say nothing," Jarrett warned, the sword a hair's breath from the boy's throat. "I do not want to kill you."

The boy's face turned pale. He slid a glance at the Maje, his eyes begging for help.

"Thee had best do as he says," she told him, despising the cowardly quiver in her voice.

48

"You're Jarrett," the boy said. "I have heard of you."

"Have you, indeed?"

"Yes. You are the most famous of all the participants in the Games."

A wry grin twitched at the corners of Jarrett's mouth. "A great honor, to be sure. What will it be, your silence or your life?"

"I will not sound the alarm," the herdboy said. "You have my word upon it."

With a nod, Jarrett swung aboard the big white stallion he had chosen for himself. "Your word, boy, remember?"

The boy nodded, his eyes narrowed as he watched the Gweneth warrior ride away in company with the silver-haired Maje. As they reached the north gate, he drew a handbow from beneath his jerkin. He had promised not to sound the alarm, he thought, but he had not promised he wouldn't kill the man.

He was smiling as he let the arrow fly, thinking of the reward that would be his when the Minister of War learned he had prevented one of the participants from escaping.

Jarrett grunted as the iron-tipped arrow buried itself in his right thigh. With an oath, he turned in the saddle, his hands putting an arrow to the Giant's bow, his eyes blazing with fury as he sighted down the shaft, released the bow string. The arrow flew straight and true, burying itself in the middle of the boy's jerkin, and Jarrett grimaced with satisfaction.

"Lying wretch," he muttered as he rode out of the gate. "You'll lie no more!"

They rode for hours. He refused to stop, refused to let her treat his wound, though it was bleeding badly. He was driven by a deep-seated need to get as far away from the Pavilion as possible, to forget the hood and the Games, the fear that never left him, even when he was alone in the darkness of his chamber, to ride away from the pain and the humiliation of his captivity. He wanted to be Lord Jarrett again, Master of Gweneth. But it was not to be. He was a renegade, deemed a traitor by the Fen sovereignty. But, more than that, life in the bowels of the Pavilion had changed him, and he knew he would never be the same again.

Chapter Five

They rode until dusk, pausing only to rest the horses. She fretted at his unwillingness to let her tend to his wound; the need to heal, to use the gift, burned through her like a flame, but he was adamant, refusing to stop while there was yet daylight.

Only when the three moons of Hovis had appeared over the horizon did he agree to stop. He was weak from loss of blood by then, barely able to stand. The shaft of the arrow stood out from his thigh, grotesque and covered with blood.

The Maje unsaddled her mare, then spread the saddle blanket on the ground, insisting that Jarrett lie down.

"Cold." He forced the word through clenched teeth, his body wracked by violent shivers. "So cold."

Nodding, she quickly gathered an armful of wood, then, squatting on her heels, she took the three largest pieces and formed a triangle. When that was done, she placed smaller bits of wood and leaves within the triangle.

Closing her eyes, the Maje held her hands over the wood.

"Dry from wet, heat from cold. Give me fire, bright and bold."

Immediately, the bits of wood within the triangle began to glow, brighter and brighter. There was a sharp crackling sound, then flames licked at the wood.

Jarrett swore under his breath as the fire's heat reached out to chase away the cold that enveloped him.

"Are you also a witch?" he asked with a wary gaze.

"Nay, my Lord. 'Tis but another of my gifts." She met his gaze, a ghost of a smile hovering around her mouth. "But then, are not all women witches of one kind or another?"

"True enough," he agreed. He shifted on the blanket, grimacing as the movement awakened the pain in his thigh.

Reminded of his wound, she drew the knife she had secreted in the pocket of her skirt and made a neat slit in his breeches. For a time, she studied the wound, wondering how he had ridden so long, how he had managed to stay in the saddle.

"Thee," she muttered, shaking her head. "So stubborn."

"Get it out." He forced the words through clenched teeth.

Yes, she thought, it had to come out, but how? Would it be easier, less painful, to push the arrow through his thigh, or to cut it out instead?

Sensing her dilemma, Jarrett took a deep breath. "Push it through," he said, knowing it would be easier and quicker.

She looked at him for a moment, seeing the taut lines of pain around his mouth. The thought of laying hold of the arrow, of driving it through healthy flesh, chilled her to the marrow of her bones, but there was no help for it. She couldn't heal his wound and relieve his pain until she had removed the cause.

Teeth clenched with determination, she took hold of the short, narrow shaft, emptying her mind of everything but the need to get it done.

A harsh cry of pain rumbled in Jarrett's throat as the arrow penetrated farther into his flesh before leaving it, and then he let out a long shuddering sigh.

He gazed at her through eyes filled with pain and fever. Then, taking her hand in his, he lightly kissed her palm.

"Thank you," he murmured, his voice heavy with fatigue; then, his eyes closing, he took her hand and placed it over the wound in his thigh.

She stared at him, her palm tingling with heat from the touch of his lips, a warmth vastly different from the internal heat that flowed from her body to his.

No man had ever kissed her. Ever. Her heart was pounding erratically, her cheeks felt flushed, and all from one kiss, and that kiss only on her hand.

Her gaze wandered over his face. His lashes were thick and very black against his pale skin. As she watched, she saw the tension drain from his expression, saw his muscles relax as she absorbed his pain, a pain she hardly felt. She was only aware of her hand upon a well-muscled masculine thigh, of the heat that burned in the center of her palm, a warmth that had nothing to do with her power to heal and everything to do with the searing memory of his lips on the delicate skin of her hand.

She started to draw her hand away, but his own hand still covered hers, lightly but forcefully.

"Thee must let me go," she said, suddenly frightened by his power over her. "Thee is healed."

He nodded, his eyes still closed. But he didn't release her hand. "Your name, I would know your name."

"Leyla." She had not meant to tell him, but somehow lacked the power to refuse.

"Leyla." He repeated the word softly, drawing it out, liking the sound of it.

He opened his eyes and gazed into her face. "Leyla."

A slow smile spread across his face, making his green eyes sparkle.

"I am free again," he murmured. He

reached for her other hand. Leaping nimbly to his feet, he swung her round and round. "Free, Leyla! Free! Do you know what that means? No more dungeons!"

He lifted her off her feet and hugged her close. "No more darkness!" he exclaimed. "No more chains. Free!"

He twirled her around again, his face buried in the cleft of her breasts and then, slowly, he came to a stop and stood her on the ground before him, one of her hands clasped between both of his. "Free."

Unfettered by the black hood and the heavy shackles, he seemed taller, somehow, broader, a little frightening in his intensity. She had never been with a man in quite this way before, alone as they were in the midst of a sheltered glen.

"Leyla . . ." She was beautiful, so beautiful standing there with the forest behind her and the gossamer light of the three moons shining upon her silver hair.

Her nearness sent a quick heat surging through him. He gasped at the unexpected suddenness of it. So long, he thought, so long since he'd even thought about a woman. So long since he'd even wanted one. . . .

"No!" She jerked her hand free, her eyes wide and frightened as she backed away from him.

"I guess you're reading my mind," he muttered, cursing her power to do so.

"I cannot help it, thy . . . emotions . . . are so strong."

He couldn't deny that. He wanted to laugh, to cry, to bury himself in her softness and let her erase every dreadful memory.

"Leyla, do not be afraid of me. I won't hurt you, I swear it on my mother's life."

He opened his arms and she went to him without hesitation.

"I believe thee, Jarrett. And I will hold thee all the night long if that is thy desire, but only in friendship. Does thee understand?"

He nodded, not trusting himself to speak.

They had no food, no water, only a fire to turn away the cold. They sat down with their backs against a log, one of the horse blankets spread beneath them, the other across their legs.

Like a mother comforting a child, Leyla put her arm around Jarrett's shoulders and drew him close to her breast, one hand stroking his hair.

"Can you read the minds of everyone you meet?" he asked.

"No."

He looked up at her curiously. "Only mine?"

"I can communicate with other Maje telepathically."

She gazed into his eyes, keenly aware of the attraction that hummed between them. She had a strong urge to hold him, to protect him, to shield him from harm. They were motherly instincts, given to all women, and yet there was nothing maternal in her feelings.

"I have never been able to read the mind of an outsider before," Leyla confessed, and wondered why she could read Jarrett's thoughts so clearly, and what it meant.

Jarrett grunted softly, pleased that she could divine his thoughts though he could not say why. At times, it was damnably inconvenient.

Closing his eyes, he gave himself over to her touch, feeling all the tension drain from his body. How good it felt, to be held in a woman's arms, to lay his head upon her breast and breathe in her warm sweet scent.

Her warm sweet scent, like sunshine after a storm, like the flowers that grew in the walled gardens at Greyebridge Castle. . . .

Gently, Leyla eased him down, until his head was resting in her lap.

"Sleep, my brave warrior," she whispered, and held him close all the night long.

He woke with the dawn, wary as a winter wolf on the prowl. Cursing the weakness that had let him sleep the sleep of the dead, leaving Leyla vulnerable and unprotected, he rolled to his feet. Grabbing the Giant's sword, he quickly surveyed their surroundings, but all was peaceful. The horses grazed in the tall grass; Leyla was asleep, her hair flowing down her back like a cape of shimmering silver.

A hand on her shoulder brought her instantly awake, her eyes wide. "Have they found us so soon?"

"No, but it's time to move on. We need food and water." He glanced down at his bloodstained shirt. "I need something else to wear."

She nodded in solemn agreement, thinking he looked somewhat like a Giddeon pirate standing there, his long black hair blowing in the faint breeze, his jaw beard-roughened, a sword clutched in his hand.

Jarrett saddled their horses, lifted her onto the back of the mare, and swung aboard his own mount. If he remembered correctly, there was a small town a short distance to the north. If luck went with them, he might be able to barter one of the horses for food and clothing. And if no one would trade with him, he was not above stealing what they needed.

He pushed the horses hard, constantly looking over his shoulder for some sign of pursuit, knowing he'd rather die than go back.

They stopped to rest the horses at mid-morning. "Leyla, I have a favor to ask of thee."

"Ask it."

"If we are captured by Rorke's men, I want your promise that you won't let them take me back alive."

She shook her head in violent refusal, her whole being rebelling at the idea of taking a life, especially his.

Jarrett took her hand in both of his. "You must promise me," he said, his hands tightening on hers. "I cannot go back."

She gazed deep into his eyes, and in their depths she saw the awful fear that tormented him: fear of being lost and alone in the darkness, fear of being helpless, fear of madness. But no fear of pain or death.

"I cannot go back," he said again, and she heard the despair in his voice, the faint note of pleading that shattered her resistance because she knew what it had cost him to ask such a thing of her.

She placed her free hand over his. "It is against all that I believe in, all that I am," she replied softly, "but I will do it for thee, Lord Jarrett of Gweneth, because I cannot refuse thee anything in my power to give."

The town lay nestled in the lee of a wooded hillside. There were few inhabitants about as they rode down the narrow street. Jarrett's stomach rumbled loudly as they passed a bake shop filled with brown bread, honey buns and cakes, biscuits.

They rode on until they came to a stable.

Dismounting, Jarrett approached the owner, inquiring if he would like to buy the mare.

The liveryman walked around the bay, checking the horse's feet, running his hands over the bay's long legs, checking her teeth.

"How much d'ye want for the beast?" the man asked.

"Ten ducates."

"Ten!" The liveryman shook his head. "Eight."

"Ten," Jarrett insisted. "And I'll throw in the saddle."

The man grunted, then nodded. "Done."

Their first stop was at an outside tavern for food. Leyla watched in amazement as he devoured a whole loaf of brown bread, washing it down with a tankard of potent Freywine, while she nibbled at a hot honey bun and drank a glass of cold goat's milk.

Next, they walked through the marketplace, buying victuals and a bottle of ale. From there, they went into a rather disreputable looking clothing store where he purchased a pair of serviceable black breeches, a black shirt, and a pair of soft black leather boots that reached to his knees.

Leyla felt her heart catch a little as she saw him in his new attire. How magnificent he looked, tall and broad-shouldered, his dark hair shining in the sun.

He looked at her speculatively. "Go," he said, pressing a coin into her hand. "Buy yourself a new dress."

A new dress! How long since she'd had anything new to wear?

He followed her into the shop, standing nearby while she tried to make up her mind. He did it for her, choosing a full-skirted gown of sunny yellow, as well as a pair of soft-soled ankle boots and a cloak. She refused to try the dress on in the store, made uncomfortable by the nearness of the shopkeeper and a trio of unsavory-looking warriors who were haggling over the price of a broadsword.

Leyla clutched her new clothes to her breast as Jarrett took her hand and led her outside. He stowed their purchases in one of the saddlebags, lifted her onto the back of the white stallion, then effortlessly swung up behind her.

Taking up the reins with his left hand, he slid his right arm around her waist, drawing her back against his chest. The shock of his nearness, the pounding of his heart, the strength of his arm about her, made it suddenly difficult to breathe.

He rode out of town as if they had all the time in the world. Only when they were out of sight did he urge the big white stallion into a lope.

They rode for several hours, heading east, always east, toward the sea. She did not have to ask to know he intended to go to

Gweneth before he took her to Majeulla. She wanted to argue, to remind him of his promise to take her home, but she understood his need to return to Greyebridge first, and so she kept silent, trusting him to keep his promise in good time.

At dusk, they came across a cave recessed deep in a wooded hillside.

Jarrett tethered the stallion well away from the entrance to the cave, where it could graze on the stubby yellow grass. Lifting Leyla from the saddle, he approached the cavern.

Pausing at the entrance, he lit a candle, which he handed to Leyla and then, sword in hand, he entered the cave.

Their muffled footsteps sounded loud in the silence. Leyla stayed close to his side, her senses filling with the scent of decay.

"There's no one here," Jarrett said, his gaze sweeping the cavern. "No one has used this cave for many months."

Leyla tipped the candle to the side, letting some of the wax dribble onto a narrow ledge, then stuck the end of the candle in the hot wax.

The cave was long and narrow, the ceiling arched, like a cathedral, the floor of hard-packed dirt.

"I'll get the saddlebags," Jarrett said. Taking the bow and quiver from his shoulder, he dropped them below the ledge, then returned to the mouth of the cave.

Thirty minutes later, they were seated around a small fire, eating dark brown bread and tangy yellow cheese.

"How did thee happen to be imprisoned by the Fen?" Leyla asked.

"It was all a misunderstanding."

"A misunderstanding?" She licked the last crumbs of bread from her fingertips. "How so?"

"I received an order from the Minister of War to slaughter a handful of Aldanites who had taken refuge in the church at Greyebridge. When I refused to obey, I was branded a coward and a traitor. My title was revoked. All my holdings, save for Greyebridge Castle itself, were forfeit to the King by Rorke's order. I was on my way to Heth, to seek an audience with the King and explain what had happened, when I was captured by Rorke and sent to the Pavilion."

"Why did they not take thy castle as well?"

"I don't know."

"Why did thee refuse to slay the Aldanites?"

"They had taken sanctuary in my church. How could I kill them? They weren't warriors or spies, only a handful of frightened women and children."

"Are they not enemies of the King?"

He looked at her in surprise. "Are you suggesting I should have killed them?"

"No. My people shun war and refuse to

fight. But fighting was thy life. Thy reputation is well known, even to us."

"I don't make war on the helpless," Jarrett replied quietly.

"How long ago did all this happen to thee?"

"Eight months."

Eight months. A soft sound of sympathy rose in her throat.

Jarrett stared into the distance, remembering how it had been, the humiliation of captivity, the pain of the Games that never seemed to end, the degradation of having to beg for mercy when all he wanted was a sword and a fair chance.

He looked around the cave, at the scrap of deep blue sky visible at the entrance of the cave, at Leyla. It was all behind him now. In spite of everything, he was still alive. He was free. And she was there beside him, her luminous blue eyes filled with understanding.

He took her hand in his, feeling the warmth of her touch. "Leyla . . ."

"Thee must not."

"Are you reading my mind again?"

"It is not necessary. I can see what thee is thinking in thy eyes."

"One kiss?"

It was wrong. It was foolish. But she could no more resist his kiss than she could have let him die.

"Leyla." He placed his hands on either side

of her face and pressed his lips to hers, lightly. He didn't close his eyes, and neither did she.

The fire that sparked between them was as bright as a Hovis comet, as hot as the pools of Mereck. "Leyla."

She jerked away from him. "No more."

"As you wish." He reached for a flask of ale and took a long swallow, then another, savoring the taste of it. The potent brew burned through him. It was so long since he'd had anything to drink except water, anything to eat except the tasteless gruel served in the dungeons of the Pavilion. So long since he'd had a woman . . .

His gaze moved over Leyla, lingering on her lips, the soft swell of her breasts, the delicate beauty of her hands.

His body stirred to life as he remembered the touch of her hands on his flesh.

Too late, she realized her danger. She gasped as his hand closed over her arm, dragging her toward him. His mouth swooped down on hers, stifling her cry of protest. His tongue plunged into her mouth, savoring the sweetness within. She bucked like a wild mare beneath him, her nails raking the side of his face.

With a harsh cry, he drew back, lifting a hand to his cheek.

Leyla scrambled to her feet and backed away from him.

"I'm sorry." He shook his head, disgusted by his churlish behavior. "I . . ." He searched for words that weren't there. "I'm sorry," he said again.

The hurt in her eyes, the look of betrayal, cut him to the quick. "Leyla, forgive me."

She nodded, then turned away from him, making her way to the back of the cave, where she had made a bed of sorts. Jarrett had insisted she take the blanket, saying he would sleep beside the fire. She drew the coarse blanket around her shoulders, her body trembling convulsively. She had been warned that outsiders were brutal, primitive, and not to be trusted. Now she had seen it for herself. Now she knew why the Maje always married their own kind. The Maje were a quiet, peaceful people, not given to violence or passion, seeking only that which was calm and beautiful, wanting only to heal where others sought to destroy, looking for serenity when others seemed to thrive on turmoil and war.

Jarrett was a warrior. In his own land, he had been a Lord, leader of his people. Once they reached Greyebridge, once he had assured himself that all was well there, she would demand that he fulfill his promise and take her home.

Leyla sat up, not knowing what had roused her. Eyes gazing into the darkness, she listened to the sounds of the night, and then she heard it again, a hoarse cry that echoed within the walls of the cave.

Rising, she hurried toward the front of the cave. Jarrett was sprawled beside the fire, his face contorted. His hands were curled into tight fists, his knuckles white, every muscle tense.

The cry that rose in his throat seemed to be torn from the very depths of his soul.

"Jarrett." She placed her hand on his shoulder. "Jarrett. All is well."

He came awake with a start, staring at her through wide green eyes void of recognition. "No!" The single word, filled with anguish, made her heart ache. He was dreaming, she thought, reliving the nightmare that had been his life for so long.

"Jarrett." She placed one hand over his forehead.

He blinked up at her. "She?" Caught in the web of a nightmare, he called her by the name by which he'd first known her.

"I am here."

I am here. How many times had she come to him in the darkness of the night, her voice low and soothing, her touch healing the pain in his flesh?

He reached for her hand, the terror receding as her other hand stroked his brow, her warmth spreading through him, driving the demons away.

"All is well," she murmured. "Thee is free, remember?"

Free. He let out a long breath, then released her other hand, embarrassed to be caught crying in the night as if he were a child afraid of the dark. "I'll be all right now," he said gruffly. "Go back to bed."

His tone rebuffed her, but she knew the cause of it and was not offended. It was his pride striking out, that fierce pride inherent in all true warriors. He had been forced to humble himself so many times, there in the dungeons, she knew he could not bear for her to think him weak. And yet she did not wish to leave him alone.

Jarrett felt the heat stir in his loins. She was so near. He could hear the soft sound of her breathing, sense her gaze upon his face, hear the soft rustle of her clothing as she stirred beside him.

"Leyla, go back to bed."

She heard the barely restrained desire in his voice and quickly rose to her feet, leaving him there, alone in the darkness with his thoughts.

Chapter Six

He was reluctant to face her in the morning. Once, he'd been a warrior, a leader of men. Now he woke in the darkness, beset by dreams that were all too real, haunted by nightmares that left him trembling and afraid.

He avoided her gaze during First Meal, then left the cave and busied himself with saddling the horse while she washed their few dishes and stowed them in the saddlebag.

He sensed her presence at the mouth of the cave even before he turned around.

She was wearing the dress he had bought her, and he knew immediately that he should have left her in rags. The gown, the color of freshly churned butter, lent a soft golden glow to her skin. She looked like the Hovis sky in mid-summer — the dress the color of the sun, her hair the color of the three moons, and her eyes as blue as the sky. The full skirt made her waist seem incredibly tiny; the bodice hugged her upper body, revealing the swell of her breasts.

Wordlessly, he took the saddlebag from her hand, swung it over the back of the saddle, and lashed it into place. "Ready?"

"Yes, my Lord Jarrett."

"Do you mock me?"

"No. I speak to thee with the respect that should be thine."

Jarrett snorted. "Respect! For a man who wakes sniveling in the night like a frightened child?"

"Thee has no reason to be ashamed."

He didn't answer. Instead he vaulted onto the back of the stallion, then, taking Leyla by the forearm, swung her up behind him.

Lifting the reins, he turned the horse eastward.

As the morning progressed, he grew increasingly aware of Leyla's arms around his waist, of her breasts pressing against his back. He tried to ignore his longing for her, reminding himself that she was a Maje. To defile her was to rob her of the gift of healing that was her birthright. To take her against her will was unthinkable. And she would not give herself to him willingly; to do so would forever ruin her chance of marriage to one of her own kind.

Leyla, married to another. It was a bitter thing to contemplate. Try as he might, he could not shake the thought that she belonged to him. She had healed him, brought him back from the brink of death, of madness. He had admitted his fears to her, slept in her arms. He would gladly kill any man

70

who dared lay a hand on her to do her harm, and yet she was not his and never would be. He was a rebel, a renegade, a traitor. . . .

Bitterness welled within him. He had refused to kill the Aldanites who had begged for sanctuary in the chapel at Greyebridge and so he had been sent to prison. And the Aldanites had died anyway, killed by two warriors sent by the Minister of War.

He felt Leyla's arms slacken their hold around his waist, felt her body slump forward against his, and knew she'd fallen asleep. He placed his arm over hers, holding her close, feeling the soft sigh of her breath penetrate the fabric of his loosely woven shirt.

A short time later, he reined the stallion to a halt in the shade of a tree beside a slow-moving river. Lifting his right leg over the horse's neck so that he sat sideways in the saddle, he gathered Leyla into his arms and slid to the ground.

She made a soft, sleepy sound, but did not awake. For a moment, he held her close in his arms, his gaze moving over her face. Her skin was smooth, perfect, her lips the color of roses, her lashes dark and thick.

Carefully, he laid her on the thick new grass beneath the tree, and then he knelt beside her, his fists tightly clenched at his sides as he watched the rise and fall of her breasts, the faint flutter of her lashes. A small smile played over her lips, and he wondered what she was dreaming about. Not dungeons, certainly, or she wouldn't be smiling. Unicorns, perhaps, or yellow-winged fairies dancing in the wind.

Leyla stirred, feeling his nearness even before she was fully awake.

"My Lord Jarrett?"

"I am here," he replied, and thought how often she had said those words, her voice soothing him in the darkness that had ever been his.

She opened her eyes, looking vaguely bewildered. "Is something wrong?"

"No."

"Why are we here?"

"You fell asleep."

"Oh. I'm sorry."

She started to get up, but he placed a hand on her shoulder, urging her to stay where she was.

"It's all right. I've been pushing you too hard these last days."

"I'm fine."

"I know." He couldn't stop looking at her, couldn't stop wanting her. Eight months. Eight months without a woman. He'd never been licentious, taking his pleasure with every woman who crossed his path, but he'd never been a monk, either.

Eight months. He swore under his breath, wondering if she had any idea of the effect her very nearness had on him. She was so lovely, her skin like rich cream, her blue eyes luminous, her lips as pink as a wild rose. The rise and fall of her breasts tempted his hand, the scent of her enflamed him. He longed to close his eyes and bury his face in the rich silver mass of her hair, taste her sweetness, caress her cheek. . . .

He saw the change in her, saw the fear in her eyes, in the quick intake of her breath. Too late, he tried to clear his mind of its wayward thoughts.

"Leyla . . ." His voice was ragged with longing and regret.

She scrambled to her knees and scooted backwards, only to come up hard against the trunk of the tree. Feeling trapped, she stared at him in silent entreaty.

"Leyla, do not be afraid of me. I would rather cut off my right arm than cause you a moment's unhappiness."

"I want to believe thee," she said. "I *would* believe thee if . . ."

"If you could not see what I was thinking. I know." His smile was small and cheerless. "I cannot help what I feel. You're so lovely, and I've been without a woman for so long. Perhaps, if your eyes weren't as blue as the flowers at Greyebridge, or your hair didn't shine like the sun at midday . . ."

His gaze moved over her like a caress. "Perhaps if your skin wasn't so fair, your mouth not quite so perfect, I wouldn't want you so badly." He shook his head. "Perhaps, if your face were pocked and your teeth were black and you didn't smell so very, very good, I wouldn't ache for you day and night, waking or sleeping."

"Jarrett, I wish I could love thee, but I cannot. I am betrothed to another."

"Betrothed!" He felt as if Thal's knife had cleaved his heart in two. "Betrothed."

"Yes, since I was a child."

"I don't believe you."

" 'Tis true, nevertheless. His name is Tor."

He stared at her for several moments; then, with a grace that was innate, he rose to his feet and walked away from her.

Betrothed! To some soft-spoken Maje who would never appreciate her, never see past her serene facade to the fire that he knew burned deep within.

He clenched his fists, longing to strike out at something, someone. His blood ran hot with a sense of betrayal, as if he'd discovered that his woman had been unfaithful to him.

He stopped beneath a tree and pressed his forehead to the rough bark. Closing his eyes, he tried to still the rage churning within him. Unbidden came the memory of her hands gliding over his flesh, healing him with a touch. A hoarse cry of despair rose in his throat as he imagined her hands touching another, not to heal, but to arouse.

Betrothed! Eight months of torture and darkness and humiliation had not hurt as much as this.

"My Lord?"

He flinched at the sound of her voice. Wiping all emotion from his face, he turned away from the tree to face her.

"I prepared Second Meal. I thought, since we had stopped, and it is near midday, thee might wish to eat." He looked at her without speaking, the hurt in his dark green eyes stabbing her to the heart.

"Do you want to marry him?" he asked gruffly.

"I . . ." Leyla shrugged. "It is my father's wish."

"Do you love him?"

"He is a temperate man, soft-spoken, and of a kind and gentle nature."

"Not a renegade," Jarrett replied with a sneer. "Not a rebel wanted for high treason and rebellion. I suppose he'll bring you midnight flowers and sea shells and whisper Majeullian poetry in your ear."

"Perhaps."

Impulsively, Jarrett closed the distance between them. Grasping Leyla by the arms, he drew her against him. "Answer me! Do you love him?"

She stared into his eyes, her expression mildly reproving. "I will learn to love him, as my mother learned to love my father."

His fingers tightened on her arms. With a low growl, he covered her mouth with his. It was a brutal kiss, meant to hurt her, to brand her as his. Only when he tasted the salt of her tears did he release her. Only then did he see the fear and the disappointment in her eyes.

Jarrett knew he should apologize, promise her it wouldn't happen again, but he rarely made promises he couldn't keep.

He ignored her the rest of the day and spread his blanket across the fire from hers that night.

She sought her bed immediately after Last Meal. Moments later, she was asleep.

For a long while, he gazed at her through the shimmering flames, the heat of the fire as nothing compared to the throbbing heat of desire that pulsed through his veins. . . .

Jarrett choked back a groan as the lash sang its cruel song. He felt the skin of his back split, felt the warmth of his blood trickling down his sides, pooling beneath him.

The blackness inside the hood was oppressive, smothering. He whispered Leyla's name, sobbing because the dream was over . . . he wasn't free — he would never be free. And Gar's whip played endlessly across his back and shoulders, until there was no flesh left, until he was only a skeleton bathed in blood and sweat.

He cried for Leyla, pleading with them to let her touch him, to take away the pain, and then one of the Gamesmen removed the hood and he saw Leyla standing beside him. "Help me," he begged, but she shook her head.

"I cannot," she replied.

"Help me!" He screamed the words, and then screamed again when she raised her arms, revealing two bloody stumps where her hands should have been. . . .

"Jarrett! Jarrett! Wake up! Please, wake up!"

"She?" Breathing hard, he jackknifed into a sitting position, his gaze darting wildly from side to side.

Leyla grabbed his hand and held it tightly. "I am here, my Lord Jarrett," she murmured fervently. "I am here."

A low groan erupted from Jarrett's throat and he fell back, flinging an arm across his eyes. It had been so real. So real.

He grasped Leyla's hand when she started to pull away. "Don't go."

"No," she promised. "I will not." Gently, she drew her hand from his. "Sit up," she instructed, and when he did so, she moved behind him and began to massage the tension from his back and shoulders.

Jarrett closed his eyes, his chin dropping to his chest as he began to relax. Sitting there, feeling the magic inherent in her hands, he made a decision that was simple and totally without honor.

He would take Leyla to Greyebridge Castle

with him, and keep her there, willing or not.

The decision was made quickly, irrevocably, and then he put it from his mind lest she should peer into his thoughts and discover what he meant to do.

Chapter Seven

In the days that followed, he was careful to keep his distance from Leyla, careful not to touch her if he could avoid it. The long hours in the saddle were nothing short of agony. There was no way to avoid her touch then. Hour after hour, he felt the heat of her arms at his waist, the soft seduction of her breasts pressing against his back. He tried riding behind her, but it didn't help. Then it was his arms around her, holding her close, the scent of her hair rising in his nostrils.

Bad as the days were, the nights were far worse. The nightmares continued to plague him so that he dreaded the darkness. He tried sleeping during the day and riding at night, but even that couldn't keep the bad dreams at bay. Night after night, he woke drenched with sweat, the sound of Leyla's voice leading him out of the darkness.

Tonight was no different. His own screams were still ringing in his ears, the phantom images still fresh in his mind, as Leyla drew him close, rocking him as a mother might rock a troubled child.

"It is all right," she murmured soothingly.

"It is all right. Thee is safe now."

Safe . . . He willed his body to stop shaking, despising himself for his weakness, for being frightened by nothing more substantial than shadowed images. But the dreams were so real; he could feel the sting of the whip, hear their laughter, smell the blood — his blood. He could feel the blades of the Gamesmen slicing into his flesh, smell the fear that rolled off him in waves, hear the sound of his voice crying for mercy. It was that above all else that sickened him. He'd never thought of himself as a coward until he'd been forced to play the Games, but he knew he'd rather die than go back and face it all again. The worst of it was, none of the Games in and of themselves had been unbearable, at least not until the end. They weren't fatal, they weren't crippling, but, taken as a whole, day after day, they had been more than he could stand.

He closed his eyes, feeling himself begin to relax under the touch of her hand, the sound of her voice.

"Leyla . . ."

"I am here."

A faint smile touched his lips. *I am here.* She spoke the words and all the demons vanished. He would take her home, he thought again, home to Greyebridge. Home to his mother. He would grant her anything she desired, clothe her in silks and satins, adorn her

with jewels to rival those in the king's crown
— anything, so long as she would remain at
his side.

"No." Leyla jerked away from him and
stood up.

"What?" Jarrett blinked up at her, confused
by her sudden withdrawal.

"Greyebridge! I will not stay there! Thee
promised to take me home."

He swore under his breath, cursing her
ability to read his thoughts.

"Leyla . . ."

"I wish to go home, Lord Jarrett. I wish to
go now."

"I need to go to Greyebridge. We can rest
there, get fresh horses, clothing, food."

"I will not go."

"I'll take you to Majeulla afterwards."

"Thee is lying."

Jarrett shook his head sadly. "I cannot let
you go." Hating himself, he took the scarf
from her hair and lashed her hands together,
not trusting her to stay with him now. "I'll
untie you in the morning."

She refused to look at him. With an air of
injured dignity, she turned her back to him
and curled up on the ground. This was what
came of trusting one not of the blood, she
thought bitterly, of letting herself care for a
man not of her race. She was a prisoner
again.

Jarrett released her hands in the morning.

He tried to apologize, but she would not look at him, would not speak to him, would not eat the food he offered her, though she did accept a drink of water.

He understood her anger, but it didn't change his mind. He wanted her. He needed her, and he meant to keep her near, for a while at least.

He lifted her into the saddle, swung up behind her, and turned the horse eastward.

The hours passed slowly. The quiet companionship they had shared was gone. He tried to talk to her several times, but he could not break through the barrier of her silent condemnation.

At dusk, he made camp in the hollow of a hill. Again, she refused to eat, refused to speak.

"Leyla, please try to understand."

She looked at him blankly, as if he were a stone or a tree, then gazed into the fire. The flames danced in her hair, turning the silver to gold.

"I won't tie your hands if you promise you won't run away."

"I make thee no promises, Lord Jarrett, except one. Thee will regret this before the night is over."

With a curt nod, he grabbed her hands and tied them together. Her look of wounded innocence cut his heart like a knife.

He stayed by the fire long after she'd fallen

asleep, staring into the glowing coals, hating himself for what he was doing to her, yet unable to face the future without her. He did not think of loving her — such a thing was impossible. She was a Maje, a healer. He was a man who had been robbed of his titles, his land, his legions. He had nothing left but a castle that had been in his family for generations.

Gradually, his eyelids grew heavy and he settled down beside the fire's embers, thinking of home, wondering if his mother was still there. . . .

He was drowning in his own blood, unable to scream for the thick red liquid that clogged his throat. Gar stood behind him, cracking a whip made of heavy chain, while Siid touched a match to a torch made of reeds. And then Thal appeared beside him, a twelve-inch knife in his hand, a knife stained with blood. His blood. He felt the whip cut across his back, felt a dancing finger of flame lick his thigh, felt Thal's blade at his throat.

And he couldn't scream, couldn't utter a sound, as his nostrils filled with the smell of fear and blood and burning flesh — his fear, his blood, his flesh.

Leyla! His mind screamed her name, begging her for mercy, for forgiveness. *Help me! Please, help me . . .*

She was dreaming of home, of gently rolling hills and verdant valleys, of blue rain and lavender sunsets. Dreaming of her mother and father, when, unbidden, there appeared a man with black hair and fathomless green eyes, a strong man, a warrior.

She tried to banish him from her dreams, but his image only grew stronger and she smiled as she heard his voice whisper her name as no other ever had . . . Leyla, Leyla, Leyla!

Her eyes flew open at the sound of his anguished scream, and then she frowned. The night was as silent as the sunrise, yet her mind was filled with his hoarse cries.

Glancing over her shoulder, she saw him thrashing about, his sweat-sheened face contorted with pain, his mouth open in a silent scream of terror.

She would not help him, she thought. She would not help this barbarian who broke his vows and kept her prisoner.

Thee will regret this before the night is over.

She tried to find satisfaction in knowing that her prediction had come true.

Another anguished cry rose in her mind, bringing tears to her eyes. She stared at his writhing form, glimpsing the unspeakable horror that held him in its power, feeling the awful pain that engulfed him.

"I will not." Even as she formed the words, she was moving toward him, laying her bound hands upon his chest, calling his name.

"My Lord Jarrett. Jarrett! Come to me, now. I am here."

"She?"

"I am here," she said again, and wondered at the quiet power of those three words.

"Hold me."

"I cannot."

He blinked up at her, not understanding until she held out her hands.

Flooded with shame, he drew his knife and cut her free.

When she reached for him, he shook his head. "No. I don't deserve your help."

" 'Tis true," she agreed, putting her arms around him, "but thee has it just the same."

He let her hold him then, his body rigid with guilt for the way he'd treated her, wondering what would happen to him if she wasn't there to wake him, to comfort him with her touch. Would he wander in his nightmare world forever, driven to madness by the vague shadows of illusion that were too strong to fight on his own?

"Relax, my Lord," she whispered. "No more demons will haunt thee this night."

"Don't." He drew away from her. "Don't waste your powers on me. I don't deserve your kindness."

She did not bother with a reply, merely drew him into her arms again, holding him close to her breast as her hands stroked his hair and massaged the back of his neck.

"Forgive me," he murmured, surrendering to the magic of her touch. "Forgive me."

" 'Tis done," she whispered, and felt the sigh of relief that rippled through him.

Moments later, he was asleep.

The tables were turned in the morning, and it was Jarrett who refused to face Leyla. He had lied to her, abused her, tied her up as if she were no more than a slave, and she had repaid his treachery with kindness.

He muttered his thanks for the food she prepared, left her to her privacy when the meal was over. Feeling like the worst kind of wretch, he sat near the edge of a small pool, staring into the glassy water, wondering how he would endure the demons of his past without her. But he had promised to take her home, to the mist-draped mountains of Majeulla, and take her home he would.

His return to Gweneth would have to wait.

Chapter Eight

The following morning, after First Meal, Jarrett lifted Leyla onto the back of the horse and turned south, toward the majestic Mountains of the Blue Mist that had been home to the Maje for eons of time.

Located in the northern part of Fenduzia, the mist-shrouded mountains were enshrined in legend and mystery. It was said that no one could ascend their heights and live save those who were born there. A fire-breathing dragon guarded the long, winding path that led to the village. Poisonous snakes and plants infested the foothills, taking their toll of unwary, and unwanted, visitors. Rivers of sparkling blue water had lured thirsty men to their deaths. Others had died more slowly, trapped in shimmering pools of quicksand. No one knew how many men had risked all in hopes of capturing a Maje and thereby being assured of their healing powers in times of need.

"Are they true?" Jarrett asked. "All the rumors I've heard about the legendary home of your people?"

"They can be."

"Can be?"

"Much depends on one's point of view."

"You talk in riddles. Is there a dragon? Are there rivers of death and pools filled with quicksand?"

"Yes. But the dragon is harmless if one knows the secret of its lair. The poison in the water can be dispersed. The pools can be crossed, if one knows the way."

"And the snakes?"

"The Maje are immune to their venom. Our mountains are a part of us, her earth is in our blood, her mysteries come to us with the first breath of life."

"Why did you leave the safety of your home? How is it that you came to be held captive by the Fen?"

"I wanted to see another part of the world. I wanted adventure. I wanted to see the ocean." She shrugged. "I had been warned never to go past Dragora's cave alone, but . . ." She shrugged again. "I was young and foolish. One day I went for a walk, and I just kept walking.

"When I reached the foothills, I saw Gar and Thal. They were hunting. I had never seen any of the Fen close up, so I hid behind a tree to watch. A short while later, Gar chased a wounded stag into the trees where I was hiding. When the stag saw me, it turned. Its horn caught Gar in the stomach. I started to run away, back up the mountain, but I couldn't leave him there. He was bleeding and in pain and I was drawn to him. His was the first serious wound I had ever seen. While I was healing him, Thal came up behind me. There was no way for me to escape."

"Did they ever . . . did they hurt you?"

"No. Gar was very grateful that I had saved his life, but not grateful enough to let me go. They kept me with them for a while, then, eager to return to the Games, they sold me to the Pavilion."

They rode in silence for a time. Jarrett tried to think about the home of the Maje, but all he could think of was Leyla. His arm was around her waist, and he could feel her warmth, her every breath, through the thin fabric of her dress. The scent of her hair, of woman, filled his nostrils.

He had to get away from her, at least for a few minutes. A shallow pool offered the perfect excuse for a rest. Reining the stallion to a halt, he slid to the ground. Turning, he lifted Leyla from the saddle, and quickly let her go.

"We'll rest here awhile," he said.

Leyla nodded. It was a lovely spot. The pool was shaded by tall trees, surrounded by large, leafy ferns and red midnight flowers.

"Shall we take Second Meal here?" she asked.

"If you wish."

She looked at him for a moment, trying to

see what he was thinking, but his mind was closed to her. "Is something wrong?"

"No. Fix the meal. I'm going to look around."

Without waiting for her reply, he turned on his heel and walked away, needing to put some space between them. She had bewitched him, he thought, beguiled him so completely he could think of nothing but her, the shape of her mouth, the texture of her hair, the color of her eyes, the sound of her voice. Never had he craved a woman's touch as he craved hers.

He walked steadily onward, following a narrow path into a grove of tall trees. As he moved deeper into the forest, his hand moved instinctively toward his sword. Years of training as a warrior rose within him, making him cautious. He found a measure of relief in the simple exercise of walking. It was a good feeling, being able to come and go as he pleased, to see the sun. The newness of it, after eight months of captivity, still had the power to excite him. His arms and legs, freed of the constant restriction of the shackles, felt light as air.

He drew in a deep breath, filling his lungs with the scent of earth and trees and grass. The world looked new, brighter, somehow. He touched the rough bark of a tree, stooped to pick a wildflower. Pausing, he listened to the warbling of a bird.

He was alive. Alive and well, because of Leyla.

The mere thought of her filled him with warmth. Eight months of captivity. Eight months of torture and darkness. Eight months without a woman . . . and now he was free, and the one woman he wanted was forever out of reach.

Leyla. The pain of wanting her, of knowing she would never be his, made him ache deep inside.

With a sigh, he turned and retraced his steps toward the pool.

He paused when he reached the edge of the forest, all his senses suddenly alert. His gaze swept their campsite. All seemed well. Leyla was sitting on a tree stump, her back toward him. The stallion was grazing on a patch of grass.

But something wasn't right.

He looked at Leyla again, at the rigid set of her spine. Eyes narrowed, ears straining, he watched and listened. And then he heard it, the faint creak of saddle leather off to the left.

Drawing his sword, he waited in the shadows, knowing that death awaited whoever made the first move.

The moments slid by. Sweat trickled down his spine, beaded across his brow, dampened his palms. And still he waited.

The attack, when it came, still took him by

surprise. He heard footsteps behind him, the excited whinny of a horse to his left, the answering call of another horse to his right.

Pivoting on his heel, he brought his sword up, parrying a blow to his neck. The Giant's sword was heavy in his hand as he dropped to one knee and thrust the blade upward, plunging it almost to the hilt in Thal's belly.

The horsemen were practically on top of him by then. Scrambling to his feet, Jarrett braced his back against a tree, giving them no room to maneuver their horses around him.

Gar dismounted first, his lips drawn back in a feral snarl. The Fen warrior attacked viciously, careful to stay out of range of Jarrett's sword, giving Siid time to dismount and come around on the other side. It was a simple but effective tactic, forcing Jarrett away from the tree and into the open.

The harsh clang of metal striking metal shattered the stillness of the glade. Leyla glanced over her shoulder, a gasp erupting from her lips as she saw the two Fen warriors advancing on Jarrett. She swung her legs over the log, the better to see the battle as she struggled to loose her hands.

She felt her heart go cold as she saw Jarrett valiantly fighting against Siid and Gar, his sword flashing in the sunlight like lightning during a storm. His green eyes were bright with the heat of battle, and there was

92

a faint smile on his lips. It occurred to her that he was enjoying himself even though she feared he could not win. He hadn't held a sword in eight months. The Gamesmen had practiced every day. And they were good, she thought in dismay. So very good. Even as she watched, she saw Gar's cutlass slice into Jarrett's arm, saw the bright splash of blood that rose in the wake of the blade.

Jarrett hardly seemed aware of the wound as he turned to parry Siid's next thrust.

With a small cry of pain and frustration, she gave one last tug on the rope at her wrists. There was a moment of triumph as her hands came free and then she was bending to untie her feet.

A harsh scream drew her attention and she saw that Gar was down, bleeding badly from a crippling wound in his right thigh. But it was the blood splattered across Jarrett's chest that held her attention. The urge to go to him, to lay her hands upon him, was almost overpowering.

Tossing the rope that had bound her feet aside, she stood up, one hand pressed to her heart, as she watched the two warriors. They were closely matched in size and reach, but Jarrett had been wounded and that gave Siid the advantage. All he had to do was wait, wait for the loss of blood to weaken his opponent.

She could not let that happen.

Picking up a rock, she crept up behind Gar

and struck him across the back of the head, rendering him unconscious. And then, going against everything she had been taught, all she had ever believed in, she reached for Gar's sword.

A movement from the corner of his eye caught Jarrett's attention. Thinking it was Gar, he risked a glance in that direction. Leyla! He swore under his breath when he saw the sword in her hand and realized that she meant to come to his defense.

That one moment of distraction gave Siid all the chance he needed and he lunged forward, his sword slipping under Jarrett's guard, piercing flesh and muscle only to be deflected by a rib.

But Jarrett was moving, too. Spurred on by pain and anger and the overwhelming need to get Leyla out of danger, he took a step forward, his sword blocking Siid's next thrust. At the same time, he drew his knife with his left hand and drove it into Siid's chest.

With a hoarse cry, Siid dropped heavily to his knees, then slumped to the ground.

Dropping the sword, Leyla ran up to Jarrett, her face pale, her eyes wide with horror. For all the time she had spent in the Pavilion, she had never seen two men locked in mortal combat.

"Is he dead?" she asked tremulously.

"Not yet," Jarrett replied tersely. "What of Gar?"

"He is unconscious. Come, let us . . . No!" She grabbed Jarrett's arm, restraining him when she realized that he meant to slay both of the fallen men. "Please."

Jarrett glared at her, his blood running hot with the need to strike the final blow, to see the three Gamesmen dead once and for all.

The look in his eyes frightened Leyla more than anything else.

"Please," she begged. "Let us leave this place." She placed her hand over his chest. "Thee is hurt."

The sweetness of her touch and the sound of her voice cooled his anger. "We'll go, if that's what you want."

She smiled up at him. "Come, lie down. Let me care for thy wounds."

Suddenly too weary to argue, Jarrett followed her to where she'd spread a blanket on the grass. Stretching out, he closed his eyes, surrendering himself to the familiar touch of her healing hands.

The passage of time was hazy. A few minutes, an hour, time lost all meaning as she placed her hands upon him, suffusing him with heat, withdrawing the pain, replacing it with peace and harmony in body and soul.

He opened his eyes when she took her hands from him, swore under his breath when he saw her walking toward Siid.

Rolling to his feet, he ran after her, catching her by the arm before she could lay her hands on the Gamesman. "What do you think you're doing?"

"He is wounded."

"Leave him."

"I cannot."

Jarrett stared at the two unconscious men, remembering . . . remembering the smell of his own burning flesh as Siid placed a live coal against his thigh, remembering the sting of Gar's whip across his back. "Leave him. Leave them both."

"Jarrett, I cannot."

"You will!" He grabbed her by the shoulders and drew her up against him, his face only inches from hers, his eyes blazing with fury. "You asked me to spare their lives. For you, I will do it, even though my blood screams for vengeance. But I will not allow you to heal them."

Before she could argue further, before she had time to rest from the strain of healing his wounds, he swept her off her feet and dropped her, none too gently, onto the back of Gar's horse. Taking the animal's reins, he mounted his own horse and rode away from the pool without looking back.

Chapter Nine

Leyla rode in furious silence. She was a Maje, sworn to use her powers to heal whenever possible. Because of Jarrett, she had done violence. Because of Jarrett, she had been forced to withhold the gift with which she had been blessed. No matter that the Fen were the enemy, that they had meant Jarrett harm. Once the violence had passed, the need to heal had risen within her, and he had denied her that right. Her birthright.

She stared at his back as her horse trailed his. Her father had been right. The men who lived beyond the Mountains of the Blue Mist were beyond understanding.

With an effort, she drew her thoughts from Jarrett and summoned Tor's image to mind. Helpless to resist, she found herself comparing the two men. Tor's skin was fair where Jarrett's was dark; Tor's hair was white as parchment while Jarrett's was as black as the inside of Dragora's cave. Tor's eyes were a warm rich brown, like the earth; Jarrett's were as green and unfathomable as the pools of Majeulla. Tor was a man of deep inner peace, sought out for his wisdom and his incomparable gift of sight; Jarrett was a warrior, a renegade, a man of violence and passion. . . .

She had seen that passion in the depths of his eyes, felt it in his arms when he held her, tasted it when he kissed her.

She lifted her fingertips to her lips, felt her heart skip a beat as she remembered the touch of his mouth on hers. She had never known a man's kiss before, never realized the power of such an ordinary act. He had grabbed her and kissed her and his touch had sizzled through her, hot as Dragora's breath, shocking her senses. Tor would not kiss her like that. He would ask her permission before daring to indulge in such intimacy. His touch would be as gentle as the morning rain, as soft as dandelion down. He wouldn't make her heart race or her blood sing. He wouldn't make her limbs go weak, or cause the world to spin out of focus. . . .

Stop it! She shook her head, bewildered at the turn of her thoughts. She was a Maje. A Maje did not marry for pleasure or carnal desire, but to perpetuate the race, that there might always be someone to heal the pain inflicted by others, someone to see beauty in the midst of ugliness, someone to speak for peace in time of war.

She stared down at Jarrett when he touched her arm, so lost in thought she hadn't been aware that they'd stopped.

"We'll rest here for the night," he said.

She nodded, her senses reeling as his hands closed around her waist to lift her from the back of the horse.

He held her for several moments, his dark green eyes gazing into hers, making it difficult to breathe. She wondered why he didn't put her down, wondered why she couldn't read his thoughts as he held her, suspended in the air, her eyes on a level with his.

"What is thee staring at?" she asked.

"At sky-blue eyes and lips that would tempt a heavenly messenger."

"Thee should put me down."

"Should I?"

There was fire in the depths of his eyes, flames as hot as the pools of Mereck, heat that threatened to melt her defenses. "Please," she whispered.

Slowly, he lowered her feet to the ground.

Slowly, he took his hands from her waist.

Slowly, he bent his head toward hers. Freed of all restraint, she was still powerless to resist and she stood quiescent as his mouth descended on hers. Feather light, his lips caressed hers, more tempting than sweet Freywine, more tantalizing than a Siren's call.

She gazed into his eyes, felt the fervent heat of his desire leap between them even though their bodies were not touching. There was only the undemanding pressure of his lips on hers, silently entreating, quietly pleading for her surrender.

"No." Unable to draw her gaze from his, she shook her head. "No. I cannot give thee what thee desires."

"I haven't asked thee for anything." His voice was deep and low, husky with yearning.

"Thee does not need to ask. Thy desire is clearly mirrored in the depths of thy eyes, in the silent entreaty of thy lips."

"It displeases thee?"

She stared at him in confusion. She should be angry. She should be offended. Why, then, was she pleased that he found her desirable?

"Thee has not answered me. Does my ardor displease thee?"

"No . . . yes . . ." She drew a deep, steadying breath, willing herself to think of Majeulla, of her betrothed, of her duty to her people. "Please let me go."

He lifted one black brow. "I am not holding thee."

But he was. His deep green gaze imprisoned her more surely than chains or iron bars.

"Jarrett, to give in to thy desire will give thee a moment's pleasure, but it will destroy everything I am, everything I hold dear. Please do not ask it of me."

"And if I did?"

"I fear I would give it to thee."

Her words filled him with joy, and pain. Summoning every ounce of self-control that he possessed, he turned and walked away from her. Even if she were willing, he couldn't take her innocence, couldn't rob her of her gift just to ease the awful ache that plagued him. She was a Maje, born to heal. She belonged in a world far different from his. High in the mist-shrouded mountains of her homeland, she would live in peace and harmony with her people. She would listen to the song of the Hoada and the whisper of the south wind. On moonlight nights, she would tell her children tales of Dragora. And, perhaps, some dark eve, she would tell them of the horrors of the Pavilion, and of the renegade warrior whose pain and misery she had alleviated over and over again.

She did not like the silence between them, but she didn't know how to mend it. He had withdrawn from her in a way that made her feel lost and alone.

In the days that followed, they rode from dawn till dusk, pausing only to eat and rest the horses. He never touched her, either intentionally or by accident. He spread his blankets across the fire, ate his meals with his back towards her, making her feel as if she were unclean, a pariah.

As the flatlands gave way to gently rolling hills and shallow valleys, she tried to tell herself it was for the best. Soon, they would reach Majeulla. He would return to his own people, and she would never see him again.

For the best. For the best. The words became a litany, repeating in her mind as they traveled across the green-gold hills toward home.

It was near dark several days later when they reached the Cyrus River. Beyond lay the rolling foothills and the Mountains of the Blue Mist.

"We'll spend the night here," Jarrett said, indicating a quiet vale, "and cross in the morning."

Leyla nodded. Dismounting, she removed the saddlebags from behind the saddle and began to prepare Last Meal. She could feel Jarrett's gaze on her back. Almost, she looked into his mind, wondering what he was thinking, what he was feeling, now that their journey was near its end. Tomorrow, they would start up the mountain. The following morning, she would be home again, back among her own people.

The thought did not cheer her as it should have.

They ate in silence, a horrible tension-filled silence that brought tears to her eyes. She yearned to touch him, to tell him that she cared for him, that she would never forget him, but she knew it would only make it harder to say good-bye when the time came.

She wished he would look at her with affection just once more.

She wished she could . . . The thought died unfinished as she felt Jarrett's hand close over her mouth. When she tried to pull away, his hold tightened in warning.

She heard it then, the faint sound of crackling leaves as something, or someone, crept toward them.

"Drop your sword, Rebel," called a familiar voice, "or the Maje dies. My arrow will not miss at this range."

Jarrett swore under his breath. He'd been so caught up in his own thoughts, he hadn't heard the approach of the intruders until it was too late.

"Do as he says," warned a second voice. "We will not ask again."

Leyla shook her head, knowing that surrender would mean Jarrett's death.

There was a sudden hiss as an arrow arched through the sky and pinned Leyla's skirt to the ground. "That is my last warning, Rebel. Throw down your sword."

Jarrett drew a deep breath; then, with slow deliberation, he tossed his sword toward the voice in the trees.

Leyla's eyes widened in alarm as Gar limped out of the shadows. A moment later, Siid came striding toward them, a smug grin on his face.

Stricken with guilt, she glanced up at Jarrett, silently pleading for his forgiveness, but he wasn't looking at her. He was watching the two men, and though his face was impassive, she could feel the tension radiating from him as he waited to see what they would do next.

"So, Lord Jarrett, we meet again." Gar made a mock bow of respect. "It was impolite of you to leave the party before the last course."

"My apologies," Jarrett retorted, his voice heavy with sarcasm. "But I did not wish to *be* the last course.

Siid's smile was cruel as he rubbed his crippled right leg. "Your wishes are no longer important. We have one more Game to play, and a comrade's death to avenge."

Gar nodded. "The last Game will be played here, in the morning. And there will be no Maje to heal you this time, even if you survive."

Jarrett's head came up with a jerk. "What do you mean?"

With snakelike speed, Gar reached for Leyla and drew her to his side. "After tonight," Gar said cryptically, "she will be powerless to help you or anyone else."

"No." Jarrett took a step forward, only to come up short as Gar laid his blade against Leyla's throat. "Do what you want with me, but let her go."

"We will do exactly as we want," Siid replied. "With you. And with her."

"I'll do anything you ask," Jarrett said.

"Grovel in the dirt. Crawl on my belly. Anything. Only let her go."

Gar's laugh was cruel. "You'll do all those things and more before you die, Rebel, I promise you that, just as I promise that your dying will take many days." He wrapped his free hand in Leyla's hair, jerking her head back as he pressed the edge of the sword to her throat. "Siid, bind him."

Jarrett kept his gaze on Leyla as Siid bound his hands behind his back. *Don't be afraid. I'll think of something, I swear it.* He sent his thoughts toward her, hoping she would read them in his mind.

He thought she nodded slightly, but he couldn't be sure.

With malicious glee, Siid drew back his fist and buried it in Jarrett's stomach, howling with delight when Jarrett doubled over, retching.

Again and again, Siid lashed out with his fists until Jarrett lay on the ground, his body drawn into itself. With a grunt, the Gamesman kicked Jarrett in the ribs, then turned away, his eyes glinting with desire.

"Bind her," Siid remarked. "I'll get the dice."

"We'll use mine," Gar informed him with a cold grin. "I've lost to you too many times."

"As you wish," Siid agreed. "I won't mind losing tonight, since the prize remains the same."

In moments, Leyla was bound hand and foot, forced to sit between the Fen warriors while they played a game of nine points to see who would be the one to deflower her.

Frightened as she was for her own fate, it was fear for Jarrett that pounded in her brain. They might abuse her. They might steal her maidenhead, but Jarrett's life would be forfeit, and it would be all her fault. If only she had let him kill the Fen as he'd wanted. If only she could go back, she would do it herself!

Leyla gazed at Jarrett. He lay so still, she wondered if he was dead. Heartsick, she willed him to move, to breathe, even as she hoped that he would never regain consciousness, that he might be spared whatever torment the Fen had planned for him.

Jarrett opened his eyes to a red mist of pain and the taste of blood and dirt in his mouth. It hurt to breathe, to think. He could see Gar and Siid sitting cross-legged before the fire, their heads bent as they rolled the dice. Leyla sat between them.

Slowly, laboriously, he strained toward the knife sheathed within his boot. Pain slashed through him as he tried to reach the knife. He curled tighter into himself, drawing his leg as close to his body as he could, stretching his arm, his hands, his fingers, praying to the All Father that he wouldn't pass out. From the cries of his captors, he knew time was running out.

With a last mighty effort, he made a grab for the blade, felt his fingertips brush the haft of the knife. So close. Grimacing with pain, he tried again, willing hands gone numb to respond. It took a moment before he realized he'd succeeded.

He glanced at Gar and Siid, making sure they were still distracted by the game; then, moving slowly and awkwardly, he began to saw at the thick rope around his wrists.

Leyla's scream warned him that the game was over.

Chapter Ten

His wrists were slick with blood, his brow sheened with sweat, by the time he cut through the rope. He closed his eyes and drew in a deep breath, willing his hands to stop shaking, blocking the pain from his mind as he concentrated on what he had to do.

Moving slowly, he glanced over his shoulder. Siid was holding a wildly struggling Leyla while Gar stripped off his breeches.

It was now or never. Gripping the knife in his right hand, Jarrett rolled to his knees and crawled stealthily toward Gar.

Struggling to stay conscious, Jarrett raised the knife. It was then that Leyla lashed out with her feet, catching Gar in the chest, driving him backward into Jarrett's blade.

Jarrett grunted with pain as Gar fell against him.

Siid drew his knife and cocked his arm, ready to throw the weapon.

Freed from her captor's grasp, Leyla rolled to her side and scrambled to her knees.

Jarrett jerked his knife from Gar's back and shoved the man's lifeless body out of the way.

It was then that Siid hurled the longboar knife.

It was then that Leyla rose to her feet.

She screamed as the double-edged blade buried itself in her back. Eyes wide with pained surprise, she sank to her knees.

With a cry of disbelief, Jarrett charged Siid, driving him to the ground, plunging his knife into the man's chest over and over again, until the warrior lay in an ever-widening pool of blood.

"Jarrett . . ."

Leyla's voice, weak and frightened, penetrated his rage. Tossing the knife aside, he hurried to her side. She lay face down, the haft of Siid's longboar knife protruding from her back. Her upper body was covered with blood.

"Leyla?"

"Thee is all right?"

"I'm fine." He choked back the gorge that rose in his throat as he stared at the knife, knowing he would have to draw that long length of steel from her flesh. "Leyla . . ."

"It hurts," she murmured.

"I know." As gently as possible, he took hold of the knife and with one quick jerk, pulled it from her flesh. He tore a strip of cloth from her petticoat and pressed it over the wound, holding it in place with one hand while he stroked her cheek with the other. "You'll be fine, Leyla," he whispered tremulously. "I promise."

She tried to smile at him, tried to reassure him, but the pain was too strong.

When the bleeding subsided, Jarrett bound the wound and made her as comfortable as possible. He sat beside her through the night, holding her hand, praying that she wouldn't die.

By morning, she was burning with fever.

Sick at heart, he saddled the stallion, lifted Leyla into the saddle, and climbed up behind her, groaning softly as his battered body protested every move. Face set with determination, he urged the horse across the river, heading for the Majeullian stronghold high in the Mountains of the Blue Mist.

It was mid-morning when he reached the foothills. Reining the stallion to a halt, he stared at the mountains rising in the distance.

Dragons, he thought. Quicksand. Poisonous water.

He gazed at the woman cradled in his arms. Her face was pale, etched with pain. Her skin was hot beneath his hand.

Filled with a sense of urgency, he touched his heels to the stallion's flanks.

They rode for about a league before they reached the foot of the Mountains of the Blue Mist. He pushed the horse hard, climbing steadily higher, through a forest thick with trees and ferns. Sometimes, the greenery above his head was so closely intertwined that it completely blocked the light. And sometimes there would be an opening in the branches that allowed a single shaft of sunlight to penetrate the darkness.

Birds twittered high in the treetops. Leaves crackled as small animals scurried out of his way. A low roar sent a shiver down his spine. The dragon?

It was near dusk when he came to a winding river. The stallion lowered its head to drink and Jarrett gave a sharp tug on the reins, afraid the water might be poisoned. He stared into the icy blue depths, wondering if it was safe to cross, wondering if the sandy bottom hid a pool of quicksand.

"Leyla?" He shook her shoulder gently. "Leyla."

Her eyelids fluttered open. For a moment, she stared up at him, her expression void of recognition, and then she smiled. "Jarrett."

"Leyla, we're in your mountains. Is it safe to cross the river here?"

She sat up a little, frowning as she glanced around. Then she pointed to her left. "There," she said. "See those two trees near the rock? And the two trees directly across the river?"

Jarrett nodded.

"It is safe to cross there."

"Can we drink the water?"

"Yes, but thee must draw it from the river

to kill the poison."

Nodding that he understood, Jarrett stepped carefully from the saddle. Moving like an old, old man, he knelt beside the river and filled a waterskin with the clear blue water. He offered it first to Leyla, hoping it would help to ease her fever. She drank greedily, protesting weakly when he took the waterskin from her mouth.

"Not too fast," he admonished. "Rest a moment, then you can have more."

Jarrett took a deep drink, closing his eyes as the cold water trickled down his throat.

He offered Leyla another drink, then poured some into his hand and let the horse drink.

Refilling the waterskin, he took a deep breath, then climbed painfully back into the saddle and rode downriver, crossing where Leyla had indicated.

It was dark by then. For a moment, he contemplated spending the night where they were. His body cried for rest. It hurt to breathe; every step the stallion took jarred his bruised ribs. But Leyla was burning up in his arms.

With a sigh, he urged the weary stallion upward.

Nightbirds called to each other. The cry of a great horned cat rent the stillness, echoing and re-echoing off the mountainside. He heard the call of a spotted wolf, the shriek of some unwary beast as it met its death.

And then he heard the roar that had sent shivers down his spine earlier. The sound was closer now, more ominous. Instinctively, he dropped the reins and reached for his sword.

Another roar shook the earth, and then he saw a faint glow, as though from a distant campfire. He gazed cautiously from left to right, noticing that the trees ahead were charred, that the ground at his feet was thick with ash.

The dragon.

He reined the horse to an abrupt halt as a flickering tongue of fire lit up the darkness.

The stallion began to prance, its ears twitching nervously back and forth, its nostrils flaring.

Jarrett tightened his hold on the reins. "Easy, boy," he murmured. "Easy now."

A second burst of flame ignited a tree, and the stallion panicked.

Jarrett swore as the horse reared, then spun on its hocks, unseating both riders. He landed hard, holding tight to Leyla, cushioning her body with his own. A roar shook the earth, and the horse bolted down the hillside.

For several minutes, Jarrett lay where he'd fallen. A mist of blackness hovered around him, calling to him with a promise of eternal peace and rest, but he shook it off, clinging to the pain that spiraled through him even as he clung to Leyla.

Gradually, the worst of the pain subsided. With a grimace, he sat up, cradling Leyla in his arms. He sat there for a long while, gathering his strength, accepting the pain, and then, summoning all his energy, he stood up.

"Leyla?" He shook her slightly. "Leyla?"

Her eyelids flickered open. Closed again.

"Leyla! I need your help."

She nodded, too weary to speak.

"The dragon, Leyla. How do we get past the dragon?"

"You must . . . speak . . . her name. Tell her . . . my name."

"That's all?"

"Dragora . . . three times. My name . . . A violent shudder wracked her body. "Wait . . . white . . . smoke." She shuddered and went still, her eyelids fluttering down to lay like dark fans against her pale cheeks.

"Leyla!" His arms tightened around her as he bent to kiss her brow, praying that she wouldn't die before he got her home, to the people who could help her. Her skin was dry and brittle, as hot as the dragon's breath.

Holding her close, he started walking up the steep slope, praying that she would live, praying for the strength to reach the top of the mountain before it was too late.

Trees stood like black sentinels along the path. The air smelled of smoke and ash. He saw several blackened skeletons lying in a grotesque dance of death, the scorched carcass of a blue tiger, the charred remains of what looked like a horse.

"Dragora!" He shouted the word.

Twin tongues of flame arched heavenward trailing plumes of black smoke.

"Dragora!"

A thin finger of flame lanced through the air.

"Dragora!"

A low rumble sounded just ahead.

"Leyla."

A white puff of smoke drifted toward him, the end curling upward like a beckoning finger.

Jarrett brushed a kiss against Leyla's cheek and then, resolutely, followed the blackened path to Dragora's lair.

There were no trees as he drew closer to the dragon's cave, only rows of charred stumps.

The dragon sat outside the cave, a great hulking, horned beast with glowing nostrils and bright yellow eyes. Its scales were dark green. The claws on its front feet were a foot long; its tail swept back and forth, like a cat's at a mouse hole. Each breath filled the air with warmth.

"Dragora," Jarrett murmured, his voice filled with awe.

Slowly, the dragon nodded, its yellow eyes

115

watching Jarrett's every move.

Jarrett waited, wondering if he'd be burned to ash, his soul sent to hell with one heated breath, and Leyla with him. No, he thought, Leyla's soul would surely fly speedily toward heaven.

And then the dragon stood up and moved to the side, revealing the entrance to its lair.

Jarrett tightened his hold on Leyla. It took all the courage he possessed to walk toward the dark passage that led to the mountain stronghold of the Maje.

He was conscious of the dragon watching him through sad yellow eyes as he closed the distance between them. Was it possible the beast knew of Leyla's illness, that it felt sorrow?

With a shake of his head, Jarrett put the fanciful thought from him, took a deep breath, and took his first step into Dragora's lair.

The inside of the cave was rank with the dragon's smell, with the odor of death and decay. Cautiously, he picked his way across the scorched ground, stepping over bones and skulls and bits of charred fur.

He was staggering with relief and fatigue by the time he reached the other end of the cave.

For a moment, he stood there, too weary to go a step farther.

In the distance, a crystal geyser bubbled

from the depths of a quiet blue pool. Tall trees shimmered and swayed in the moonlight, their golden leaves rustling softly in the early spring breeze. Giant blue ferns, blood-red midnight flowers, and lacy peacock-blue willows swayed in the breeze, permeating the air with a heady fragrance.

Beyond the pool rose a graceful building that seemed to be made of glass. A single light glowed like a beacon of welcome in one of the lower windows.

Just a few more steps and he could rest. A few more steps . . .

His arms felt like lead, his legs like reeds, as he made his way toward the light. Each breath sent daggers of pain through his side, and still he went on, doggedly putting one foot in front of the other, promising himself that he could surrender to the beckoning darkness as soon as Leyla was safe.

But the darkness wouldn't wait. . . .

Chapter Eleven

He opened his eyes to darkness that was quiet and complete. For a moment, he thought he was back in the Pavilion. Stark fear clutched at his heart. And then he heard the sound of singing — a single clear voice rising in a prayer of thanksgiving.

Removing the blanket from his face, he blinked against the rosy light filtering through a tall casement window. With a yawn, he sat up, glancing around the room. It was large and square, pale yellow in color, with an arched ceiling. The only furniture in the room other than the bed he occupied was a large thronelike chair, and a small square table that held a crystal basin. There were windows in three of the walls, and the fourth was covered with a large tapestry that depicted a raven-haired snow maiden astride a golden-horned stag.

Jarrett swung his legs over the side of the bed, then paused. Frowning, he pressed a tentative hand over his ribs. There was no pain, no bruise.

Someone had healed him while he was unconscious.

They had also taken his clothing, leaving him nothing to wear but his whiskers.

Rising, he went to the basin. It was filled with warm water. There was a large towel, a small square cloth, a long-handled razor, and a cake of finely milled soap beside the basin.

With a grunt of pleasure, Jarrett washed from head to foot and shaved off a two-day growth of beard. Wandering to the east window, he watched the sun give birth to a new day. And all the while, he thought of Leyla. Surely she had been healed as well. Was she nearby? Would he be allowed to see her before he left? The thought of never seeing her again filled him with a deep sense of loss.

An emptiness in his belly reminded him that he hadn't eaten for quite some time. Grabbing the sheet from the bed, he wrapped it around his waist and headed for the door, hoping that whoever had healed him would offer him something to eat.

He was reaching for the knob, which appeared to be made of solid gold, when the door swung open.

"Good morrow, my Lord Jarrett. Thee is well?"

Jarrett nodded at the tall, fair-haired man.

"First Meal will be ready soon if thee should care to join us." The man handed Jarrett a dark green robe made of softsilk. "The refectory is downstairs, to the left."

"My thanks," Jarrett murmured.

"Thee is welcome." The man's smile was pleasant. Serene.

Jarrett stared after him for a moment, then slipped the robe over his head. It was long, the hem brushing the floor. The sleeves came to his elbows, and the neck was shaped like a V. It made him feel like a Gweneth Monk.

Stomach growling, he left the room and made his way down the stairs. He had no trouble finding the refectory — he just followed his nose.

The room was long and narrow. The tables, also long and narrow, were covered with purple damask. The goblets were of gold, the plates of silver.

The man who had come to Jarrett's door rose from the head of the near table. "Welcome, Lord Jarrett." He indicated a chair to his right. "Please, join us."

Feeling totally out of place, Jarrett moved to the offered chair and sat down. Immediately, a girl dressed in muted shades of gray appeared at his side, a tray in her hands. With a smile, she filled his plate with something that might have been porridge, only it was thicker and smelled of wild berries and honey. Still smiling, she lifted a pitcher of frothy goat's milk and filled his goblet.

Jarrett glanced at the man on his left, who said, "Please, eat."

Whatever it was, it was the best meal

Jarrett had eaten in more than eight months.

He ate in silence, noting that there was very little conversation at the tables and that there were no women in the room other than the serving maid.

The girl brought three other courses and refilled his goblet twice. As he ate, the room gradually emptied, until only Jarrett and the fair-haired man remained.

"Thee has done our people a great service," the man remarked when Jarrett pushed away from the table. "We had thought Leyla forever lost to us."

"Is she well?"

"Yes. Thy arrival was most timely."

Jarrett nodded, understanding what had been left unsaid. Had he delayed his journey, she would not have survived the night.

"We are eager to repay thy kindness," the man went on. "Only name thy reward, and it shall be thine."

Jarrett shook his head. "I don't want anything, except perhaps a horse, if you've one to spare." He smiled wryly. "One accustomed to dragons."

"To be sure."

"Where is she?"

"Taking First Meal with her family. Unmarried men and women do not share a table except at Last Meal."

"I understand Leyla is betrothed."

"Yes." A wide smile played over the Maje's

lips. "She is to be my wife."

So, this was Tor. Jarrett studied the man more closely. The Maje was tall, though not quite as tall as Jarrett, well-muscled. His skin was pale, but not sickly looking. His hair was thick and white, his eyes a deep dark brown, filled with gentleness.

A vague memory tugged at the corners of Jarrett's mind. "It was you who healed me."

"Yes."

"My thanks."

Tor nodded. "Will thee stay with us long? I will make Leyla my wife when next the moons are full. It would do me great honor to have thee at our wedding."

A sharp pain ripped through Jarrett's heart. Wedding! So soon? The time of the full moons was only a fortnight away.

Tor regarded Jarrett for a moment. "Thee art a man of great courage, Lord Jarrett. Leyla has spoken of the Pavilion and what thee suffered at the hands of the Fen."

Jarrett grunted softly. He felt strangely betrayed that she had spoken of their time together to anyone else, especially to this man, whose clear brown eyes seemed able to divine the innermost secrets of his soul.

"Great courage," Tor repeated. "Many men would not have survived such an ordeal."

Jarrett shrugged. "I didn't feel very courageous at the time."

The Maje smiled. "Courage takes many

forms. For thee to leave here will no doubt take a great deal of fortitude."

"I don't understand."

"Thee has strong feelings for Leyla."

"Did she tell you that?"

Tor shook his head.

"Are you reading my mind against my will?"

The Maje looked insulted. "Of course not. The feelings of thy heart are clearly revealed when thee speaks of her."

"You've got nothing to worry about. She told me all about you, how you've been betrothed since she was a young girl."

"Yes. I have always loved her."

Jarrett took a deep breath, released it in a long sigh, and then stood up. "My thanks, again, for your hospitality."

Tor rose to his feet in a fluid movement. "Please make our home thine. We ask only that thee does not enter the small chapel located in the west wing. It is considered hallowed ground."

Jarrett nodded. He started to ask where Leyla was, if he might see her, and then bit back the words. Seeing her again would only make it that much harder to leave.

"May I tell Leyla that thee will honor us by attending our wedding?"

Jarrett shoved his hands into the pockets of the robe and clenched his fists. He very much wanted to hate the man standing before him, but the Maje exuded such kindness, such concern, that it was impossible. To Jarrett's dismay, what he really felt for the man was envy, not only because he was to marry Leyla, but because he was so clearly at peace with who and what he was.

"Please stay and let us try to repay thy kindness," Tor said, his voice filled with quiet dignity. He made a gesture that encompassed the crystal fortress and the lands beyond. "Surely thee would not mind spending a short time in this place? I think thee might find it to thy liking."

It would be an insult to refuse, Jarrett thought. And he had to admit he was intrigued by the place. As long as he was here, he might as well take advantage of it. To his knowledge, no outsider had ever been allowed into the fortress of the Maje. "I'd be honored to stay."

"If thee has need of anything, thee has only to ask. Second Meal will be served at mid-day, in this room." Tor bowed. "Until then, Lord Jarrett."

No one bothered him as he strolled through the house. It was a place unlike any he had ever seen. The walls were of a kind of crystal. Light penetrated every room, picking up all the colors of the rainbow. The furniture was of polished ebony, the cushions of feather-soft velvet. The floors were like mirrored glass; the globes of the lamps were of hand-blown glass, the most delicate he had ever seen.

The Maje greeted him politely, careful to keep their curiosity under control lest they offend him. The men were all tall, regal in their bearing, formal yet polite.

The women, dressed in flowing robes of softsilk, were beautiful beyond description.

Feeling like a thorn among roses, Jarrett left the house and made his way to a walled garden located near a small shrine housed beneath an arch of white stone.

With a sigh, he dropped down on a wrought-iron bench and closed his eyes. The mingled scents of spring flowers and earth rose all around him, their sweet fragrance soothing him somehow. Beyond the garden wall, he heard the sound of gentle laughter, and in the distance, the ringing of a bell.

The Majeullian stronghold was like a monastery. Except for the presence of women, he might have been in Gweneth Abbey, surrounded by monks who thought only of service and sacrifice. For the first time in his life, he envied them. They had no time for worldly ambition; their thoughts weren't tormented by silver-haired goddesses who were out of reach, or by blue eyes that captured a man's heart and soul and haunted his dreams.

Leyla. Her name whispered through his mind.

When he opened his eyes, she was standing before him, a vision of femininity clothed in a robe of periwinkle blue that made her look sensual and innocent at the same time.

"Thee is well?" she asked.

He nodded, unable to speak past the lump in his throat.

"May I?" She inclined her head toward the bench.

Unable to think, unable to take his eyes from her face, he nodded again.

"This is my favorite place."

She sat down beside him, obviously unaware of the effect her nearness had on him. He took a deep breath, and her scent filled his nostrils, sweeter than the smell of the flowers.

"Thee has met Tor?"

"Yes."

"It was his touch that made thee whole again."

"I know." Jarrett gazed into her eyes, aching to feel the touch of her hands upon him just once more.

"We are to be married soon."

The words cut into his heart like Thal's knife. "He told me." Jarrett took a deep, calming breath. "I wish you both every happiness."

"I thank thee." Her smile was as bright as

the sunshine that warmed the garden. "My mother and father desire to meet thee. They have asked that thee would join us for Last Meal."

"All right."

"I will come for thee this evening." She stood up, her smile warm as a summer day. "Until then, my Lord Jarrett."

"Until then," he agreed. And knew he couldn't stay for the wedding, knew it would kill him to stand by while she said the words that sealed her to another man.

Chapter Twelve

Leyla dressed with care that evening, choosing a full-skirted, gauze-like gown of crystal blue. She left her hair unbound, knowing Jarrett preferred it that way. Her only adornment was a ribbon that matched the color of her eyes.

Because it was too early to go to dinner, she sat at her dressing table, gazing at her reflection in the mirror. It was good to be home. Her parents had welcomed her with tears and smiles, touching her both physically and mentally to make sure she was well. Tor had greeted her with his usual cool reserve, but she had seen the gladness that brightened his eyes when he drew her into his arms for a long hug of welcome.

Today, she had spent the afternoon with Tor, making plans for their wedding, telling him of her experiences in the Pavilion, making light of the hardships, the barbaric food, her imprisonment, assuring him that the Fen hadn't molested her. She hadn't told him of the nights she'd huddled in her dark cell, weeping in despair, fearing she would never see her family or her homeland again.

Nor had she told him about the extra time she had spent in Jarrett's cell after she had healed his wounds; or how Jarrett's presence had made her own captivity more bearable. She had felt an awful sense of guilt as she blocked her thoughts so Tor could not sense her true feelings for Jarrett, feelings she was reluctant to acknowledge.

She looked at herself critically, wondering what Jarrett would think when he saw her. She had bathed in rose-scented water, washed her hair twice, then dressed with infinite care, telling herself she was doing it for Tor when she knew, deep within her heart, it was for Jarrett. She'd chosen the blue gown, not only because it made her eyes sparkle and complemented the color of her hair, but because of the way it outlined her figure. Because she wanted to look pretty for Jarrett.

A gentle chiming of bells told her it was time to summon their guest to Last Meal. She couldn't stifle her excitement at the thought of seeing Jarrett again, hearing the soft resonance of his voice.

Leaving her room, she hurried down the wide, candlelit hallway to the south wing, and knocked lightly on the door of Jarrett's room.

He opened the door at once, making her wonder if he, too, had been eagerly awaiting the time when they could be together again.

For a moment, they gazed at each other in silence.

Leyla felt her heart catch in her throat. He had never looked more handsome. He wore a loose-fitting red shirt that revealed a dark vee of bronzed skin, tight black breeches that outlined his muscular thighs, and knee-high black boots. His hair, freshly washed, glistened like carbonite, his green eyes were bright and clear. He looked like a Giddeon pirate, she mused. All he lacked was a cutlass.

Jarrett drew in a deep breath, awed, as always, by Leyla's ethereal beauty. The gown she wore exactly matched the color of her eyes. The square neck, edged with a froth of lace as delicate as a spider's web, revealed a tantalizing glimpse of smooth ivory flesh. Her hair fell in careless waves around her shoulders, shimmering like a cloud of silver silk. She flushed under his prolonged gaze. He found it most becoming.

"Thee is ready?" she asked.

Jarrett nodded, wondering if she could hear the rapid beat of his heart even as he hoped she wasn't reading his mind.

With a smile, Leyla took him by the hand, and knew immediately that it had been a mistake. The warmth of his touch went through her like heat lightning, bright, unexpected, devastating. And he felt it, too. She knew it by the sudden tensing in his arm, the

130

sharp intake of his breath.

"We'll be late." She released his hand, only to have him capture hers. "I . . ." She gazed up at him, her pulse racing. "We should go."

Jarrett nodded. Mesmerized by the sight of her, by the beguiling scent of roses that lingered in her hair, he slowly pulled her toward him, his arm slipping around her waist.

"No, thee mustn't . . ." She pulled back, her gaze darting up and down the long corridor. "Please, it isn't seemly."

He held her a moment longer and then, with regret, he let her go. Wordlessly, they walked down the hallway toward the family dining hall.

Leyla's parents could only be described as regal, Jarrett decided as they sat down to dinner. Her mother, Vestri, was a slender, dark-haired, dark-eyed woman. Her father, Sudaan, was a shade taller than Jarrett. He had a mane of iron-gray hair and eyes as blue as his daughter's. His grip, when he clasped Jarrett's hand, was firm and strong. They quickly put Jarrett at ease, their sincere smiles of welcome and inquiries about his health making him feel like a guest in the stronghold instead of an intruder.

Vestri sat at the foot of the long, damask-covered trestle table, Sudaan at the head. Leyla sat beside Tor, whose arm rested possessively across the back of her chair. Jarrett sat across from Leyla, fully aware of Tor's scrutiny.

The meal, consisting of light brown bread, vegetables and fruit, some of which Jarrett had never seen before, was leisurely. Each course was served with its own special wine.

Leyla ate without tasting a thing, all too conscious of Tor's presence beside her. Guilt did not make for a good appetite, she thought, but she couldn't help wishing it was Jarrett who sat beside her, Jarrett who filled her wine glass, Jarrett whose arm rested on the back of her chair.

After dinner, before anyone could suggest a diversion, she asked Jarrett if he'd like to go for a walk. He hesitated before answering, and she saw him glance at Tor, as if asking for permission.

Leyla stood abruptly, her back straight, her cheeks hot. "If thee would rather not . . ."

"I'd enjoy a walk," Jarrett said. Rising quickly to his feet, he thanked her parents for the meal, bade Tor good sleep, and followed her from the room.

In the hallway, Leyla whirled around to face him. "I've changed my mind."

"Why?"

She shrugged, unable to explain her feelings, not certain she understood them herself.

"Leyla, I'm sorry."

"For what?"

"For whatever I've done that's upset you." He smiled down at her, his green eyes filled with warmth. "I really would like to go for a walk."

"Very well."

Outside, they strolled side by side. Not quite touching, she was nevertheless aware of his every movement.

It was a clear night, the three moons shining brightly, the air fragrant with the scent of night-blooming midnight flowers and giant cactus ferns.

Gradually, they left the brightly lit crystal fortress behind and descended into a verdant valley watered by a narrow, winding stream. Fluffy pink cattails skirted the sandy shore; graceful willows swayed to the music of the breeze.

"Pretty place," Jarrett remarked.

"I often came here when I was a young girl. Each morning and evening, the unicorns come here to drink with their young."

"Unicorns?"

Leyla nodded. "Has thee never seen one?"

"Never . . ."

"Perhaps it is because thee lacks the faith and innocence of a young maiden," Leyla mused with a gentle smile.

"I don't think I was ever innocent," Jarrett replied. Or young, he thought ruefully.

As far back as he could remember, he'd seen too much of reality, of hardship and war, to believe in unicorns or winged fairy maidens. He'd learned to ride before he could walk, doing mock battle with a small wooden sword. As soon as he could lift the real thing, he'd been tutored in the ways of war. At the age of twelve, he'd ridden into battle against the Serimites for the first time. At the age of thirteen, he'd seen his father killed. At the age of fourteen, he'd avenged his father's death. . . .

"Thy thoughts are troubled."

Her voice was as soft and welcome as the first spring rain, calling him back to the present.

"Sorry."

"Would thee care to go riding on the morrow?"

He knew he should tell her no. Every minute he spent in her company would only make it that much harder to leave. "Very much."

"I will come for thee after First Meal."

"Leyla . . . what about Tor?"

"What about him?"

"Won't he mind, you spending so much time with me?"

Her gaze met his, open and direct. "He will not like it, but thee is here as our guest. It is my duty to entertain thee."

"Your duty?" His voice was harsh. By Hadra's Fire, he didn't want her spending time with him because it was her "duty."

Her gaze, warm and serene as a summer's morn, met his without flinching. "My duty," she repeated. "And my wish."

"Leyla!" He moved toward her, but she held out her hand to ward him off.

"Thee mustn't."

"Leyla . . ."

"I am betrothed," she said, as much to remind herself as him. "Tor is an honorable man. I must not betray his trust in me."

"I understand."

"I do not think so," she murmured.

"Then tell me."

Leyla shook her head. How could she tell Jarrett that she was afraid to let him touch her, afraid that one kiss would shatter her tenuous resolve to marry the man her parents had chosen for her? How could she tell him she loved him with every fiber of her being, and then let him go?

"Let us talk of something else," she suggested. "There is a waterfall beyond that meadow. Would thee care to see it?"

His eyes told her he understood exactly what she was doing. "Sure."

They walked across the wide, grassy meadow in silence. Long before they reached it, they could hear the thunder of the falls, see the frothy spray as it splashed against the rocks.

Jarrett had to admit that the waterfall was an awesome sight, appearing almost out of nowhere, cascading over gigantic white boulders into a turbulent river, making the dancing drops of water sparkle like crystals. Downriver, the surging water slowed, forming shallow pools near the shore. The moonlight danced on the face of the water, turning the quiet pools into mirrors of silver.

But it was the woman at Jarrett's side who captured his gaze again and again. She looked like a storybook princess. The wind blew her hair away from her face and molded her gown to her figure so that he could see every graceful curve. Her lips, as soft and pink as the cattails that grew along the shore, were slightly parted, issuing an unspoken invitation he could no longer resist.

Before she could protest, before he quite realized what he was doing, he drew her into his arms and kissed her, the pounding of his heart louder than the roar of the waterfall. She tasted sweeter than Sylvan honey. Her lips were soft and pliant beneath his, bidding him to linger, but he dared not. Another moment of such incredible pleasure would surely strip away what little self-control he had left.

With regret, he forced himself to let her go.

He had expected her to slap him, or, at the least, berate him for his barbaric behavior. She did neither, only took him by the hand and led him back the way they had come. She bade him good sleep at his door, and left him in his room, befuddled and be-witched, and completely beguiled.

As promised, Leyla arrived at his door im-mediately after First Meal.

Jarrett stared at her, surprised to see her wearing snug brown breeches, a long-sleeved, loosely woven lavender shirt, and soft-soled boots.

"Thee does not approve?" she asked, a hint of amusement lurking in the depths of her eyes.

"Oh, I approve, all right. I just never ex-pected to see you wearing anything so . . ." He hunted for the right word. Breeches were considered masculine attire, but he'd never seen anything that was more feminine, more revealing, or more provocative, in his life. "Forget it," he said.

Her laughter sparkled like early morning dew. "The horses are ready. Are thee?"

"Lead the way."

They followed a narrow, tree-lined trail up the mountain. The air was cool, crisp, and invigorating. The sky was a bright azure blue, the tall, yellow-green grasses still damp.

Jarrett's horse tossed its head, prancing in its eagerness to run.

Jarrett glanced at Leyla. "What do you say? Shall I give him his head and let him go?"

"I will race thee to the top," she replied, and dug her heels into her mount's flanks.

The mountain-bred mare gathered its haunches and sprang forward, quickly taking the lead.

Shouting an ancient Gweneth war cry, Jarrett urged his horse into a gallop, and the big black gelding lined out in a run.

It was a heady feeling, to be racing up the side of a mountain in the early hours of the morning. His heart pounded with the sheer exhilaration of it, and he drummed his heels against the black's flanks, wishing he could outrun the bitter memories of the last eight months.

As they reached the crest of the mountain, Jarrett drew back a little on the reins, grinning as Leyla's mount surged into the lead.

Leyla's face was flushed with victory when he drew rein beside her a few moments later.

"You ride like a Gweneth warrior," Jarrett remarked, his voice tinged with admiration.

"Thee let me win."

"Why do you say that?"

"Dusault has never beaten the black before."

Jarrett shrugged. "There is a first time for all things."

Leyla grinned at him, then slid from the back of her horse. Taking a flask from her saddlebag, she offered Jarrett a drink.

It was brandywine, smoky and sweet, and he took a long, appreciative swallow. Dismounting, he handed her the flask.

"I love it here," Leyla said. She took a small drink, then laid the flask aside. "There is a legend among the Maje that the goddess Judeau gave birth to her twin sons on this peak. The first-born son touched his mother's heart and became the first Maje. The second-born son touched the soft inner flesh of her thigh, and became the father of all other races."

"What happened to Judeau's husband?"

"He was killed by an evil sorcerer, and when he died, his soul united with the sun. Judeau went into mourning. She gave all her riches away, except for the jewels her husband had left her. These she threw into the night sky, and they became the stars. When she died, her soul merged with the moon nearest to our world. Whenever you see the sun pass in front of that moon, you know their souls are touching."

Jarrett smiled at Leyla, charmed by the fanciful tale, enchanted by the woman. She glanced up at him and their gazes met, and held.

"Leyla . . ."

She shook her head, afraid of what he might ask of her, afraid of what her answer might be. Her body yearned for his touch. He was tall and strong, more virile, more masculine, than any man she had ever known. She loved the color of his hair, the depths of his eyes, the feel of his skin that she knew so well. And she loved him. The words trembled on the tip of her tongue, but she dared not say them. Once put into words, she could never take them back. To say it would be the first step toward disobedience to her parents, to her people.

Jarrett studied her face, wondering at her silence. "I'm leaving tomorrow."

It was the last thing she had expected him to say. "Tomorrow? But why? The wedding . . . thee promised to stay."

"I cannot."

"But I do not want thee to leave."

"I cannot stay," he said, his voice thick with anguish. "I cannot watch you marry Tor."

"I do not want to marry him."

She spoke the words so softly that he was sure he had imagined them.

Leyla bowed her head, ashamed because she had no wish to be obedient to her parents' wishes, confused by her feelings for a man who was so different from her own people. All her life, she had known she would marry Tor. They had grown up together, knowing that one day their lives would be joined. Her parents called him son. But it was Jarrett who made her blood tingle with excitement, Jarrett who had given her life meaning in the foul dungeons of the Pavilion, Jarrett who had risked his life to bring her home. Right or wrong, it was Jarrett who held her heart.

"Leyla, look at me."

"No, I am too ashamed."

"Ashamed? Of what?"

"Everything. Nothing." She looked up at him then, her eyes filled with tears. "I have never disobeyed my parents, or the Law of the Maje. Until I was captured by the Fen . . ." *until I met thee . . .* "my life had order, serenity."

She shook her head, her expression as bewildered as that of a child told that the truths she'd been taught were wrong. "Please do not go away."

Leaving her was the last thing he wanted. But he couldn't stay, couldn't watch her marry another man. To do so would be the worst kind of torture.

Agitated, he ran a hand through his hair. If only he could just grab her and carry her to Gweneth. "I cannot stay. Do not ask it of me."

"I beg it of thee." Knowing it was wrong, she placed her head against his chest. Closing her eyes, she listened to the strong, steady beat of his heart.

"Leyla." He wrapped his arms around her and held her close, his lips moving in her hair as he whispered her name over and over again.

They stood that way for a long while, content to be in each other's arms, to pretend, if only for a little while, that nothing else mattered.

She leaned against him, secure in his strength. He was so different from Tor, from her father, from any man she had ever known. The Maje were peaceful, serene, full of wisdom. They had no weapons save their agile minds and whatever gifts had been bequeathed to them. Were it not for the terrors and dangers of the Mountains of the Blue Mist, her people would have been overrun long ago, subjected to tyranny and captivity.

But Jarrett was different. He was a fighter, a warrior. He used a sword as if it were an extension of his body. Clubs and knives and the shedding of blood were second nature to him, and she knew intuitively that he would die for her if need be.

With Tor, she would be always at peace. Each day would be the same as the last, with no pain and no surprises. He would treat her with kindness and respect. They would have children who would be blessed with the gifts of the Maje. They would grow old together, but there would be no magic between them. His touch would not make her heart soar, his kisses would not make her heart sing or drain the strength from her limbs.

A life with Jarrett would be fraught with turmoil, but she would also know the wonder of discovery. Their children would be born in passion. The nights in his arms would be filled with flash and fire, like a comet crossing the heavens, and she knew she would gladly turn her back on her own people, on the life she'd been born to live, to be with Jarrett. If only he would ask her.

"Leyla." His hand stroked the wealth of her hair, the curve of her cheek. "What do you want from me?"

"Whatever thee wishes to give."

"My heart? My soul? My life? They have all been yours since the day you first placed your hands upon me."

"I do not want thy gratitude, Lord Jarrett."

"It isn't just gratitude."

"What then?"

"Can you not see it in my mind, hear it in my thoughts?"

"I would rather hear it from thy lips."

"I love you, Leyla," he murmured. "I think I have always loved you."

"As I have loved thee," she replied ardently. "From the first day I was brought to thee, I loved thy courage, the sound of thy voice. I knew it was wrong, but I was glad they had imprisoned thee."

"I cannot be glad for the pain," Jarrett said with a grin, "but I am glad of thee."

"Thee will not leave? Promise me."

"I will not leave thee, but what of Tor?"

"I will annul our betrothal."

"Are you sure this is what you want? I have nothing to offer you but a castle fallen into ruin. That and my love."

"It is enough," she replied, her heart swelling with joy. "Enough and more."

Chapter Thirteen

Telling her parents she had decided to annul her betrothal to Tor was the hardest thing Leyla had ever done. For a long moment, they stared at her, too stunned to speak.

And then her father cleared his throat. "I cannot believe thee is serious. What has happened to change thy mind? Has Tor behaved toward thee in an unseemly manner?"

"No, Father. I . . . we have been apart a long time. I . . ." She bit down on her lower lip, wondering how to explain that she'd fallen in love with an outsider. Her mother saved her the trouble.

"It is because of the man, Jarrett, is it not?" Vestri surmised. "Thee has healed him often, and a bond has formed between thee."

Sudaan stared at Leyla, his gaze sharp. "Answer thy mother."

"Yes," Leyla admitted. "I have fallen in love with my Lord Jarrett. It is my wish to marry him."

Vestri and Sudaan exchanged glances.

"No," Sudaan said curtly. "I will not permit it."

"Nor I," Vestri added. "He is an outsider,

a man of violence. His ways are not ours, his faith is not ours. Our people are few in number, my daughter. Thee must not betray thy heritage."

"I will not marry Tor," Leyla exclaimed. "I do not love him. I never will!"

"We will not discuss it," Sudaan said gruffly. "I have made my decision. Thy betrothal to Tor stands."

Sudaan's expression hardened as he took a step toward his daughter. "Know this. Should thee marry against my wishes, I will invoke the Recantation."

Leyla stared at her father in horror, the threat of being stripped of her powers rendering her momentarily speechless. Surely he would not do such a thing! To her knowledge, the Recantation had been used only once in the history of recorded time.

"Go to thy room, child," Vestri said quietly. "When thee has had time to think, thee will see that thy father has only thy best interests at heart."

Leyla clasped her hands to her breast, summoning the courage to ask, "What of Jarrett?"

"He leaves in the morning." Her father's voice was firm, with no hope of reprieve.

"Tor has invited him to the wedding," Leyla said, grasping for any excuse that might keep Jarrett in the stronghold.

She glanced at her mother beseechingly. "It

would be discourteous to send him away."

"I will speak to Tor," Sudaan said. "Considering the circumstances, I am sure he will understand."

Sudaan wrapped his arm around Leyla's shoulders and hugged her to his side.

"I bid thee good sleep, daughter," he said, his tone softening as he gazed into her luminous blue eyes.

"Good sleep, Father," she replied, forcing the words past the growing lump in her throat. "Mother."

Blinking back her tears, Leyla fled for the solitude of her own room. She should have known they would not approve, but in her happiness, she had dared to hope they would understand, they would share her felicity.

She paced her room for several minutes, her thoughts troubled. She could never marry Tor now. Once, she had thought she would grow to love him, but she knew now it would never happen. She loved Jarrett — not just because of the bond that had formed between them in the Pavilion. She loved his courage, his kindness, the warmth that was ever in his eyes when he looked at her. She loved the sound of his voice, the touch of his hand in her hair, the knowledge that he didn't want to live without her.

She thought of what her father had said — and knew she would willingly sacrifice all her powers for the chance to be Jarrett's wife.

With a sigh, she went to her window and stared down into the walled garden below. A movement in the shadows caught her eye, and she felt her heart give a leap of joy.

Impulsively, she grabbed her cloak. Hurrying down the corridor, she left the fortress and ran to the garden, hoping he was still there.

Jarrett turned at the sound of her footsteps. "Leyla," he exclaimed, pleased beyond words to see her.

"Jarrett, oh Jarrett," she wailed softly, and hurled herself into his arms.

"What is it?" he asked gently, grieved by her tears. "What has happened?"

"My parents refuse to let me cancel the wedding. They said I must marry Tor, that I must fulfill my heritage."

It was what he had expected, what he had feared. Ever since he'd promised Leyla he would stay, he had been plagued by doubts, wondering if he was doing the right thing.

Leyla was so young, so innocent. She had no real knowledge of life beyond the shelter of her mountain, no true concept of the hardships of daily existence. She had been reared in a society where there was no conflict, no contention, only harmony and beauty. Even in the Pavilion, she had been treated with courtesy and respect. No one had abused her. She hadn't gone hungry, or been forced to do menial tasks.

How could he even think of taking her away from her beloved mountains? He had no idea of what awaited him at his castle in Gweneth, no way of knowing if his home was still standing. And if Fenduzia and Aldane went to war, Gweneth would be caught in the middle. Jarrett had sworn an oath of allegiance to Tyrell, but he was related by blood to Morrad, the ruler of Aldane.

Bending down, he pressed a kiss to the top of Leyla's head. He had known it could never be, he thought bleakly. From the very beginning, he'd known she could never be his.

Leyla wrapped her arms around Jarrett's waist, holding him with all her strength. She could hear the strong steady beat of his heart beneath her cheek, feel the hard wall of his chest beneath her fingertips.

She sighed as his arms curled around her, holding her tight. This was where she yearned to be, only here, only forever.

But it was not to be. She knew it as soon as she heard the sound of footsteps.

And then her father's voice cut across the stillness of the night, thick with anger and sharp rebuke. "Leyla!"

Jarrett swore softly as he met Sudaan's gaze. For a moment, his arms tightened around Leyla and then, reluctantly, he let her go.

Only then did he notice that Sudaan had not come alone. Tor stood behind Leyla's father, and behind him, a half-dozen men. They were not armed; the Maje kept no weapons of war. But then, he wasn't armed, either.

"Daughter, Tor will take thee to thy room."

Leyla looked at Jarrett, her eyes pleading for him to do something, but he only shook his head. And then Tor was leading her away.

Sudaan waited until Leyla had left the garden before he spoke again. "I would have the truth from thy lips," he demanded. "Has thee defiled my daughter?"

"No."

Sudaan gazed at him for a long moment, and Jarrett knew the Maje was probing his mind, seeking to know if he spoke the truth.

"We have made thee welcome as a guest," Sudaan remarked. "We are grateful for thy kindness in returning our daughter."

Jarrett curled his hands into fists. "But?"

"But I think it will be better for thee and for Leyla if thee departs on the morrow."

"And if I refuse?"

Sudaan inclined his head toward the men who had fanned out around him. "We will convince thee. These men will escort thee to thy room. Tor will see thee on thy journey on the morrow."

"In other words, I'm your prisoner?"

"Thee has said it."

Knowing it was useless to argue, Jarrett left the garden and made his way back to his room, followed by the six Maje.

When he closed the door, he heard a key turn in the lock and the muted sound of voices as the Maje decided who would take the first watch.

He was a prisoner again, though this time his jail was infinitely more hospitable.

Too agitated to sleep, Jarrett paced the floor. Restless as a caged blue tiger, he prowled the confines of the room. They weren't going to let him see Leyla again. He knew it as surely as he knew he had no choice but to leave in the morning. No choice at all. The Maje would see to that. They'd taken his weapons, and weren't likely to give them back. And even if they handed him his sword, he couldn't fight them all.

He went to the window and stared into the darkness, his future looming before him as black as the sky now that he knew she wouldn't be there to brighten it.

They came early the following morning, bringing First Meal into his room along with a change of clothing and a ewer of hot water to wash with.

An hour later, Sudaan and Tor came for him.

"Tor and one of our young men will escort thee to the path that leads to Dragora's lair," Sudaan said curtly.

"Where's Leyla?"

"My daughter's whereabouts need no longer concern thee."

"I love her."

"Our ways are not thy ways," Sudaan said, his voice tinged with compassion. "Forget what thee has seen here and return to thy people."

Jarrett drew a deep breath. "Can I at least tell her good-bye?"

Sudaan shook his head. "It will only make thy parting more difficult."

"Please." Jarrett forced the word through his teeth. *Please. Please.* The plea echoed down the corridors of his mind. How many times had he begged for mercy in the dungeon of the Pavilion, only to have his words thrown back at him? But he didn't mind begging this time. He would have debased himself to any degree required for the chance to see her one last time.

Sudaan held Jarrett's gaze for stretched seconds, his brow furrowed in concentration.

Jarrett stood firm, not caring that the Maje was reading his mind, judging the depths of his feelings for Leyla. In a moment, he became aware of another presence, and knew that Tor was also probing his thoughts.

Sudaan grunted softly, and then he nodded. "I will send her to thee."

"No!" The exclamation burst from Tor's lips. "She is my betrothed. I will not permit it."

"She is my daughter," Sudaan said, his voice sharp with reproval. "This man saved her life and returned her to us. I will allow them a few minutes to say Godspeed."

"I am against it!"

Tor's deep brown eyes glittered with uncharacteristic anger, making Jarrett wonder if all the tales of Majeullian docility might be a myth. He could feel the other man's animosity reaching toward him, see it in the depths of his eyes, in the clenching of his fists.

"I will send her to thee, Lord Jarrett," Sudaan repeated. "Tor, let us depart in peace."

Tor glared at Jarrett. "Do not make the mistake of thinking we are soft or weak," he warned. "Force and fear are not the only strengths."

Jarrett loosed a sigh of relief as the door closed behind his visitors. They would let him tell her good-bye. He would see her one last time. For now, that was all that mattered.

It seemed like hours before she knocked at his door, though he knew it had only been a few minutes, and then she was there, close enough to touch.

For a time, he could only look at her, imprinting her image in his mind: the pale opalescence of her skin, the shimmering silver of her hair, the deep blue of her eyes, the rosy hue of her lips. Soft, sweet lips that tasted of Sylvan honey. She wore a flowing gown of powder-blue softsilk. There were matching slippers on her feet. She looked like an angel recently come from the courts of heaven.

"Leyla." Her name whispered past his lips.

"I am here."

Her familiar reply made his heart ache with sweet regret. He longed to go to her, to enfold her in his arms and feel her lifeforce, her caring warmth. He yearned to bury his face in the wealth of her hair, to cover her face with kisses. To hold her close and never let her go.

Instead, he murmured her name again, the anguish in his voice betraying every thought, every desire.

"My Lord Jarrett, I came to thank thee for bringing me home." She blinked back the tears that burned her throat and eyes as she delivered the carefully rehearsed speech. "I wish to thank thee for making my life in the Pavilion more bearable, for having the courage to flee thy captivity and the generosity of heart to take me with thee. I am honored to have known thee, and wish thee every happiness."

She was crying openly now, and she saw him through a blur of tears that made him no less handsome. Green eyes, as green as Dragora's scales. Skin the color of sun-kissed

Majeullian earth, warm and rich and brown. Hair as black as ebony. She committed each feature to memory. A nose as straight as a blade, a strong square jaw, the high cheekbones inherent to all Gweneth males. Large hands capable of unspeakable violence. Indescribable tenderness. Arms corded with muscle, strong legs that could carry him up the side of a mountain and across rivers. Broad shoulders that could bear any burden placed upon them.

"Jarrett." She laced her fingers together to keep from reaching for him.

"I know," he murmured brokenly. "I know."

It was time to go. Her father had allowed her only a few minutes to say farewell, and that grudgingly.

"Jarrett." She couldn't seem to say anything but his name. Heart filled with anguish, she could only look at him, wishing that things could have been different between them, wishing she were an outsider, or that he were a Maje, so that they could have joined together. Obedience to the Law. Fidelity to truth. Loyalty to kith and kin. Suddenly, the tenets by which she had lived her whole life meant nothing; only the knowledge that he was leaving, that she would never see him again, had any meaning at all.

She gazed into his eyes as she closed the distance between them, saw his expression change from doubt to hope as she wrapped her arms around his neck and kissed him.

Sparks. Lightning. The flaming tail of a comet.

Jarrett's mind whirled as her lips touched his. He loosed a ragged breath when she took her mouth from his, and then he was kissing her, his hands moving restlessly up and down her arms. She pressed her length against his, her soft moan of pleasure igniting his desire still more. She was light and warmth, the giver of life, and he knew he would rather die than spend the rest of his days without her.

"Leyla, come with me."

"I cannot. Thee must know I cannot."

"I know." He rested his chin on the top of her head, breathing in her scent, reveling in the silkiness of her hair, the satin-smooth skin beneath his hand.

Soon, they would come for him and he would have to leave her. Nothing the Gamesmen had ever done to him, no agony of the flesh, had ever caused him as much pain as the thought of never seeing Leyla again.

He drew away from her, then took her hand and placed it over his heart. "I hurt," he said. "Deep inside."

Leyla nodded, her eyes clouded with tears. "I know." Taking his hand, she placed it over her breast. "Feel my heart, my Lord Jarrett, and know that I share thy pain, that I grieve because there can be no healing for thee, or for me."

Her trembling fingertips stroked his cheek, caressed his lips. "I will never love Tor. I will never give him a child. I will never truly be his."

"No." Jarrett shook his head, her words shredding his soul. "Do not deny thyself the pleasure of a man's love because of me." Unconsciously, he used her quaint speech. "Do not deny thyself the love and comfort of a child. I want only thy happiness, Leyla. Do not let thy love for me bring thee anything else."

"Kiss me," she begged. "Kiss me and never stop."

His arm curled around her waist and he dragged her length against his, his kiss brutal, possessive, aching with need. Her hands curled over his shoulders and she clung to him, fervently returning his kiss. She could feel the wild beating of his heart, the heat of his desire inflaming her own.

The sound of her father's footsteps penetrated the haze of passion. Summoning every ounce of will power she possessed, Leyla twisted out of Jarrett's arms and went to stand by the window, looking out into the garden below.

A moment later, the door swung open and her father and Tor stood in the doorway.

Tor stared hard at Jarrett, his dark brown eyes filled with suspicion and mistrust.

"Leyla, it is time for Lord Jarrett to depart."

"Yes, Father." She turned away from the window and crossed the room, extending her hand to Jarrett. "Travel in safety and peace, my Lord Jarrett. May the goddess Judeau bless thee with health and strength all the days of thy life."

Jarrett took her hand in both of his and squeezed it hard. "And may the All Father grant thee a long and happy life." He could feel her hand trembling in his, see the tears that clung to her lashes. "Farewell, Leyla, I will never forget thee."

"Nor I thee."

"It is time; Lord Jarrett." Tor's voice cut across the stillness of the room.

"I'm ready," Jarrett replied curtly. Releasing Leyla's hand, he walked out of the chamber.

The sound of her tears followed him down the hall.

Tor's companion was waiting outside. Wordlessly, Jarrett mounted the horse they'd brought for him, absently stroking the animal's neck as he gazed at the shimmering crystal palace.

A moment later, Tor joined them.

With one last glance at the Maje stronghold, Jarrett followed Tor and the other man out of the courtyard.

Chapter Fourteen

Jarrett rode between Tor and his companion, the ache in his heart growing heavier with each league that went by.

He would never see her again.

They reached the head of the serpentine path that led to Dragora's lair at mid-day.

"Do not come back here," Tor warned. He handed Jarrett his sword and knife. "Thee will not be welcome."

"Take care of Leyla," Jarrett said. He sheathed the sword, slipped the longboar knife into the sheath inside his boot.

Without another word, he urged his horse down the narrow twisting path that led to the dragon's cave.

He rode for over an hour, hardly aware of his surroundings. The ache in his heart seemed to intensify as he put more and more distance between himself and Leyla. It was like riding away from a part of himself. The best part.

His horse, a big-boned gray gelding, snorted and rolled its eyes as they neared Dragora's lair.

For a moment, Jarrett thought he'd find

himself afoot again, but after flicking its ears back and forth, the gray approached the cave without hesitation.

"Dragora!" Jarrett called, and waited for the flame.

"Dragora!" He called the dragon's name a second time, and saw the thin finger of flame brighten the far end of the cave.

"Dragora!" A low roar caused the earth to tremble.

"Leyla."

A white puff of smoke rose into the air.

Jarrett took a deep breath, let it out slowly, and urged the horse into the maw of the enormous cavern.

Dragora sat on her haunches at the entrance to the cave, a freshly killed carcass at her feet. The dragon's tail, as long as its body and forked on the end, swished back and forth, stirring dust and ash.

Jarrett stared up at the dragon. Wide-set, intelligent yellow eyes stared back at him.

Knowing he might be courting death, Jarrett urged the gray nearer to the great horned beast.

"Dragora." Slowly, carefully, he lifted his hand and touched the scaly hide. It was warm and rock-hard beneath his palm. "Guard my beloved well," Jarrett murmured, and urged the horse down the path, past the blackened trees and the charred skeletons.

He was half-way down the mountain when

he reined the gray to a halt. He would spend the night here, he thought. One last night on her mountain, breathing the air of her homeland, sleeping on ground that she had walked on.

Unsaddling the gelding, he tethered the horse to a nearby tree, then sat cross-legged on a patch of short blue grass, gazing sightlessly into the distance.

He would never see her again.

The three moons rose high in the sky, their dazzling silver light reminding him of Leyla's hair. Lying on his back, his hands folded beneath his head, he gazed at the stars, his mind conjuring up images of fathomless blue eyes and an angel-woman's soft smile. He thought of all the times she had come to him in his cell, remembering how he had yearned to see her face just once, remembering how her touch had soothed his bruised flesh and eased the torment in his soul.

How many times had she drawn his pain, his despair, into herself? Never complaining, never letting him know how much anguish it caused her to absorb his pain. So many long, lonely nights when he had lain in his lonely cell, strapped to a hard metal table or chained to the floor, yearning for her touch, the sound of her voice, the warmth of her presence. She had made him whole, in body and spirit, over and over again.

And now she was gone, forever lost to him.

Heartsick and soul-sick, he closed his eyes, knowing he would dream of her, ache for her, for the rest of his life.

Heart pounding with fear, he held his breath as they lowered him into the pool. The water was cold, chilling his bare flesh. He felt it creeping up his legs, shriveling his manhood, rising up his chest, past his neck, seeping into the hood. He held his breath, his body thrashing wildly. Why didn't they pull him up? His lungs were on fire, his heart was pounding with soul-shattering fear. Never before had they left him under water so long. Blackness swirled before his eyes, darker than the inside of the hood, deeper than the pool.

They were going to let him drown.

He opened his mouth to scream, and his throat filled with dark, cold water.

"Leyla!" His mind screamed her name, and then he was drifting down, down, lost in eternal darkness. . . .

"Jarrett! Jarrett! Wake up, I am here."

He struggled through layers of blackness to the surface, following the sound of her voice. He felt the warmth of her hands upon his shoulders, felt the dampness of her tears, like raindrops, on his cheeks.

"Leyla?" He opened his eyes to find her kneeling beside him. "Am I still dreaming?"

"No. Oh, Jarrett!" She threw her arms around him and held him close, wishing she could do something to banish the awful nightmares that haunted his dreams.

Jarrett wrapped his arms around her waist, gripping her tightly as he buried his face in the hollow of her breasts, breathing in the warm, sweet scent of her. His heart was still pounding, his body shivering convulsively as the last images of the dream faded. It had been so real, so very real. The cold water, the darkness . . .

"Leyla, what are you doing here?"

"I ran away."

Her words scattered the last vestiges of the nightmare. Pulling back a little, he gazed into her eyes. "You ran away?"

She nodded, her blue eyes dark and solemn.

"Leyla . . ." He laid his hand against her cheek. "Are you sure this is what you want?" He hesitated a moment, his gaze probing hers. "That I'm what you want?"

"Very sure."

"They'll come after you."

"Yes."

"We'd better go then." Jarrett frowned as a sigh of relief whispered past her lips. "What is it?" he asked.

"I was afraid thee might turn me away."

"Why would you think that?"

Her shoulders lifted in a slight shrug. How could she tell him that she had been afraid he wouldn't want her, afraid that, as much as he desired her, he would not want to spend

163

the rest of his life with her.

He saw the doubts in the clear blue depths of her eyes. "I don't think I could live without you," Jarrett said quietly. "Nor would I want to."

Her smile was radiant, her eyes filled with love and tenderness. "Kiss me, my Lord Jarrett," she entreated softly. "Just one kiss before we go."

"One or a thousand, beloved," he murmured as he drew her close. "You have only to ask."

Gently, his lips touched hers, and in that kiss was his pledge of infinite love and loyalty, and her wholehearted reply.

They traveled the rest of that night and into the morning, leaving the Mountains of the Blue Mist far behind.

At noon, they were well beyond the Cyrus River. A short time later, Jarrett reined his horse to a halt.

Dismounting, he lifted Leyla from the saddle of her mount. For a long moment, he held her close, his hands lightly caressing her arms, her back, his gaze intent upon her face, as if to assure himself she was really there. Not a dream, not an image of hope conjured from the depths of his despair, but a flesh-and-blood woman.

"We'll rest here awhile," he said. Reluctantly, he let her go. "I'll gather wood for a fire."

"Jarrett." She threw her arms around him and held him tight.

"It will be all right," he murmured, but in his heart he wondered if she would come to regret her hasty decision to follow him. He had nothing to offer her, nothing but his love and a solitary castle overlooking the Azure Sea.

They were on the road again within the hour. Jarrett pushed the horses hard, driven by an overpowering need to reach Greyebridge Castle. Tor would come after Leyla, he had no doubt of that. His only hope was that the Maje would turn back when he reached the Cyrus River rather than expose himself to possible capture by the Fen or by one of the roving bands of flesh peddlers who would sell him to the highest bidder.

He traveled warily, knowing that the prospect of being captured by the flesh peddlers was a possibility they had to face as well.

The next several days passed quickly. They traveled swiftly, pausing only for food and to rest the horses. Nights, they took advantage of whatever shelter they could find.

Jarrett slept with one hand on his sword, never completely relaxing his guard. Always, he was aware of the danger they were in, and of the beautiful woman who slept peacefully at his side. He was awed by her faith in him, her trust in his ability to protect her from harm.

Her nearness was a constant torment, a never-ending temptation. His arms yearned to hold her, his hands wanted only to bury themselves in the soft halo of her hair, his lips hungered for the taste of her. But he could not take her by force, nor could he bring himself to beg for her favors. She was not a woman of low character, not some concubine to be used and cast aside. He cared for her too deeply to defile her, loved her too desperately to betray her trust.

He looked at her now, sleeping beside him, her hair spread over her shoulders like a mantle of liquid silver, her lashes like pale shadows against her cheeks. Innocent in the ways of love between a man and a woman, she slept on, completely unaware of the twin demons of need and desire that pulsed within him, causing him to ache in a way that was both bitter and sweet.

At Greyebridge, he would ask for her hand in wedlock. He would not touch her until their union had been blessed by the Church. He would wait, he vowed, wait until she was his by right of marriage, even if it killed him.

Jarrett knew a moment of blessed relief when they reached the Fenduzian Coast. Away in the distance, across the Azure Sea, lay the green and gold Isle of Gweneth.

He stared out at the calm water. Once, he had loved the vast blue expanse of the sea, the quiet lapping of the waves as they kissed the sandy shore, but now, thanks to the months he'd spent in the Pavilion, the idea of being on the water filled him with trepidation. All too clearly, he remembered the horror of being lowered into a deep black pool, defenseless, powerless.

Well, there was no help for it. If he wanted to go home, they must go by boat. And since he dared not book passage on one of the large Fenduzian ships for fear of being recognized, they would have to trust one of the local fishermen to take them across.

Jarrett could not disguise his apprehension as he stepped into an ancient-looking vessel the following morning, even though the old seaman who owned the boat assured them it was quite safe.

Jarrett kept his eyes focused ahead, his heart pounding with excitement as the tiny speck in the distance grew larger.

He was going home.

They reached Gweneth late in the afternoon. Leyla gazed up at the huge old castle that stood like a lonely sentinel on a windswept promontory.

Upon reaching the coast, Jarrett paid the old fisherman, then unloaded their belongings. Slinging their packs over his shoulder, he started up the long gravel path that led to the castle. The countryside, which had once supported any number of horses, gentlesheep, and goats, seemed deserted. The cottages they passed stood in disrepair, doors askew, woven thatches fallen in.

Greyebridge Castle had been named for the massive dark grey stones of which it was made. He knew the rough texture of each stone, had scratched his name on more than one when he'd been a boy. A ragged banner woven of red and black and emblazoned with the head of a white stag fluttered from the gatehouse.

Leyla glanced at Jarrett as they crossed the drawbridge and entered the bailey, disquieted by the absence of people. Surely a castle as large as this should have housed hundreds, yet it was as quiet as a tomb. The yew trees, the shrubs, the bushes, were all in a sad state of neglect.

As they approached the keep itself, she saw a huge yellow mastiff, its bones showing clearly through its mangy hide, sleeping in the shade of a rotting tree. From off in the distance, she heard the unhappy lowing of a cow.

"Where is everyone?" she asked.

Jarrett shook his head as a feeling of uneasiness settled over him. When he'd been arrested eight months ago, the castle had been home to over three hundred people. Now, the gatehouse was deserted. There were no sounds of life from the stable. The gardens, which had been his mother's delight, had gone to seed. The only sign of life was a dog that would have been better off dead.

Resolutely, he opened an iron-strapped wooden door and stepped into the Great Hall.

The silence within the keep was absolute. For a moment, he stood just inside the door, his gaze sweeping the Hall. Once, the room had been filled with intricately carved tables and chairs, couches covered in rich damask and velvet. Enormous candelabras that held hundreds of candles had provided light. Huge tapestries had decorated the high stone walls.

Now the room was virtually empty. The rushes were old and dirty, and a monstrous cobweb fluttered from one corner of the ceiling.

Face set in grim lines, Jarrett crossed the room, his footsteps echoing loudly as he approached the spiral staircase that led upstairs to the family's living quarters. Leyla trailed behind him.

His steps were heavy as he made his way to the fourth floor. "Sherriza?" he called as he reached the landing. "Mother?"

The sound of cautious footsteps drew his attention. Turning, he saw a small, bent figure moving slowly toward him.

"Tannya?"

"Lord Jarrett!" She hurried toward him,

her face wreathed in smiles. "Praise the All Father, is it really you?"

"It's me, Tannya," Jarrett said gently. He gazed down into the wrinkled face of the woman who had been his nurse. She seemed to have aged twenty years in the past eight months.

"We feared you were dead," the old woman remarked. Lifting a corner of her apron, she dabbed the tears from her eyes.

"There were times I wished I was," Jarrett muttered under his breath. "Where's my mother?"

"In her room, Jeri. She's . . . she's not well."

Jeri. It had been his nursery name, one he'd thought never to hear again. "What's wrong with her?"

Tannya shook her head. "I fear she has lost the will to live." Fresh tears glistened in the old woman's pale blue eyes. "Everyone has left Greyebridge. We've nothing to eat, no wood to warm us now that the furniture is gone. The axe is so heavy . . ."

Jarrett put his arm around her frail shoulders. "It will be all right," he said reassuringly. "There's food in one of the packs downstairs. Will you prepare something while I see my mother?"

Tannya nodded. She took a few steps, then stopped as she saw Leyla standing in the shadows. "Who is this?"

"Her name is Leyla. She's my . . . my friend. Go along now, Tannya. There will be time for explanations later."

He watched his old nurse out of sight; then, taking Leyla by the hand, he walked down the hall to his mother's chambers.

The room was cold and dark. No furniture remained save the huge bed in which he'd been born. The hangings, once a bright cerulean blue, were in need of cleaning.

Fearing what he would see, he made his way to the bedside. His mother lay like a skeleton upon the bed. Her skin, once clear and fair, was now tinged with gray. Her hands, once plump and dimpled, looked like claws as they moved restlessly over the bedclothes. Her hair, once as glossy as a raven's wing, lay in limp strands upon the pillow.

"Mother . . ."

Her eyelids flickered open. "Tannya, is that you?"

"It's Jarrett."

"Jarrett?" She stared up at him, her gray eyes vague and unfocused. "No. That cannot be. My son is dead." A shadow of a smile lifted the corners of her mouth. "I will join him soon."

Jarrett turned toward Leyla, his eyes filled with silent entreaty. "Am I too late?"

"I will do what I can," Leyla murmured. Moving closer to the bed, she placed her left hand on the woman's brow, her right hand

171

over the woman's heart. Eyes closed, she summoned the Power, felt it swell within her veins, felt its heat pulse in her hands.

Leyla groaned softly as she absorbed the woman's unhappiness, the pain of a broken heart, the weakness of a body that had been denied sufficient food almost to the point of death.

Jarrett stood at the foot of the bed, awed by the miracle taking place before him. He saw the lines of pain disappear from his mother's face, saw the color bloom in her cheeks.

But at what a price! Leyla's face was etched with deep lines of pain. A soft moan escaped her lips and then, as if devoid of all strength, she slid to the floor.

With a low cry, Jarrett rushed to her side. Lifting Leyla in his arms, he hugged her close, knew a moment of heart-wrenching relief when he realized she was still breathing. He glanced over his shoulder at his mother, and when he saw that she was sleeping peacefully, he hurried from the room.

He carried Leyla down the hall to the room that had been his and placed her reverently on his bed. After covering her with a heavy quilt, he sat beside her and took her hands in his, willing his strength into her body. Hardly aware of what he was doing, he began to pray, quietly beseeching the All Father to spare the life of the woman he loved.

172

He lost track of time as he sat there. He was vaguely aware of Tannya coming and going in the room, drawing the draperies across the window to shut out the night, bringing him a plate of food which he never touched.

Hours passed, or it might have been days. He continued to hold Leyla's hands in his, frightened by her stillness. On the verge of despair, he knelt by the bedside, lifting his voice toward heaven in a desperate plea, begging the All Father to take his life instead of hers.

It was near dawn when Jarrett felt her hand move in his, heard the welcome sound of her voice calling his name.

"I am here, beloved," he said, hardly able to speak for the joy that pounded in his heart. He rose from his knees and sat on the edge of the bed. "I thought . . . I was afraid . . ."

She smiled up at him. "I should have warned thee," she said contritely.

"Warned me?"

"When the healing is very severe, it drains my strength. Your mother was very near death." Leyla sat up, her expression worried. "Is thy mother well?"

"I don't know."

"She's very well," came a voice from the doorway.

Jarrett glanced over his shoulder as his

173

mother entered the room. Gone was the gray, waxy look. Her skin was clear and unblemished, her eyes were bright, her hair as lustrous as polished ebony.

Jarrett squeezed Leyla's hand. "Bless you, Leyla," he whispered fervently.

Rising, he took his mother into his arms and held her close, a soft sigh escaping his lips as his mother hugged him in return.

"Welcome home, Jeri," Sherriza said, her voice thick with unshed tears. "I never thought to see you again."

"Nor I you."

"So," she said, giving him one last hug, "who is this child I find in your bed?"

"This is Leyla. It was her touch that healed you."

"Ah, a Maje. I have never met one before. Welcome to our home, Leyla. I regret that I have little to offer you, but what I have is yours."

"I require nothing in return, my Lady," Leyla replied, struggling to hide her embarrassment at being found in Jarrett's bed. "It is my duty to heal whenever I can."

"Nevertheless, I owe you a debt I can never repay."

Sherriza took Jarrett's hand, her gaze searching his face. "Tell me, Jeri," she said, "tell me all."

With a sigh, Jarrett covered his mother's hand with his own and told her, in as few words as possible, about being captured on his way to see the King, of being taken to the Pavilion. He made light of the tortures he had endured, dwelling instead on the comfort he had found in Leyla.

"It seems I owe you an even greater debt," Sherriza said, giving Leyla a look of deep gratitude.

"No, Milady. I am only glad that I was there, that I was able to ease his pain."

Sherriza nodded. There were not words enough, nor enough lucre in all the known world, to repay Leyla for Jarrett's life.

"I cannot believe that Rorke would dare abduct you in such a fashion. And to reinstate the Games without Tyrell's permission . . ." She spread her hands in a gesture of bewilderment. "What did he hope to gain by stripping you of your title and locking you away in that dreadful place?"

Jarrett shook his head. "I don't know, but I mean to find out. Let us speak of it no more, for now."

"Ah, Jeri," Sherriza murmured, "it is good to have you back. Well," she said, her voice steadier now, "when you are ready, Tannya has prepared First Meal. I shall see if I can't find a change of clothes for our guest. Perhaps, after we have broken our fast, she would like to bathe."

Sherriza smiled at her son affectionately, then wrinkled her nose as if she had caught scent of something unpleasant. "Of you, I demand it."

"Yes, my Lady," Jarrett replied.

With a parting smile at Leyla, Sherriza left the room.

"Thy mother is lovely," Leyla said. Swinging her legs over the side of the big square bed, she stood up, refusing to meet Jarrett's eyes. "What must she think of me?"

"What do you mean?"

"She found me in thy bed like some common strumpet."

"Leyla, my mother knows I would not bring such a woman into her house, or my bed. You have nothing to be embarrassed about. Come now, let us go down to First Meal."

Two hours later, Leyla accompanied Jarrett on a tour of the castle. She had enjoyed a leisurely bath, then dressed in a gown of emerald green that had been left on her bed. Matching slippers adorned her feet.

She slid a glance at Jarrett as they walked down a long hall. He wore a pair of snug black breeches, costly black boots, and a wine-red shirt. He looked at home here, she thought. Jarrett of Gweneth, Lord of the Manor.

Greyebridge Castle was square in shape, with massive towers at each corner. They started on the first floor, which was below ground level. It held a guard room, storerooms, and the granary.

The second floor housed the Great Hall, the kitchens, and the servants' quarters.

The chapel was located on the third floor, as was the sewing and weaving room. There were also several small apartments to accommodate guests.

The fourth floor was where the family resided. Sherriza occupied the east tower, Jarrett, the west. Leyla had been given the south tower. There were several large apartments located along the hallways between the towers.

Jarrett said little as they toured his home. Once, it had been a place filled with people, a city unto itself. Now it was virtually deserted. The servants had left soon after his disappearance. His men had been pressed into the service of the King. Only Tannya and his mother had been allowed to remain in the castle.

In the months that he'd been gone, the keep had fallen into disrepair. The grounds were barren, unkempt. The cottages on the hillsides had been abandoned; the moat had filled with debris. The mews and the stables were empty of the fine falcons and destriers that had once been the pride of Greyebridge.

And he was an outlaw.

The words rang in the back of his mind as they toured the dungeon located in the bowels of the castle. The air was heavy and damp and suddenly, he couldn't breathe. His heart began to pound as, all too clearly, he recalled his cell in the Pavilion, the constant darkness within the hood. He stared at the torch in his hand, his nostrils filling with the remembered stink of his own scorched flesh.

"Come," he said, and grabbing Leyla by the hand, he practically dragged her up the narrow stone staircase that led into the courtyard.

He dropped the torch into a bucket of water, then drew several deep breaths, filling his lungs with the fresh sweet scent of freedom.

"Jarrett?" She placed her hand on his arm, her eyes dark with concern. His face was suddenly pale, his breathing harsh and erratic.

"I'm all right."

"Thee must not think of that place," she said. "Thee is home now."

"I know, but I can't forget . . ." He wiped a hand across his eyes, haunted by the nightmare images that were never completely out of his mind.

In the beginning, before Leyla had been assigned to take care of him, there had been no one to heal him. The worst of his wounds had been treated by one of the Giants. Sometimes they had left him alone until his wounds healed, sometimes not. But then Leyla had come. With her there to heal him, it was no longer necessary to excuse him from the Games for several days at a time. In that respect, her coming had been both blessing and curse; a blessing because he didn't have to endure the pain of his wounds for days at a time, a curse because her healing power made it possible for him to participate in the Games more often, much to the delight of his tormentors.

"Jarrett, think of something else."

He nodded, knowing she was right. He had to put the past behind him. Perhaps then the nightmares would stop. Perhaps then he could think of the future.

"Leyla." Murmuring her name, he drew her into his arms and held her close. She was his strength, he thought as his lips brushed hers. She was his future.

Taking her by the hand, he led her toward the portal at the rear of the castle. The gate opened onto a large meadow. A narrow path led to a small lake surrounded by yellow willow trees and giant ferns. A wooden bridge spanned the lake; there was a covered porch where one could sit in the shade and enjoy the solitude.

Hand in hand, they circled the lake, then Jarrett knelt on the grass and drew Leyla down beside him. For a long moment, he gazed into the depths of her eyes — eyes as deep and blue as the lake, as calm as a midsummer day.

"Leyla . . ."

"My Lord?"

"Tender words and pretty phrases do not come easily to a man who has spent most of his life in battle." He took her hand in his. It was small and warm and soft, everything his was not. Just as she was everything he was not, he mused. And yet he loved her wholly, deeply.

He took a deep breath, wishing he were as skilled with words as he was with a sword. "Leyla, I had thought to ask thee to be my wife, but . . ." He shrugged helplessly. "I have nothing now to offer thee."

"Nothing, my Lord Jarrett?"

"Nothing," he repeated, his voice harsh with regret.

"Thee holds thy love cheaply then."

"My love? Thee has that already."

"It is all I will ever ask of thee."

"My love won't put food in your mouth, or clothes upon your back. It won't keep you from the king's wrath if his men come here looking for me."

Leyla lifted her chin defiantly. "Had I desired a life of ease and security, I would have married Tor."

"Does that mean you'll be my wife?"

"Any day thee chooses."

"I'll ride into the village tomorrow and fetch the priest."

"I will go with thee."

"No, it's too dangerous. I'll bring Father Lamaan here, if he'll come. It is my wish that we be married in Greyebridge chapel."

"Then it is my wish, as well."

"Are you sure this is what you want, Leyla? You will lose your gifts when we are wed."

Leyla shook her head. "That is only a myth."

"A myth? I don't understand."

"It was never true," she explained. "It was a lie told in hopes of protecting our women from harm if they fell into enemy hands."

Jarrett smiled with relief. It had bothered him, knowing she would be sacrificing her powers, a part of herself, to be his wife.

He squeezed her hand, and then frowned when she lowered her gaze. "What is it?" he asked. "What troubles you?"

"Nothing, my Lord."

"Leyla, I cannot read your mind as you read mine, but I can see that something is bothering you. Tell me what it is."

"My father . . ."

"What about him?"

"He threatened to revoke my powers if I married against his wishes."

"Can he do that?"

"Yes, by means of an old and seldom-used rite."

"Will he do it?"

"I do not know, but it matters not." She made a vague gesture of dismissal. "It is a small price to pay to be thy wife. Do not trouble thyself about it."

"It is not a small price. It is a part of you that will be forever lost. Are you sure you're ready to give it up? I want no regrets between us, no doubts."

"I have no doubts, my Lord Jarrett, only love for thee."

She gazed up at him, her eyes luminous, her lips slightly parted. Her name was a sigh on his lips as he pulled her into his arms and rained kisses upon the soft velvet of her mouth, the tip of her nose, the pulsing hollow of her throat. He could feel the beat of her heart, the warmth of her breasts against his chest.

His fingers burrowed into her hair, reveling in the silky softness. A deep breath brought him her scent, warm, fragrant, feminine. It stirred him to the core of his being, to the depths of his desire. He had yearned for her, dreamed of her, long before he'd seen her face or knew her name. In the awful despair of the Pavilion, she had become all things to him — mother, sister, friend, a haven from pain, warmth on a cold night, a ray of sunshine in the constant darkness in which he had lived.

Now, knowing her, he could not help but love her, could not help but want her.

With a groan, he pressed her back on the grass, his body covering hers as his tongue ravaged her mouth. She was life and breath and he would be lost without her.

One last kiss, and he drew away, his breath ragged.

With a rueful grin, he stood up. "We should not be out here alone," he said, offering her his hand. "You are far too beautiful, and I am much too weak."

"My Lord?"

"I fear you will not be an innocent on our wedding night if we stay here much longer."

A sudden flood of color washed into Leyla's cheeks as she grasped his meaning.

Hand in hand, they walked back to the keep.

Tomorrow, he thought, tomorrow she would be his in every sense of the word. He would live for her; die for her, if necessary.

Tomorrow, she thought, tomorrow all the mystery would be gone, and she would know what it meant to be a woman. Jarrett's woman.

Chapter Fifteen

Jarrett kept off the main road as he made his way toward the small village located some two and a half leagues from the castle. He knew he had no business being seen in public. Everyone knew he was an accused traitor. By now, it was probably common knowledge that he had escaped from the Pavilion. No doubt there was a price on his head. But someone had to fetch Father Lamaan, and he couldn't send Leyla or his mother, not without a proper escort.

He walked briskly, enjoying the gentle caress of the wind on his face. It felt so good to be free, to see the sun, feel the earth beneath his feet. Freed of the restricting shackles, his arms and legs felt as light as the air.

It was near mid-day when he reached the village. For a time, he stood out of sight behind a tree, watching the villagers come and go. There was no sign of any of the king's men. Indeed, the village was relatively quiet, but there was nothing unusual about that. Third Day was not normally a busy day.

He drew the hood of his cloak over his

head and then, with one hand on his sword, he crossed the road and entered the small white brick church located at the south end of the village.

It was dark inside, cool. A single candle burned on the altar. A lone figure clad in a long brown robe knelt at the intricately carved wooden railing before the altar.

"Father?"

The priest rose at the sound of Jarrett's voice, a smile of welcome lighting his florid face as he turned around.

"My Lord Jarrett," Father Lamaan murmured. He made the sign of the cross, then held out his hand. "Is it really you?"

"Aye." Jarrett swept the hood from his head as he walked down the narrow aisle and took the priest's hand. "It's good to see you again, Father."

"And you, my Lord." A frown creased the cleric's brow. "But, tell me, where have you been all this time, my son?"

"In the dungeons of the Pavilion."

"Ah. We heard a rumor to that effect, but could scarce believe it."

"Believe it, Father." Jarrett shoved his hands into his pockets, his fists clenching.

"The Pavilion," the priest said with a shudder. "How is it that you escaped?"

"By the grace of the All Father," Jarrett replied fervently, "and the help of a very courageous lady."

"Was it . . . very bad?"

"The Games are still being played there, Father," Jarrett replied flatly. "Does that answer your question?"

"But that's impossible!" Father Lamaan exclaimed. Everyone knew that the Games had been outlawed long ago; that the Pavilion had been turned into a prison to hold incorrigibles. "Impossible," he said again. "The King would never permit it."

"The King doesn't know."

"And you survived the Games." There was a note of awe in the priest's voice.

"My lady happens to be a Maje, Father. It is only because of her that I am here today."

"A Maje . . . I have never met one."

"You will. We are to be wed."

"I see." The priest looked thoughtful for a moment. "It is said that when a Maje weds an outsider, her powers are lost."

"So they say," Jarrett replied, unwilling to reveal what Leyla had told him about the myth, even to a holy man.

"And this does not trouble her?"

"She says not."

"And it does not trouble you?"

"Of course it does! But . . ." Jarrett shrugged. "I cannot live without her."

"I see."

"I doubt it, and I cannot explain it, except to say that it seems as if we are already one. She knows me as no other does, or ever will.

We would like you to perform the ceremony. Today, if possible. You'll like her, Father. She has a beautiful soul."

"Is a marriage wise at this time?"

"Is marriage ever wise?" Jarrett replied with a grin. "It will not be a large affair, just Tannya and my mother."

"And how is your mother? She was not well when I visited with her a fortnight ago."

"She's much improved."

"May the All Father be praised! Well, if there's to be a wedding, we had best be on our way."

"I'm afraid we'll have to walk back to the castle, Father."

"I am used to walking, my Lord." The priest paused, as if he feared saying something offensive. "Have you . . . I mean . . ." He cleared his throat. "Is there food enough at Greyebridge?"

"There's nothing at Greyebridge," Jarrett said bitterly. "In the King's absence, Rorke has taken everything except the castle itself."

"I feared as much. Wait here."

Jarrett stared suspiciously at the priest for a long moment, then glanced away, ashamed of what he'd been thinking. The good Father had been a friend to Jarrett's family ever since he could remember.

A sad smile tugged at Father Lamaan's mouth. "Were I in your place, my Lord, I would not trust anyone, either."

"Forgive me, Father."

The priest laid a gnarled hand on Jarrett's shoulder. "I'll not be gone long."

Alone in the chapel, Jarrett drew the hood of his cloak over his head and stepped into the shadows. The silence within the church was absolute. He stared at the flickering light of the candle, remembering the awful stillness of his cell in the bowels of the Pavilion, where the only sound had been that of his own harsh breathing and the echo of his screams. . . .

The Pavilion, a place of darkness, of despair, of days and nights without hope, until she came. Leyla. Her name rose on his lips, soft as a child's sigh, fervent as the prayer of a dying man.

He whirled around, his hand reaching for his sword, as the heavy oak door swung open, but it was only Father Lamaan, his aged shoulder sagging beneath the weight of a heavily laden sack.

"Are you ready, my Lord?"

With a nod, Jarrett took the sack from the priest, slung it over his own shoulder, then followed the old man out of the church.

Neither said a word until they were safely out of sight of the village, and then the priest spoke.

"You took a grave chance, coming here. There are signs posted about the village that offer a goodly reward for your capture."

Jarrett grunted softly. It was what he had expected.

Father Lamaan fell silent after that, his expression thoughtful. He had heard stories of the Pavilion, whispered bits and pieces of the horrors that had once taken place there; indeed, who had not heard at least one tale of the sadistic Games that gave the place its reputation? But they had been outlawed eons ago by every province in the realm. It was a miracle Jarrett had survived, Maje or no Maje.

The priest shook his head in silent wonder. A Maje. All his life, he had wanted to meet one. Now, it seemed, he would have his chance.

They reached Greyebridge an hour after dusk.

Sherriza made Father Lamaan welcome. The priest was an old friend of the family. He had been there to comfort Sherriza when her second child was born dead; he had been there when Jarrett's father was killed, offering prayers for the soul of the deceased, holding Sherriza while she wept bitter tears.

Leaving the priest with Sherriza, Jarrett went in search of Leyla. He found her in her room, a piece of delicate embroidery in her lap.

Leyla's heart skipped a beat when she glanced up to see Jarrett in the doorway. Each time she saw him was like the first

189

time. Just looking at him warmed the inner-most core of her being. He was so tall, so very masculine, everything within her was drawn to him.

Laying her needlework aside, she hurried into his arms. "I missed thee," she mur-mured, thinking how she had worried over his absence, fearing that he might be recog-nized in town, or captured by the king's men.

Jarrett held her close. She felt so good in his arms, so right. "I brought the priest. Do you wish to be wed this evening, or wait until the morrow?"

Leyla tilted her head back, her eyes spar-kling. "This evening, most assuredly, my Lord."

"I will send my mother to help you get ready." He kissed her gently on the cheek, his hands kneading her shoulders. Soon, he thought. Soon, she would be his. "Be quick, beloved."

An hour later, Leyla entered the family chapel to take her place at Jarrett's side. It was a beautiful place. The pews and the altar were of burnished oak. Wrought-iron cande-labras held dozens of tall white candles, filling the chapel with a soft glow. A shaft of moonlight fell on the stained-glass window behind the altar.

Sherriza and Tannya, both dressed in their finest, moved up to take their places beside

Leyla, but Jarrett had eyes only for his bride. She wore a full-skirted gown of gold and silver cloth; a gossamer veil covered her face. She looked like a goddess recently descended from heaven, an angel who had come to earth to steal his breath away. Her lustrous silver hair fell in loose waves down her back save for one silken curl that fell over her left shoulder. She held a single, long-stemmed midnight flower in her hand.

He couldn't seem to take his gaze from her face, not even when the priest began to speak the words that would unite them now and forevermore.

Jarrett spoke the proper words when the time came, slipped a heavy gold band over Leyla's slender finger and then, with the priest's blessing, he lifted the veil from her face.

For a long moment, he gazed into the depths of her eyes, overcome with the love he saw reflected there. And then, very gently, he kissed her, silently reaffirming his pledge of love and devotion.

And then he kissed her again. And again.

Reverently, he lifted a hand to stroke her cheek. "Beloved," he murmured in a voice thick with emotion. "My own."

"Always," Leyla replied quietly. She basked in the love and adoration shining in her husband's eyes. Never had he looked quite so handsome, so masculine. So desirable. He wore snug black breeches, black boots, and a dark green tunic that matched the color of his eyes. Her gaze moved over him lovingly, caressing the width of his shoulders, pleased by the smile that was for her alone.

A soft cough drew her attention to the fact that they weren't alone. Cheeks flushed, she turned to find Sherriza and Tannya standing at her elbow, grinning at each other.

"Welcome to the family, child," Sherriza said. Stepping forward, she pressed her cheek to Leyla's. "If he mistreats you in any way, you come to me."

"Or to me," Tannya said, giving Leyla a hug. "He was a terrible bully as a lad. Don't let him get away with it now."

"I won't," Leyla said, and then the priest was hugging her and wishing her well.

"My turn," Jarrett insisted, and drew Leyla into his arms, holding her to his side as if he would never again let her go.

For Leyla, the next hour passed in a haze of laughter, excitement, and anticipation. Using the food stuffs Father Lamaan had brought, Tannya had prepared a wedding dinner, complete with golden honey cakes for dessert.

Sherriza kept the conversation light, the wine glasses filled. The priest spoke of the latest gossip in the village, of the marriage of the blacksmith to the baker's daughter. He told of Jorrad's wife giving birth to twins, and how Jorrad had accused her of being unfaithful because of it.

Leyla listened in astonishment, amazed that a man of the church would know of such things. She was ever aware of Jarrett's eyes caressing her, of his nearness. He found numerous excuses to touch her hand, her arm. When he smiled, her heart soared. The sound of his laughter filled her with joy. It was so good to see him at ease in his own home, surrounded by those who loved him, as she loved him. She prayed that being home again would banish his nightmares forever.

A warm rush of heat flooded her cheeks when Jarrett stood up and announced it was time for bed. Sherriza and Tannya exchanged knowing looks; the priest seemed suddenly intent upon the contents of his wine glass.

"Good sleep, my mother," Jarrett said, bowing in Sherriza's direction. "Tannya. Father."

"Good sleep to you, my son," Sherriza replied. She smiled at her new daughter, felt a little tug of nostalgia as she remembered her own wedding night. Jarrett's father had been every bit as handsome, as tall, as strong. All the young women in the village had turned their eyes in Shammah's direction, fascinated by his prowess as a hunter and fighter, by the curling black of his hair, the deep green of his eyes; but, to her eternal gratitude, Shammah had chosen her for his wife. Sherriza uttered a silent prayer, hoping that Leyla would find the same enduring happiness in Jarrett's arms that she had found in his father's.

Hand in hand, Leyla and Jarrett climbed the spiral staircase that led to Jarrett's room. There was freshly washed bedding on the huge four-poster bed, the covers had been turned back, a fire crackled in the raised hearth.

Leyla gave a little start when Jarrett closed the door. They were alone now. Quite alone.

"Leyla . . ."

She swallowed hard. "My Lord?"

"I have not changed."

"My Lord?"

"You look at me as if you think I'm going to attack you like some wild beast."

Embarrassed, she looked away. She had wanted this moment, had been wanting it almost from the first day she had seen him in that horrid little cell in the bowels of the Pavilion, but now . . .

She looked up at him, wondering how she could make him understand, how she could explain her sudden apprehension. She had never known a man. She wanted Jarrett. She feared the loss of her powers. So many doubts and fears crowded her mind. How could she explain them to Jarrett?

"Do not be afraid of me, beloved. I will not hurt you." He took a deep breath. "Nor

194

will I touch you, until you wish it."

Her gaze slipped away from his. "It is thy right."

" 'Tis true, but I will respect your wishes, now and always."

"It's just . . . I mean." Still not meeting his eyes, she took a deep breath. "I am sorry, my Lord."

Murmuring her name, Jarrett gathered Leyla into his arms and held her close, one hand lightly stroking her hair. "You are so beautiful. Your hair outshines the sun, and your eyes . . . ah, beloved, your eyes are as blue as the Azure Sea."

At his words, a single tear slid down her cheek. He was so kind, so patient. His arm was warm and strong around her waist, his hand gentle in her hair. His scent swirled around her, filling her nostrils with the aroma of wine and leather and fine-spun cloth. Of man. Her man. Her husband, if she but had the courage to let him show her the secrets she yearned to know.

Sweeping Leyla into his arms, Jarrett carried her to the comfortable old leather chair beside the fireplace and sat down.

Settling her on his hip as if she were a sleepy child, he pressed his lips to her hair.

"Only let me hold you," he said. "Nothing more."

"Would thee perchance grant me one kiss, my Lord?"

He obliged her willingly. She tasted of sweet wine and tangy cheese, of apples and spice. The scent of wild roses lingered in her hair and rose from her skin, tantalizing his senses. Her breast was warm where it pressed against his chest, her mouth a honeycomb filled with secrets he yearned to explore.

He was breathing as though he had run a great distance when he took his lips from hers. "Leyla, beloved . . ."

"I am here," she whispered, her eyes dark with trepidation and desire. "I will always be here."

Jarrett gazed into her eyes and knew a sudden, gut-wrenching fear. She had never known a man, and he had not had a woman in almost a year.

He groaned low in his throat. He needed her more than his next breath, and yet he was afraid, so afraid. He wanted their first time together to be filled with tenderness, and yet he was afraid to touch her for fear he wouldn't be able to control the desire that was clawing at his insides like some beast on a rampage. What if he hurt her? Or frightened her so badly that she refused to let him touch her ever again?

Almost a year without a woman. Just touching her was torture of the most exquisite kind. How often had he dreamed of her only to wake in a cold sweat to find himself alone, imprisoned in a world of darkness?

But she was here now, enfolded in his arms, a magical creature with hair like moonlight, her innocent blue eyes filled with love and trust.

"Jarrett?" Her hands caressed his face as she gazed into his eyes. The arms holding her close were trembling; a muscle twitched in his jaw. "Is something wrong?"

His throat was as dry as the Serimite desert. Slowly, he shook his head. "I'm afraid."

"Afraid? Thee?" Astonished by his reply, she drew back to look at him more clearly. "Of what?"

"Of hurting you." He covered one of her hands with his, noting how very different they were. His hand was large and brown, heavily calloused, made for hard work and fighting; hers was small and slender, smooth and unblemished, created to give solace. "It's been so long. . . ."

"Do not be afraid, my Lord," she whispered tremulously. "I do not fear thy touch or . . . or thy desire."

He kissed her again, and yet again, felt her breath quicken, the rapid beating of her heart, saw the wonder that filled her eyes.

One slender hand curled around his neck, the other delved inside his shirt to stroke his chest. Her touch was like fire, burning away his self-control, incinerating the last of his doubts.

He lowered his head to nuzzle the slender curve of her neck, marveling anew at the warmth that radiated from her, the sweetness. He touched her, and everything else faded from his mind. She was truly a magical creature, able to heal his wounds, to read his thoughts, to conjure fire. . . .

A faint smile tugged at the corners of his mouth. Fire. She had truly lit a fire in him, he mused. It burned him now, blazing in his loins, threatening to consume him.

Leyla let her head fall back against Jarrett's arm, giving him access to her throat, reveling in the hot little kisses that rained down on the sensitive skin of her neck. There was magic in his touch, she thought, a magic stronger and more potent than any she had ever known.

She shuddered with pleasure as his mouth covered hers yet again, his tongue sliding over her lower lip. Her lips parted on a sigh and his tongue delved into her mouth, unleashing a torrent of sensations, quickening a response from deep within her, a warmth that unfurled like a leaf and permeated her whole being, brighter, warmer, than sunlight.

She offered no protest when he carried her to the bed and removed her gown and silken undergarments, bending to kiss the curve of her shoulder, the hollow of her throat, the silken heat of her breasts. With a ragged sigh, he quickly stripped off his shirt, boots, and breeches, and then stretched out beside her, drawing her into his arms.

Moaning softly, Leyla turned toward him, her body opening to receive him as a flower opens to the sun.

The unexpected beauty of it, the brilliance, caught them both unaware, and then they were moving together, two halves of the same whole, forever joined, forever one.

Like a river flowing into the sea, his seed spilled into her, flooding her with heat, and life. . . .

Chapter Sixteen

Leyla stood at the tower window, gazing across the courtyard at the rising sun. The sky was afire, splashed with broad strokes of crimson, as red as the virginal blood that had stained her thighs.

She glanced over her shoulder to where Jarrett lay asleep. Even in repose, he was splendid to look upon. His hair was spread like thick black silk against the white satin pillow covering. His jaw was shadowed with dark stubble. His skin was the color of dark copper touched with gold.

Her husband. She had lain in his arms all the night long, learning the contours of his body, her fingers measuring the width of his shoulders, the length of arms and legs corded with muscle. She had touched him and tasted him; she had filled her nostrils with the warm musky scent of him, heard the hunger in his voice when he murmured her name.

She did not regret her marriage or the loss of her innocence. She had found only joy in the arms of her husband, in the touch of his lips, in his whispered words of love. And yet . . .

She gazed down at her hands, resting lightly on the window sill. Her power to heal was gone. Of that there was no doubt. She felt the loss of her gift keenly, as though a part of her soul had been cut away, leaving her outwardly whole and yet forever incomplete.

She hadn't heard a sound, but suddenly Jarrett was standing behind her, his hands on her upper arms, his chin resting on her shoulder.

"What is it?" he asked.

His breath was warm, stirring the hair at her nape. "Nothing."

"Tell me."

She turned in his arms and laid her head against his chest, listening to the sure, steady beat of his heart. How could she tell him what she was feeling when she didn't fully understand it herself?

She felt the sudden tensing of his body. Looking up, she saw that his jaw was tightly clenched, his eyes dark with self-reproach.

"Are you sorry?" he asked. "Is that what's wrong?"

"No," she replied quickly, fervently. "No, I am not sorry. Thee must not ever think that."

"Then what is it that troubles you?"

She drew a breath that seemed to come from the very depths of her soul. "My powers are gone."

"You're sure?"

"Quite sure." A single tear glistened in the corner of one eye. "I did not believe he would do it," she said, very softly. "I guess I did not want to believe it. I thought it was only his anger that made him speak so."

Jarrett's arm tightened around her waist as a raw aching pain clawed at his insides, sharper than Thal's longboar knife, more agonizing than the touch of Gar's whip. He had taken more than her innocence, he had robbed her of her birthright.

"I'm sorry, beloved."

"It is not thy fault. I came to thee freely, willingly." She placed the palm of her hand against his cheek. "I would do it again." Her eyes searched his. "Thee does not believe me."

"I do."

"I see doubts in thy mind, my Lord Jarrett, and thee must never doubt my love for thee. Be assured that I will speak only the truth to thee."

"You can still read my mind?"

"Yes." The thought pleased her greatly. "I have lost only the power of healing." She gestured at the hearth. A small fire burned within, giving light and warmth to the room. "As thee can see, I can still conjure fire."

"Perhaps the gift of healing will return, in time."

Slowly, she shook her head. "No, my Lord. Once revoked, the gift of healing cannot be restored."

"My Lord," he said, smiling down at her. "Why do you continue to call me that?"

"If fits thee so well. Does thee wish me to stop?"

"No." His hands moved restlessly over her shoulders, reaching up into the wealth of her hair, sliding down her arms, then locking around her waist. "Leyla, beloved, you make me weak."

She gazed into the depths of his eyes, as clear and green as the Aldanian glass so prized by the Maje. Her smile was softly seductive as she took him by the hand.

"Come," she said, leading him toward the bed. "I need no mystical power to make thee strong again."

"You have more power than you know," he muttered, and drawing her down beside him, he covered her body with his, surrendering to the power in her hands — not the power of healing, but the power of love.

It was late afternoon when hunger drove them down to the Great Hall.

Sherriza looked up from the altar cloth she had been mending, a knowing smile lighting her face. Her son looked relaxed and happy as he placed a possessive arm around his bride's shoulders. And Leyla was radiant, her summer-sky eyes aglow with love and adoration when she looked at her husband.

"Did you sleep well, my children?" Sherriza

asked, her voice tinged with tender amusement.

"Very well indeed, my mother," Jarrett replied. Noting the blush creeping into his wife's cheeks, he drew Leyla closer to his side. "Where's Tannya?"

"Preparing Second Meal." Sherriza met his gaze. "She thought you might be ravenous when you finally decided to come down."

"She was right."

Jarrett held a chair for Leyla, then sat down beside her, his hand reaching for his bride's as if he could not bear to lose contact with her, even for a moment. His gaze was intent upon her face, his eyes filled with adoration. And Leyla returned his gaze, her deep blue eyes brimming with love and devotion.

Sherriza felt a tug at her heart. It was obvious that they were very much in love, and she uttered a silent prayer that it might always be so.

Moments later, Tannya entered the Hall, fussing at Jarrett for missing First Meal, smiling at Leyla, asking if there was anything special she desired.

When they were all seated at the table, Jarrett asked after the priest's whereabouts.

"Father Lamaan left this morning," Sherriza said. "He said to tell you he'll be back soon. He helped us plant the seedlings before he left."

Jarrett nodded. The good father had managed to obtain quite an assortment of young vegetable plants to restock their garden. Due to the short growing season, it was critical to plant as early as possible.

"He said he'd bring a cow and a few sheep when he returns. And some cloth, if he can manage it."

Jarrett grunted softly. Greyebridge had never been forced to accept charity before. Always, it had been Greyebridge Castle that had helped alleviate whatever need there had been on the island, but those days were gone, at least for now. Much as it galled him to accept help, he could not let his pride keep food off the table; he could not let the women of his household suffer because of his insufferable arrogance.

My Lord Jarrett. He was a man who had always been accorded a great deal of honor and respect, not only because he was lord of Greyebridge, but because he was a hunter without equal, a man of insight and daring. His courage was well-known, his skill with a blade almost legendary. No one had dared cross him, or mock him, until the Pavilion. . . .

In the bowels of the Pavilion, he had learned that there were things far worse than enduring the pain of the flesh. Harder to bear than the torture he had been subjected to had been the contempt in the eyes of the men who had played the Games, the constant degradation of the whip, the humiliation of being shackled like a dog, the constant ridicule, the scorn, the jeers they had hurled at him.

"Not so lofty now, my Lord," they had cried as they forced him to his knees again and again.

Almost as bad had been the taunts the Giants had hurled at him: *"Here's your food, my Lord Jarrett,"* they had sneered when they brought him his meals, meager as they were. *"Sorry, we're all out of silver trays and crystal goblets."*

He felt Leyla's hand tighten on his and he shook the memories away. What was past was past. It was time to look forward, not back.

Filled with a sudden restless energy, he began to move through the castle, assessing what needed to be done, determining which tasks should be started immediately, which could wait.

He sent the women to search the fields for whatever wild fruit or vegetables they might be able to find while he set several snares in the woods behind Greyebridge.

The next few days passed swiftly. There was much to do, and far too few hands to do it.

Father Lamaan returned, bringing a ewe and a ram, apologizing profusely because he hadn't been able to procure a cow.

On the afternoon of the fourth day, two

heavily armed men rode into the courtyard.

Leyla was sitting outside with Jarrett, watching as he fashioned a chair from a tree trunk, when the men rode up. Her first thought was to run, but Jarrett made no move to flee, nor did he reach for his sword. Instead, a slow smile spread over his face.

"Dann! Paull! By thunder, it's good to see you!"

The two men dismounted and for the next few moments there was a lot of laughing and back-slapping.

"What brings you here?" Jarrett asked at length. "I thought you were serving in the King's army."

"A few of us managed to avoid being taken," Dann answered. "We've been hiding out in the hills. Father Lamaan told us you were here. Can you use us?"

"Indeed. Where are your families?"

"In the hills also."

Jarrett shook his head, touched by their loyalty, by their unspoken belief in his innocence. He had been branded a traitor, accused of consorting with Aldanite spies. No one had come forward in his behalf. Rorke had claimed that the King refused to hear him, though Jarrett was beginning to wonder if Tyrell had ever been made aware of his arrest.

He held out his hand, bidding Leyla to join him. "This is my wife, Leyla," he said, slipping his arm around her waist.

"My pleasure, my Lady."

"Welcome to Gweneth, my Lady."

"Thank you," she murmured, flattered by the admiration she saw in their eyes.

"Come inside," Jarrett invited. "Tannya will have food prepared."

Paull shook his head. "Our women will worry if we do not return home before dark. With your permission, we will return on the morrow." He glanced around the courtyard. "We have a small herd of sheep. Some goats. A cow."

"Your generosity will not go unrewarded."

"It is not generosity, Milord," Dann replied with a grin. "All wear the mark of Greyebridge Castle."

"How came you by them? My lands and livestock were forfeit to the Crown."

Paull's pale blue eyes sparkled with mischief. "Would you believe they followed us into the hills?"

"Followed you?"

"Aye, Milord," Dann said, stifling a grin. "It took but a rope and a firm hand. Until the morrow, then."

"Wait! What is the word in the village? Do the people think me guilty of treason?"

"No, Milord. But they have been warned not to help you on pain of death. There are others from Greyebridge hiding in the hills. In time, they will come home."

"I cannot promise you safety if you stay," Jarrett warned. "If Rorke learns of my presence here . . ." Jarrett shrugged. "Think on it carefully before you decide to return."

"Greyebridge is our home," Dann replied. "And you are our Lord." He bowed in Leyla's direction. "Until the morrow, my Lady. My Lord Jarrett."

"Until the morrow," Paull repeated.

Jarrett draped his arm across Leyla's shoulder as he watched the two men ride out of the courtyard. "I hope they do not regret their decision." Jarrett let out a deep breath. "Tyrell should return to Heth soon. When he does, I'll go to him and explain what happened."

"What if he won't listen?"

"He will," Jarrett said emphatically.

He kissed Leyla soundly, then reached for the ax he had dropped earlier. "It looks as though we will need many more chairs," he said with a grin. "Go tell Sherriza that Dann and Paull are coming home."

The next few weeks were happy ones. Dann and Paull brought their families to the castle, and the walls rang with the sound of children's laughter. In a short time, the men built two tables and enough chairs to seat everyone. New wardrobes were constructed, new shelves and trunks made. Dann's wife, Sarrah, spent hours beating the dust from tapestries and bed hangings. Paull's wife, Janna, washed the floors and the windows. Tannya reigned in the kitchens, enlisting the help of the older children. Sherriza spent hours in the garden, planting, weeding, watering.

Leyla found herself in charge of the house. She knew it was her right, her duty, but it did not come easily to her. She was not comfortable giving orders, settling disputes, planning menus. She felt as if she were usurping Sherriza's place, but Jarrett's mother insisted that was not the case. Leyla was Jarrett's wife. As such, she was now the lady of the manor.

Gradually, a few others returned to Greyebridge, renewing their allegiance to Jarrett. First, Harran, the cobbler; then Jorrad, the blacksmith; Terrek, the cooper. They brought their wives and families, their livestock.

They brought news, as well. Tyrell was marching toward Heth; Rorke had been called to Cornith to preside over a minor border dispute between two adjoining landholders.

Jarrett breathed a sigh of relief. With Rorke at Cornith, there was nothing to fear, at least for the time being. It would give him time to get Greyebridge on its feet again before he left for Heth.

And now Greyebridge Castle vibrated with life. Roosters announced the coming of dawn, the lowing of cattle and oxen could be heard, mingled with the sounds of sheep and horses.

Soon, Greyebridge looked the way Leyla imagined it had before Jarrett's arrest. New rushes covered the floors. The tapestries and hangings had all been aired and brushed clean. The mattresses had been turned, the bedding laundered.

When Jarrett decided they deserved a holiday, she wholeheartedly agreed. They had worked hard for weeks. It was time to dance.

The women immediately began cooking, and when Sherriza remarked that she had a taste for fresh pork, Jarrett decreed that she would have it.

So it was that early on a clear summer morn he took up his bow and a quiver of arrows and went in search of game.

He experienced a sense of peace as he prowled through the sun-dappled forest. As a boy, he had spent hours within the woodland, chasing rabbits and foxes and the other furry creatures that inhabited the timberland. As he grew older, he hunted the great gray stags, and the wild pigs that were more vicious than any other beast of the forest.

On silent feet, Jarrett made his way deeper into the woods, his eyes and ears attuned to each shifting shadow and sound. A change in the wind carried the heavy scent of the Sea of Darkness, located on the far side of the island, and with it came the heady fragrance of the wildflowers that grew in abundance along the shore.

And then, ever so faintly, he caught the musky odor of a wild boar. Fitting an arrow to his bowstring, Jarrett moved through the woods, soundless as the sunlight.

He found the boar sniffing around a rotten log, its long narrow snout rooting in the soft earth.

Jarrett was taking aim when the island wind, always as unpredictable as a woman, shifted yet again, carrying his scent to the boar.

The animal's head came up with a jerk. Its little pig eyes searched the shadows as it sniffed the wind, and then, with a high-pitched squeal, it charged forward, its short stocky legs propelling it toward Jarrett with astonishing speed.

Forcing himself to remain calm, Jarrett sighted down the long shaft, waiting until the last possible moment before he let the arrow fly.

The shaft struck home, killing the animal almost instantly, though the boar's momentum carried it another three yards before it skidded to a halt mere inches from Jarrett's feet.

Drawing his knife, he skinned the carcass, gutted it, and hung it from a tree. He would return later with a horse to carry the meat home.

With his bow slung over his shoulder, he started for home, his mouth already watering. It had been almost a year since he'd had fresh meat of any kind, and his stomach growled as he envisioned the meals to come: succulent pork, stuffed sausage . . .

It was near dusk when Greyebridge Castle came into view. Jarrett came to an abrupt halt as he reached the edge of the timberland, his gaze drawn to the red and black banner that hung upside down from the top of the west tower.

It was a warning to stay away.

Drawing his sword, Jarrett followed a narrow deer trail around the side of the hill to the front of the castle. Hunkering down behind a great clump of blue ferns, he stared at the scene before him. A dozen mounted men wearing the King's colors waited near the drawbridge. He could see another dozen or so strung out on the bridge itself. No doubt there were more inside the keep.

Melting into the gathering shadows of sunset, Jarrett made his way to the east side of the castle. A small boat waited there, hidden in a dense thicket.

Sheathing his sword, he dragged the boat from cover and eased it into the moat. Praying that the ancient craft would stay afloat, he lowered himself into the boat and rowed across the narrow channel to a small opening cut into the castle wall, cleverly hidden by a tangled mass of water vines that grew up out of the moat, clinging precariously to the rough stones of Greyebridge.

It was awkward, trying to keep the boat from capsizing while he pushed the vines aside, then levered himself out of the boat and into the opening.

His hands were scraped and bloody by the time he managed to drag himself into the narrow passageway. On hands and knees, he made his way through the thick darkness, shaking off the memory of other dark places that had closed him in.

There were two hundred hand-hewn stone stairs from the passageway to the fourth floor. He had counted them often in carefree days gone by. He counted them now. When he reached one hundred, he made a sharp right turn, then crawled quietly along the damp stone floor until he came to a narrow door which opened into the Great Hall. The door, known only to members of the family, had been designed and painted in such a way that it looked as though it were a part of the hunting scene that covered the entire north wall from floor to ceiling.

Rising to his feet, Jarrett peered through a slit to the right of the door, his gut clenching at what he saw. Sherriza, Tannya, and Leyla stood in the center of the Hall surrounded by several of the King's men, while the King's brother-in-law asked questions, one after the other.

Rorke! So much for the rumor that he had gone to Cornith.

"Where is Jarrett?" Rorke asked brusquely. "We know he's been here. He was seen in the village. Has he left? Did he speak with anyone other than family while he was here? Have any Aldanites been seen in the area?"

Sherriza shook her head after each question, her expression placid.

"He managed to escape from the Pavilion, something that's never been done before. Do you know who helped him? Do you know where he might have gone?"

Again, Sherriza shook her head.

"The punishment for refusing to answer the King's questions is imprisonment in the King's Tower," Rorke said, his anger rising. "Do not think you will be spared because you are related to the Lord High Ruler of Aldane."

Sherriza looked unimpressed by the threat.

Tannya shivered, visibly shaken by the mere mention of the Tower. Her brother had died within its walls.

Leyla remained unmoving, her hands clasped together, her chin thrust forward in unspoken defiance. The King's brother-in-law was tall and lean, with dark brown hair, a full beard, black eyes, and a nose as thin as a blade. A hideous scar bisected his left cheek. She wondered if he could tell how frightened she really was.

Rorke's narrow-eyed gaze lingered on each woman's face. "You will all be sent to the King's Tower if you do not tell me what I wish to know."

"We know nothing," Sherriza replied calmly. "You may search the castle. You may threaten us. You may flog us. But there is nothing we can tell you except that he is not here."

Rorke fingered the scar on his cheek as he contemplated flogging Jarrett's women. It would give him pleasure to do so, simply because he knew it would cause Jarrett a great deal of pain. Jarrett, who had been his childhood friend.

They had played together, learned to ride together, hunted in the king's forest together. As they grew older, Rorke began to realize that he would always be second best. When they went wenching and drinking together, Jarrett always managed to end up with the most desirable woman.

They had trained together, but it had been Jarrett who excelled with the sword, the crossbow, the lance. Always, it had been Jarrett who had been the better horseman, the wiser strategist, the most skilled at hand-to-hand fighting. Jarrett who might have replaced Rorke in the old King's affections if he hadn't been sent away for disobedience. It was Jarrett's one weakness, his refusal to obey orders without question, to be humble in the face of authority, to be silent in the face of discipline, deserved or not.

When the old king died, his brother, Tyrell, had inherited the throne. With a great deal of cunning and patience, Rorke had gained Tyrell's confidence. He had courted Tyrell's sister, Darrla, earnestly and unceasingly, not because he loved her, but because he coveted the throne, and an alliance with the royal house put him that much closer to the King.

Rorke stared at the young woman with the silver hair. She was a distant cousin, Sherriza had said. A dreamy child who had been sent to Greyebridge to put distance between her and an unwanted suitor. Perhaps, when this trouble with Jarrett was over, he would get better acquainted with the girl.

From his hiding place behind the wall, Jarrett listened to every word. Hands curled into tight fists, he glared at Rorke. It was all he could do to keep from bolting through the door and wrapping his hands around the man's throat. But killing the King's brother-in-law would accomplish nothing but his own death, and that of those he loved.

"I know he has been here," Rorke remarked. "I think perhaps we will await his return. Taark, take the Lady Sherriza and the young one to the dungeon and lock them up. You, Tannya, prepare food for my regiment at once. Gayd, go outside and tell the men we'll be staying the night. Yorri, Parre, see to the first watch."

Jarrett swore under his breath as three of the King's men escorted Leyla and his mother from the Hall.

The dungeon was dark, damp, and cold. Sherriza was locked in the cell nearest the door. Leyla was thrust into a cubicle at the far end of the corridor. After making sure the locks were secure, the men left, taking the only source of light with them.

Leyla shuddered as the moldy hay piled in the corner of her cell began to rustle. She screamed as something scurried over her foot. "Sherriza!"

"I'm here, child. Do not be afraid."

"Something touched me."

"A rat, most likely."

"A rat." Leyla shuddered with revulsion. "Sherriza." Leyla's voice dropped to a whisper. "Jarrett is near. I could feel his presence in the Hall."

"Are you certain?"

"Yes."

"I hope he has the good sense to stay away."

"When have I ever shown good sense, my mother?"

"Jeri!" Sherriza exclaimed. "What are you doing here?"

"Did you expect me to leave you in

Rorke's hands? Where are the others? Paull and Dann, Jorrad . . ."

"Paull and Jorrad were killed trying to defend the castle. Dann and several other men were badly wounded."

Jarrett swore under his breath, berating himself for thinking that he could return to Greyebridge and make everything right again. He never should have let his people come home. They'd been safe before, living in the hills. Now the survivors were Rorke's prisoners.

"You must go, Jeri," Sherriza urged. "If they find you, they'll take you to the Tower, or worse, back to the Pavilion."

"I know." He took his mother's hand and squeezed it reassuringly before he continued down the corridor to the last cell. "Leyla?" He could scarcely see her for the darkness.

"Here. Oh, Jarrett, it was awful. Our people fought so hard, but they were badly outnumbered. So many were hurt, and there was nothing I could do to help them."

The anguish and regret in her voice tore at his heart. But for him, she could have healed the wounds of his people. But for him, she wouldn't be here now. But for him, his men would still be alive. The fact that he had warned them of the danger lessened his guilt not at all. They were his people, his responsibility, and he had failed them.

"Jarrett, what are we to do?"

What, indeed? he thought bleakly.

Reaching through the bars, he cupped her face in his hands. Her cheeks were damp with tears. "Don't weep, beloved," he murmured, and leaning forward, he kissed away her tears. "Don't be afraid. I'll be nearby."

"No. There are too many of them. Does thee hope to fight them all?"

"No, only to out-smart an old rival. Kiss me now, quickly, and then I must go."

The touch of his lips boosted her courage, and then he was gone, silent as a shadow.

Moments later, one of the king's men entered the dungeon bearing a lantern and two tin plates. He slid a plate under the door of each cell, shrugged in apology at the poor fare, and left the dungeon, plunging them into darkness once again.

Chapter Seventeen

Leyla sat in a corner of her cell, her legs drawn up to her chest, her arms folded around her knees. She was afraid to close her eyes, afraid to sleep for fear she'd wake to find rats, or worse things, crawling on her skin or nesting in her hair.

The darkness was oppressive, and she wondered how Jarrett had survived in the Pavilion for so many months, how he had endured the long dark nights, the endless days of pain, the thick black hood. She knew she would have gone mad if she'd been forced to wear that awful hood for more than a day. It was a constant reminder that death was never far away, a subtle form of imprisonment far more cruel than the shackles that had bound him, or the cell that had caged him.

The darkness. It was stifling in its completeness. She held up her hand and saw only blackness. She had never realized she was afraid of the dark until now, but then, she'd never been completely alone in darkness like this.

How slowly the hours passed! The stone

floor was cold and damp. The chill crept into her, climbing up her legs, her arms, her back, until she was shivering uncontrollably.

How long until dawn, she wondered, and then laughed. What difference did it make? She wouldn't be able to see the sun. It could be morning now and she'd never know it.

A faint light appeared at the far end of the passageway. Leyla scrambled to her feet and moved toward the front of the cell, her heart pounding with hope.

But it wasn't Jarrett come to rescue them. It was Rorke. He stopped at Sherriza's cell.

"Are you ready to answer my questions now?" he asked, his voice curt.

"I have nothing to tell you," Sherriza replied.

"Perhaps you'll think more clearly on an empty stomach."

"Your threats do not frighten me, Rorke. Do to me as you wish, but I would ask that you let my cousin go. She has no part in this."

"You try my patience, woman. Now, hear my decree. You will be sent to the King's Tower this very day. Perhaps a night or two in the company of the King's Executioner will loosen your tongue. As for the girl . . ." Rorke shrugged. "I shall keep her here with me. I shall abide here awhile, just in case Jarrett shows up. She can keep me company."

"I warn you, Rorke, do not lay a hand on that child. You will sorely regret it if you do."

"A threat, my Lady?"

"A warning."

"Take her," Rorke said, and four men appeared out of the shadows. Unlocking the cell door, they escorted Sherriza out of the dungeon.

Torch in hand, Rorke walked to Leyla's cell. "So, have you anything you would like to tell me?"

Leyla stared at him, at the cruel twist of his mouth, the cold black eyes, and shook her head.

"This is no place for a lady such as yourself. Tell me what I want to know and I'll see that you're taken to your home in safety." His gaze narrowed imperceptibly. "You know where he is, don't you? Don't you!"

She had never told a lie in her life. It took all her will power to speak one now. "No. I would tell thee if I did."

"Would you? I wonder." His gaze moved over her in a long assessing glance. "We shall see what song you sing after a few days without food and water, my little silver-haired angel. And if that doesn't loosen your tongue, there are other ways." His black eyes glittered. "Ways that I'll find most pleasant."

Leyla stared after him as he walked away, her gaze fixed on the light of the torch as it grew fainter and fainter, and then disappeared.

And now she was truly alone.

No one came to her for what seemed like days. She lost all track of time. Hunger gnawed at her belly, her throat grew dry. She huddled in her corner, shivering from the cold, from the fear that held her fast. Where was Jarrett? Why didn't he come for her? Had he been captured? But surely, if he'd been taken prisoner, he'd have been brought here. Had he decided the risk was too great and abandoned her?

No! She would not believe that.

She tried to think of something pleasant: the unicorn meadow at home, the touch of Jarrett's hands, but she couldn't seem to concentrate on anything other than the awful fear that she'd been left here to die, alone, in the dark.

When she heard the muffled sound of footsteps, she didn't bother to look up, assuming it was Rorke coming to see if hunger had loosened her tongue.

"Leyla."

His whispered voice went straight to her heart. Scrambling to her feet, she hurried toward the cell door. "Jarrett! Oh, Jarrett." Tears of joy and relief burned her eyes.

"Shhh, it's all right."

She heard the harsh rasp of a key in the lock, and then the door swung open and she was in his arms, holding on as if she would never let go. He was here. She breathed in the scent of him, let her arms twine around his neck. She could hear his heartbeat beneath her cheek. Yes, he was here. He was real.

She clung to him when he tried to loosen her hold. "A moment more," she begged.

"Leyla, there's no time for that now. Come, we've got to get out of here."

He took her hand and led her down the passageway. It was narrow and cold, so dark she couldn't see him ahead of her. They walked for a long distance, then turned left.

She felt Jarrett's arms wrap around her, and then he was pulling her close, his hands moving over her shoulders and back, caressing her face.

She pressed herself against him. "Is something wrong?" she asked anxiously.

"No." She heard the smile in his voice. "I just can't wait to hold you any longer."

For several moments, they stood in each other's arms. And then, reluctantly, he let her go. "We have to crawl the rest of the way," he said, "but it isn't far."

The stones were hard and cold beneath her hands and feet as she followed Jarrett along the narrow passageway. She felt his tension as they made their way through the darkness, knew he was fighting memories of another kind of darkness.

At last, she saw light ahead. Moments later, they were in a small vessel headed across the moat.

When they reached the far side, Jarrett caught hold of a sturdy vine and climbed up the side of the moat.

"Grab hold," he called, tossing the vine to her, "and I'll pull you up."

She knew a moment of sweet relief when she was standing beside him.

"Let's go," he said, and taking her hand, he led her into the cover of the trees.

"What now?" she asked when they were out of sight of the castle.

He shook his head. "I'm not sure. I can't very well storm the King's Tower alone, and I can't leave my mother in there to rot at Rorke's leisure. Rorke." He spat the name as if it tasted bad. "I can't believe the King knows what's going on."

Jarrett ran a hand through his hair. "I can't believe Rorke was acting on Tyrell's orders when he sent me to the Pavilion. I can't believe Tyrell would think I'd turn traitor, that he would strip me of my lands and title because I refused to kill those women and children."

Jarrett swore under his breath. "Tyrell's a hard man, but he's never made war on helpless folk before. Why would he change now? Why wasn't I allowed to plead my cause before the King?"

"Do you think he will help thee?"

"I don't know."

He shook his head again. There were too

many things he didn't know, too many things that didn't make sense.

"Come," he said, taking her hand, "we'll rest until nightfall, and then I'll see if I can't steal a couple of horses."

She was too weary to argue, too worried to do more than follow him deeper into the forest. Exhausted mentally and physically, weak from hunger, she curled up in his arms as soon as they found a place to hide. Moments later, she was asleep.

When she woke up, Jarrett was sitting beside her slicing into a loaf of black bread. Her stomach growled loudly, bringing a flush to her cheeks as she sat up.

With a grin, Jarrett handed her a chunk of bread and a flask of wine.

"Go on," he said, "it's all for you. I've eaten."

She took a bite of the bread. It was fresh from the oven, and she was certain nothing had ever tasted so good. The wine was warm and sweet.

"Where did thee get this?" she asked when she'd taken the edge off her hunger.

"From Tannya."

"She is well?"

Jarrett nodded. "They won't hurt her. She's too old to be a threat, and if they did away with her, they'd have to cook for themselves."

He stared out into the darkness. The outline of Greyebridge Castle rose in the distance, shadowy, mystical. Home. The only home he'd ever known. And now Rorke was there. Was it possible that Greyebridge was what Rorke had been after all along? Had sending Jarrett to the Pavilion been the first step toward that end? With Sherriza locked in the King's Tower, there was no one to protest if Rorke decided to take over Greyebridge Castle.

Jarrett frowned thoughtfully. Rorke was the King's brother-in-law. He had security and wealth and the King's confidence. His wife had a small estate near Heth, as well as several other places of residence. But Rorke didn't have lands or a castle of his own.

And Greyebridge was a castle almost without equal. If Rorke could gain possession of Greyebridge, he might be able to persuade the King to restore the surrounding lands and holdings that had been forfeit to the Crown when Jarrett was accused of treason.

"My Lord?"

He turned to see Leyla watching him carefully. "Feeling better?" he asked.

Leyla nodded. She licked the last of the bread crumbs from her fingers, took a sip of wine, and handed the flask to Jarrett.

He took a long drink, wiped his mouth with the back of his hand. "Ready?"

"Where are we going?"

"To see the King."

"Is that wise?"

"You mean is it safe, don't you?"

"Yes."

"I hope so, but one way or another, I have to get my mother out of the Tower. And I have to know if Rorke was acting on the King's orders when he sent me to the Pavilion."

Taking Leyla by the hand, Jarrett helped her to her feet, then drew her into his arms. His gaze held hers for a long moment, and then, ever so tenderly, he kissed her, his lips moving in a gentle caress over her mouth and nose, her closed eyelids, the curve of her cheek.

He had been wrong to take her away from her home in the mountains, he thought, wrong to make her his wife when his life was in such turmoil. And yet, selfishly, he was glad of her presence at his side.

Leyla smiled up at him. "I would not have let thee leave me behind," she remarked, her eyes sparkling like costly jewels. "I would have followed thee to the bowels of Hadra and back again."

"Would you, my beauty?"

"Thee knows it's true."

"I fear such devotion will bring you harm, beloved. More harm than you can imagine."

"I am not afraid."

"You needn't be. I'm frightened enough for both of us."

Bending, he kissed her again, his lips claiming hers in a kiss filled with passion and possession. He longed to press her down on the grass, to take her, there, in the shadowed woodlands, to brand her as his for all time, but Rorke was too close, the chance of discovery too great.

He hugged her close one last time and then he released her. "It's time to go," he said. Finding a leafy branch, he erased their footsteps, then scattered dirt and leaves over the smooth ground. It would not fool a good tracker for long, but it might stall Rorke's men for a while.

Two horses waited for them in a clearing a short distance away. Jarrett lifted Leyla onto the back of a long-legged bay mare, swung onto the back of a blue roan, and turned his horse north, toward the sea.

Chapter Eighteen

They located a small ship flying the Fenduzian flag moored off the coast.

Jarrett watched it for a long while, and when he was satisfied that there were only a few men aboard, he left Leyla with the horses and boarded the ship. He dispatched two of the sailors by striking them over the head with the hilt of his sword. The third sensed his presence and turned to fight. It was a brief skirmish, quickly over, and when it was done, Jarrett dumped the man's body into the sea.

Hurrying now, he returned for Leyla. Regretfully, he was forced to leave the horses behind. A short time later, they were underway, headed across the narrow channel toward the Fenduzian border.

Leyla stood at the rail, the wind in her face, as she watched Jarrett maneuver the sleek craft. His jaw was thick with black stubble, and the breeze tossed his long black hair over his shoulder. A bit of moonlight glinted off the hilt of his sword. She had often compared him to a Giddeon pirate, she mused, but never had he looked the part more than he did this night.

He turned his head, his hooded gaze meeting hers, and she felt her stomach curl with pleasure at the fervent look in his eyes. Ah, those dark eyes that made her heart beat fast and her blood sing; those fathomless green eyes that had haunted her night and day since first she'd seen them.

"What are you thinking?" Jarrett asked.

"Nothing."

"You do not play fair," he chided gently. "I lack the power to read your thoughts as you so readily read mine."

"I was admiring thee, my Lord Pirate," she admitted shyly, and felt the heat climb into her cheeks.

"Were you?"

She nodded, and he held out his arm, bidding her come to him.

She moved instantly to his side, sighing as his arm slid around her waist. She would have risked any danger, she thought, any peril, just to be near him, to feel his strength, see the caring in his eyes, hear the sound of his voice murmuring her name.

The pale Hovis moons were low in a cloudless sky when Jarrett anchored the ship in a small cove sheltered from the wind by a ridge of jagged yellow mountains that looked like dragon's teeth. For a time, he contemplated spending the night on board, but the thought of being enclosed, of being unable to take flight should the need arise, changed his mind.

Finding a large knapsack, he filled it with what provisions he could find and added candles and flint, two bowls, a flask of ale. There were blankets in a small cabin below decks, as well as a limited supply of men's clothing. He found a clean white linen shirt and a pair of tan breeches that fit him well enough.

After a moment's consideration, Leyla slipped off her long gown and donned a pair of buff-colored breeches and a red-and-black striped seaman's shirt.

"How do I look?" she asked.

"You'll do for first mate," Jarrett answered with a wicked grin. His gaze moved over her in warm appreciation. The breeches clearly outlined her shapely legs; the shirt, though at least one size too large, did little to disguise the feminine curves beneath.

"I had best be thy only mate," Leyla chided. "As thee shall be mine."

Jarrett nodded, his expression suddenly sober. "Naught but death shall part us," he vowed, and felt a sharp pain at the thought that, by marrying her, by keeping her with him, he was undoubtedly putting her life in grave danger. If they were captured by Rorke's men, she would be of no more value to them than any other woman now that she no longer possessed the ability to heal. They would use her until they wearied of her, and then dispose of her.

Leyla took his hand and pressed it over her heart. "Not even death shall part me from thee," she whispered fervently, "for I shall follow thee even there."

"No." He placed his hand over her lips. "For my sake, you must live. You must not risk your life for mine. Promise me."

She saw the anguish in his eyes, the silent pleading. Slowly, she nodded.

A deep sigh escaped his lips, and then he kissed her with all the love in his heart, his hands sliding into her hair, delighting in its softness.

Someday, he would buy her jewel-encrusted combs and a golden tiara for her hair, costly gowns and laces, though such riches would never shine as bright as the woman herself. Someday.

"Come," he said. "We must find a place to pass the night."

Tor stood in the Great Hall, his face impassive as he endured Rorke's scrutiny. In vision, he had seen Leyla imprisoned in the dungeon of Greyebridge, and he had followed the Sight to this place, determined to take her back home no matter what the cost. But, upon waking that morning, he had realized that Leyla was no longer in the castle. She had left Gweneth sometime late last night, bound for the King's Palace in Heth.

"So," Rorke asked after a time, "why have you come here, Tor of Majeulla?"

"To take my woman home."

Rorke sat forward in his chair, his elbows braced on his knees. "The silver-haired one?"

"Yes. But she is no longer here."

"How can you know that?" Rorke demanded, for news of her disappearance had not yet been made known.

"I have the Sight, my Lord."

Rorke stroked his beard thoughtfully. If he could find the silver-haired woman, he might find Jarrett as well. "Where has she gone?"

"She travels the back roads toward Heth with the man you seek."

"You are sure of this?"

Tor nodded. "Quite sure, my Lord."

Rorke nodded. A motion of his hand brought two guards swiftly forward. "Bind him."

Tor did not resist as his hands were lashed behind his back, though he could easily have killed the two men with the power of the amulet he wore around his neck.

"Thee has no need to restrain me, my Lord," Tor remarked, his expression placid. "I will guide thee to the renegade, Jarrett, in exchange for the woman's return."

"I do not need your help to capture him," Rorke replied, his voice thick with scorn.

"Does thee wish to take him alive?"

"Most assuredly."

"He will resist." Tor's gaze settled on Rorke's face. "Leyla no longer possesses the power to heal him should he be mortally wounded in the struggle."

"You have this power?"

Tor nodded. "We should leave with all due haste, my Lord."

"There's no hurry. The King has stopped at Cornith. There is no one of consequence at Heth."

"As thee wishes, but Jarrett is known to be a traitor to the Realm. His life will be in danger if he is seen."

Rorke grunted. By Hadra, the Maje was right. Anyone who came across Jarrett would try and claim the reward, and though Rorke had specified that Jarrett was to be taken alive if possible, there was always a chance the renegade might be killed if it came to a fight, and Rorke didn't want Jarrett dead, not yet.

Due to the King's absence, Rorke had been obligated to attend to the King's business at Heth and Cornith during the eight months that Jarrett had been imprisoned in the Pavilion. He had been furious when he learned that Jarrett had escaped, a feat heretofore unheard of.

Rorke fingered the scar on his cheek. He would not rest until Jarrett was returned to the Pavilion — until he, Rorke, had a chance to play the Games one last time, with Jarrett as the Pawn.

He smiled as he thought of it; his hands itched to participate in the Challenge, and he wondered which of the three major Games Jarrett feared the most — fire, water, or steel.

To have the upper hand at last. He stroked the scar on his cheek, his fingers sliding up and down the ridged flesh as he pictured it in his mind: Jarrett bound hand and foot in heavy chains, the hood in place, completely at his mercy.

There were no words to describe the satisfaction it would give him to see the Lord of Gweneth bleeding from every inch of flesh, to hear him pleading for mercy, his haughty spirit humbled at last. As Rorke had been humbled. His fingernails cut into the palms of his hands as he remembered that day on the field of battle long ago when he had begged Jarrett to take his life rather than let him be captured by the Serimites, but Jarrett had refused and they had been taken captive.

Jarrett had managed to slip his bonds and escape, but Rorke had been taken prisoner and tortured. No matter that Jarrett had returned a fortnight later and rescued Rorke and the other Fen who had been taken captive. Rorke had never forgotten the pain and the humiliation he had endured, had never forgiven himself for his cowardice, had never forgiven Jarrett for the scar on his cheek, souvenir of a Serimite sword.

A wave of self-disgust rose within him, bitter as bile, when he remembered how the Serimite guards had broken his will and humbled his spirit.

On their return to Heth, Jarrett had been hailed as a hero of the first order, invited to sit at the King's table with the royal family. Rorke had never forgotten how everyone from the Queen to the lowliest stable hand had come up to him, slapping him on the back as they welcomed him home, all of them saying what a brave man Jarrett had been, how grateful Rorke must be.

Grateful, indeed! His face had been hideously scarred. The woman he had loved had turned her back on him, repulsed by his appearance. Her adoring gaze, which had once been only for him, had turned to Jarrett, who had showered Caandis with attention and lavish gifts until another woman caught his fancy. When that happened, Rorke had humbled himself, begging Caandis to come back to him, but she had refused, her eyes wide with revulsion at the thought of sharing his life, his bed. And he had killed her for it.

His appearance hadn't mattered to Darrla. He had wooed her with infinite patience, treating her as a woman rather than the heir to the throne. He had been properly respectful, humble, not quite begging for her favors, but letting her know, in subtle ways, that he was dying of love for her. He had plied her with gifts of sweets and soft furs, a puppy to keep her company on cold lonely nights.

His persistence had paid off. She had turned her back on tradition and chosen him, a commoner, to be her husband.

Darrla was a good wife. She had borne him three beautiful daughters and two fine sons, but he had never forgiven Jarrett for those weeks in the Serimite prison, or for Caandis, and he never would.

A cruel grin twisted Rorke's lips. All the pain and ugliness of the past would be forgotten when he had Jarrett in the dark bowels of the Pavilion. . . .

"We leave within the hour," Rorke said brusquely. "Be ready."

Chapter Nineteen

Leyla woke slowly, teased from sleep by the feather-soft kisses that Jarrett was raining over her face and neck. Her eyelids fluttered open and she saw him bending over her, his beautiful dark green eyes alight, sparkling like emeralds held up to the sun.

Just a look, she thought sleepily, the merest touch of his lips, and she burned for his caresses.

Her arms twined around his neck as she drew him down, sighing with pleasure as the length of his body covered hers. He wore no shirt and his skin was warm beneath her questing fingertips. She never tired of looking at him, of touching him. Her hands drifted over the spread of his shoulders, the width of his back, marveling at the hard muscles that bunched and quivered beneath her hand.

"Good morrow, my Lord Jarrett," she murmured.

"Good morrow, wife."

Wife. The title, and all it stood for, sent a shiver of delight down her spine.

He kissed her again, his hands moving in slow appreciation over her body. She was soft and yielding, more intoxicating than mulled Freywine, warmer than the sun. Her hair was spread around her like liquid silver, glinting in the sunlight.

She gazed up at him, her eyes filled with desire, her lips curving in a seductive smile as her hands slid down his chest and belly, slipping between their bodies, inside the waistband of his breeches, to enfold him in the palm of her hand.

It was like being held by lightning. The heat of it shot through him, stunning in its intensity. With a groan, he captured her lips, plundering the soft sweetness of her mouth as she caressed him. His hands were restless now, possessive as they moved over her, stripping away her clothing, branding her as his.

He buried his face in the wealth of her hair, inhaling the beguiling fragrance that was hers, and hers alone.

"Leyla, beloved . . ." He searched for the words that would convey the depths of his feelings, but the power to think clearly seemed to fade as she moved beneath him.

"Come to me," she whispered fervently.

"Leyla." Her name was a groan on his lips.

"I know," she murmured huskily, and guided him home.

A long while later, Jarrett released a deep sigh. "We should be on our way," he remarked.

Leyla nodded. Lying on her side, with Jarrett's hard masculine body folded around hers, moving was the last thing she wished to do. She felt warm and safe in his arms.

Jarrett pressed his face to her neck, breathing in her scent. Closing his eyes, he let his mind wander, wondering if he should forget about trying to find out why he had been sent to the Pavilion, why the King had refused to hear his petition. Maybe he should just take Leyla and leave the realm. They could find a place to live in Aldane. Though the Aldanites were the sworn enemies of Fenduzia, there was an alliance between Aldane and Gweneth. He had relatives there, friends . . .

For a time, he let himself pretend that was what he would do, even though he knew he would not leave Fenduzia. He could not leave his mother in the King's Tower. He could not let Rorke take Greyebridge without a fight.

"Wife, your husband is hungry."

"Truly?" Leyla chuckled softly. "I thought I had just satisfied thy hunger, my Lord."

"Indeed," Jarrett said, nipping at her ear lobe. "Thee satisfies me in every way." With a sigh of regret, he sat up. "Someday you will have servants to do thy bidding, but for now, I fear it falls to thee."

She didn't argue. Walking to a small stream, they washed quickly, then Leyla prepared First Meal while Jarrett gathered their gear together.

A short time later, they were walking toward Heth.

Tor rode behind Rorke, his thoughts turned inward. They had left Greyebridge at dusk the night before. A large ship had carried them across the sea, and they had been riding hard ever since, stopping at dawn to let the horses rest while the men ate First Meal.

In his mind, Tor saw the place where Leyla had passed the night — the trees, the small stream. Jarrett had been there, too. He felt a sharp stab of jealousy as he thought of Leyla lying in another man's arms. They had grown up together, betrothed since childhood.

He had loved her even then, the slender girl with hair like liquid silver and eyes as blue as the sky above the Mountains of the Blue Mist. He had watched her grow from a long-legged child into a beautiful young woman, always dreaming of the day when she would be his. Often, he had been tempted to carry her off into the woods and possess her, but he loved her too dearly to offend her or cause her pain, so he had remained aloof, polite but distant, waiting for the day when she would be his.

And then she had been captured by the Fen and imprisoned in the Pavilion. For months, he had lived on the edge of despair, fearing for her life, dying inside because there was nothing he could do to help her.

And then, miraculously, she had returned to the stronghold, alive and well, more beautiful than ever. And in love with another man, an outsider.

And now she was Jarrett's wife.

The knowledge knifed through him, slicing into his heart, rotting his soul. Jealousy and hatred were emotions he had never experienced. Until now, his whole life had been one of peace and serenity, of love for his people, for all living creatures. The thought of taking a life had been as abhorrent to him as it was to every Maje. Until now.

In his mind, he conjured up an image of Jarrett, and with slow, deliberate intent, he imagined what it would be like to cut the heart from the Gweneth warrior's body.

It was an idea that should have sickened him. Instead, it brought a smile to his face.

Jarrett would die, at his hand or another's, it mattered not. Either way, Leyla would be his once again.

An hour later, they passed the place where Leyla had spent the night.

Tor straightened in the saddle, his heart pounding. She was near. He urged his horse into a lope, heard Rorke's startled cry, then the thunder of running horses as Rorke and his men followed him.

Jarrett swore under his breath as he saw the rising cloud of dust behind them, heard the muffled sound of hoofbeats. He knew, with cold certainty, that it was Rorke.

He turned to face Leyla, saw the concern rising in her eyes.

"Tor is coming," she said. "I feel his mind seeking my presence."

"Tor?"

"He is coming for me."

"By Hadra, he'll not have you!"

Leyla placed her hands on Jarrett's shoulders and gazed deep into his eyes. "He will be here soon." She closed her eyes for a moment, her mind joining with Tor's. "Rorke is with him," she said, her voice rising in alarm. "He holds Tor prisoner. Thee must go now, while there is time."

"I'm not leaving you."

"Thee must! They will not hurt me."

"Leyla . . ."

"Does thee wish to be imprisoned in the King's Tower? Or worse, to be returned to the Pavilion?"

The Pavilion. The mere thought chilled Jarrett to the depths of his soul. He could face death, he could face torture at Rorke's capable hands, but he could not endure the weight of chains again, nor could he bear to think of the constant darkness, deeper than the blackest of nights, that lived within the hood, waiting to drag him down into the depths of despair.

"Go," Leyla urged. "I am not afraid, except for thee."

"I'll come for you as soon as I can," Jarrett vowed. He drew her close and kissed her, long and hard. "Leyla . . ."

"Go!"

He held her close a moment more, his face buried in her hair, and then he melted into the dappled shadows of the forest that bordered the province of Heth.

Moments later, Tor rode up, closely followed by Rorke and a regiment of the king's men.

"Leyla!" Vaulting from the saddle, Tor ran toward her. "Thee is well?"

She nodded curtly.

"Where is the rebel?" Rorke demanded.

Leyla met Rorke's harsh gaze. "Milord?"

"Jarrett. Where is he?"

"Not here," she replied, blinking back a sudden flood of tears. "Not here."

Rorke's gaze swept the area. "Captain Taark, take your men and search the woods." Dismounting, he tethered his horse to a low-hanging branch. "You've done well, Tor of Majeulla. I shall see that you are suitably rewarded."

"I seek no reward, Milord. I will take my woman and return home."

Rorke studied the Maje's face for a long

moment, his expression thoughtful. "I think not."

"I have done as I promised," Tor said, his voice sharp. "I expect thee to do the same."

"I gave no word to keep," Rorke retorted. His gaze moved over Leyla, lingering on the swell of her breasts and the soft, sweet curve of her hips that even the baggy seaman's shirt and breeches could not hide. And her hair. He had never in his life seen hair like that. "You will both accompany me to Heth. Perhaps, when I have settled with Jarrett, I will let you go."

"Milord . . ." Tor forced the word through clenched teeth.

"Mind your tongue, Maje, else you lose it."

Leyla placed her hand on Tor's arm in silent entreaty. There was nothing to be gained by making Rorke angry, and everything to lose.

She whirled around at the sound of footsteps, gasped when she saw two of the King's men emerge from the forest dragging Jarrett's limp form between them.

"Is he dead?" Rorke asked sharply. "I said I wanted him alive!"

"Not dead, Milord," Taark replied. "Only unconscious." The captain of the guard rubbed his bruised knuckles, a look of satisfaction on his face. "He put up quite a struggle when we brought him down."

"He's bleeding." The words were torn from

Leyla's lips. Only Tor's hand on her arm kept her from running to her husband. Blood dripped from his nose; his breeches were dark with it.

"He is not bad hurt," the captain assured Rorke as they lowered Jarrett to the ground. "Only an arrow wound in his thigh."

Leyla sent a pleading glance at Tor. "Heal him."

Ignoring the urge to do just that, Tor shook his head. "No, I will not."

"Thee must!"

"Do as the girl says," Rorke ordered brusquely. "I want this man alive."

With a curt nod, Tor knelt beside Jarrett. He hesitated for a moment, his eyes filled with loathing, and then, with a sigh of resignation, he placed his hands over the long bloody gash in the back of Jarrett's right thigh.

A thoughtful frown furrowed Rorke's brow as he watched Tor. He had heard of the remarkable healing powers of the Maje, of course, but he had always been skeptical of their purported abilities, certain their healing was based on tricks and chicanery rather than truth. He doubted no longer.

He could almost feel the mystical power flowing from the hands of the Maje. He watched Tor's face, saw his lips compress and his eyes darken as he absorbed Jarrett's hurt into himself.

When the Maje lifted his hands from the wound, the skin beneath was whole as before. There was no sign of injury, no bruise, no scar.

"Bind the rebel," Rorke ordered tersely. "And the Maje, too."

Furious at Rorke's treatment, Tor reached for the amulet that dangled from a fine gold chain around his neck, but the charm was jerked out of his hand before its power could be invoked.

Helpless now, he could only submit to Rorke's men, who bound his hands tightly behind his back, then knelt beside Jarrett, binding him in a similar manner.

The soldier handed the amulet to Rorke, who held it up to the light, studying the harmless-looking hunk of crystal. "Tell me, Maje, what is this fetish and how does it work?"

"It has no power except in my hands," Tor replied.

"What magic does it possess?"

"The power to take life."

"Such a thing is possible?" Rorke frowned. "The Maje are sworn to save life. How came you by such a charm?"

"I bought it from the witch at Hannadragorra." He felt Leyla's censure. Their people were forbidden to possess such amulets, but he had bought it when he left Majeulla. Certain he could not defeat Jarrett in a fight, he had bought the charm, intending to use it against Jarrett should the need arise, even though to use it would put his soul in darkest jeopardy.

"How does it work?" Rorke demanded. "What words are said?"

"There are no words, Milord, only the strength of my thoughts."

"I see." With a thoughtful frown, Rorke slipped the charm around his neck. "Get the rebel on his feet and let's go."

The journey to Heth was one Leyla would never forget. Rorke dropped a rope around Jarrett's neck, taking great delight in jerking on the rope, or putting his horse into a trot, forcing Jarrett to run or be dragged. Tor walked beside Leyla's horse, his hands securely bound behind his back.

The days passed slowly, long hours under a relentless sun, with only her thoughts to help pass the time. On those occasions when she dared to probe Jarrett's mind, she caught images of rage and black despair as he contemplated a return to the Pavilion. Tor's thoughts were equally dark and ominous. It shocked her to sense anger and hatred in his mind, for such emotions were alien to their kind.

Nights, she sat beside the fire, her gaze on Jarrett. She yearned to go to him, to remove the rope that bound his hands behind his back, to rest her head on his shoulder and have him tell her everything would be all right even though it was a lie.

She was ever aware of Tor's presence. He watched her constantly, his eyes filled with silent accusation, his expression ominous. She had never thought of Tor as a violent man. Always, he had been a man of infinite peace and patience. But his inner serenity had been shattered, and it was all her fault. It was a heavy burden to bear, but not so heavy as her grief at what awaited Jarrett when they reached the King's Palace at Heth.

As their journey neared its end, Rorke began to mock Jarrett, grinning with malicious pleasure as he taunted him about what awaited him at the Pavilion, going on and on about what a pleasure it would be to lock the heavy shackles in place, to drop the hood over his head, to see him chained to the wall, bound and helpless.

"I shall leave you there a day or two," Rorke decided, "so that you shall have sufficient time to wonder what Games we shall play." His hand caressed the hilt of his sword. "I prefer steel, myself, but I shall have the Maje probe your mind to see which Game you dread the most."

Rorke took hold of the rope around Jarrett's neck and yanked on it, forcing Jarrett to his side. His gaze bored into Jarrett's. "And when I am done with you, my

Lord Jarrett, I shall get to know the silver-haired child better."

"No!" Jarrett glared at Rorke. "By Hadra, I swear I'll kill you if you lay a hand on her."

A slow smile spread over Rorke's face. "Such concern for a distant cousin," he mused. "I begin to think you have strong feelings for the girl."

A muscle worked in Jarrett's jaw as he realized he had just given Rorke a powerful weapon to use against him.

Chapter Twenty

They reached the palace two days later. Jarrett was taken immediately to the Pavilion. Tor was imprisoned in one of the cells in the King's Tower.

Rorke escorted Leyla to a well-appointed chamber on the third floor.

"I think you will be comfortable here, child," Rorke said. "I shall send one of the maids to attend you. If you need anything, you have only to ask."

"I need nothing from thee, Milord, save my freedom."

"All in good time. For now, it pleases me to have your company."

"What are thy plans for Tor and Lord Jarrett?"

"Their fate concerns you?"

"Yes. Tor is my countryman."

"And Jarrett?"

"He is . . . he is my cousin."

"Your cousin?" Rorke looked skeptical. "I think not."

"Please let us go."

"Perhaps, in time. My family has gone to Cornith to be with the King. Emissaries from

Tyrell have gone to Aldane to discuss the possibility of peace."

Rorke made a vague gesture with his hand. "I do not care for Cornith this time of year, so I have decided to stay here and amuse myself at the Pavilion." He grinned at her, a cold, cruel grin. "I think my Lord Jarrett will provide a pleasant diversion, don't you?"

"Please, Milord, do not leave him in the Pavilion. I will do anything thee asks of me if thee will only spare him."

"Anything?"

She hesitated, knowing what that one word implied. "Yes, Milord," she replied at length. "Anything."

Rorke's eyes narrowed. "What is he to you?"

"My cousin, as I . . ."

A low-pitched growl erupted from Rorke's throat. "Do not lie to me or I shall bring him here and have him drawn and quartered before the sun sets!"

"No, please!"

Leyla dropped to her knees, her hands folded in supplication. Drawn and quartered! It was a terrible fate in which the victim was cut open and his heart ripped out while he still lived.

"He is my husband."

"He loves you?"

Leyla swallowed hard, frightened by the feral gleam in Rorke's eyes. "Yes."

Rorke gazed sightlessly out of the window. "As I once loved Caandis," he murmured under his breath. "Who says the fates aren't kind?"

He stared down at Leyla's bowed head. So many choices. He could defile the woman in front of Jarrett, or he could make her watch while he slowly tortured her husband to death.

Or perhaps he would do both.

It had taken the combined strength of two Giants to strip away Jarrett's clothes and shackle him to the wall, and two more to hold him while the hood was fitted in place.

He let out a roar that could be heard throughout the Pavilion as the door to his cell was slammed shut and he was left alone in the darkness once again. Heart pounding with dread, he struggled against his bonds, the thick metal cutting into his skin until his wrists were slick with blood.

All for nothing. All for nothing. The words echoed and re-echoed inside his mind. He had known a few weeks of freedom, and now he was back in the Pavilion to meet the death that should have been his. But, worse than that, he had put Leyla's life in danger as well. Leyla! He closed his eyes, concentrating on her face with all the power he possessed, willing her to hear him. *Forgive me,* he cried. *Beloved, please forgive me.*

His breath caught in his throat when he heard the door to his cell open. Fear, raw and primal, rose up within him.

"Ah, my Lord Jarrett." Rorke's voice dripped with satisfaction. "How well you look."

Jarrett felt his body tense as he waited for Rorke to strike. The sword? A flame? Please, not the water!

He flinched as he felt a hand on his shoulder.

"Well, Tor of Majeulla?" Rorke's voice sounded from the far side of the room. "What is it that he fears the most?"

"Tor, don't!" Jarrett forced the words through clenched teeth.

"Afraid, my Lord Jarrett?" Rorke jeered. "And we've not yet begun."

Jarrett let out a long, shuddering breath. By Hadra, he was afraid, afraid that Tor would reveal what frightened him most. Afraid that the Maje's hatred and his desire for vengeance were stronger than his feelings for Leyla.

"Tor, for the love of heaven . . ."

"You will tell me what my Lord Jarrett fears most, Tor," Rorke warned, "or the woman will suffer the consequences."

Forcing Leyla from his mind, Jarrett closed his eyes and concentrated on knives — the Fen's deadly longboar knives, the broadswords of the Aldanites, curved Serimite blades. Sharp knives, dull knives, all cutting into his flesh.

He felt Tor's hand tighten on his shoulder, felt the incredible power of the Maje's mind as it probed his own, slipping easily through his defenses to find his weakness.

Leyla. Fear for Leyla. That was what frightened Jarrett the most. Fear that she would be made to suffer because it would cause him more pain than anything else. And beyond that, dwindling in comparison, was a horrible fear of water.

Strange, Tor thought, it was not the pain of knives or flame that Jarrett feared, it was the smothering darkness of the pool.

"Well?" Rorke's voice was sharp and impatient. "What is it the rebel fears beyond all else?"

"The water, Milord. He has a deep and abiding fear of the pool."

Jarrett swore under his breath, hating the Maje for revealing the Game he most dreaded, and yet feeling a surge of gratitude that Tor had not mentioned the thing he feared above all else. Fear for Leyla's life.

"The water?" Rorke frowned. "Are you certain of this?"

"Yes, Milord. He fears the dark, the quiet, the sense of utter helplessness. It is the thing that haunts his dreams, the one thing that threatens to drive him beyond reason."

"I see." Rorke stared at the hooded man.

"Tell me, my Lord Jarrett, what happened to Siid and Gar and Thal? I was told they went to search for you and never returned."

Jarrett shrugged. "Perhaps they returned home."

"Perhaps. Maje, I would know the fate of my friends."

Tor concentrated for a moment, and then let out a sigh. "They are dead."

"He killed them?"

"Yes."

"I thought as much. You've done well, Maje. I shall see you are suitably rewarded."

"In the King's Tower?" Tor asked, his voice thick with sarcasm.

"I shall see that you are moved to one of the castle apartments and properly attired."

"I wish for nothing, Milord, save that thee should honor our agreement and let me take my woman home."

"*Your* woman! She is *his* wife."

"He will soon be dead, will he not?" Tor replied calmly. "And then she will be mine, as she was meant to be mine from the beginning."

"I shall make a deal with you, Tor of Majeulla. I shall dispose of the rebel at my leisure, and when I have pleasured myself with the woman, you may take her home."

Tor stared at Rorke, unable to believe what he had heard. "Milord, has thee no honor?"

"None. If you do not find my offer satisfactory, be assured I can devise one even less to your liking."

Tor glanced at Jarrett. The Gweneth warrior stood against the wall, his arms and legs stretched to painful limits, every muscle in his body taut and quivering with rage. The hatred emanating from him was a tangible presence in the cell, a living, breathing entity with a life of its own. He tried to probe Jarrett's mind, but the force of the warrior's hatred drove out all other thought, all reason.

"As thee wishes, Milord," Tor replied at last.

"Rorke, no!"

"You bellow like a bull about to go under the knife," Rorke remarked, and then he laughed softly. "I think I shall hold that possibility in reserve," he mused aloud. "I'm only surprised I did not think of it sooner. Perhaps I shall bring the woman here to watch. Perhaps I will insist that she wield the blade."

Drawing upon every bit of concentration he possessed, Tor sent his thoughts to Jarrett, willing the other man to receive his thoughts, to control his anger.

Whatever he does to her, I have the power to heal. Whatever loathsome thing he may ask of her, I have the power to make her forget.

Jarrett nodded imperceptibly. *I understand. I beg of thee, let no harm come to her.*

Be assured I will give my life for hers if neces-sary.

Jarrett drew a deep breath and expelled it in a long, shuddering sigh. He had no choice but to believe the Maje would do as he said.

"Do what you will with me, Rorke," Jarrett said, his voice low. "It matters not. I would ask one thing only."

"Ask it then."

"Swear that you will not use it against me."

"I make no promises where the woman is concerned."

"This is not about . . . about Leyla. Swear to me, Rorke, upon your mother's honor."

"I swear."

"On your mother's honor."

"On my mother's honor."

"It is my wish that on the morrow you re-lease my mother from the Tower and send her to my uncle, Morrad, in Aldane."

"It shall be done."

Jarrett nodded. There was nothing more he could do. He had ensured his mother's free-dom; he would have to depend on Tor to get Leyla safely home.

Moments later, Rorke and Tor left the cell.

Alone, Jarrett surrendered to the all-consuming darkness within the hood. Closing his eyes, he thought of Greyebridge, of warm summer days upon the moors, of cool au-tumn nights before a blazing fire. He thought of his mother, singing softly as she sat at the loom, of Tannya's wrinkled smile, of riding his horse across fields of flowering grass.

And lastly, he thought of Leyla, the touch of her hand upon his flesh, the sound of her voice whispering that she loved him.

And in the quiet of his chamber, he prayed that the All Father would see her safely home where she belonged.

Leyla blinked in surprise when Rorke led her into the dining hall that evening. Seated at the long table were a score of people, Tor and Sherriza among them.

Rorke indicated that she should take the seat to his right, which placed her next to Sherriza and across from Tor.

Sherriza took Leyla's hand in hers. "Are you well, child?"

"Yes, my Lady. And you?"

Sherriza squeezed Leyla's hand reassuringly. "I am well."

She didn't appear well, Leyla thought. She was pale beneath the dusting of powder on her cheeks, thinner than before.

Leyla glanced at Tor, her mind seeking to link with his. *What is the meaning of this? What is happening?*

She is being sent to Aldane on the morrow.

What of Jarrett? When he refused to answer, she tried to draw the answer from his mind, but he had shut her out.

A moment later, a half-dozen servants entered the room bearing trays laden with food: whole roast chickens, baked hams, mutton and veal. There were platters of cheese and breads, four kinds of vegetables.

Rorke ate heartily, unaffected by the tension at the table as he conversed with his men. Everything he had ever wanted was within his grasp. Jarrett would soon be only a memory. Sherriza would be banished to Aldane. The Maje would remain his prisoner. Tor of Majeulla was a man of rare gifts, gifts Rorke intended to explore fully.

As for the silver-haired woman, he would sample her delights and then, regretfully, he would send her back to her own people. It would not do to anger Darrla. She was still the King's sister, and though she was usually the most compliant of women, she refused to permit him the luxury of a mistress. It would not be wise to anger her unduly. Tyrell had no heirs. When he died, Darrla would inherit the throne, and after Darrla, her sons. A smile twisted Rorke's thin lips. His sons. Jerrian and Norrman.

It was during the last course that Leyla found the courage to speak to Rorke.

"My Lord, what has happened to my husband?"

"He awaits my pleasure in the dungeons of the Pavilion."

"I should like to see him."

Rorke's smile was cruel. "And so you shall, my dear. So you shall."

A cold chill slithered down Sherriza's spine as she recognized the implied threat in Rorke's words.

"Rorke, I warn you, the King will not condone my son's death."

"I have said nothing of his death, madam."

Sherriza shook her head. "I do not know how you convinced Tyrell to have Jarrett stripped of his lands and titles, but I am certain the king was not told the full story of what happened in the chapel at Gweneth. Tyrell is an honest and fair man. He would never have denounced Jarrett for refusing to kill helpless women and children."

Rorke snorted. "They were not helpless women and children. They were Aldanite spies in league with your son."

"You cannot prove that!"

"I obtained a confession from one of the women before she died, madam. She named Lord Jarrett of Greyebridge Castle a traitor. The punishment for treason is death. He is lucky he still has his head."

"What bribe did you offer the woman, that she would bespeak such a horrible lie?"

Guilt flickered in the back of Rorke's devil-black eyes and Sherriza knew she had guessed right.

Rorke grunted softly. Sherriza was more perceptive than he had supposed. He had, indeed, offered the Aldanite woman a bribe. He had promised to spare the lives of her children in return for her mark upon a written confession. She had died reminding him of that promise.

"I thought so," Sherriza said. "Anyone who knows Jarrett knows he would never betray his king or his country."

"So you say, but I will have his confession, written in his own hand, before the new moon, and that will put an end to all doubt of his guilt."

"Do to him what you will, my son will never confess to such an outrageous lie!"

"I think he will," Rorke replied confidently. "And when I have it, I will see that you receive a copy."

"Tyrell will hear of this," Sherriza warned. "He will not look kindly upon you for sending Jarrett to the Pavilion. Nor do I think you will escape unscathed when he learns that you have reinstated the Games."

A dark flush of anger washed into Rorke's cheeks. Everything she said was true. For a moment, he thought of having Taark dispose of the troublesome woman, but then he remembered his vow to Jarrett, sworn on his own mother's honor. He comforted himself with the knowledge that, in the long run, Sherriza was no threat. Jarrett would be long dead before she reached Aldane. And Tyrell, too.

Rising, he clapped his hands, once, sharply. Immediately, four of the King's men came forward.

"A ship awaits my Lady Sherriza," Rorke said, speaking to the captain of the guard who stood to the right of his chair. "These men will accompany her to Aldane."

"Yes, Milord," the captain replied.

"See to it."

"Rorke, I beg you, let me see my son before I go."

He glanced at Leyla. Wanting her to think well of him, he decided to be generous. "As you wish. Captain Taark, escort the Lady Sherriza to the Pavilion."

Sherriza stood up. Turning to Leyla, she embraced her. "My thoughts and prayers will be with you," she murmured. "Have you any word for Jarrett?"

"Only give him my love and tell him I wait for the day when we can be together again."

With a nod, Sherriza turned away and followed Taark out of the dining hall, followed by the four King's men who had been instructed to see her to Aldane.

The harsh rasp of a key turning in the lock roused Jarrett from a restless sleep. Still shackled to the wall, he turned toward the door, all his senses suddenly alert.

He tensed as a hand settled on his shoulder. Expecting Rorke, he was taken aback to hear his mother's voice.

"Jeri, it's me." Sherriza stared at the hideous black hood that covered her son's head and neck like a shroud.

Her heart twisted with pain and despair as she noted the taut muscles in his shoulders, arms, and legs, a tenseness that revealed not only his discomfort, but also his rage. And his fear.

"Are you well?" she asked.

"Well enough."

She shook her head as she glanced around the barren cell. The walls and floor were made of stone. An iron-bound table fitted with leather straps stood to one side. There were no windows, no other source of light save for the candle she held in her hand. A covered chamber pot stood in one corner, its malodorous smell permeating the air.

Placing the candle in a holder near the door, Sherriza removed the hood from Jarrett's head and tossed it aside. "Beastly thing," she muttered.

"You should not have come here." Jarrett looked away, unable to bear the pity in his mother's eyes. "This is not how I wish to be remembered."

"What do you mean?"

"Rorke wants me out of the way. Permanently out of the way."

"For all his threats, he would not dare! Not without the King's knowledge and approval."

Jarrett met his mother's horrified stare with a level gaze. "You know he would," he replied quietly. "Have you seen Leyla?"

"She sends her love, Jeri. She would have come if she could."

"He means to have her." He ground the words through clenched teeth. The thought of Rorke holding Leyla, touching her, possessing her, was like a blade twisting ever deeper in his gut.

"I feared as much, but there is nothing I can do. Nothing you can do but hope he tires of her quickly and sends her home."

Cursing under his breath, Jarrett tugged against the heavy chains that shackled him to the wall, heedless of the pain as the thick iron cuffs cut into his flesh. "I've got to get out of here!"

"Jeri, stop," Sherriza begged. She placed her hands on his wrists, hoping to stop his frenzied struggles, sickened by the warm stickiness of his blood beneath her fingertips. "Please, stop."

With a sigh of resignation, he slumped against the wall.

"Listen to me," Sherriza urged. "Rorke is sending me to Aldane. I'll talk to Morrad. He'll heed what I say. Somehow, we'll get word to Tyrell. I'm certain he doesn't know the whole story."

Jarrett's gaze rested on his mother's face. "There won't be time."

Sherriza shook her head, fearing he was right, yet not wanting to believe that the man who had once been her son's best friend was capable of such treachery.

"Jeri, don't give up hope. I'll . . ." She bit back her words as the captain of the guard entered the cell.

"It is time to go, my Lady," Taark said.

"Jeri, don't despair," Sherriza begged as Taark led her out of the cell and gave her into the keeping of his men.

She glanced over her shoulder, her heart aching at the thought of leaving her son in such a dismal place. And yet, more terrible than the thought of leaving him was the thought that she might never see him again. And then they were leading her away.

Turning back into the room, Taark picked up the hood, running his fingers over the heavy black fabric for a few moments.

Like most men who visited the Pavilion, he had tried the hood on, and immediately taken it off. There was something malevolent about that bit of black cloth, something that called up a man's most primal fears.

He stared at Jarrett, saw the look of dread in the rebel's eyes as he stepped closer and then, with a shrug, he dropped the heavy black hood over the prisoner's head and snugged it down tight.

Jarrett's muscles tensed as the hood settled into place. He took a deep breath, willing himself to relax as the material molded itself to his face. Stifling, sinister, it blocked every trace of light, filling his mind with images of the darkest corner of Hadra.

He bit back the urge to beg Taark to dispense with the hood for one night only, knowing the captain of the guard would take it as a sign of weakness. No doubt Taark would be amused by such a request. But how could anyone know the horror of the hood unless they'd worn it?

Taark stared at the hooded man for a moment longer, feeling a grudging sympathy for the Gweneth rebel, and then he blew out the candle and left the cell, closing the door behind him.

Whistling softly, he made his way down the narrow corridor, suddenly anxious to feel the sunlight on his face.

Chapter Twenty-one

Jarrett's head came up as the cell door swung open. He heard the muffled sound of footsteps as someone entered the room, felt the faint smoky heat of a torch as it was placed in the holder to the left of the doorway.

And then he heard Rorke's voice, low and mocking. "So, my Lord Jarrett, I hope you find your lodgings to your liking."

Jarrett stiffened as he felt the hard edge of fine Fenduzian steel against his chest.

"Are you asleep under there?" Rorke asked, tugging on the edge of the hood. "Perhaps this will wake you."

Jarrett sucked in a deep breath as Rorke dragged the tip of the sword across his chest. He shuddered as the cold steel pierced his flesh like frozen fire, bit down on the inside of his cheek as the warm sticky wetness of his blood trailed in the wake of the blade.

"Still nothing to say?" Rorke asked, resting the point of the blade in the hollow of Jarrett's throat.

"What do you wish to hear, Rorke?"

"Ah, so you can speak." Rorke lifted the blade, then drew the point down the length of Jarrett's chest to rest against his groin. "Yes, I believe I will have you gelded," Rorke mused. "It will prove a pleasant diversion on a dreary evening."

Jarrett silently cursed the hood that kept him from seeing his enemy's face. "What do you want of me?"

"A direct question," Rorke remarked, sheathing his sword. "I'll give you a direct answer. I want Greyebridge. I've wanted it ever since I was old enough to know it was to be yours."

"Why? You have lands and holdings of your own."

Rorke made a sound of derision as he jerked the mask from Jarrett's head. "It all belongs to Darrla. I want a plot of ground that is mine, only mine."

"There are other castles you can have."

"I want Greyebridge, and I mean to have it." Rorke fingered the hideous scar on his cheek. "I've never forgiven you for this. Or for Caandis. Or for those hellish days I spent in a Serimite dungeon. I want Greyebridge." Rorke paused, and then nodded. "And I want the crown."

"The crown!" Jarrett exclaimed softly. "You are even more ambitious than I supposed."

Rorke nodded. "I want it all," he admitted. "Only two things stand between me and the throne. Tyrell. And Darrla."

Jarrett took a deep breath, fighting to keep

his growing anxiety under control. "Tyrell won't live much longer. When he dies, you'll rule with Darrla."

"I don't want to share the throne. With Darrla out of the way, Jerrian is next in line. But he's just a boy, and the crown will be mine." Rorke frowned thoughtfully. "The King is old. A bit of poison in his ale, and none will be the wiser."

"What of Darrla?"

"What of her? Women are easily disposed of, even sisters to the King."

The man was mad, Jarrett thought, he must be mad, to plot not only the death of his wife, but the King's as well.

Jarrett took a deep breath. He had no fear of death for himself; only fear for what would become of those he loved.

"What of my mother?" he asked.

"She sails for Aldane."

"And Leyla?"

Clasping his hands behind his back, Rorke walked the length of the narrow chamber and back again. It was a dismal little cell, cold and dark, heavy with the smell of sweat and blood and excrement.

Jarrett felt his heart pound with fear. "What of Leyla?" he repeated.

"She is my guest. I find her to be a woman of rare beauty. She would make a fine queen, don't you think?" He nodded, pleased with the idea. "She is so lovely, so young. So easily molded. And since she is not one of us, she would never be a threat to me, or to the throne."

"Don't touch her, Rorke, I warn you!"

Rorke's laughter filled the small cell. "You warn me!" He drew his blade and slapped the flat of it across Jarrett's chest. "You insolent knave, there's nothing you can do to stop me."

Rorke smiled, pleased with his cunning. "Yes," he mused aloud. "I shall have it all. And when I am King, I shall move the throne from Heth to Greyebridge, and I will rule from there, with Leyla at my side."

A harsh cry of rage was torn from Jarrett's throat as he strained against the shackles that bound his arms and legs to the cold stone wall.

And with that rage came a deep and abiding fear that Rorke would do as he threatened. The man was capable of murder. He had killed Caandis, he had killed the Aldanite women and children in Greyebridge chapel, thereby stilling their tongues forever. He would not hesitate to kill his wife if he thought it would further his ambition. And Tyrell was old, so old. No one would suspect foul play if he should be found dead in his chambers.

"Rorke, don't do it. I beg of you, let Leyla return to her own people."

"Aye." Rorke smiled. "Beg me, my Lord

Jarrett," he said with a sadistic smile. "I should like that."

"I'll do whatever you ask, just let her go in peace. She's a gentle woman, Rorke, she'll never be happy at court."

Rorke yawned. "You'll have to do better than that."

"Unchain me, and I'll go down on my knees, if that's what it takes. Only promise me you'll let her go."

"I make no promises now. I shall wait until I have taken her to my bed. If she pleases me, I shall keep her. If not, I might let her go. Then again, I might not." Rorke smiled smugly, his eyes cold and cruel. "Whatever happens to her, you will not be here to see it."

"Rorke! By Hadra, you'll never be free of me if you hurt her."

"You have gall enough for ten men, my Lord Jarrett," Rorke mused as he dropped the hood in place once more. "But I fear it will avail you nothing. Think of her in my chambers while you await the waters of the pool. Perhaps I shall let you see her one last time." Rorke shrugged. "Perhaps not. Rest well, my Lord."

Knowing it was useless, Jarrett pulled against his bonds. The heavy chains bit deep into the flesh of his wrists and ankles, but his fury was stronger than the pain.

He bellowed with rage, his mind filling

with images of Leyla struggling in Rorke's embrace. Rorke! What manner of man was he, to speak so easily of murdering the mother of his children, of murdering his King?

Fury seared Jarrett's soul. Rorke wanted Greyebridge. He wanted the throne. He wanted Leyla, and, by Hadra, he would have them all, and there was nothing Jarrett could do about it.

A low cry of anguish rose in Jarrett's throat as he slumped against the cold stone wall, the ache in his heart as black as the darkness that lived within the hood.

Chapter Twenty-two

When Leyla woke in the morning, she was surprised to find a maid testing the water in a small bathtub.

"Milady." The maid curtsied, then gestured at the clothing she had laid out at the foot of the bed. "Lord Rorke bids you join him at First Meal."

It was in Leyla's mind to refuse; she had no desire to dine with Rorke again, but it occurred to her that, should she annoy Rorke, he might take it out on Jarrett.

Rising, she bathed quickly, allowing the maid to help her dress in a gown of velvetsoft burgundy. The sleeves were slashed, and the underskirt was a froth of silver ruffles.

Tor and Rorke were waiting for her in the dining hall.

Both men turned her way when she entered the room. Tor's expression was grim; Rorke's smug.

She sat down where Rorke indicated, her back stiff. There was no conversation at the table this morning. Leyla ate what was placed before her, not tasting anything. She glanced at Tor from time to time, but he refused to meet her probing gaze, or to let her probe his thoughts.

When Leyla finished eating, she pushed her plate aside, folded her hands in her lap, and fixed her gaze on Rorke, waiting for him to acknowledge her.

Rorke let out a heavy sigh of exasperation. Shoving his plate aside, he met Leyla's stare. "He is fine, for now," he said, his voice gruff as he answered her unspoken question.

The look of relief in Leyla's eyes filled him with unreasoning anger.

Shoving back his chair, he stood away from the table. "I have business to attend to. I shall expect you both at Last Meal. Make no attempt to leave the castle," he warned, and without waiting for a reply, he left the hall.

"Tor, what are we to do?"

"Leave, of course. We cannot stay here." The Maje glanced at the doorway. "I will not play Rorke's games."

Leyla leaned across the table. "Does thee have a plan?" she asked hopefully.

"Not yet."

"I want to see Jarrett."

"No, it is not possible."

"If thee won't take me, I'll go alone."

"Leyla, it is not wise."

She sat back in her chair, her shoulders squared, her chin raised defiantly. "I do not care. I must see him. Thee cannot stop me."

"He won't like it," Tor warned, and she knew he wasn't speaking of Rorke.

"I have to see him. I have to know he's all right."

Tor stared into the distance, his expression blank, as he concentrated on Jarrett. In moments, images formed in his mind.

Jarrett. Chained to the wall. The black hood over his head. A bloody gash made a path of bright crimson across his chest. His thoughts were filled with darkness and despair. And fear, not for his own well-being, but for Leyla.

"He is well," Tor said, his voice empty of emotion. "In a dark room. Alone."

"I must go to him."

"No." Tor's hand closed over her arm. "Thee will do him no kindness. Rorke is sure to find out, and it will only anger him the more. We must bide our time."

"Tor, I will not leave here without Jarrett."

"I thought as much." He loosened his hold on her arm, letting his fingertips caress the back of her hand, then slide over her wrist. Her skin was smooth and warm. "Promise me thee will not try to see him."

"No."

"Leyla, should thee displease Rorke, he is sure to lock thee in thy room. We will have no chance to escape if we're denied the freedom of the castle. Thee must be patient."

He was right, of course. "Very well," she agreed. "I will not try to see him."

"Good. I am going outside to have a look around. Go to thy room and rest. We must make Rorke think we have resigned ourselves to our situation."

Leyla nodded. Perhaps Tor was right.

Tor watched her out of sight, then left the keep. There were few people outside save for the King's men. Most of them were engaged in a game of some kind; the rest stood watch at the various castle gates.

Tor strolled about the yard, seemingly interested in nothing more than a leisurely walk. As if he had every right to do so, he went to the stable and saddled a horse, then rode out of the castle toward the Pavilion.

Once out of sight, he urged the horse into a gallop. A short time later, he entered the walled city.

The Pavilion was a large oval building made of dark stone and wood. Flags fluttered over the outdoor arena adjacent to the Pavilion.

No one stopped him as he approached the arena, where several men were showing off their equestrian skills.

Acting as though he were a regular visitor, Tor entered the gate, then stood at the rail, watching the riders. To a man, they rode as though they had been born on horseback, executing difficult maneuvers with ease. And the horses . . . Tor had never seen such beautiful animals. They moved with the grace of dancers, their hooves seeming to glide over the soft sand, their necks arched, their manes and tails snapping like banners in the wind.

No one paid him any attention as he left the arena and walked toward the immense double doors that led to the Pavilion. He paused, his hand on the heavy latch, staring at the life-size figures carved in the wood. He hadn't had time to examine them closely when he'd come here with Rorke, but now he studied the carvings carefully.

Two men, naked to the waist and armed with curved swords, were etched in vivid detail. Clearly outlined were the taut muscles, the numerous cuts, the glaring intensity as they focused on each other. It was obvious that this was a representation of how the Games had once been, a fight between two evenly matched warriors, a battle meant to prove a man's skill and test his courage. But the Games had changed until they had become nothing more than a mockery, no longer Games of Skill but Games of torture and butchery.

With his finger, Tor outlined the muscular arm of the carved figure on the left. He could almost feel the blood that oozed from the gash in the man's shoulder, smell the dust in the air, hear the cheers of the crowd. In Majeulla, a carving depicting such a barbaric display of swordsmanship would have been an abomination.

With a shake of his head, he opened one

of the doors and stepped inside.

Crossing the main floor, he made his way to the narrow iron steps that led to the dungeons, nodding affably at a Giant he passed on the way down. They were peculiar creatures, near eight feet tall, with hunched shoulders and hands that could span a sapling. Their skin was dark, their eyes yellow beneath shaggy black brows.

Tor expected at any moment to have his presence challenged, but there were few people about. No one questioned his right to be there, and he decided it was because of his attire. He no longer wore the soft flowing robes of the Majeullian people, but the tight-fitting, somber-hued clothing of the Fen. Obviously, they had mistaken him for one of Rorke's cronies.

At the top of the last stairway, he took a torch from one of the wall sconces. As had happened before, a torrent of sensations flooded his mind as he reached the last level: the smell of blood and sweat and fear, pitiful cries for help that never came, bitter feelings of despair and anguish, the harsh crack of the lash. And over all, pain, waves and waves of pain. Men had died here. Hundreds and hundreds of men.

But now only one remained.

He paused when he reached a narrow wooden door located at the far end of the cell block.

He looked up and down the corridor; then, taking a deep breath, he put his hand on the latch and opened the door.

The cell was as he remembered it; dark as Dragora's cave, it smelled almost as bad. For a moment, Tor stood in the arched doorway, absorbing the atmosphere. The torch in his hand made grotesque shadows on the gray stone walls.

Stepping into the room, he placed the torch in the holder located to the left of the doorway before he closed the door.

Jarrett was chained to the wall, his head and shoulders covered by the thick black hood. He saw the Gweneth warrior's body tense when he entered the room. Hatred emanated from the man, strong, implacable hatred. And mingled with that hatred was a rage so malignant, so violent, that Tor took an instinctive step backward.

He studied Jarrett carefully, noting the way the warrior stood there, his very stance filled with defiance. His hands were curled into tight fists; there was dried blood on his wrists and ankles. Several welts criss-crossed his torso; a thin ribbon of dried blood marked his chest like a crimson sash.

Tor closed his eyes. He concentrated on Jarrett, felt the warrior's heart pounding with the force of his hatred. He caught snatches of thought — concern for Leyla, for his mother, a potent thirst. He sensed a mild feeling of discomfort caused by the wound in Jarrett's shoulder, and over all, a layer of tightly controlled fear as Jarrett waited in the darkness, wondering who it was that stood before him.

Jarrett felt the sweat bead on his brow and trickle down his back as the silence in the room stretched on and on. All his nerves were strung out, taut as a bowstring, as he waited for the unseen person in his cell to say something, do something. Was it Rorke standing there, lash in hand, or just one of the Giants, come to taunt him because there was nothing else to do at the moment?

By Hadra, why didn't the man say something?

"Jarrett, it's Tor."

Jarrett frowned. Tor? What was he doing here?

"I'm alone," Tor said. "Thee has no need to fear."

"Where's Leyla?" Jarrett asked, his voice hoarse. "Is she well?"

Tor stared at Jarrett for a long moment before answering, fascinated by the hood. The Fen wizard who had created it must have been a master of cruelty, he mused, for there was little that men feared more than the endless darkness of the unknown.

With a grimace, he reached forward and removed the hood. "Leyla is in the castle," Tor said, his fingers examining the covering.

The hood was indeed a remarkable piece of workmanship, Tor thought. There were no seams to be found, and though the material was thick, it was not heavy. But most frightening of all, it seemed to possess a life force of its own, and even though it lay unmoving in his hand, he sensed a malevolence inherent in the very cloth itself.

"Why are you here?" Jarrett asked.

Tor glanced up, his expression bewildered. "Did thee say something?"

"A curious piece of workmanship, is it not?" Jarrett mused, his voice dark and bitter. "But you cannot truly appreciate it for the cunning piece of torture it is unless you put it on."

"No." Tor shook his head violently, the very prospect of donning the hood chilling the blood in his veins.

"Why are you here?" Jarrett asked again.

Tor held the hood at arm's length. "I care not for Rorke's plans."

"Rorke's plans! You know nothing of his plans."

"What does thee mean?"

"He was here last night. It's in his mind to dispose of his wife and the King and put Leyla on the throne."

"Leyla! But he vowed to release her after . . . after he had his way with her."

"He has changed his mind. He wants Greyebridge, and he wants the throne, and he cares not how he gets them."

"I see."

"You must get Leyla out of here."

"I said as much to her only moments ago. She will not leave without thee. And so I have come to make thee an offer. I will find a way to get thee out of here, and in return, thee will accompany us to Majeulla, where thee will release Leyla from her marriage vows."

"No."

"Thee would rather stay here and face the pool?"

"She is my wife. I will never willingly give her to another."

"And if I cannot persuade her to leave this place without thee, what then? Is it thy wish that she share Rorke's bed? Has thee forgotten he fancies her?"

Jarrett swore a vile oath. "I haven't forgotten." He forced the words through clenched teeth. Forgotten! He'd thought of little else.

"How long does thee think he will wait to take her?"

Jarrett shook his head helplessly. "Isn't it bad enough I have to endure Rorke's threats without listening to yours as well?"

"We both want her out of here. Rorke will not wait forever. Only give me thy promise that thee will release Leyla from her marriage vows."

"Suppose I were to agree. Do you think we can just walk out of here?"

"I walked in. No one paid me any mind. Now that you are the only prisoner here, there are few Giants on guard. It might not be too hard to make our escape." Tor shrugged. "Thee managed it before, with only Leyla to help thee."

Jarrett felt a flicker of hope. What Tor said was true.

"We dare not wait too long," Tor said, thinking aloud. "A few days, at most, so that I can learn the routine of the guards."

Jarrett nodded.

"Have I thy promise to release Leyla from her marriage vows?"

"No. Only my promise to help you get to Majeulla."

Tor shook his head. "I want thy promise, Lord Jarrett, else I leave thee here to rot."

"I cannot believe you would see Leyla come to harm at Rorke's hands."

"I will take her away by force, if necessary, though that might endanger her. I do not believe thee would put her life at risk." Tor glanced at the door. "We are wasting time, my Lord Jarrett. I will not come here again."

"My promise will have no meaning."

"I would have it anyway."

"Why?"

"I know thee to be an honorable man.

Once thee has given me thy word, thee will keep it. As I will keep mine."

"What if she refuses to stay with you?"

"I will judge the depths of that gorge when I come to it. I want only thy word, and thy solemn vow that thee will not reveal this conversation."

"You want her to believe I no longer want her for my wife."

"Yes."

"She will never believe it."

"We shall see. Thy word, Lord Jarrett. Do I have it?"

"You have it. I will release Leyla from her vows when we reach the Mountains of the Blue Mist if she so wishes."

"That will do." Tor stared at the hood in his hands, thinking he had never seen a more cruel instrument of torture. Heaving a sigh, he glanced at Jarrett, an apology in his eyes as he dropped the hood in place.

Shrouded in the hood's living darkness, Jarrett listened to the sound of Tor's footsteps as the Maje crossed the floor toward the torch, then made his way to the door and left the cell.

Chained to the wall, trapped within the hood's infinite darkness, Jarrett offered a silent plea to the All Father, praying that Tor would find a way for them to escape before Rorke had his way with Leyla. And though he asked nothing for himself, he hoped the

All Father would take pity on him and grant his petition before he had to endure the awful terror of the pool.

Chapter Twenty-three

"Thee has seen him?" Leyla's voice was rough with the strain of the past few hours, her eyes filled with anxiety and hope.

"Yes."

"Is he well?"

"He is unhurt."

"Thee is keeping something from me."

Tor shook his head. "He has a minor wound. It is nothing to speak of."

"Did he ask for me?"

"Yes." Tor held up his hand, holding off further questions. "I have a plan, Leyla. I think we can get out of here without much trouble. No one bothered me when I entered the Pavilion. If we dress Jarrett in suitable clothes and act as if we have every right to roam the castle at will, I think we can escape without much trouble."

"Truly! Oh, Tor, that is wonderful news!"

"Hear me out."

Her eyes lost their sparkle at the sound of his voice. "What is wrong?"

"There is a condition."

"What sort of condition?"

"I will help thee free Jarrett only if thee

agrees to return to Majeulla with me."

She stared at him as if his words had no meaning. And then she shook her head. "It is impossible. I am Jarrett's wife."

"He has agreed to release thee from thy vows."

"I don't believe thee."

"It is true, nevertheless. Thee may ask him thyself once we are away from this place."

"And if I refuse to disavow my troth and return to Majeulla with thee?"

"Thee must do as thee thinks best. But I would remind thee that Rorke has sworn to kill Jarrett. And to take his pleasure with thee."

"And thee will do nothing to help Jarrett unless I yield to thy wishes?"

He said nothing, only stared at her, his dark eyes opaque, his mind closed against her.

"I do not believe thee would do this, Tor. It is not our way to watch others suffer. Shield thy mind as thee might, I sense the hatred within thee. It makes thee a stranger to me."

"I want only that which was promised me," Tor replied. "That for which I have waited my whole life." He crossed the short distance between them. "I have loved thee since thee was a child. I have waited for the day when thee would be mine."

His hand rested lightly on her shoulder,

then slid down her arm. "What has patience gotten me, Leyla?" he asked bitterly. He took her hand in his. "When we return to Majeulla, I will claim what is rightfully mine."

A coldness settled over Leyla's heart as she gazed into Tor's eyes. The gentle Maje she had known was gone, and in his place stood a stranger. It was in her mind to tell him nay, but logic told her that Tor was her only hope of getting Jarrett away from the Pavilion. She was too well-known in the dungeons. The Giants would not let her pass unchallenged. They knew she had helped Jarrett escape before; they would not let her near him again.

"If thee can get Jarrett away from the Pavilion, I will do as thee asks, Tor. I will return to Majeulla with thee. I will be thy wife if Jarrett will release me from my vows."

Tor nodded. He was not proud of deceiving her, but she had been promised to him since childhood and he meant to have her as his wife. He had waited patiently for her to grow up. Though there had been many women who would have been proud to be his wife, he had shunned the company of other women, keeping himself untouched so that he might go to her without blemish, as he had expected her to come to him. But Leyla was no longer untouched. Jarrett had taken her innocence. Tor would never forgive him for that.

"How soon?" Leyla asked.

"A few days. I must observe the guards before I can formulate a plan of escape. Until then, we must do as Rorke bids, no matter how distasteful it might be."

The next three days passed without incident. Rorke seemed to have no interest in either Tor or Leyla, insisting only that they join him in the dining hall morning and evening. Leyla wondered what business kept him occupied during the day. Occasionally, she tried to pry into his affairs, but he refused to reveal anything. Tor had tried to probe Rorke's mind, but thus far he had been unsuccessful.

"He has great control over his thoughts," Tor remarked that afternoon. "He is aware of my power, and he therefore thwarts me at every turn."

"What does thee think he is up to?"

Tor shrugged. "I think he has plans to take control of Greyebridge. Once he has a fortress, I think he will try to gather an army and overthrow Tyrell. The King has no heirs, no direct kin. I believe Rorke hopes to put his own issue on the throne."

"Can he do it?"

"Perhaps. But it is not our concern." He leaned toward her, his voice low. "After dark, there is but one guard at each castle gate. I saw only one Giant in the Pavilion. There were no guards in the lower levels. Now that the place is abandoned, some of the King's men train in the arena, but they will be gone by nightfall.

"This eve, I will challenge Rorke to a game of nine points. While we are thus engaged, thee must go into his chamber and take a set of his clothes for Jarrett to wear. Tomorrow eve, at tenth hour, I will go to the dungeon and free Jarrett. Thee must meet us by the north door of the Pavilion so he can change clothes."

Leyla nodded. It might work. With Jarrett disguised as Rorke, it just might work. It had to work.

"By what manner did thee escape before?"

"We went through the kitchens, out into the stable yard, and then out the east gate. Are the helldogs still there?"

"I saw none." He let out a sigh. "Tomorrow, then, at tenth hour."

"Tomorrow," Leyla agreed.

She was ill at ease during Last Meal that evening. Tor's plan sounded so simple, yet there were so many things that could go wrong, and Jarrett's life hung in the balance.

She ate slowly, steadily, answering when spoken to, immediately forgetting what had been said. Jarrett wished to renounce their marriage. The thought cut through her like a knife. Resolutely, she put it from her mind. She would not believe it until she heard it from his own lips. She looked up, realizing that Rorke had spoken to her. "Milord?"

"Your thoughts appear far away, mistress," he remarked.

"Yes, Milord, I was thinking of my home and my family."

"I hear the Mountains of the Blue Mist are quite lovely."

"Yes, Milord."

"You will be there again soon."

Fear snaked through Leyla's heart. Did he know of their plans? "Milord?"

"Have you forgotten I promised to send you home?"

"No, Milord," she replied quickly. "Will it be soon?"

"Not too soon." His dark eyes moved over her breasts, his lingering glance betraying his intent. "I fear I have neglected you these past few days, but I shall soon remedy that."

"Please, Milord, I beg of thee, do not shame me."

Rorke turned to stare at Tor. "You are unusually silent. Have you nothing to say?"

"Thy mind is made up, Milord. Naught that I can say will change it." Tor's gaze clashed with Rorke's. "Thee has given me thy word that thee will release us at thy leisure."

"And you are content to wait?"

"My people are not inclined to make war, Milord Rorke. Unlike the Fen, we are instructed not in the art of war, but to walk the paths of peace."

Rorke grunted. "There is no strength in peace, Tor of Majeulla. Power is for those who have the courage to take it."

"Thee has said it, Milord."

"I grow bored with this conversation. I have had no diversion since we arrived." His gaze washed over Leyla, hot as the pools of Mereck. "Taark, bring me the prisoner. I desire some entertainment."

"Yes, Milord."

Leyla's eyes grew wide. "Milord . . ." She stared helplessly at Tor.

Tor leaned forward. "Milord, I had hoped to engage thee in a game of nine points."

"On the morrow, perhaps. I have not seen my Lord Jarrett these last three days. I would know how he fares."

Tor nodded. Sitting back in his chair, he sent a message to Leyla, bidding her mind her tongue and keep silent no matter what Rorke might do.

Minutes later, Taark ushered Jarrett into the room.

Leyla's heart twisted with pain as she stared at her husband. His chest was covered with a dozen minor cuts and welts. The hood covered his face, his hands were shackled behind his back.

"Ah, my Lord Jarrett," Rorke said, his voice a mockery of welcome. "We bid you welcome. Your lovely wife sits here at my side. Your rival for her affections is here, also. Have you anything to say?"

Slowly, Jarrett shook his head.

"No words of love for this beautiful silver-haired creature? Ah, I am indeed disappointed in you. Perhaps a few strokes of the lash will loosen your tongue. Taark!"

Leyla's nails bit into her palms as Taark laid the lash across Jarrett's bare back. He flinched as the thick leather strap cut deep into his flesh.

Leyla flinched as well, a small sob escaping her lips. She felt Jarrett's pain as if it were her own, felt the warm trickle of blood that oozed down his back. His rage, as black as the bowels of the Pavilion, seared her mind, frightening in its intensity.

"Milord," she whispered, "please . . ."

Rorke's smile was cold. "You wish me to stop?"

"Yes, please."

The sound of her voice, meekly acquiescent, elicited a wordless cry of despair from Jarrett. He knew Leyla only too well, knew she would do whatever she thought necessary to spare him any further pain.

Pleased by Jarrett's reaction, Rorke nodded at Taark, and the lash fell again.

"Please, Milord," Leyla begged. "I'll do anything thee asks of me, only spare him."

"Leyla." The warning hissed through Jarrett's clenched teeth.

Leyla faltered for only a moment. He would be angry if she defied him, she knew it as surely as she knew the three moons of Hovis would rise that night, but it couldn't be helped. She could not stand idly by and let him be whipped, not if there was a way to stop it.

Rorke looked thoughtful for a moment, and then a wry smile tugged at his lips. "Anything, madam?" he mused, his expression turning smug. "A kiss, I think. One kiss, freely given, to stay the lash."

"Leyla, no!" Jarrett ground the words out between clenched teeth.

"So, he does speak," Rorke mused. "Taark, remove the hood."

Jarrett's gaze settled on Rorke's face, his eyes ablaze with defiance.

Rorke grinned insolently, and then turned to Leyla. "One kiss, madam," he reminded her. "One kiss, freely given."

Heart pounding with revulsion, Leyla pressed her lips to Rorke's. She gasped as his hands grasped her shoulders, his grip brutal. She tried to pull away, but he held her fast, his tongue plundering her mouth with sickening intimacy.

Just when she thought he would never let her go, he released her, his expression insolent as he turned to face Jarrett.

A feral scream of fury erupted from Jarrett's throat as he lunged toward Rorke.

Striking out with his right foot, he struck Rorke full in the chest, driving him over backward.

Leyla screamed as Taark drew his sword. But Tor was moving, too. Snatching up a stool, he brought it down over Taark's head, then plucked the captain's sword from his hand.

"Do not move, my Lord Rorke," Tor warned, the blade steady in his grasp. "Jarrett, step away."

Jarrett backed up, his breath coming in hard gasps as he watched Rorke gain his feet.

"What do you hope to gain by this?" Rorke asked. "Put that sword away. A word from me will have a dozen men in this room."

"Say it, and die," Tor warned. "Leyla, release Jarrett."

With a nod, she hurried to Taark's side. Finding a ring of keys on his belt, she quickly unlocked Jarrett's shackles.

He rubbed his wrists a moment, then pulled her into his arms and kissed her, hard and quick. Untying the sash from Taark's waist, he ripped it in half and tied the captain's hands behind his back.

"You will never make it out of the keep," Rorke warned as Jarrett used the remaining strip of cloth to bind his hands.

"You will not make it through this night," Jarrett retorted, his eyes cold and hard as he drew Rorke's sword from its sheath.

"Jarrett, no!" Leyla rushed to his side. "Please, I cannot abide for thee to kill him."

"I cannot let him live."

"Please, my Lord." She placed her hand on his arm, felt the hard ridge of muscle quiver beneath her fingertips. "Please."

"You do not know what you're asking. He will not rest until one of us is dead."

She heard the fury building in his voice, saw it in the harsh glint of his eyes, in the labored rasp of his breathing.

"He wants Greyebridge, Leyla. He will not rest until he has it, and the throne as well."

"The throne?"

"Aye, the throne. He wants it badly enough to kill for it."

Leyla glanced at Rorke, then at Jarrett. "Please, no killing."

"As you wish." Jarrett studied Rorke a moment, knowing it was a mistake to let the man live, yet unable to refuse Leyla's request. "I have another idea."

Twenty minutes later, five people entered the walled city surrounding the Pavilion. It was the hour after Last Meal and the arena was deserted.

Quickly and silently, Jarrett dispatched the Giant who stood guard at the door of the Pavilion.

Leyla shivered as they made their way down to the lowest level. She had hoped never to return to this place.

Jarrett locked Taark in one of the cells, and then they were standing before the narrow chamber that had imprisoned Jarrett.

She stood in the corridor while Jarrett ushered Rorke into the cell and shackled him to the wall.

"Ah, my Lord Rorke." Jarrett pulled the hood from inside his shirt and turned it this way and that in his hands. "I hope you find your lodgings to your liking."

Rorke grimaced as Jarrett threw his own words back at him.

"I can tell you now the food is sorely lacking," Jarrett went on, "and the creature comforts are poor."

"You'll not get away with this, Jarrett, I warn you. . . ."

"I grow weary of your warnings, Milord," Jarrett exclaimed, and stepping forward, he dropped the hood over Rorke's head.

Rorke's reaction was swift. His whole body tensed as the hood settled over his head and shoulders.

"You would be wise to be content with what you have, Rorke. You may take the throne, but Greyebridge will never be yours. I warn you now that not even Leyla will be able to save you if I see your face again."

"Jarrett!" Rorke strained against the chains that imprisoned him, every muscle taut, as the hood molded itself to his face like a

300

second skin, its darkness embracing him wholly, completely.

"Only now do you begin to understand the true meaning of hell," Jarrett said quietly. "Rest well, my Lord."

Leaving the cell, Jarrett closed and locked the door. "Come, we have no time to waste."

While Tor kept watch, Jarrett saddled three horses. Earlier, he had changed into a loose-fitting white shirt and a pair of velvetsoft black breeches that belonged to Rorke. Now, mounted on Rorke's favorite horse, and with the hood of one of Rorke's dark cloaks covering his head, he rode through the gate, unchallenged. Tor and Leyla rode in his wake.

Chapter Twenty-four

It had been so easy, she wanted to laugh. And later, when they stopped in a small clearing to rest the horses, Leyla did laugh, releasing the tension that had been building within her ever since they'd been forced to leave Greyebridge. Jarrett was alive and well, and they were free.

She smiled at her husband as he helped her from her horse. Nothing else mattered but that he was there beside her. She hugged him close, frowning when he winced.

"What is wrong?" she asked.

"Nothing."

"Thee is wounded!" she exclaimed. "I had forgotten." Ignoring his protests, she removed his shirt and ran her hand over the long gash in his back. There was an ugly red welt across his back, too. "Tor, we have need of thee."

"No, we don't," Jarrett asserted.

Leyla placed her hand on his arm. "Jarrett, it will take but a moment."

Jarrett shook his head as Tor came toward them. "Leave me be, Maje. The wound is not serious."

"But it pains thee," Leyla argued, frowning up at him. "It is foolish to suffer when there is no need."

"I can bear the pain better than his touch."

Leyla glanced from one man to the other. "I do not understand."

"It doesn't matter," Jarrett said. He placed his arm around Leyla's shoulders and drew her to his side. "So, Maje," he asked, his tone skeptical as he regarded Tor. "Can you use that sword?"

High color stained Tor's cheeks as he shook his head. "No."

"I thought as much." Jarrett gave Leyla's shoulders a quick squeeze, and then he released her. "If you're going to carry a weapon, Maje, you'd best know how to use it."

Tor shook his head, his expression one of near revulsion. "I cannot."

"You will learn; and now."

"From you?"

"Who better to teach you?"

Tor scowled, irritated by the warrior's arrogant grin.

For the next hour, Leyla watched as Jarrett instructed Tor in the use of a sword, showing him at length the correct stance, how to grip the sword, warning him not to choke the hilt.

Over and over, Tor practiced the lunge and basic parries, swinging the sword from side to side and in circular and low-line moves.

Feint, lunge, disengage, thrust, slash, parry. Tor was clumsy with the blade. His thrusts were awkward and unsure, his feints weak.

"Come at me as if you mean it," Jarrett chided, his sword arm extended. "Don't hold back."

Time and again, Leyla watched as Jarrett flicked the sword from Tor's grasp. He was agile on his feet, as light as thistledown as he eluded Tor's blade. His eyes, as green as the moss that grew in the mountains, were filled with exhilaration as he breached Tor's defenses.

He was a man without equal, she thought, and beautiful to watch, so beautiful she forgot that it was forbidden for Tor to even hold a weapon of destruction. For a Maje, the taking of a life was a sin without equal, without forgiveness.

But she did not think on that now. Sitting on a fallen log, Leyla could scarce take her eyes from her husband. The three moons of Hovis shone down upon the two men, making Tor's white hair gleam like winter frost, casting silver shadows on Jarrett's long black mane.

Jarrett had removed his shirt, and the moonlight caressed him like a lover's eager hand. A fine sheen of perspiration covered his copper-hued skin; the wound Taark had inflicted looked like a dark ribbon across his broad back. Surely the Creators had designed a masterpiece when Lord Jarrett of Gweneth was conceived. Broad of shoulder, slim of hip, long of leg, he moved with the fluid grace of a blue tiger on the hunt.

The muscles rippled in his arms and back with each thrust and parry, causing her heart to pound and her insides to dance with excitement. Never had he looked so strong, so masculine. So desirable. And he was hers . . .

Her joy in that thought died a quick death as she recalled that Jarrett had said he wished to release her from her vows. Much as she longed to disbelieve, she knew Tor would never lie to her. Jarrett wished to end their marriage.

Tears burned her eyes. Silent as a drifting shadow, she stepped down from the log and made her way into the darkness beyond the clearing. She would not let Jarrett see her tears. If he wished to end their marriage, she would not argue, she would not ask why. She would leave him with her honor and her dignity intact. . . .

Tor grunted as the flat of Jarrett's blade struck his shoulder, numbing his whole arm so that his sword fell to the ground. He had not expected sword fighting to be so difficult. With his mind, he could easily discern Jarrett's thoughts. He knew what the Gweneth warrior was going to do before he did it, yet he was powerless to avoid the other man's blade. Had they been fighting to the death, he would have been dead a dozen times.

Grudgingly, Tor had to admit that Jarrett was a masterful teacher. By the end of the hour, he could wield the sword with at least a bit of skill, and Jarrett was no longer able to disarm him with such ease.

Tor was breathing hard when Jarrett called an end to the lesson.

"Not bad, Maje," Jarrett said, though it galled him to give Tor any kind of compliment. "You might be able to defend yourself against Leyla should the need arise."

Tor scowled at him, his fist tightening around the hilt of the sword. For a moment, he thought of lunging forward, of burying his sword to the hilt in the arrogant warrior's chest. But the consequences of such an act were beyond comprehension. He stared at the weapon in his hand, wondering at the turn of events that had brought him here, that had him turning his back on everything he had ever believed in, everything he knew to be right and true.

"Think twice, Maje," Jarrett warned. "I'd hate to have to kill you."

With a muttered oath, Tor lowered the blade.

Only then did Jarrett notice that Leyla was missing. His gaze swept the clearing, but there was no sign of her. Sheathing his sword, he walked toward the log where he'd seen her last, his gaze sweeping the ground. Her tracks were barely visible in the waning moonlight.

"Leyla?" He called her name as he followed her trail into a grove of locust trees. By Hadra, whatever had possessed her to go off by herself? It was dangerous for her to be wandering around alone. There were wild animals in this part of the country, slime pits, pools of shimmering quicksand, bands of outlaws who bartered human flesh.

And then he saw her, kneeling on the ground beside a moss-covered tree trunk, her face buried in her hands, her hair flowing down her back and over her shoulders like a cloak of silver angel's hair.

Thinking her hurt, he hurried to her side. "Leyla?"

"My Lord?"

"What's wrong?"

"I would know why thee wishes to be free of me," she said, her voice muffled by her hands. "Has thy love died?"

"What?"

"Perhaps thee thinks to send me away to keep me from harm?"

Roughly, he grasped her by the shoulders and drew her around to face him. "What are you talking about? You're my wife."

"Until we reach Majeulla," she replied bitterly.

Jarrett's eyes narrowed ominously. "Can you not wait until then? Are you so anxious to be rid of me that you'd risk your life by running off into the night?"

He stood up then, his chest heaving with silent rage. "Shall I send Tor to you? Mayhap you will not find his presence so undesirable."

Jarrett whirled around, only to come face to face with Tor.

"Did you think to have her now, Maje?" Jarrett challenged.

Tor shook his head, put off by the anger that blazed in the depths of the warrior's dark green eyes.

"You may have her, Maje, when we reach the Mountains of the Blue Mist. But until then, she is mine. And I would be alone with her this night." Jarrett's gaze locked with Tor's. "Do you take my meaning?"

For a moment, Tor's hand caressed the hilt of his sword. Then, with a curt nod, he turned on his heel and went back the way he'd come. No man in his right mind would dare to challenge the warning in Jarrett's eyes.

Leyla scrambled to her feet as Jarrett moved toward her, his booted feet making no sound on the spongy sod.

He was like a great blue tiger stalking its prey, she thought, graceful and lethal. His beautiful green eyes glittered with barely suppressed fury and desire.

"Jarrett . . ."

His mouth descended on hers, shutting off her words. She tasted blood, his or hers, she couldn't say, and then he was carrying her down, pinning her body to the ground with his considerable weight, trapping both her hands in one of his.

She wanted to ask why he wanted to be free of her, to hear from his own lips that he no longer loved her, knowing that, even then, she would not believe it. But he was kissing her again, his free hand burrowing into her hair, holding her head immobile as his tongue plundered her mouth.

She writhed beneath him, her breasts crushed against the unyielding wall of his chest, her legs well caught between his. She could feel every heated inch of him, from shoulder to thigh, as he continued to kiss her, his lips moving over her face. His breath was warm, his words muffled and indistinct.

With his free hand, he dispensed with her clothing, then his own. Breathless, she stared up at him, her heart hammering within her breast. He looked like an avenging angel, with his long black hair swirling around his face and his eyes blazing green fire. His skin glowed like heated copper in the moonlight, and she felt a deep answering hunger uncurl within the depths of her being. How magnificent he looked, her rogue warrior. His body was taut so that every muscle stood out in bold relief.

He murmured her name as he plunged into her, taking her violently, using her as he might have used a concubine.

She should have hated it, and him. Instead, she arched beneath him, drawing him deeper into herself, her anger dissolving into tears as Jarrett breathed her name again.

Her nails raked his back as his rhythm increased. "I love thee, my Lord Jarrett," she whispered, tears stinging her eyes. "I will always love thee."

Her words pierced the hard veneer of Jarrett's anger. Abruptly, his assault lessened and he took her gently, his hands softly caressing the smoothness of her skin as ecstacy blended with ecstacy, their bodies, fully joined, melding together in a dance older than time.

Later, holding her close, he rained feather-light kisses along her neck.

"Why, Leyla?" he asked, his voice gruff. "If you love me, as you say, why do you wish to renounce our marriage?"

"Thee is the one who wishes it, my Lord, not I."

"What are you talking about? Who told you such a thing?"

"Tor. He said thee wished to end our marriage."

Jarrett swore a vile oath. "I said no such

thing. Tor swore he would not help you get away from Rorke unless I agreed to free you from your vows when we reached Majeulla."

Leyla echoed Jarrett's oath. "He told me he would not help thee to escape unless *I* renounced our marriage."

"Then you do not wish to be free of me?" Jarrett asked.

"Never! And thee?"

"My life means nothing if you are not there to share it with me." Jarrett stroked Leyla's cheek, delighting in the softness of her skin, the radiance in her eyes. "He must love you very much."

Leyla lowered her gaze. "We have been betrothed since I was a child."

"And he cares for you deeply," Jarrett repeated.

"Yes."

Jarrett tried to be angry with the Maje, tried to hate him, but it was impossible. What man, knowing Leyla, could help but want her for his own?

"I'd kill him for his lies if I didn't feel so sorry for him," he muttered ruefully.

Leyla snuggled closer to Jarrett, her head resting on his shoulder, one arm over his chest. How could she have ever believed that Jarrett would let her go? They were bound to each other, heart to heart and soul to soul. She had no life without him, wanted no life without him.

"What will we do now?" she asked. "Thee cannot go back to Greyebridge."

"We'll go to Majeulla," Jarrett said, thinking aloud. "You'll be safe there."

"I will not stay there without thee," she said. "Do not even think of taking me there unless thee plans to stay as well."

"My life is not my own," Jarrett said, "nor will it be until I can convince the King that I am innocent of treason. And the only way to do that is to go to Cornith and beg an audience with Tyrell. I know he'll listen to me."

"Rorke will never allow it."

"Rorke be damned!" Turning on his side, Jarrett rested his chin in his hand and gazed down at Leyla. "I don't want to leave you, beloved, but I will not put your life at risk again. I'll come back for you after I've seen Tyrell."

"No. I will not be parted from thee again."

"Leyla . . ."

"No! Do not think thee can trick me, or persuade me with pretty words and promises. My place is at thy side, and I will not leave thee."

"Ah, my brave warrior woman. Perhaps I instructed the wrong Maje in the use of the sword."

"If necessary, I will fight beside thee, my Lord Jarrett."

"I know." Bending toward her, he kissed her, savoring the softness of her lips, the sweetness of her mouth, the blue fire in the depths of her eyes. He had no doubt that she would fight to the death for him.

Sensing his thoughts, Leyla smiled up at him. "We are agreed then?" she queried softly.

"Aye, beloved, we are agreed. I will not leave thee." He traced the outline of her lips with his fingertip. "We will see Tor safely to Majeulla. Mayhap we will spend the winter in your mountains."

"Thee has never seen the Mountains of the Blue Mist in winter," Leyla mused, pleased at the prospect. "There is nothing more beautiful than our mountains when they are covered with snow."

"Is it really blue?"

"Yes."

"As blue as your eyes?"

Leyla shook her head. "It is a pale blue, paler than the bluebird's egg, but it shimmers in the sunlight. Thee must see it! And perhaps, if thy heart is pure, thee will see a unicorn, as well."

It was early the following morning when Jarrett and Leyla returned to the clearing. Tor glared at Jarrett, his hand itching to draw his sword and plunge it into the Gweneth warrior's heart.

"What now?" Tor asked curtly.

"We ride for Majeulla," Jarrett answered.

Tor grunted in surprise, then frowned. "Why does thee wish to go there?"

"I promised to take you home," Jarrett replied gruffly. "And I keep my promises."

"Thee also promised to release Leyla from her marriage vows."

"If it was her wish," Jarrett reminded him. "It is not." Jarrett shook his head. "You are a rare knave, to play us one against the other." His hand caressed the hilt of his sword. "And a lucky one. Did I not understand how easy it is to love her, you would be dead now."

Tor's hand closed over his sword hilt. "I but await thy pleasure, my Lord Jarrett."

"You're a brave man, Maje, or a fool, I know not which, but I have no wish to kill you. There is a town a few leagues from here where we can get something to eat, and supplies for our journey."

Tor held Jarrett's gaze for several moments; then, with a sigh, he went to saddle the horses, his mind filling with images of Majeulla. Perhaps, safe within the Mountains of the Blue Mist, he would recover the serenity that had once been his.

Chapter Twenty-five

The journey from Heth to the Cyrus River passed peacefully enough. At least, Tor and Jarrett managed to refrain from killing each other, and for that, Leyla was grateful. Very little was said as they made their way across the fields and forests. Autumn was in the air; the days were cool, the nights frigid.

Wrapped in the circle of Jarrett's arms, she hardly felt the cold as she reacquainted herself with the hard planes and contours of his body. She wondered if she would ever tire of touching him, of being touched by him.

Each time they made love, she marveled anew at the masculine beauty of the man who was her husband. Would the width of his shoulders ever cease to amaze her? Would she grow indifferent to the muscles that rippled in his arms and legs? Would there be a time when she would no longer notice the rich texture of his skin, the way the sunlight glinted in his hair, the deep green of his eyes?

She'd heard it said that such things became less important, less noticeable, with the passage of years, but she could scarcely fathom such a thing. Jarrett was the center of her life, the joy of her existence. Had he been short and ugly, she would still have loved his valiant heart, his courageous soul.

Now, riding beside him, she could not keep her gaze from sliding in his direction. He rode as he did everything else, effortlessly, with a natural grace that was wonderful to watch. He moved in perfect rhythm with the horse, as though he knew what the animal would do before it was done.

When he turned to smile at her, she felt the heat of his gaze, warm and soft and filled with promise.

They camped that night on the banks of the river. Across the way, she could see the rolling foothills, and beyond the foothills, their peaks already topped with snow, were the Mountains of the Blue Mist.

Her heart felt suddenly light as she thought of seeing her parents and her homeland again.

Tor remained sullen and silent, as he had been since they left Heth. Each evening, he practiced with his sword, his movements becoming faster, more agile. It troubled her that he seemed so intent upon mastering the weapon, that he deigned to carry an instrument of death. Most worrisome of all was her deep-seated fear that he meant to use the blade against Jarrett, and that Jarrett would kill him.

They ate a simple meal of black bread and goat cheese washed down with strong Fenduzian ale.

Later, sitting beside Jarrett, Leyla gazed into the fire. The flames, blue and green and bright yellow, were mesmerizing. Her mother could see images of the past or foretell the future in the dancing light of a fire.

A small sigh escaped Leyla's lips. She would be no more than an outsider when she reached home. Her powers were gone, though she could easily read Jarrett's thoughts as he sat there beside her.

He was thinking of his own mother, of Greyebridge, of vengeance.

Leyla placed her hand on his arm, smiling at him when he glanced her way. "We will be home soon."

"Your home," he said quietly. "I fear my home is forever lost to me."

"I will be thy home," Leyla replied softly. "No one can take me from thee, nor will I ever leave thee."

"Leyla . . ." He was reaching for her when he heard a twig snap to his right.

Instantly, Jarrett was on his feet, his sword in his hand, his gaze sweeping the darkness.

"What is it?" Leyla asked, her voice hushed.

Jarrett shook his head, then felt his blood run cold as a blood-curdling cry rent the stillness of the night. Before the last shriek had died away, they were surrounded by nine mounted men armed with swords and lances and long bows.

Jarrett grabbed Leyla and drew her close to his side, his sword held at the ready. Tor sidled up beside him, his sword in his hand.

"Canst not fight us all," one of the flesh peddlers said. With an affable smile, he stroked his beard, which was the same bright red as his shaggy hair. "Best drop your weapons before I cleave you in half."

"Better to fight to the death than go down like a cowardly cur," Jarrett retorted.

"We will not permit you to die," the peddler retorted sharply. "There is no money in dead flesh."

"Have you the courage to face me one at a time?"

"We have the courage, my friend," the man assured him, "but we were not born stupid. Drop your weapon and stand away from the woman."

"No. She is my wife and you will not have her."

"We will."

"Some of you will die first." Jarrett squared his shoulders. "I've faced worse odds and won."

"My men are in no hurry to die," the man said, his tone still agreeable. "Put down your sword, and no harm will come to the woman."

Jarrett shook his head. "You must do better than that."

"This is my final deal. We will sell your white-haired companion. We will keep the woman to cook for us. And you will become our swordsman. There is lucre to be made in the towns hereabout if you are as good with a sword as you seem to think you are. And if you are not . . ."

The man shrugged. "We will sell you into slavery in the mines of Mereck if you fail to prevail in the arena, and then we will amuse ourselves with the woman before we sell her to one of the Fen brothels."

"Let the woman go free."

The man shook his head. "She is fair to look upon, with her slanted eyes and silver-colored hair. By the fires of Hadra, I've never seen hair that color in all my living life. Tell me yea or nay, my friend. I grow weary of waiting."

"I will fight your men, one at a time, to the death or not, as you wish. If I win, you will let us go. If I am bested, I will do as you say."

The flesh peddler stared at Jarrett in astonishment. "You are that confident of your ability?"

"Try me and see."

Leyla looked at Jarrett in horror. "No!"

"Leyla, do not interfere." He shook her hand from his arm, his gaze intent upon the flesh peddler's face. "Have we a deal?"

"You intrigue me, my friend. We have a deal. Tell your companion to drop his weapon."

"Tor, do as he says."

Tor's hand tightened on his sword. "Thee must be mad," he hissed. "Thee cannot possibly hope to best them all."

"Do as I say."

With a sigh of resignation, Tor dropped his sword.

Immediately, two men took hold of him, dragging him away and binding his arms behind his back.

The other flesh peddlers dismounted, forming a loose circle around Jarrett.

"To the death?" Jarrett asked.

The red-haired flesh peddler shook his head. "I think not. Good men are not easy to come by these days."

"First disabling blow, then?"

"Aye. Lahairoi, draw your sword."

Leyla watched in horror as a tall, heavily bearded man drew his sword and stepped into the circle. Clad in skins and furs, he looked like a bear in human form.

For a moment, the two combatants studied each other, and then, with a clash of steel, they engaged.

It was horrible. Ugly. Frightening.

Leyla tried not to watch, but she could not take her eyes from Jarrett. He fought exultantly, his movements fluid, his dark green eyes flashing with defiance, his expression intense as he focused on his opponent. His blade slashed through the night, quick as a serpent's tongue.

The sound of metal striking metal pierced the darkness, making her cringe with fear, fear for Jarrett's life, for Tor, for her own well-being should anything happen to Jarrett.

She knew a moment of intense relief when Jarrett crippled the other man, but it was short-lived as another stepped in to take Lahairoi's place.

Jarrett disabled the second man in a matter of minutes, but there was another outlaw to take his place, and then another.

Jarrett was breathing heavily now. Stripping off his shirt, he wiped the sweat from his face and chest; then, tossing his shirt aside, he picked up his sword to face the fifth man.

He knew at once that this opponent was a man to be reckoned with. He held his sword easily, confidently. They lunged and parried for fully five minutes, and then the outlaw's sword slipped past Jarrett's guard, opening a long bloody gash the length of Jarrett's left arm.

There was a jubilant cry of victory from the watching outlaws as one of their own finally drew blood.

Their joy was short-lived as Jarrett drove his blade into his opponent's right shoulder, before he disarmed the man.

The next two men each took a terrible toll on Jarrett's strength before he managed to disarm them.

Leyla was weeping now, her heart aching for his pain. He was a warrior unlike any she had ever seen, a man of indomitable courage and pride.

Covered with blood and sweat, his breath coming in hard, short gasps, Jarrett faced the man who was the leader of the flesh peddlers.

But the red-bearded man did not play fair. Dismounting, he drew Jarrett's attention while four of his men, all bearing wounds inflicted by Jarrett, came up behind him and wrested him to the ground, quickly relieving him of his sword and lashing his hands behind his back.

With an oath, Jarrett scrambled to his feet, his eyes blazing with anger. "Your word! You gave me your word!"

"Fool. Do you think I've become rich by making deals that offer me no profit?"

A muscle worked in Jarrett's jaw. He had been a fool, but what else could he have done? Tor would have been little help in an all-out battle, and in a fight to the death, Jarrett knew he couldn't have beat them all. Their number alone would have defeated him, and in the process, Leyla might have been hurt or killed. He couldn't risk that.

"It shall be as I said," the flesh peddler decreed. "We will sell the white-haired one, and you shall fight in the arena. If you win, you will be well cared for. If you lose too often, we will sell you to the mines."

Jarrett shuddered imperceptibly. The salt mines of Mereck. Incorrigible prisoners were sent there to die. No one had ever escaped; no one had ever survived the stifling heat and the hard work for more than a few months.

He took a deep breath. "And my woman?"

"So long as you bring me a profit, she shall be unharmed."

"Sir?" Leyla stepped forward, her cheeks damp with tears.

"I am Keturah."

"Keturah, our companion is a Maje. I beg of thee, let him heal my husband's wounds."

Keturah frowned thoughtfully. "A Maje? A healer, you mean?" He grunted at Leyla's nod. "Perhaps we will not sell him. If our new warrior is badly wounded, it would be to our advantage to have someone who could heal him. If we do not need to wait for his wounds to heal, he will be able to fight more often."

"Sir, my husband . . ."

"You may bind his wounds, but I do not wish him healed just now. I think he will be more easily controlled if his strength is limited."

"But . . ."

"I have spoken, woman! Do not trouble me again. Lahairoi, bring the Maje to me. We shall see what manner of healer he may be."

Jarrett sat in tight-lipped silence while Leyla treated his cuts. Though he had lost a good deal of blood, none of his wounds was serious.

He watched through narrowed eyes as Tor was called forward to heal the wounds of one of Keturah's men. It was clear from the expression on Keturah's face that he was mightily impressed with the Maje's powers, and equally clear that the flesh peddler would not sell Tor for any price. A man who had access to the kind of power Tor possessed was not likely to part with it for something as paltry as lucre.

"We will reach Kedar on the morrow," Keturah informed Jarrett. "Your first fight will be there, at eventide. The Maje will heal your wounds before you enter the arena. Rest well, my friend."

Chapter Twenty-six

Kedar was a large village located in a verdant valley south of the Cyrus River. Like most towns in the region, there was an arena where various types of contests, similar to the original Games of Skill, were held on a regular basis. Just now, sword fighting was the most popular amusement. Contestants were usually slaves who fought to the death, though occasionally village champions competed against each other, vying for fame and lucre.

At dusk, Jarrett stood in one of the tunnels, his hands bound behind his back while he waited his turn in the arena. Earlier that day, Tor had worked his magic, healing Jarrett's wounds.

Leyla stood close beside him, her face pale, her eyes sad and worried. "Perhaps thee should tell Keturah thy name," she suggested. "It might be he would free thee if he knew thee to be related to the Lord High Ruler of Aldane."

"And perhaps he'd turn me in for the reward Rorke has placed upon my head," Jarrett muttered. "I've told him my name is

Dumah and that we come from the hill country of Fenduzia, near Cornith. We will leave it at that, for now."

Keturah came striding down the tunnel. He was a huge man, thick of bone, with not an ounce of fat. A man who had no pity for those who were less strong, less intelligent, than himself. A man totally lacking in honor.

"You fight next," Keturah said, his sharp brown eyes raking over Jarrett. "Your opponent is unbeaten in this arena." He reached into his shoulder pouch and withdrew a black mask. "You will wear this when you fight. It will add a bit of mystery."

"No!" Eyes filled with loathing, Jarrett took a step backward, his heart pounding with dread. "No mask!"

"You will do as I say, Dumah," Keturah warned. "I will suffer no insolence from the likes of you."

Jarrett shook his head. "No. I will not wear it."

"I have wagered much on your success this night," Keturah said, his voice edged with anger. "I warn you now, do as I say, or be prepared to watch your woman suffer the consequences of your disobedience."

"Not only have you no honor," Jarrett muttered under his breath. "You do not fight fair."

"But I always win." Keturah summoned Lahairoi. "Loose his hands."

Two of Keturah's other men stepped forward, their swords at the ready, while Lahairoi cut Jarrett's hands free.

Keturah took hold of Leyla's arm. "Should you try to escape from the arena, the woman will die," Keturah warned. He fixed Jarrett with a hard stare. "Do we understand each other, Dumah of Cornith?"

"Aye, flesh peddler. We understand each other well."

"Put on the mask."

Jarrett shuddered with revulsion as he slipped the thin cotton mask over his head. It was nothing like the heavy black hood he'd worn in the dungeons of the Pavilion. This cloth was lightweight, inanimate. Slits had been cut in the material so that he could see clearly. No hint of silent, subtle menace lurked within this mask; it did not mold itself cunningly to his skin, or pulse with a life of its own.

A moment later, his name was announced, and he walked out of the tunnel and into the Kedar arena, which was illuminated by hundreds of torches.

Shouts of derision and hoots of scorn rose on the evening air. He was the challenger, an unknown, with no one to champion him.

Hands clenched, he waited for his opponent to enter the arena.

A roar of approval swept through the crowd as his adversary entered the field. He was a Giant, his yellow eyes glittering with anticipation, his hulking frame clad in nothing but a pair of tight green breeches and knee-high boots. Wide copper bands encircled his massive biceps.

The Giant raised his arms over his head, accepting the cheers of the crowd. And then he turned to face Jarrett, a slow smile spreading over his face. *An easy victory,* his expression seemed to say.

Three heavily armed men entered the field then, followed by the Master of the Arena bearing two swords. The hilts were of polished brass, the blades of gleaming Fenduzian steel. The Arena Master offered the first one to the Giant, the second to Jarrett, and then the Master of the Arena took his place at the entrance to the main tunnel while the three armed men took their positions at the three arena entrances.

Jarrett eyed the Master of the Arena thoughtfully. If either swordsman refused to fight, or showed cowardice, it was the Arena Master's duty to slit the man's throat.

The Master of the Arena raised his arm, held it up for a long moment, then let it fall to his side. It was the signal to begin.

With a roar, the Giant charged Jarrett, the sword in his hand poised to strike at Jarrett's heart. Jarrett pivoted sharply on his heel, a soft oath escaping his lips as he felt the sword's breath whisper past his chest.

The Giant, for all his bulk, was quick and agile. He turned, graceful as a cat, his guard up, as he faced Jarrett.

For the next twenty minutes, Leyla sat on the edge of her seat, hardly breathing, her heart hammering as she watched the contest. She was grateful that it wasn't a fight to the death. The Giant had drawn first blood, the edge of his sword catching Jarrett high in the thigh. But now, well into the fight, both men were covered with dust and sweat and blood.

The crowd cheered wildly each time their champion struck a blow, screamed with indignation when Jarrett's sword found its target.

She sobbed, "No, no, no," when the Giant feinted to the left, stooped, grabbed a handful of dirt, and flung it into Jarrett's face. Momentarily blinded, Jarrett stumbled backward, and the Giant lunged forward, his blade driving toward Jarrett's heart.

Suddenly, it seemed as if everything had slowed. She watched in horrified fascination as Jarrett shook his head . . . took a step forward . . . turned to the left so that the blade, only inches from his chest, sank into his shoulder instead.

She screamed as he jerked back, then brought his own sword up, slashing wildly at the Giant's sword arm, the blade biting deep into muscle and bone.

A high-pitched scream of pain erupted

from the Giant's throat as his sword fell from a hand gone numb.

Eyes wild, chest heaving, Jarrett lunged forward, pressing the edge of his blade against the Giant's throat.

"Do you yield?"

The Giant glared down at him; then, with a curt nod, he dropped to his knees and bowed his head in defeat.

Shivering uncontrollably, his body sheened with sweat and blood, Jarrett stood in the middle of the arena while the crowd cheered their new champion.

Two brawny men clad in black entered the arena. Collecting the Giant's sword, they escorted him out of the arena.

Moments later, the Master of the Arena rode toward Jarrett. Dismounting, he took Jarrett's sword, then placed the red victory cloak around Jarrett's shoulders. And the crowd, their loyalty as constant as mercury, cheered again.

Jarrett took a deep breath; then, gathering what little strength he had left, he walked across the arena and into the tunnel, his ears ringing with the crowd's enthusiastic applause.

In the next fortnight, Jarrett fought eight times. Three, against slaves, were fights to the death; five ended with the first crippling blow. He won each contest, and the name of Dumah, the Masked Swordsman of Keturah, began to spread across the southern provinces.

Though Keturah was a crude, uneducated lout, a man totally without honor, he proved to be a generous master. Pleased with his new discovery, he treated Jarrett like the valued slave he was, making sure he was well-fed and well-clothed.

But the clothes were of no consequence, and the food tasted like ashes in Jarrett's mouth. He had spent eight months in the bowels of the Pavilion and now he was a prisoner again, forced to fight like a wild animal in order to survive, to insure Leyla's well-being. In that, at least, Keturah had spoken the truth. Leyla was not mistreated or abused by Keturah's men. She cooked their meals when they were between towns, and Keturah allowed her to sleep at Jarrett's side.

It was torture of the most exquisite kind, being near her but unable to touch her. Lying beside her, with the three moons of Hovis overhead, he ached to bury himself in her warmth, to lose himself in her sweetness and forget, if only for a moment, that his life was no longer his own. Ah, that short, sweet taste of freedom when he'd had no one to answer to but himself, when he'd been the master of his own fate.

Worst of all, his nightmares had come back to haunt him, resurrected, no doubt, by the mask he was forced to wear when he fought in the arena.

He grinned ruefully as he recalled the night after his first fight. Leyla had told him that his screams had roused the whole camp. She'd smiled as she described in great detail, how Keturah's men had rolled out of their blankets, swords in hand, certain they were being attacked by a horde of Serimites. Caught up in the horror of his nightmare, he'd been unaware of the turmoil around him until Leyla's voice pierced the blanket of darkness, softly pleading for him to return to her.

Leyla had begged Keturah to let Jarrett fight without the mask, but the flesh peddler had refused, ridiculing Jarrett's fears.

"They are only dreams, after all," Keturah had said. "They will pass."

But they didn't. Eight times he fought in the arena. Eight times the nightmare drew him down into a black abyss where he relived the terrors of the Pavilion, the horrible memory of the hood clinging to his face like a second skin, enclosing him in a smothering cocoon of darkness.

And now he stood in the arena again, his sword stained bright red with the blood of his opponent, his body splashed with blood, listening to the cheers of the crowd. He saw Leyla standing inside the tunnel, her expression one of mingled relief and concern.

Glancing past Leyla, Jarrett saw Keturah accept a small pouch filled with the lucre he had won. And beside Keturah, his expression impassive, stood Tor.

Moments later, the Master of the Arena rode forward to collect his sword and drape the red cloak of victory around his shoulders. And then he was walking toward the tunnel and Leyla's waiting arms.

She drew him close, embracing him fiercely, before Lahairoi came to bind his hands and lead him away. As soon as they were out of the tunnel, Keturah removed the mask, allowing Leyla to bathe the sweat from Jarrett's face and neck.

At their camp, well away from the town, Jarrett's leg was shackled to a tree and Tor was called to heal his wounds.

Jarrett endured Tor's touch because he had no choice, but it galled him to accept the Maje's help. They had a peculiar relationship, Jarrett mused. The animosity between them was strong, yet they were bound together, Tor's very existence dependent on Jarrett's survival. They had nothing in common save that they both loved Leyla.

When Tor's ministrations were complete, he went off by himself, needing time alone to recover his strength.

Jarrett glanced up as Keturah came toward him.

Keturah's gaze ran over Jarrett, assessing

him in much the same way a man might examine a valuable animal after a day's hard work.

"You fought well, my friend," he remarked. He patted the heavy pouch hanging from his belt. "Well, indeed."

Jarrett stared up at the flesh peddler. "I want a favor."

"A favor? Peradventure I was of a mind to grant it to you, what would you ask?"

"I want a night alone with my woman."

"It is not possible."

"It is. There's a small clearing not far from here. You can shackle my leg to a tree so that I can't escape. You can post guards, at a distance, if you think it necessary. But I want a night alone with Leyla. Now. Tonight."

Keturah dragged a hand over his beard. Jarrett was a warrior, and a warrior, like any man worth the name, needed a woman.

"I would have your word that you will not try to escape."

A cold smile twisted Jarrett's lips. "I give you my word," he said, his voice thick with contempt, "as you gave me yours."

"A man who takes the word of an outlaw deserves what he gets," Keturah replied affably. "But you, my Lord Jarrett, are a warrior, and a man of honor."

"You know who I am?"

"Your fame is not unknown to us."

"A night," Jarrett said again. "One night

with my woman."

"Done," Keturah agreed.

And so it was that Leyla found herself lying on a blanket beneath the shelter of a yellow fern tree with Jarrett at her side. His left ankle was securely chained to the trunk of the tree, but his hands were free. Keturah had thoughtfully provided them with fresh bread and cheese and a flask of watered wine, warning Jarrett of dire consequences should he try to escape.

But Jarrett had no thought for food. His hands and his lips were hungry for other things. He drew Leyla into his arms, holding her tight against him, reacquainting himself with the warmth of her skin, rediscovering the silken hills and valleys of her body, the fragrance of her hair. She fit into his embrace, filling the emptiness of his heart as she murmured his name, whispering words of love and encouragement.

Keeping a tight rein on his passion, he pressed her back on the blanket, his mouth slanting over hers, drinking from her lips, craving the taste of her as a starving man craved nourishment. He shuddered with pleasure as her hands moved over him in return. Her touch was warm and gentle, chasing the hatred from his soul, the rage from his heart.

With a sigh, he surrendered to the magic of her hands. Her touch was like fire, igniting his blood, arousing his desire until his self-control was shattered. Rising over her, he lifted her hips to receive him, her name a groan as he buried himself in satin flesh and fire. . . .

Leyla lay awake long after Jarrett had fallen asleep, his head cradled against her breast, her arms holding him close, as if she could ward off the nightmares that were sure to come to him.

She studied his face in the moonlight, loving the sensual line of his mouth, the proud cheekbones, the sharp outline of his nose, the strong square jaw. His hair, as black as the bowels of the Greyebridge dungeon, made a dark splash against the blanket. Her gaze moved over him lovingly, caressing the broad shoulders and chest, the long legs that lay over hers.

She tried to fight the fears that crowded her mind. He was a strong man, a valiant fighter, a warrior without equal, and yet she knew he could not win in the arena forever. Sooner or later he would lose. He had killed or maimed nine men. What would she do when it was Jarrett's body lying in a bloody heap in the sand? What if he sustained an injury that even Tor could not heal? What if he were killed?

Her dismal thoughts fled as Jarrett's body twitched convulsively. A low groan rose in his throat, and then an anguished scream cut across the stillness of the night.

Leyla jackknifed into a sitting position, her hand shaking his shoulder. "Jarrett! Jarrett, wake up."

"No!" His hands clawed at his face. "Take it off!"

"Jarrett, wake up!" She made a grab for his hands, only to fall back, stunned, as a wildly flailing fist caught her flush on the jaw.

For a moment, she saw stars and bright comets, and then she realized that Jarrett was on his feet, his body in a crouch. His breath came in ragged gasps as he stared at an enemy only he could see.

"Jarrett." She spoke his name softly. "Jarrett, I am here."

"She?"

"Yes. I am here. Come to me, my Lord Jarrett."

Tears burned her eyes as she watched him. A terrible fear clutched at her heart, a horrible fear that one day he wouldn't be able to fight his way out of the awful nightmare that plagued him, that he would sink so deeply into the bad dreams that haunted him that he would never return.

"Jarrett?"

He shook his head as awareness crept into his eyes. "Leyla?"

"I am here." She went to him then, wrapping her arms around him, feeling the violent shudders that wracked his body. "Come, sit beside me."

She poured him a cup of wine and when he had drunk that, she poured him another. Gradually, his trembling ceased, the wildness left his eyes, and his breathing returned to normal.

Wordlessly, Leyla put her arms around Jarrett and held him close. She felt like crying when he looked at her, his eyes filled with torment and humiliation.

"I'm worse than a mewling infant," he muttered.

"Jarrett . . ."

"It's true!" He tugged against the chain that bound his ankle, his eyes blazing with self-loathing. "What kind of man is terrified by dreams?"

He jerked against his tether again, harder this time, oblivious to the fact that the heavy chain cut into his skin. "And you. What kind of life is this for you? You should have stayed with Tor."

"Thee does not mean that."

"No." He held out his arms and she went to him gratefully, pressing her face to his chest, absorbing his warmth, his strength. She did not need to probe his mind to know he was feeling utterly helpless and completely discouraged.

With a sigh, he stretched out on the blanket, his head in her lap, her hand clutched in his.

She sat there for a long time, listening to

his breathing slow as he fell asleep, wondering how to tell him that a new life was growing beneath her heart.

Chapter Twenty-seven

"Please," Leyla said.

She knelt at Keturah's feet, her hands clasped to her breasts. "Please, I beg of thee, let him fight without the mask."

Keturah shook his head. "It stays."

"Is there no pity in thee? Can thee not see what it does to him? He will fight as well without it."

Keturah grunted softly. "The mask stays."

Leyla glanced over her shoulder to where Jarrett sat, his back against a tree, his arms bound behind his back. Tor sat a short distance away, a glass of ale in his hand. Of the three of them, only Jarrett was kept shackled.

"Please," she said again.

"No. The mask is necessary." He relented a little at the pleading look in her deep blue eyes. "Too many people might recognize him without it."

Leyla blinked at the flesh peddler in astonishment. "Thee knows who he is?"

"Of course."

"But . . . ?"

He silenced her with a wave of his hand. "You want to know why I have not taken him to Rorke for the reward? Only think about it. An outlaw like myself can hardly approach the King for a reward. And, in time, Lord Jarrett will win more lucre than the reward Rorke is offering for his head."

Thoroughly disheartened, Leyla went to sit beside Jarrett. Four days had passed since their night together. In that time, he had withdrawn into himself, hardly speaking to her. He was fighting again at mid-day. Already, she could see the tension building within him as he prepared himself to meet another opponent, to kill or be killed. And, hiding deep inside, waiting for the time when he was at rest, lurked the nightmare.

She glanced over at Tor, her gaze locking with his as she sent him her thoughts. *We have to get away from here.*

How?

I do not know, but it must be soon else Jarrett will perish.

Tor nodded imperceptibly. They couldn't go on like this much longer. When he probed Jarrett's mind, he received little more than thoughts of death and destruction. It was only a matter of time before the warrior exploded into violence.

Jarrett stood up as Keturah and Lahairoi walked toward him. It was time to go to the arena in Sidonni, time to face another swordsman, time to kill or be killed.

A soul-shattering weariness engulfed him.

He was tired of fighting, sick of the smell of blood and death, of the taste of fear on his tongue. A heavy lassitude settled over him as he stared at the heavy chain on his ankle. It would be so easy to escape it all. So easy. He had only to let his guard down in the arena to end it all.

But then he saw Leyla watching him, her silver hair shimmering in the sunlight, her blue eyes warm with love and encouragement, and he knew he could not leave her to face the flesh peddlers alone. While he lived, she was accorded a degree of respect. If anything happened to him, she would be at their mercy, to be used and abused and finally sold into a life even more degrading than the one he now lived. He would find no peace in the grave knowing that he had left her in the hands of Keturah and his flesh peddlers.

He stood passive as Lahairoi shackled his hands behind his back, then removed the chain from his ankle. He thought of Keturah, of the mask, of being enslaved, letting his hatred grow and spread within him until it threatened to choke him.

One way or another, today would be his last fight.

Leyla stood in the shade of the tunnel, her eyes riveted on Jarrett. He stood in the middle of the arena, sword in hand, facing his opponent, a dark-skinned man whose body was covered with grotesque tattoos in the manner of the Jovites. A cold winter sun bathed the combatants in a blaze of light, shining off the long blades.

She shivered as she watched the two men circle slowly back and forth, her heart pounding with dread as she went over the plan Jarrett had laid before her on their way to the arena.

They were in a small arena in a small town. They would never have a better chance, Jarrett had said. Several of Keturah's men had gone ahead to the next town to scout around. It was now or never, Jarrett had told her, and she had heard the underlying note of desperation in his voice, seen it in the depths of his green eyes.

She glanced at Tor, who stood a little behind her. *Will it work? Can it possibly work?*

She wanted assurance, but he only shrugged. He had tried to see into the future, but he saw only vague shadows and an endless darkness that left him with a feeling of great unease. He had tried to convince Jarrett to postpone his escape, but to no avail. In truth, Tor could not fault the man for his impatience. He was as weary of captivity as was Jarrett.

The harsh ring of metal striking metal drew Leyla's attention and she turned her gaze back to the arena. The fight had begun.

Jarrett faced his opponent, all his energy,

all his thoughts, focused on the other man. For this brief period of time, nothing else existed, not Leyla, not Keturah, not Greyebridge. There was only the dark-skinned man weaving gracefully before him, his dark eyes narrowed in concentration as he adroitly parried Jarrett's thrusts.

The man was a master swordsman and Jarrett knew he would have to be on guard every moment just to survive, and now his whole world centered on the other man. Time lost all meaning and he saw only the other man, heard only the sharp chime of steel striking steel and the labored rasp of his own breath. Only vaguely was he aware of the cheers of the crowd, of the dust that filled his nostrils, of the smell of sweat and blood. His sweat. His blood.

He winced as the dark-skinned man's blade slipped under his guard and pierced his left side. Oblivious to the pain, Jarrett took a step back, feinted to the left, and brought his sword up in a smooth swift motion, sinking the blade to the hilt in the chest of the tattooed man.

For a long moment, there was only silence. The dark-skinned man remained on his feet, his eyes clouding with pain and shock as he stared at the blade embedded in his flesh. The sword slipped out of his hand.

Jarrett swallowed hard and then, with a jerk, he withdrew his blade. The life went out of the wounded man's eyes and he sank slowly to the ground, a bright splash of blood staining his chest.

And now the crowd was on its feet, cheering for Dumah, the Masked Swordsman of Keturah.

As if acknowledging the crowd, Jarrett moved slowly toward the tunnel where Leyla waited. He turned as the Master of the Arena rode toward him to collect his sword.

Covered with sweat and blood, his heart pounding, Jarrett waited for the man to close the distance between them. And then the Master of the Arena was leaning toward him, his gloved hand outstretched to receive Jarrett's sword.

With a wild cry, Jarrett drove his sword straight up into the man's throat; then, grabbing the man by the arm, he pulled him out of the saddle, grabbed the man's sword, and swung onto the horse's back.

Stunned by the unexpected violence, the crowd fell silent, and then roared to life, some screaming for Jarrett's blood, others urging him on.

Ripping off the mask, he rode toward the tunnel, tossing one of the swords to Tor. Leaning over his horse's neck, he caught Leyla around the waist and dropped her, none too gently, across the horse's withers. Not stopping to see if Tor followed, Jarrett rode out of the tunnel, his heels drumming against the horse's flanks.

Outside the arena, he reined the horse to the left, heading out of the village toward the low foothills beyond. He glanced over his shoulder only once. Tor was behind him, mounted on Keturah's big black stallion.

Jarrett pushed his mount steadily onward. The wind stung his wounds and whipped his hair into his face, but he rode on, ignoring the blood that welled from the deep gash in his left side and dripped onto Leyla's back. More blood welled from a cut in his right thigh. He knew she must be uncomfortable, riding belly down over the horse's withers, but he dared not stop to let her right herself.

They rode hard for over an hour before Jarrett drew his winded mount to a halt. Taking Leyla by the arm, he lowered her to the ground, then slid down beside her. A moment later, Tor rode up.

A pithy oath escaped Jarrett's lips as he glanced up at the Maje. Tor's face was as white as his hair, and his eyes were glazed with pain. His shirt, once a pale green, was wet with blood.

"We made it," Tor murmured, and toppled from the saddle.

Leyla ran to him. Kneeling at his side, she brushed a lock of hair from his face. "Tor? Tor, can thee hear me?"

A faint smile lifted the corner of his mouth. "I hear thee."

Leyla sent a pleading glance at Jarrett. "Do something!"

Slowly, Jarrett shook his head. Tor had sustained a wicked sword wound deep into his belly. There was nothing to be done.

Hand pressed over the bleeding gash in his side, Jarrett sank to his knees on the other side of the Maje. "You fought well," he said.

Tor smiled weakly. "Keturah . . . will not . . . follow you."

Jarrett nodded, his heart filled with remorse. The Maje, born to heal, had sacrificed his own life, and taken the life of another, to save his and there was nothing Jarrett could do for him save sit and watch him die.

Leyla ripped a strip of cloth from the hem of her skirt and placed it over the horrible wound in Tor's abdomen, watching in horror as the cloth quickly turned from white to red. She placed her hand over the gaping wound, tears of despair washing down her cheeks as she lamented her helplessness.

With an effort, Tor placed his hand over hers. "I would . . . have . . . cherished thee . . . always . . . always . . . loved thee."

"I know." A fresh wave of tears flooded her eyes. "I know."

Tor's gaze sought Jarrett's. "Take care . . . of her."

"I will."

Tor's pain-glazed eyes moved over Jarrett.

"Thee . . . is wounded."

"I'll be all right."

"Thee cannot . . . protect her . . . if thee . . . is dead." Summoning every ounce of strength he possessed, Tor lifted his hand and placed it over the deep gash in Jarrett's left side. "Leyla . . . help me."

Wracked with silent sobs, she placed her hand over Tor's, holding it in place, feeling the power of his gift pulse sure and strong through his fingertips. A low groan rumbled from deep in his throat as he absorbed Jarrett's suffering into his own pain-wracked body.

Jarrett's eyes burned with unshed tears as he felt the rejuvenating heat of the Maje's touch flow into him.

"I am . . . afraid . . . I lack the strength . . . to heal . . . the others. . . ."

A low gurgle rattled in Tor's throat, a soft sigh escaped his lips, his hand went suddenly cold, and Jarrett knew the life had gone out of the Maje.

"No!" Leyla's anguished gaze met Jarrett's across Tor's body. Lifting Tor's hand to her breast, she held it tight, as if she could will her life force into him. "No, please, no."

"Leyla, I'm sorry."

"It's all my fault." She kissed the back of Tor's hand, then laid it across his chest. "All my fault. If he had not come after me, he would be alive now."

"Leyla . . ."

She buried her face in her hands, rocking back and forth, her tortured sobs terrible to hear.

Rising, Jarrett went to her. Gathering her in his arms, he held her close, his hand stroking her hair as he murmured soft words of comfort, his own guilt like a knife in his heart. He had taken Leyla from the Maje, taught Tor to fight, to kill, and now Tor was dead. If it was anyone's fault, it was his, not Leyla's.

But there was no time for regret now, no time to mourn. Keturah might be dead, but there was always a chance that his men, angered by the death of their leader, might come after them.

"Leyla, we have to go."

"No, I cannot leave him."

"Leyla . . ."

"No!" She twisted out of his embrace, her eyes wild with grief, and then she gasped. Tor had healed the worst of Jarrett's wounds, but a dozen other cuts and gashes marred his flesh, the worst of which was the wound in his thigh. Lifting her skirt, she unfastened her petticoat and stepped out of it.

"What are you doing?" he asked, thinking she meant to use her undergarment as Tor's shroud.

"Thee is bleeding."

Jarrett glanced down at his thigh. "We've got to get out of here before Keturah's men decide to come looking for us."

"At least let me bandage it."

She felt his impatience, his need to be moving, as she bandaged the wound.

She didn't argue as Jarrett lifted her onto the black's back. She saw him grimace as he concealed Tor's body in a thicket of tangled brush and vines before mounting his own horse. And then they were riding north, toward the Cyrus River, toward home.

But Leyla, casting a last glance at Tor's bloodstained body, knew that Majeulla would never be the same.

Chapter Twenty-eight

They rode for hours, not stopping until well after dark. Leyla was exhausted when Jarrett helped her from her horse, but the touch of his hand drove all thought of sleep from her mind. He was burning with fever.

He swayed unsteadily on his feet as she unsaddled the horses, then gathered an armful of leaves and covered it with one of the horse blankets.

He stretched out on the makeshift bed without argument, his eyelids fluttering down. For a moment, she hovered over him. They had no food, no water, no shelter. What was she to do?

Standing there, she heard the faint whisper of purling water. Following the sound, she discovered a small stream at the foot of a gentle slope. Tearing the hem from her skirt, she dipped it in the cold water, then hurried back to Jarrett's side and bathed his face and neck with the cool cloth.

She washed the wound in his thigh as best she could, wrapped it in a strip of clean cloth, then sponged the dried blood from the numerous cuts on his chest. Time and again, she made the trip to the stream, soaking the cloth, drawing it over Jarrett's chest and arms and legs, praying that he wouldn't die, that the fever would go down. She wished fleetingly that Tor had lived long enough to heal all Jarrett's wounds, then felt a deep sense of guilt for even thinking such a thing.

She wept softly for Tor's death, for the creeping fear that was stealing over her as the night deepened around her. In the distance, she heard the howl of a black-furred wolf, the answering cry of its mate. A great gray owl swept past her head, searching for prey. Nearby, she heard the reassuring snuffle of the horses.

She stayed at Jarrett's side all through the long, cold night, gathering him into her arms when he shivered with a chill, wiping his body with cool cloths when the fever raged through him.

She could feel him drifting away from her and she began to talk to him, begging him not to leave her.

"A child, Jarrett, we are to have a child. Do not leave me. Please do not leave me."

Towards dawn, she drew the other horse blanket over both of them and fell into a restless sleep.

He was smothering, drowning in heat instead of the dark water of the pool. It took him a moment to realize he wasn't dreaming.

He opened his eyes to find he wasn't smothering at all. The heaviness across his face wasn't the hated mask, but the silky softness of Leyla's hair. She was lying on her stomach, one arm flung across his belly, her head nestled in the hollow of his shoulder.

He brushed her hair from his face, then groaned softly as he tried to sit up.

Leyla woke instantly, her expression one of alarm. "What is wrong?"

"Nothing," he said, then frowned. "Are you all right?"

"Of course. Why?"

"Last night, I seem to remember hearing your voice calling to me."

"Yes."

"You mentioned a child."

"Yes."

A child. He'd hoped it had all been a dream.

"Thee is not pleased?"

Pleased was hardly the word, he thought ruefully. He was wounded, on the run. His silence brought a look of immeasurable sadness to her face.

"Beloved." He took her hands in his, wishing he could give her the kind of life she deserved. "I just wish the timing was better."

"Babies rarely consider such things."

The hurt in her voice pierced him to the quick.

"We will speak of it later." She lifted a

hand to his brow, and frowned. "Thee is still warm."

"I'm fine. A little sore, that's all."

She didn't believe him. She examined his thigh, relieved that there were no ugly red streaks spreading from the wound. She ran her hands lightly over his chest, making small sounds of distress as she examined the half-dozen minor cuts that criss-crossed his torso.

"I'm fine," he said again. In truth, he was feeling more than a little light-headed, but he attributed it to the hunger that was making itself known. "We need to go."

She didn't argue. Jarrett looked pale, his skin was damp, his eyes had the look of someone who was ill. The sooner they got to Majeulla, the better.

She watched Jarrett carefully as he saddled their horses. Though he tried to hide it, she saw the way he winced when he lifted the saddles in place, saw the fine sheen of sweat that broke out on his brow as he insisted on lifting her onto the stallion's back. He paused a moment, his head pressed against the horse's neck, before he mounted his own horse.

Needing food, they stopped at the first village they came to. Jarrett bartered Tor's sword for food and ale, as well as a waterskin, eating utensils, and a warm cloak for Leyla. Then they were riding again, nibbling on fresh black bread and cheese as they went.

They rode all that day and into the night, stopping only to rest the horses. Jarrett's fever rose that night and Leyla held him close, worried that his wounds were becoming infected, fearing he might die before they reached Majeulla.

He seemed better in the morning and they rode as before, eating in the saddle, stopping only long enough to let the horses rest.

That evening, they crossed the Cyrus River and bedded down in the foothills of the Mountains of the Blue Mist.

After making Jarrett comfortable, Leyla searched the hillside, looking for the tiny orange berries of the Boarsh plant. Its root, when ground to pulp and boiled with water, was effective against fever.

Jarrett eyed the pewter cup suspiciously. "What is it?"

"Drink it while it is hot," she exhorted. "It will make thee feel better."

Without further argument, he took a drink, shuddering as the bitter brew slid down his throat. "Tastes awful," he muttered, but she lifted the cup to his lips, urging him to drink the rest.

A sudden lethargy settled over him almost immediately. He gazed up at her through heavy-lidded eyes. "Have you poisoned me?"

"No. 'Tis only to help thee sleep. Thee will feel better when thee wakes, I promise."

"Hold me."

A rush of tenderness flooded Leyla's heart as she wrapped Jarrett in her embrace. She caressed his cheek, running her fingertips over the black beard that roughened his jaw and shaded his upper lip.

"I'm happy about the baby," he murmured, his eyelids fluttering down. "Truly, I am. I just wish . . ."

"I know. Sleep well, my Lord Pirate." She bent to kiss his cheek and then, with a sigh, she stretched out beside him, covering them both with her cloak.

Leyla woke to find Jarrett much improved in the morning. A familiar light gleamed in his eyes as he propped himself on one elbow and gazed down at her.

"Good morrow, wife."

"Good morrow, husband. Did thee sleep well?"

"Very well." His gaze moved over her face in a slow glance that made her blood heat, and then he tossed the cloak aside, a question in his eyes.

"Now, my Lord Jarrett?" she asked, her voice husky.

"Will it harm the babe?"

"No, but thee has been ill."

"Thee can make me well." His hand slid over her breast and down one thigh.

"Thee thinks so?"

"I know so."

Cupping his face in her hands, she drew him down toward her, pressing her lips gently to his. "Is that better?"

"Oh, yes," Jarrett murmured.

"And this?" She kissed him again, longer this time, a little cry of pleasure sounding in the back of her throat as he tucked her beneath him.

Jarrett's lips grazed her cheek, the length of her neck. "More."

"Anything to aid thy healing, my Lord Jarrett," she replied, and kissed him again, and again, their breath mingling as their hearts began to beat in the sweet rhythm of love.

Slowly, oh, so gently, he made love to her there, with the lacy branches of the trees forming a canopy above and the earthy scent of fallen leaves surrounding them.

She threaded her fingers through the ebony silk of his hair, loving the feel of it in her hands. His beard-roughened jaw abraded the tender skin of her breasts, his tongue trailed fire wherever it roamed. Her hands moved over his shoulders and back, restlessly, drawing him close, closer. His name spilled from her lips as she arched to meet him, her body welcoming him home, filling her, making her complete as only he could.

Later, he sat beside her, his hand on her belly as he tried to imagine his child growing within her body.

"It will be all right," she murmured,

placing her hand over his. "Truly."

And when she looked at him like that, how could he doubt it?

It was near dusk when they passed through Dragora's cave. Leyla felt her heart begin to pound with trepidation as they rode up the narrow path to the Fortress. Her parents loved her, she had no doubt of that. But would she still be welcome at the stronghold? Would her father forgive her for defying him?

With each passing moment, her uneasiness grew. What if her father refused to receive Jarrett?

Sudaan was waiting for them when they rode up to the front door. Dismounting, Leyla walked toward her father, waiting, hoping, for some sign of welcome.

Jarrett watched as father and daughter gazed deeply into each other's eyes. After a long moment, Sudaan held out his arms and Leyla embraced her father.

"Leyla." Sudaan hugged her, his arms holding her tight. "Welcome home, child."

"Father."

Looking over Leyla's head, Sudaan leveled a hard gaze at Jarrett. "I had not thought to see thee again."

Jarrett shrugged. "I will leave if you wish."

Sudaan shook his head. His daughter had made her choice, and he had made his. "Are thee well, daughter?" he asked, his gaze searching her face.

"Yes."

"Have thy feelings for me changed?"

Leyla shook her head.

"I warned thee of the consequences should thee defy my wishes," Sudaan said quietly. "Thee must know I took no pleasure in recanting thy powers, nor do I find satisfaction in it now."

"I understand, Father. Thee did as thee felt was best, as I did."

"I would hear thy forgiveness from thy lips," Sudaan said.

"I forgive thee. Let us speak of it no more."

Sudaan nodded, the tension draining out of him as her words poured over him.

Releasing Leyla, he took her by the hand and entered the Fortress. "Thy mother awaits thee."

Feeling about as welcome as a heathen in a nunnery, Jarrett dismounted and followed Sudaan and Leyla to their apartments.

Vestri was waiting for them. She hurried forward, arms outstretched, to enfold Leyla in a warm embrace. "I've missed thee, my child."

"I've missed thee." Leyla placed her head on her mother's shoulder, basking in her nearness. "Tor is dead."

"We know. It was not thy fault." Vestri drew back, her gaze meeting Leyla's. "We felt thy pain, child, thy grief. It was not thy fault."

"What of his parents?"

"They have gone to the Summit to mourn his loss."

Leyla felt her father's gaze. Lifting her head, she saw him nod, confirming that he held her guiltless in Tor's death, and she felt the burden of her remorse ease just a little.

Stepping away from her mother, Leyla went to Jarrett and took his hand in hers.

Leyla's parents exchanged glances and Jarrett wished that, just this once, he had the Maje's ability to probe minds.

"Thy husband is welcome here," Sudaan said after a lengthy silence. "We trust he will abide by our laws while thou art here."

Sudaan nodded at the sword sheathed at Jarrett's side. "Thee will have no need of a weapon."

"I understand."

"Will thee stay here, with us?" Sudaan asked, speaking to Leyla.

A faint flush rose in her cheeks. "I think not."

Sudaan nodded. "Thee may dwell in the apartments in the west wing." His gaze skimmed over Jarrett, then settled on Leyla. "Will thee join us for dinner?"

Leyla looked at Jarrett, awaiting his decision. "It's up to you," he said, though he really wasn't up to spending the evening with her parents.

"Yes," Leyla said, smiling. She hugged her father and mother again, then took Jarrett by the hand and led him out of the room toward the west wing.

"I don't think your parents are very happy with your choice of a husband," he remarked dryly.

"They wished me to marry within my own clan," Leyla remarked, "and they were very fond of Tor." She reached up to caress his cheek. "They will come to love thee, in time."

"And if they don't?"

"Then I will love thee for them as well as for myself."

Jarrett lay back, his long body relaxing in a tub filled with fragrant suds while Leyla washed his shoulders and back. He obligingly lifted first one arm and then the other as she moved around beside him, his eyes closing as he savored her touch.

She paused when she reached his chest, her fingertips tracing the half-healed lacerations.

"I'm all right," he murmured reassuringly.

He felt a sudden heat that had nothing to do with the temperature of the water as she began to wash his left leg, her hand drifting slowly upward along his thigh, tantalizing him with her touch.

Leyla grinned as, slowly and deliberately, she drew the cloth over Jarrett's belly. A low groan erupted from his throat as she began to wash his other leg.

She squealed in mock terror when he grabbed her and pulled her into the tub, dress and all. She opened her mouth to berate him but his lips closed over hers, effectively silencing her protests. For a moment, as he quickly divested her of her garments, she wondered if he had grown another pair of hands, and then she forgot everything as he drew her against him, his skin feeling soft and silky in the scented water.

She gazed into his eyes, pleased by the desire she saw there. His voice was low and husky as he whispered that he loved her. She watched his hands trace meaningless patterns over her breasts, loving the bronze of his skin against the paleness of her own, the heat of his touch.

A familiar warmth sparked to life deep within her, rising upward and outward, until it engulfed her. She let her hands roam over him, a great surge of tenderness filling her heart, and with that tenderness came the welcome knowledge that he was hers, only hers, as she was his.

With a great splash, he rolled on top of her, his mouth claiming hers in a searing kiss as his body meshed with hers, uniting them body and soul.

When they woke in the morning, winter

had come to the Mountains of the Blue Mist. A fine layer of azure-colored snow covered the hillsides and clung to the trees.

Jarrett stared out the window, fascinated by the faint blue glow that seemed to envelop everything in sight.

He smiled as Leyla came up behind him, her arms wrapping around his waist, her breasts warm against his back.

"Does thee like it?"

Jarrett laid his hand over her arm and gave it a squeeze. "It's beautiful."

They spent the day in their room, loving and sleeping and loving again. At dusk, they bundled up in heavy clothes and boots and gloves and went for a walk in the moonlight.

Hand in hand, they strolled along a narrow path that had been brushed clean of snow.

"Thee is well?" Leyla asked.

"I'm fine."

"My father could heal thy wounds."

"I'm all right. Stop worrying about me."

"It is a wife's place to worry about her husband. I know thy wounds are not serious, but they still pain thee. And there will be scars."

Jarrett shook his head. The last thing he wanted was to be indebted to Leyla's father. The cuts were healing, and they didn't hurt that much. And if they left a few scars, well . . .

"Does that bother you?" he asked. "My

being scarred, I mean?"

Leyla grinned up at him. "What thee really wants to know is if I will still find thee desirable."

Jarrett frowned at her. "You've been probing my mind again," he accused.

"I am sorry."

"No, you're not."

"I will always find thee desirable," Leyla said, answering his unspoken question. She pressed his hand to her stomach. "Will thee still find me desirable when I am misshapen with our babe?"

"Always, beloved. In the bloom of youth, or lined with the passage of many years, fat or lean, you will ever be the desire of my heart." He drew her into the circle of his arms and kissed her, thinking that eight months in the Pavilion had been a small price to pay for the woman in his arms.

The days passed by. On clear afternoons, they walked in the snow, marveling at the beauty of the winter-kissed landscape, laughing at the antics of the snow rabbits. Evenings, they made slow, sweet love before a roaring fire, the heat of the flames as nothing compared to the heat that flared between them.

When the weather was harsh, they sometimes spent afternoons with Vestri and Sudaan. Jarrett was never at ease with Leyla's parents. He felt their silent disapproval, knew they lamented the fact that their only child had defied their wishes and married an outsider.

But even her parents' silent disaffection could not mar his delight in Leyla, his joy at being with her. Here, safe in the mountains of her homeland, he could sleep without fear. No nightmares came to haunt his sleep. He had no fear of being captured and returned to the Pavilion. He had no need for weapons, no need to shed blood or take a life. Here, in the stronghold of the Maje, he was free.

Chapter Twenty-nine

The days and weeks slipped past, peaceful as a sigh. Gradually, Leyla's parents learned to accept their new son-in-law, and Jarrett found much to like and respect about Sudaan and Vestri.

As their acceptance of each other increased, they began to spend more and more evenings together, sometimes sitting before the fire playing games that challenged their mental agility, sometimes reading, often talking of the future, of the baby that would be born in the summer.

Jarrett could not help thinking that the knowledge that he was the father of their grandchild had helped to alleviate their dislike.

It was on one such evening, while Jarrett and Sudaan were hunched over a chessboard, that Tor's parents came to call.

Sudaan introduced them as Bree and Sturgid. They were handsome people, both tall and slender, with white hair and brown eyes. They were both dressed in long black mourning robes.

Jarrett nodded, bowing formally to Bree,

shaking Sturgid's hand. He knew a moment of deep discomfort as they studied him, and he wondered how much they knew of their son's death, and if they blamed him for it.

"Please," Vestri said, "won't thee be seated?"

Bree nodded, moving with regal grace as she crossed the floor and sat down on one of the cushions before the fire. Her husband sat beside her, his hand grasping hers.

Sturgid lifted his gaze to Jarrett's face. "We would hear of our son's death."

Haltingly, Jarrett told of their capture by the flesh peddlers, of how they had escaped, how he had been wounded.

"Tor was grievously injured," Jarrett said. "With his last breath, he healed my wounds. It is because of him that I am alive now. He fought bravely."

"He fought bravely . . ." Bree repeated his words, her voice filled with anguish. "I cannot believe that my son was responsible for bloodshed, that he died in violence." She gazed into her husband's eyes, her face as pale as her hair. "What of his soul, my husband? Has it been lost forever?"

"He also saved a life," Sturgid replied quietly. "Surely the Creators will take that into account."

Jarrett glanced at Leyla and saw that tears were coursing silently down her cheeks.

"Where did he learn to fight?" Bree asked,

her voice thick with tears. "Who would have taught him such a despicable thing?"

Taking a deep breath, Jarrett stood up. "I taught him."

"How could thee do such a vile thing?" Bree exclaimed. "How could thee jeopardize his immortal soul?"

"I didn't know it was considered a sin of such magnitude. He never mentioned it."

Sturgid sent Leyla a sharp glance. "Did thee remain silent, as well?"

Leyla nodded. At the time, fighting had seemed to be the only answer, the only road to survival. She had not taken time to think of the consequences. She'd been too worried about Jarrett's life to think of anything else. She knew now that she'd done a terrible thing. Tor had died with blood on his hands.

"I am sorry," she murmured. "I shall pray this night for his soul."

"And I shall pray for thine," Bree replied. "I hope the Creators can forgive thee for what thee has done, for I know I never shall."

Sturgid stood up then. Offering Bree his hand, he helped her to her feet. They bowed to Sudaan and Vestri, and then left the apartment.

A heavy stillness hung in the air as Sudaan and Vestri exchanged glances.

Jarrett went to stand beside Leyla, offering her the strength of his nearness.

"Let us go to chapel," Vestri said at last.

It was not a suggestion, not the way she said it.

Jarrett took Leyla's hand, and they followed her parents down the staircase to the candlelit chapel.

It was like nothing Jarrett had ever seen before. An enormous altar covered with a red cloth dominated the room. A giant sun-burst hung suspended from the vaulted ceiling; silver moons and bright stars were painted on the east wall. The west wall showed a verdant garden abloom with a riotous mass of flowers. A pair of unicorns stood in the midst of the foliage, their golden horns catching the light of the sun.

Vestri, Sudaan and Leyla knelt at the altar, their heads bowed.

Jarrett stood behind them, listening to their prayers, which were spoken in a language he did not understand. So much had happened between himself and Leyla in such a short time, he had never given any thought to her religion, or to the fact that it was vastly different from his own.

A Gweneth warrior hoped to die in battle, with the blood of his enemies on his hands and a war cry on his lips. He believed in one God, the All Father, who ruled the heavens above and the earth below. The All Father was a warrior being who was endowed with infinite wisdom and strength, and who admired those qualities in His worshippers.

It seemed the gods of the Maje did not condone violence of any kind, not even in self-defense. With that knowledge, Jarrett came to realize what a remarkable sacrifice Tor had made in his behalf.

Leyla's eyes were red with tears when she rose from the altar. Here, in the solitude of the chapel, the awful significance of the manner of Tor's death had made itself known. Because of her, because she had betrayed him, he had left their homeland, his inner peace shattered by jealousy. He had learned to fight, he had learned to kill. And in killing, had found his own death. Blood for blood. According to their beliefs, one who died with blood on his hands was denied entrance to the Afterlife and was doomed to wander through eternity forever.

Heartsick, she bade her parents good sleep, then hurried to Jarrett's side, in need of his touch, his strength, his wisdom.

Wordlessly, he put his arm around her and led her back to their apartments. When they arrived, he closed the door, shutting out the rest of the world.

"Why did I not stop him?" Leyla asked, her voice thick with self-condemnation. "Why did I not remind him that it was forbidden for him to fight?"

"There was nothing you could have done," Jarrett replied quietly. "He would only have died that much sooner."

"No! I remained silent because of thee, because I could not bear to lose thee!"

"Leyla . . ."

Anguished tears welled in her eyes and slid down her cheeks. "I let my love for thee blind me to everything else, and now Tor is dead and his soul is forever lost in darkness."

"What do you want me to do?"

"Do? There is nothing to be done. I betrayed Tor and everything he believed in. Everything I once believed in."

"Leyla." He tried to take her in his arms, wanting to comfort her, but she pushed him away. "No, do not touch me."

"Damne, Leyla, Tor was a grown man! He knew what he was doing. You can't blame yourself for what happened."

But she wasn't listening. Wracked by grief and guilt, she curled up on the bed and wept bitter tears. She had let her love for an outsider blind her to everything she was, everything she believed in.

Jarrett watched her sob for several minutes and then, feeling as though his heart were being torn to shreds, he left the room.

Leyla kept to their apartments the next day, refusing to eat, refusing to see anyone.

Wrapped in a thick fur cloak, Jarrett prowled the grounds. He would not beg for her attention. If she wanted to be alone, so be it. But, deep inside, he hurt for her, for the awful doubts and recriminations that Tor's parents had planted in her soul.

And when another day passed, and another, he began to be concerned for her health, and for that of their child.

On the morning of the fourth day, he swallowed his foolish pride and went to her. She looked as pale as death. Her eyes had lost their warmth, her hands were cold.

"Leyla. You've got to eat something, for the child's sake if not your own."

"I will," she said, but she made no move toward the bowl of soup beside her.

He lifted the spoon and held it to her mouth. "Eat, beloved."

She shook her head, and he put the spoon down.

"Leyla, what can I do? Do you want me to leave?" It would kill him to leave her, he thought, but he would do it, and gladly, just to see her smile again.

"Leave?"

"Will it make you happy if I go away? I never meant to hurt you. Please tell me what to do."

"It doesn't matter. Nothing matters. I can't sleep. I can't eat. I keep seeing Tor lying in a pool of blood. Sometimes I think I hear him calling to me, begging me to put his soul at rest."

"How can you do that?"

"I can't!" she sobbed. "No one can. Oh, Jarrett, what am I to do?"

She let him hold her then, and he cradled her in his arms, stroking her hair as he held her close. He could not bear to see her in such pain, to know she was hurting and there was nothing he could do to help. No pain of the Games, no torture he had ever endured, had been as bad as this.

He held her until she fell asleep in his arms, and then he went in search of Tor's father.

Chapter Thirty

Sturgid stared at Jarrett with obvious dislike. "Why has thee come here?"

"Because of Leyla. She's blaming herself for Tor's death."

Sturgid's gaze slid away, and then returned to Jarrett. "I had not meant to cast blame on her."

"If you need someone to blame, blame me. I'm the one who took Leyla away from him. I'm the one who taught Tor to fight. If it hadn't been for me, he'd be alive now. I accept the responsibility for his death."

"I see."

"I want you and your wife to go to Leyla and tell her it wasn't her fault."

Sturgid shook his head. "Bree will never . . ."

"I'm not asking you to do this," Jarrett interrupted. "I'm telling you."

"Thee is threatening me?"

"No. I'm begging you." Jarrett's gaze slid over Sturgid's face in a long, assessing glance. "Or is it revenge you want? Perhaps, for all your pitiful mouthings of peace and love, you will not rest until Leyla's guilt makes her ill enough to lose the child. A life for a life. Is that what you want? Then take mine."

Sturgid's face was suddenly drained of color. He took a step backward, as if to distance himself from Jarrett's accusation, and then he sat down heavily, covering his face with his hands.

"Tor was our only son. Bree almost died giving him life. She has doted on him, and loved him, perhaps more than is wise. And I . . . Sometimes it is hard to ignore one's dark side, but I will speak to Bree, I swear it. I will remind her of how much our son loved Leyla. Tor would not wish harm to befall her, or her child." Sturgid looked up. "Nor would he wish harm to befall the man for whom he sacrificed his life."

Jarrett felt hope and relief course through him at the other man's words. "Thank you."

"Forgive us. We meant thee no harm."

"There's nothing to forgive."

Jarrett extended his hand and Sturgid took it.

"May all that is good go with thee."

"And with thee," Jarrett replied.

Leyla was still asleep when he returned to their apartments. He sat beside her on the bed, hurting because she hurt, wondering if that was what it was like to be a Maje, to feel another's pain so deeply that it became your own.

Carefully, so as not to awaken her, he lifted a lock of her hair, marveling at its beauty. It was like soft silk in his hands, so fine and pliable.

He lost track of the time as he sat there, his thoughts drifting. He wondered if his mother was still alive, if she was well, if Rorke had returned to Gweneth. Rorke. The man must be mad if he thought he could dispose of his wife and Tyrell and take the throne.

Leyla stirred, drawing his attention. Glancing down, he saw that she was awake. Her face was too pale for his liking. There were dark shadows under her eyes, eyes that were dull and filled with unhappiness.

He poured her a glass of water from the crystal pitcher beside the bed. She tried to push it away, but he held it to her lips until she took a few swallows.

"Leyla?"

"I'm sorry, my Lord Jarrett."

"Sorry?"

"I should not have pushed thee away. Forgive me."

"My arms ache for thee," he said, using her quaint speech. "My heart grieves for thy pain. Help me to help thee."

Two bright tears surfaced in her eyes. "Hold me then, for the night is coming, and I fear the darkness."

Jarrett swept her into his arms and cradled

her against his chest, overcome with the urge to protect her, to shield her from all hurt and harm.

"Do not be afraid, beloved," he murmured into the wealth of her hair. "No one will harm thee while I am here with thee."

She burrowed into his arms, as if seeking his strength. "Thee cannot protect me from that which I fear."

"I don't understand."

"I'm afraid Tor's shade will come to haunt me, that he will wish to torment me for what I've done."

Ghosts? He hadn't known the Maje believed in ghosts.

He was wondering what he could possibly say to calm her fears when there was a knock at the door.

He pressed a lever beside the bed, and the door swung open.

Leyla drew back when she saw Tor's parents standing in the doorway.

"Enter, please," Jarrett said. He slid Leyla onto the bed and stood up. "Welcome."

Sturgid nodded and clasped Jarrett's hand. Bree stood silent.

"Will you sit?" Jarrett asked.

Sturgid shook his head. "Bree wishes to speak to Leyla, in private."

Jarrett hesitated a moment, then nodded. Going to Leyla's side, he took her hand in his and gave it a squeeze. "I won't be gone long," he promised.

She looked up at him as if he were about to throw her into a bottomless pit.

"It will be all right, beloved," he murmured. "Trust me." He nodded in Bree's direction, then followed Sturgid out of the room, closing the door behind him.

The next hour passed slowly. When Sturgid suggested they go into the main salon, Jarrett agreed because he didn't know what else to do. Sturgid suggested a game of Balonchar, a dice game similar to nine points, but Jarrett couldn't concentrate and in the end, the two men sat staring out into the gathering twilight.

After what seemed like an eternity, Bree joined them. She looked at Jarrett, her expression solemn, and he knew she would never approve of him, or forgive him for his part in her son's death.

"I have made my peace with Leyla," she said, her tone coldly formal. "I now ask thee to forgive me, as well. I behaved badly and for that, I apologize."

"I accept your apology," Jarrett replied, equally formal, "in the spirit in which it is given."

Bree nodded her head and turned away.

Sturgid let out a heavy sigh. His wife was a stubborn woman, but she had a good heart, and he trusted that she had put Leyla's guilt to rest. They had not been there at the time of Tor's death. They would never know his last thoughts. Jarrett had said their son died well. It was all the comfort they would ever have.

"Good sleep, my Lord Jarrett," Sturgid said.

"And to you," Jarrett replied.

Before going upstairs, Jarrett went into the common kitchen and fixed Leyla a cup of green herb tea and a bowl of broth, praying that she would take the nourishment he offered. If she refused, he would have to force her to eat before she did serious harm to herself and the child.

He drew in a deep breath and let it out in a long sigh before he opened the door.

She was sitting up in bed. She was still pale, and he could see she had been crying, but her eyes had lost their haunted look.

"I brought thee something to eat," he said, stepping into the room and closing the door behind him.

"I thank thee."

"Is everything all right?"

"Yes."

He put the tray on the bedside table, then sat down beside her. "What happened?"

"I would rather not speak of it."

"Very well."

"Do not be offended, my Lord." She placed her hand over his. "Bree told me her thoughts, and I told her mine, and we wept together for a life that was too soon over. Much of what passed between us was not spoken."

"I am only glad that you're feeling better. Will you eat now?"

Leyla nodded and he sat beside her while she ate, wondering what had been said, and unsaid.

The rest of the winter passed uneventfully. Their mountain home was beautiful. Covered in a fine layer of pale blue snow, it took on a fairy tale kind of beauty he had never dreamed of.

The Maje passed their days reading or playing complicated games of skill that required great mental concentration. They spent long hours in quiet meditation.

Jarrett learned to appreciate their peaceful life even as he came to realize that he would go slowly insane if he had to spent much more time in their company.

As the last days of winter passed into spring, he grew increasingly restless and spent a great deal of time outside, taking long hikes, sometimes running for miles for the sheer joy of it. He missed the physical exertion that came from hard work. He missed having fresh meat on the table. Most of all, he missed Gweneth. He had been born there; the land was as much a part of him as his hands and feet. He needed to go home, to see to the affairs of the castle. More important, he needed to find out if his mother still lived.

His interlude on the Mountains of the Blue Mist was over. All he needed now was the courage to tell Leyla they were leaving.

The morning after he made his decision to leave, Leyla roused him from bed before dawn. Urging him to dress warmly and quickly, she hurried him out of the fortress. Taking him by the hand, she led him to the small green valley she had showed him on his first visit to Majeulla.

The sky was glowing when they reached the valley. The stream was high, the water faintly tinged with blue from the run-off in the mountains.

As they made their way across the verdant grass, the sun rose over the mountains, bathing the valley in a soft golden light even as it splashed the sky with bright hues of orange and crimson.

"Look," Leyla whispered. "There."

Jarrett followed her gaze, felt his breath catch in his throat as he saw a unicorn emerge from a leafy thicket. Its golden horn caught the rays of the sun as it lowered its head to drink. A moment later, a foal joined its dam.

Speechless, Jarrett watched the two animals nuzzle each other. The dam left the stream and moved beneath a giant fern to graze on the new grass while the foal nursed.

He smiled at Leyla as he took her hand in his and gave it a squeeze. Side by side, they stood there, mesmerized by the incomparable beauty of the unicorns, knowing they were sharing a moment that few were privileged to see.

It would be hard to leave this place now, Jarrett thought. There was something about the unicorns that made him want to stay, to always be a part of the magical world in which they lived. Looking at their sleek white coats, knowing he was seeing a myth come to life, made him believe that anything was possible. And even as he realized that he would not be happy here even if he could watch the unicorns every day, he knew Leyla had brought him here hoping that he would decide to stay, that he would be content to put his old life behind him once and for all.

But there was no place for him here. He was a warrior, not a healer. He was a man of action. He would never be content to spend his days in idle contemplation, or in the peaceful pursuit of knowledge simply for the sake of knowledge. He would never be happy to till the soil and watch things grow. He needed to return to Fenduzia and clear his name of the charges against him. He wanted to restore Greyebridge to its former greatness. There were matters at home that needed his attention, people who depended on him for their livelihood.

He glanced at Leyla and saw that she was staring up at him, her luminous blue eyes damp with unshed tears.

"I'm sorry." The words were a whisper, but he had no sooner spoken them than the unicorns took flight.

"How soon does thee wish to leave?" she asked.

"Reading my mind again?"

She nodded. "I wish I had not."

"I can't stay." His hand caressed her cheek, then slid to her nape, his fingers threading through her hair. "I must go back to my own people. I need to find my mother, to seek an audience with Tyrell. I will understand if you want to stay here."

"Stay here? Without thee?" She shook her head. "No, my Lord Jarrett. My place is, and ever shall be, with thee."

Their farewells had been said and now Jarrett and Leyla were riding down the path toward Dragora's cave. Leyla had been subdued since they left the fortress, and he knew she was trying to put up a brave front, but he could see the tears she was trying so hard to hide.

Her sadness tore at his heart. He loved her with every fiber of his being, would do anything to make her happy, yet he couldn't stay in her homeland any longer.

Last night, he had told her he would understand if she decided to stay. Saying the words, waiting for her decision, had taken every ounce of self-control he possessed, yet he could not take her from her home against her will, not if it would cause her sorrow. She hadn't even taken time to consider staying behind. *My place is with thee,* she had said, repeating her earlier words, and that had been the end of the discussion.

Sudaan and Vestri had taken the news of their departure with quiet regret. Sudaan had made sure they had enough supplies to see them across the Cyrus River.

Jarrett absently patted the neck of Keturah's big black stallion. It was a fine animal, with a strong, arched neck, a deep chest, and long powerful legs. Leyla was mounted on Dusault, a sturdy, mountain-bred bay mare. She had not taken the mare when she ran away from home to be with him and he realized that, by taking the horse now, she was symbolically cutting all ties with her people.

Jarrett reined the black aside when they reached Dragora's lair, watching as Leyla spoke the words that would allow them to pass through the dragon's cave.

When they reached the far side, Leyla dismounted. Lifting her skirts in one hand, she walked up to the huge beast, a wistful smile playing over her face as the dragon lowered its huge head.

Jarrett drew a deep breath as Dragora gently nudged her shoulder. The dragon's bright yellow eyes closed as Leyla scratched the hollow beneath its ears.

"Farewell, my old friend," Leyla whispered. "Guard my homeland well."

Dragora snorted softly, a faint puff of white smoke issuing from its blood-red nostrils.

"Farewell," Leyla said again, and then she turned away, hurrying toward her horse. Climbing into the saddle, she urged Dusault down the long path lined with fire-blackened trees and charred skeletons. She never looked back.

That final good-bye affected Jarrett more deeply than anything else.

Chapter Thirty-one

They traveled by night, seeing no one along the way. After crossing the Cyrus River, they made their way to the coast, where Jarrett hired a ship to take them to Aldane.

Soon, he would know if Rorke had spoken the truth, if his mother still lived.

Jarrett and Leyla said but little during the short voyage across the sea. Jarrett was pre-occupied with thoughts of his mother, of seeing his uncle, Morrad, again. He had not seen his father's brother for twelve years. Morrad was a large man, with hair as red as flame and eyes as hard and brown as hickorywood. He ruled his kingdom with a firm but fair hand. And his wife and six sons, as well.

Jarrett led the horses down the gangplank, helped Leyla onto the back of her horse, and then they were riding south, toward Morrad Castle.

Leyla watched the passing countryside with a sense of awe. Aldane was a beautiful land, lush and green, with rolling hills and gentle swales. Great stands of timber grew on the hills; flowers bloomed in bright profusion, there were lakes and streams without number. She saw herds of cattle and long-haired ponies, flocks of gentlesheep and curly-haired goats.

They rode for several hours, pausing now and then to refresh themselves from the stores her father had packed.

It was late afternoon when she spied Morrad Castle looming in the distance. It was a formidable-looking fortress. As they drew nearer, she saw a score of armed men guarding the entrance to the castle. Other men patrolled the catwalks and bastions.

Jarrett reined his horse to a halt and identified himself to the captain of the guard. A runner was dispatched into the keep to see if Morrad would receive visitors.

"Is Aldane at war?" Leyla asked as she glanced around.

"I don't know," Jarrett replied. "But something must be wrong."

A short time later, the runner returned. "You may enter, Jarrett of Gweneth. The High Lord of Aldane awaits you in the West Hall."

"My thanks," Jarrett replied.

The captain of the guard edged his horse beside Jarrett's. "Your sword, my Lord."

"What?"

"I will take your sword. No one is allowed to enter the castle bearing arms."

Jarrett hesitated a moment, then surrendered his sword.

The sound of their horses' hooves clattering over the cobblestones echoed the hammering of Leyla's heart. She had a feeling that something was gravely amiss within the castle, a premonition that death awaited them within its walls.

"Jarrett . . ."

"I know," he said, his gaze meeting hers. "I feel it, too."

There were a dozen armed guards at the entrance to the keep, and guards at each door they passed.

Jarrett pressed his right arm against his side, reassured by the presence of the knife beneath his loose-fitting shirt. A second knife rested securely within his left boot.

The guards stationed at the door of the West Hall came to attention as Jarrett and Leyla approached.

Jarrett hesitated only a moment and then, holding Leyla's hand in his, he crossed the polished hardwood floor toward the dais, his gaze fixed on the man who sat on the elaborately carved wooden throne.

"Rorke."

"Welcome, my Lord Jarrett. I've been expecting you. Your mother will be here shortly."

Jarrett's hand tightened on Leyla's. "Where's my uncle?"

Rorke uttered a low sound of distress. "No longer with us, I'm afraid."

"And his men?"

"Those who refused to swear allegiance to the crown were executed. The rest now wear my colors."

"I see." Jarrett glared at Rorke. The man spoke of killing so easily. "Is Darrla here with you?"

"Not yet."

"And Tyrell?"

"He has returned to Heth." A cold smile twisted Rorke's lips. "He is in poor health. I'm afraid he will not see another winter."

Jarrett grunted softly. It all made sense now. Rorke had gone to Cornith, intending to dispose of the king, but after learning that Tyrell was ill, he had decided to wait. Why take a risk, however slight, of being caught trying to poison the king, when he was already dying? In a few short months, Darrla would take the throne, and Rorke would be her consort, for as long as she lived. Knowing Rorke, it would not be long, and then his oldest son, Jerrian, would become king, and Rorke would at last have the power he craved. There was just one thing he didn't understand.

"Why did you make war on Aldane?"

"I did not. Morrad attacked the Fenduzian coast in the dead of winter. I was sent to meet his forces. He was killed in battle. His wife and sons fled."

"Jeri!"

He turned at the sound of his mother's

voice, opened his arms to embrace her as she flew at him. He choked back tears of relief as he held her close. He had not thought to see her again.

When he could let her go, Sherriza embraced Leyla. "My dear, you look well." Sherriza held Leyla at arm's length, her gaze running over her daughter-in-law's swollen belly. "When is the child due?"

"In late summer."

"This reunion is very touching, to be sure," Rorke said in a bored tone. "Could you, perhaps, save it for later?"

"What are your plans now?" Jarrett asked.

"The same as before. To have Greyebridge."

"You have Aldane. You'll soon have the throne. Why do you need Greyebridge as well?"

"Because it's yours."

"You'll never have it!" Sherriza exclaimed. "I'll see it torn down, stone by stone, first."

"Spare me your threats, madam."

"I'm surprised you haven't taken Greyebridge by now," Jarrett remarked.

"All in good time," Rorke replied with a wave of his hand.

He looked enormously pleased with himself, Jarrett thought, but then, why shouldn't he? Everything seemed to be going his way.

"Greyebridge isn't going anywhere," Rorke went on, "and neither are you. In any case, I have had other, more urgent matters to take care of."

"What of Leyla and my mother?"

"I believe we discussed that before."

"Let them go."

"I think not. But I will give you my promise that no harm will befall them in exchange for your signed confession stating that you did indeed conspire with Aldane against Tyrell."

Jarrett frowned. "To what end?"

"Can you not guess?"

Jarrett nodded. "I would have thought you'd be content to take my life, Rorke. Would you have my honor, as well?"

"Exactly so."

Jarrett kept his expression impassive, refusing to let Rorke have the satisfaction of seeing how deeply the idea of being thought a traitor disturbed him, and then he shrugged. What difference would a signed confession make? Those who knew him would know it for the lie it was. He didn't care what others thought.

"How soon?"

"On the morrow, I think, just after dawn. There is a deep pool behind the mews that should serve our purpose."

A gasp escaped Leyla's lips as the meaning of Rorke's words washed over her, and then she slid to the floor, her face as white as wool.

Jarrett dropped to his knees beside her and gathered her into his arms. "Leyla. Leyla!"

Her eyelids fluttered open. Upon seeing Jarrett, she threw her arms around his neck and held him close. He spoke so calmly of dying. Didn't he know she could not live without him?

Jarrett rose to his feet, cradling Leyla to his chest. "I need a room for my wife."

"Taark will see to her. You and I still have much to discuss."

"I will take her to her room and make sure she is comfortable, and then I will return."

Rorke's fingers caressed the polished arm of the throne for several seconds, then he nodded.

"Very well. Do not be long. Take the first chamber at the top of the stairs."

With a curt nod, Jarrett left the hall. Refusing to think of anything but Leyla's safety and comfort, he carried her up the stairs and into the room Rorke had indicated.

After closing the door, Jarrett stood Leyla on her feet and began to undress her.

She placed her hand over his, forcing him to stop. "Jarrett, what are we going to do?"

"You're going to get into bed, and then I'm going down to talk with Rorke."

"He means to have Greyebridge and the throne."

"Aye." He took her hand from his and continued undressing her until she stood before him in only her shift. His eyes caressed her and then he bent and placed a kiss on her breast, just over her heart.

"Jarrett . . ."

"There is nothing to be said, Leyla." Sweeping her into his arms, he carried her to the bed and drew the covers up to her chin. "Rest now."

"Thee expects me to rest when thy life is in danger?"

"I am safe enough, for now. Please, Leyla, think of the child." *The child I will never live to see.*

"Jarrett, I'm afraid."

"I know."

Her throat tightened with unshed tears as he kissed her, his lips achingly sweet. He placed his hand on her swollen abdomen, gave her a smile that made her heart melt, and left the room.

Four guards waited outside the door. Three had their swords drawn.

The fourth quickly tied Jarrett's hands behind his back, then gave him a shove.

"Lord Rorke's waiting."

Followed by the four men, Jarrett returned to the West Hall.

Rorke had been pacing the floor. At Jarrett's entrance, he resumed his place on the throne.

"You cannot win, Jarrett," he said, waving the guards aside. "You will do as I say, or your mother and your wife will suffer for it."

Jarrett choked back the angry words that rose in his throat, knowing that Rorke was right. There was nothing he could do, not now. "Where is my mother?"

"In one of the rooms belowstairs."

"Your promise, Rorke, I want your promise, sworn on your mother's life, that no harm will come to my mother or Leyla. Or to my child."

Rorke let out a sigh. "Very well."

Jarrett drew a deep breath. "What are your plans for me?"

"Can you not guess?"

Hands tightly clenched, Jarrett nodded once, slowly. Thanks to Tor's mental powers, Rorke knew of Jarrett's deep-seated fear of the Pool. "Until then?"

"The dungeons, of course. I cannot take a chance of your escaping again."

"I want to stay with Leyla until the baby comes."

"No. You will die in the pool tomorrow, as I said. Slowly. Painfully."

Jarrett fought down a rising tide of panic. "I will sign nothing until after the child is born."

It was a weak threat, a last endeavor to buy a little more time. His only hope was that Rorke wanted his confession of guilt badly enough to postpone his death.

Rorke stood up, his hands clenched, his

face mottled with rage.

"I would remind you that you are in no position to dictate terms, my Lord Jarrett. You will do as I say, or I will have your mother beheaded before your eyes, and the child cut from your wife's body!"

"Then do it!"

Rorke took a step back, his eyes mirroring his astonishment. "You doubt me?"

"No."

Dropping to his knees, Jarrett gazed up at Rorke, his eyes blazing with impotent fury, his face burning with humiliation.

"You will soon have everything you desire, everything that I have ever loved. I am begging you to send my mother home, to let me spend my last days with my woman, to see my child. It will cost you nothing. I give you my word as a warrior that I will not try to escape. I will sign whatever papers you wish once the child is born, only let me see my son before I die."

Rorke stared at the man kneeling before him. Never, in all his life, had he expected to find Jarrett of Gweneth groveling at his feet. It was a good feeling. Perhaps he was being over-zealous in his eagerness to see the man dead. It would do no harm to let him live another few months. Indeed, the anticipation of the actual event would only make Jarrett's death that much sweeter.

Rorke grinned. And Jarrett's death would

be that much more bitter, much harder to accept, once Jarrett had seen his child, held it in his arms. Ah, how much more painful to go to his grave knowing he would never see the child again.

"Very well," Rorke agreed, "but I warn you now that should you make any attempt to escape, should you disobey me once, your mother will pay the ultimate price. I will keep her here to ensure your obedience."

"I believe you."

"I hope so. I will allow you four hours a day with your woman. You will be confined to the dungeon the rest of the time."

"You are most generous, my lord."

Rorke summoned Taark with a wave of his hand. "Take my Lord Jarrett to the dungeon. He is to have no visitors. You will see that he is taken to his wife's room for no more than four hours each day. His mother will be given suitable quarters, and she is to be given anything she requires for her comfort. Tomorrow, you will ride to the village and find a midwife."

Rorke sat down, his hands gripping the arms of the throne. Soon, he thought, soon everything he had ever wanted would be his.

Chapter Thirty-two

Jarrett flinched as the heavy iron door closed behind him. He stood there for a long time, absorbing the darkness, inhaling the musty scent of decaying straw, the lingering stink of old sweat and vomit.

He quietly cursed the length of chain that tethered him to the wall, connected to his right ankle by a thick iron cuff. There was no need to chain him, he thought bitterly. He wasn't going anywhere.

His steps measured the length and breadth of his prison, the infernal chain clanking with every movement. His hands slid over the cold stone walls, acquainted themselves with the straw-filled pallet, the slop jar that reeked of old excrement, the small barred panel set into the door that was the cell's only opening.

Standing on tiptoe, he stared into the hallway. It was empty of life, of light. No guards were needed to keep watch within the dungeon, though he had no doubt that there were two stationed outside the entrance.

Four months. He could go quietly mad in less time than that.

Sherriza took Leyla's hand as they made their way toward the dining hall where they were to take the evening meal with Rorke and the captain of the guard.

"Be strong, child," Sherriza urged. "Do not let Rorke frighten you. He will do nothing until he has what he wants."

"And he will have it," Leyla said in despair. "Greyebridge. The throne. There's no way to stop him."

Sherriza's hand tightened on Leyla's. "That's not all he wants, child. He wants you to share the throne with him."

"What?" Leyla stared at her mother-in-law. "Who has told you such a thing?"

"I had it from Rorke's own lips only this morning. He has always been jealous of Jeri, and he will not be content until he has all that Jeri possesses."

"But . . . but Rorke has a wife," Leyla exclaimed. "The king's sister!"

"Men have killed to obtain thrones before. Mothers, fathers, siblings, all have been slain by ambitious men."

"No." Leyla shook her head. "No."

"Listen to me, child. You must do nothing, nothing, to make Rorke angry. Do you understand? Jeri's life hangs in the balance."

"What difference does it make if Rorke is angry? He is planning to send thee back to Heth, to kill my husband, and thee worries that I might make him angry!"

"We have time, Leyla. We have the time until your child is born to find a way to thwart Rorke's plans. You must be strong, stronger than you've ever been before."

"I don't understand."

"Rorke has agreed to let Jarrett live until your child is born."

"Truly?"

"Truly. If you are agreeable, if you flatter Rorke, we might persuade him to make Jarrett's stay in the dungeon more comfortable." Sherriza drew Leyla closer. "All is not lost. There are some within the castle who have sworn allegiance to Rorke, but who are still loyal to Jeri because he is Morrad's nephew," she whispered. "If we are patient, a way may be found to send word to Tyrell."

"I understand. I will do whatever thee thinks best."

"Good."

Hand in hand, the two women entered the dining hall, both determined to do whatever was necessary to help Jarrett.

Leyla looked up in surprise as Jarrett entered her chamber. "My Lord . . ."

He crossed the room swiftly and drew her into his arms. Closing his eyes, he held her close, inhaling the warm sweet fragrance of her hair and skin. His lips drifted over her bared shoulder, savoring her soft flesh.

"Leyla." His hands slid over her arms, caressed her breasts, then rested on her expanded girth. He smiled as he felt his child's kick. "Are you well?"

"Yes. And thee?"

"Fine, now."

He drew her down on the bed and buried his face in the hollow of her neck. Her hair was like finely spun silk in his hands. With a low groan, he covered her mouth with his, taking nourishment from her lips as though he were a man starved for food and she was a banquet meant only for him.

He murmured her name again and again as he held her and caressed her. Her nearness banished his fears, the sound of her voice overshadowed the memory of the long night he'd spent in the dungeon.

Leyla cradled him in her arms, assuring him that she loved him, that all was well with the child, that somehow they would find their way back to Greyebridge. Knowing that he needed to be a part of her, she slowly undressed him, raining kisses on his chest and belly, watching as his eyes grew cloudy with passion.

Rising from the bed, she slipped out of her gown and let it fall to the floor at her feet.

His breath caught in his throat as he gazed at her bared flesh. Her skin was the color of fresh cream. Her breasts were full, her belly distended with his child. She had never looked more beautiful. Or more desirable.

She stood there a moment, basking in the love that was reflected in the depths of his eyes and then, opening her arms to him, she joined him on the bed.

When he would have pressed her to the mattress, she shook her head and then, slowly and tenderly, she began to caress him, telling him with each kiss, each touch, that she loved him beyond words. She took satisfaction in knowing that she could arouse him, and as she fanned the embers of his passion, her own desire blossomed, until she was trembling with need.

"Now, my lord Jarrett," she urged, lifting her hips to receive him.

And in the warmth of her arms he found the strength he was looking for.

Their days fell into a routine as the weeks went by. Sherriza and Leyla were given the run of the castle. They took their meals with Rorke, sat with him in the evening. Neither woman made any pretense of liking his company, yet they did not defy him in any way. If asked to sing, Sherriza complied with good grace. If Rorke was in the mood to talk, they talked. If he wished for silence, they acquiesced. When Sherriza remarked that Leyla needed exercise, he agreed to let them walk within the bailey each evening.

Occasionally, Rorke demanded to be alone

with Leyla. At such times, he spoke to her as if they were old friends, telling her of his childhood, of his sons.

He made no attempt to hide his desire for Leyla, or to deny that he intended to seduce her when her child was born. He dressed her in fine gowns of softsilk and velvet, offered her the jewels from Morrad's treasury, adorning her in a sparkling array of precious gemstones set in gold and silver. Though he did not attempt to bed her, he often caressed her with his eyes, the bright heat of his barely controlled passion evident in the depths of his gaze. His hands ofttimes stroked her arms, her shoulders, and each touch was a promise of what was to come.

Leyla found his touch repulsive, but she dared not show it for fear of making Rorke angry. She knew what he was capable of, knew that he would not hesitate to punish her by mistreating Jarrett.

Often, she looked at Rorke and wondered what had twisted him into the man he was now. He should have been well satisfied with his life. He had three daughters and two fine sons, a lovely wife who was sister to the king. He was the second most powerful man in the realm, he had lands and wealth, the king's trust. Yet it was not enough.

The time passed with painful tedium for Jarrett. Confined to his cell, there was little to do but pace or sleep or stare into the darkness, contemplating his fate. His nightmares returned to haunt him, and he often woke shivering in the middle of the night, the sound of his own cries echoing off the stone walls. He lived only for the time he was allowed to spend with Leyla. For those few short hours, he forced all thought of the future aside, wanting nothing to mar their time together.

Like Jarrett, Leyla lived only for those hours when Jarrett was with her. He refused to speak of the past or the future, which troubled her a great deal. When she let herself probe his mind, she encountered only despair, and she feared he had given up all hope.

Once, when she remarked on this, he told her he had given Rorke his word that he would not escape if he were allowed to live until the child was born, and she knew then that he had made such a bargain because of her, to ensure that no harm would befall her during the last months of her pregnancy. He was sacrificing himself for her and for their babe.

"But surely you need not hold to such a promise," Leyla argued. "Rorke has no honor. He has betrayed you in the past. He would do it again."

"My honor as a warrior is all I have left," Jarrett replied quietly. "I gave Rorke my word that I would not try to escape, and I will keep it. All that matters now is our child."

"And what of me? What am I to do without thee?"

"Raise my son."

She wept then, tears flooding her eyes and washing down her cheeks while he held her close.

Jarrett came awake slowly, his nerves taut, his heart pounding as he realized that someone was staring at him through the narrow slit in the door.

"My Lord? My Lord, it is Mettric. I was your uncle's steward."

Jarrett nodded at the man. Mettric was tall and extremely thin, with lank brown hair and pale skin. Only his eyes seemed alive, their gray depths filled with a vibrant glow. "Aye, Mettric, I remember you."

"You are not alone, my Lord. There are those of your uncle's men who await only the chance to take Rorke unaware."

"How many?"

"I am not certain, my Lord, as we dare not meet together often for fear of arousing suspicion. Some of us chose to swear allegiance to Rorke rather than face death. Some of us feel that an allegiance sworn under such circumstances is not binding."

Jarrett grunted softly. Were it not for the fact that Rorke had threatened his mother's life, he would feel the same.

"It is your mother's intention to go to Heth and plead your cause to the King."

Rising to his feet, Jarrett approached the door. "It's madness to try such a thing. If she's caught . . ."

"Indeed, my Lord, but she has left this night. She forbade me to tell you of her plans until they were accomplished." Mettric glanced up and down the dark corridor. "Take heart, my Lord. We may yet see the better side of this."

"My thanks, Mettric. If all goes well, I will see that you are amply rewarded."

"Good sleep, my Lord Jarrett," Mettric said, and then he was gone, blending into the darkness.

Good sleep, Jarrett mused ruefully as he paced the floor. How could he be expected to sleep now? If his mother was caught outside the castle, she'd be killed. If she managed to reach Heth, if she could convince the King that Jarrett was innocent of treason, there might be a chance that all was not lost. And yet . . .

Jarrett swore under his breath, wondering if his mother had stopped to consider that Rorke might put everyone in the castle under the knife and make a run for it if he thought his own life was in danger.

Rorke entered the dungeon early the following morning. Flanked by four armed men, he burst into Jarrett's cell. "Where is she?"

"Who?"

"Your mother." As he spoke, Rorke tapped a heavy riding crop against his left thigh. "She's gone."

"I have not seen her since our arrival," Jarrett replied.

"But you know where she is, don't you?" Without waiting for an answer, Rorke struck Jarrett across the face with the heavy crop. "Has she gone to Heth?"

Jarrett pressed the back of his hand to the gash in his cheek. "I would not tell you if I knew."

"But you do know," Rorke said. He struck Jarrett again, deepening the gash. Blood splattered in the wake of the crop. "And you will tell me. Taark, bring the woman here."

"No!" Jarrett took a step forward, only to come to an abrupt halt as four swords swung in his direction.

"Has she gone to Heth?"

Jarrett clenched his jaw, his mind searching frantically for some way to tell Rorke what he wanted to know without betraying Mettric's trust. He flinched as Rorke struck him again, the crop landing with a sharp crack against the side of his neck.

"I have not seen my mother," Jarrett said again, "but if she has left Aldane, then she would go to Heth."

Rorke stared at Jarrett through narrowed

eyes. Was he speaking the truth? They would soon know.

Jarrett's head lifted at the sound of Leyla's footsteps in the corridor. A moment later, Taark pushed her into the cell.

"Jarrett!" She started toward him, her face paling at the sight of the blood dripping from his cheek, only to be brought up short as Rorke grabbed her by the arm.

"Sherriza has left the castle," he said curtly. "Where has she gone?"

Leyla's eyes widened in horror as Rorke raised his arm and she saw the blood dripping from the end of the crop. Jarrett's blood. "I do not know."

"Do not lie to me."

"Rorke, in the name of heaven, leave her alone!"

"Then tell me what I wish to know."

"I can't tell you what I don't know."

Rorke's gaze moved from Jarrett's face to Leyla's and back again. And then, without warning, he struck Jarrett hard across the face, splitting his lower lip and peeling a bit of skin from his jaw.

Leyla screamed, her stomach churning as Jarrett's blood was spattered across the front of her dress.

"Perhaps you will tell me what I wish to know," Rorke said, his hand tightening on Leyla's arm, "before I destroy his pretty face."

"She went to Heth," Leyla said, the words spilling from her in a rush. "She's gone to seek the King's help."

"When did she leave?"

"Late last night."

"Who helped her?"

"I do not know."

"I think you do, and I will flay the flesh from his face unless you tell me."

"I do not know, truly. No!" She grabbed Rorke's arm as he made to strike Jarrett again.

With an oath, Rorke shook her off and she reeled backward, slamming into the stone wall. She stood there for a moment, her expression stunned, her eyes blank, and then, her arms folded across her stomach, she slid to the floor.

"Leyla!" Ignoring the swords that threatened him, Jarrett ran to her side. He lifted her into his arms, his hand smoothing the hair from her face. "Leyla."

She groaned as she opened her eyes. "The baby . . ."

Jarrett lifted his gaze to Rorke's face. "Let me take her to her room."

"Not until you tell me all you know."

"I've nothing to tell. By Hadra, Rorke, I've been locked up. Do you think my mother's been visiting me at night? Do you think I've been coming and going at will?"

He cast a frantic look at Leyla, who was

groaning softly. "For the love of heaven, Rorke, let me take her out of here. Even if my mother has left for Heth, even if she manages to convince Tyrell of my innocence, she cannot get there and back for at least a fortnight. You have nothing to fear before then."

Rorke stared at Jarrett for a long moment, his mind working furiously. He had hoped to remain at Aldane until Tyrell died. It would have been an easy thing then, to return to Heth, dispose of his wife, and take the throne. But Sherriza's escape made that impossible. He had to assume that the King would listen to what she said, that he might even believe her.

Rorke tapped his finger on the hilt of his sword as he considered his choices. Castle Aldane was virtually invincible. He could stay and make a fight of it, or he could march his men to Heth. If he timed it right, he could arrive in Heth while the King's forces were en route to Aldane. With most of the King's men gone, he could easily overthrow the castle, dispatch Tyrell and Darrla, and assume the throne.

"Take the woman to her chamber." Rorke's cold black eyes settled on Jarrett as he spoke to one of the guards. "Find a girl to sit with her until the babe is born."

Jarrett's throat grew tight as he watched two of the men carry Leyla from the cell. "Rorke, you gave me your word."

"And you gave me yours."

"I've told you all I know."

"Perhaps." Rorke turned on his heel and went to the door, followed by the remaining two guards. "No one is to enter this cell again, Porrter. The prisoner is to be denied food and water. Is that understood?"

"Yes, Milord."

"Summon Taark to the West Hall."

"Rorke!" Jarrett's angry voice filled the cell. "Rorke!"

He lunged forward, rushing toward the doorway, but the chain brought him up short, and then Porrter shut the door, plunging him into darkness and despair.

He lost track of the time as he paced the cell, the chain around his ankle clanking with each step. How long did it take for babies to be born? He cursed Rorke with all the fury in his soul, damning the man for his treachery, silently berating his mother for her foolhardy plan to help him. By leaving Aldane, she had only made things worse.

Driven to near madness with worry for Leyla, he lashed out at the walls that imprisoned him, driving his fists against the cold stone until his knuckles were swollen and bloody.

And then, because he had nowhere else to turn, he dropped to his knees, buried his face in his hands, and prayed to the All Father for a miracle.

Chapter Thirty-three

Leyla writhed on the bed, gasping as her body sought to expel the child. She tried to ignore the pain, tried to remind herself that it was Jarrett's babe, but the cause of the pain was no longer important and she clung to the sheet the kitchen maid had tied to the foot of the bed, weeping softly.

She was vaguely aware that Rorke came into the room on occasion, impatiently questioning the girl, asking if something couldn't be done to make the child come more quickly.

And then, when she thought the baby would never be born, the girl urged her to push hard. Feeling as if she were being torn apart, Leyla did as she was told. Moments later, the girl placed the baby in her arms.

" 'Tis a boy, Milady," the girl said.

"Is he all right?"

"Perfect. See for yourself. He has all his fingers and toes in the right place."

With great care, Leyla examined her son, all her pain forgotten as she marveled at the beauty of the infant in her arms. He had a mop of black hair, dark blue eyes, and a dimple in his chin. She felt a sweet pain in her breasts when he began to nurse, a dull ache in her heart as she thought of Jarrett, shut up in the dungeons below.

She begged Rorke to let Jarrett come to her, but he refused, advising her to get some sleep as they were leaving in the morning.

"Leaving?"

"For Heth. Sherriza has put the throne within my grasp."

"I don't understand."

"No reason why you should. Be ready in the morning."

Chapter Thirty-four

Time had lost all meaning. He slept. He woke. He paced the dark cell, haunted by fears worse than any nightmare he'd ever known. Hunger gnawed at his belly, thirst plagued him constantly. He prayed until his knees ached and his voice was raw.

Leyla. Please let her be all right. Please let the child be well. Leyla . . . Leyla . . .

He sat up with a start, his head turning toward the door. Had he heard something, or was it only his imagination playing tricks on him again? How many times had he thought he'd heard someone in the corridor only to have it turn out to be nothing?

Fear rose in his throat, making his heart pound like thunder as he saw a flicker of light. Had Rorke come to finish him off at last?

He stood up, his back to the wall, his gaze fixed on the light.

"My Lord?"

He tensed at the sound of a key in the lock, and then the door swung open and Mettric stood there.

"My Lord?"

For a moment, Jarrett could only stare at him. He swallowed hard, then licked his lips. "Leyla?"

"She is well, my Lord." Kneeling, Mettric unlocked the shackle on Jarrett's ankle.

"Where is she?" Jarrett demanded. "What of the child?"

"Rorke has left for Heth. He has taken them with him."

"When did they leave?"

"Early yesterday morning. I would have come to you sooner, but Rorke left several of his men behind to keep an eye on the castle. It took time to subdue them all."

Jarrett swayed on his feet. Leyla was alive and well. A silent prayer of thanks rose in his heart as he followed Mettric out of the dungeon.

"I have food and wine waiting, my Lord," Mettric said. His eyes betrayed his concern as he urged Jarrett to sit down. "I will warm water for your bath while you eat."

"There's no time for that. Saddle my horse."

"Nay, my Lord. You will be no use to your woman and child unless you eat and get some rest. We will catch Rorke, my Lord, have no fear."

Jarrett nodded. The man was right. He needed food and rest, and a bath after months in the dungeon would be a kindness to any who came near him.

Twenty minutes later, he was submerged in a tub of hot water. He scrubbed away the filth on his body, washed his hair twice, and slipped into the robe Mettric had left him.

He glanced around the room, recognizing it as the one Leyla had occupied. Sitting on the bed, he lifted a handful of the spread and pressed his face against it. Her scent filled his nostrils, and he stretched out on the bed, his face buried in her pillow. Thinking to rest for just a few moments, he closed his eyes. Leyla and the child were well. Belatedly, he realized that he had neglected to ask if he had a son or a daughter. . . .

The air had turned cold when he woke. A glance out the window told him the sun was setting. He'd been asleep for six hours.

Swinging his legs over the edge of the bed, he dressed in the clothes Mettric had left for him. Rorke's clothes, he thought bitterly.

Mettric was waiting for him downstairs. "A ship awaits us, Milord. My grandson has gone ahead to procure horses." He handed Jarrett a sword and a longboar knife.

"You've done well, Mettric." Jarrett buckled the sword at his waist, then slid the knife into his boot. "I won't forget it."

Mettric nodded, embarrassed by Jarrett's praise. "We waste time, Milord."

"Aye," Jarrett agreed. "Let us go."

Jarrett stood in the bow of the ship, his heart keeping time with the pull of the oars.

Hurry. Hurry. Hurry.

When they reached the shore, Mettric's grandson awaited them.

They rode hard all that night, not resting until dawn, and then only for a few hours.

Three hours later, they were riding again. It was mid-day when they came to a fork in the road. Jarrett reined his horse to a halt, his expression thoughtful. The road to the left was shorter; no doubt it would be the route taken by Tyrell's men. Would Rorke choose to meet the King's men in battle, or would he choose the long way around in order to avoid a confrontation?

"Mettric, take the long road in case the King's men come that way. If you see them, tell them to return to Heth immediately."

"Aye, Milord. Good speed."

"And to you also."

Jarrett pushed his horse hard until dusk, then allowed the horse an hour to graze and rest before swinging into the saddle again.

An hour after sunset, he came upon the King's men. Identifying himself, he asked to be taken to the commander.

"Commander Haarkness," the sentry said, entering the commander's tent. "This man claims to be Jarrett of Gweneth."

"And so he is."

Haarkness was a man well into middle age. Tall and broad-shouldered, he possessed the air of authority that came only with long years of experience. His hair and eyes were brown, his beard grizzled.

"I am surprised to see you here, my Lord," Haarkness mused. "We were told you were being held prisoner in Aldane."

"I was, but I've no time to explain now. I need your help. Rorke is riding for Heth. He plans to dispose of the King and assume the throne."

Haarkness waved his hand in a gesture of dismissal. "Nonsense."

"You must believe me," Jarrett said urgently. "The King's life is in danger. There is no time to waste."

"Rorke is the King's brother-in-law. What reason would he have to usurp the throne? It will be his by right of marriage. And soon, from what I hear of the King's health."

"He will not be content to be the queen's consort," Jarrett retorted impatiently. "He wants the throne for himself."

Haarkness shook his head doubtfully.

Jarrett swore under his breath. "What orders were you given?" Jarrett asked.

"I was directed to remove Rorke from Castle Aldane, forcibly if need be, and return you both to Heth as quickly as possible. There was no mention of a threat to his majesty."

Jarrett took a wary step backward, his sword still drawn. "Perhaps the King isn't sure whom he can trust."

Haarkness drew himself up to his full

height. "I have served his Majesty for twenty years," he replied indignantly.

"But there may be traitors elsewhere who would ride ahead to warn Rorke of danger."

Haarkness nodded. "I believe you, my Lord Jarrett. Brunnel, tell the men to prepare to ride for Heth."

"I'm going to ride ahead," Jarrett said. "I want to be there should Rorke arrive before you."

Moments later, he was riding out of the encampment, headed south, toward Heth.

It was near dusk the following day when he reached the palace. No sooner had he crossed the moat than a half-dozen armed men surrounded him, quickly relieving him of his weapons.

"I must see Tyrell," Jarrett said, wincing as his arms were jerked behind his back and lashed together.

"And he wishes to see you," one of the men replied ominously.

Flanked by four men, Jarrett was ushered into the Great Hall to await the King's pleasure.

He glanced around the hall, recalling the last time he'd been there, the night Tor and Leyla had helped him escape from Rorke. A mural recounting the victories of the ruling monarchy of Heth adorned all four walls. Narrow stained-glass windows overlooked the courtyard. Two intricately carved thrones made of white oak stood on a raised dais at the far end of the room. Long trestle tables were situated on each side of the room. A hundred candles burned in sconces along the walls. The stone floor was covered with a mat of tightly woven reeds, and over this, at varying intervals, were laid brightly colored carpets.

Jarrett stood there for perhaps twenty minutes before the King entered the Hall, followed by several of his retainers.

Watching Tyrell take his seat on the throne, Jarrett knew the rumors of the man's ill health were well-founded. Tyrell's skin was the color of old parchment, his cheeks were hollow, his brown eyes, once shrewd and bright, were sunk deep in their sockets. Though the room was warm, he wore a heavy, fur-lined purple cloak trimmed in sable around his frail shoulders, and thick fur-lined boots covered his feet.

Darrla entered the hall behind the king and sat down on the throne beside him. She studied Jarrett, her face impassive, as she waited for her brother to speak.

A shove from behind sent Jarrett to his knees. He knew he should bow his head, that he should humble himself before Tyrell, beg for his forgiveness and understanding, but he couldn't do it. He had always been loyal to the crown, and to Fenduzia. He had nothing to hide, no reason to grovel. Head high, he met the King's probing gaze.

Tyrell stared at Jarrett for several minutes. When he spoke, his voice was a harsh rasp that told of constant pain.

"I would have the truth from your own lips," the King declared.

"I am no traitor, sire. That is the truth."

"What of the spies found in Greyebridge Chapel?"

"There were no spies, only a handful of frightened women and children who had escaped the battlefield and taken refuge in my church."

The King leaned forward, his eyes as hard and bright as moonstone.

"Rorke has a confession, signed by an Aldanite woman, saying that you incited the rebels, that it was your intent to usurp the throne."

"I know of no such confession, but I know Rorke. He would not hesitate to blackmail the woman."

Tyrell sat back in his chair. "Your lies fall easily from your tongue. Perhaps I should have it cut out."

"Your majesty, I have never betrayed you. It is Rorke you have to fear, not I. He wants the throne, and he means to have it." Jarrett's gaze met Darrla's for the first time. "He intends to rule alone, madam, through your son, Jerrain."

Darrla shook her head. "I don't believe you."

"Ask my mother."

Darrla's shoulders sagged, as though a great weight had been placed upon them. "We have. Your words confirm everything she has said. Is it true you were confined to the Pavilion? That Rorke had the Games reinstated?"

"Aye, madam. I was there for eight months." He shuddered with revulsion as he recalled the endless days and nights spent in a small dark cell.

Jarrett looked at the King. "Rorke has high ambitions, sire. He marches on the castle now. He has my wife and child with him."

"I hear she is quite lovely," Darrla remarked.

Abruptly, her shoulders straightened and her eyes blazed with anger and the deep-seated pride that was ingrained within all those of the royal house.

"She will never sit on my throne," Darrla exclaimed. "Nor will he! Haggar, release Lord Jarrett at once."

"How many men are left here?" Jarrett asked, rubbing his wrists.

"Not enough to fight off Rorke, should he decide to attack the castle."

"Haarkness is on his way back."

Tyrell leaned forward, one bony elbow resting on his knee. "Haarkness? Are you certain of this?"

"I met him on the road. He should be here within a matter of hours."

"And Rorke?"

"I don't know, your majesty. Soon, I would think."

"Haggar, summon the men. Have them prepare for battle. Dispatch two scouts to locate the whereabouts of Rorke and Haarkness. And call my ministers to attend me in my room at once."

"Aye, sire!" With a salute, Haggar hurried from the room to do the King's bidding.

Jarrett bowed as the King rose to his feet.

"We apologize for the wrongs that have been done you, my Lord Jarrett," Tyrell said. "My sister will see to your needs."

"My thanks, sire."

Tyrell nodded, his steps heavy as he left the hall.

"Ryaan, tell Lady Sherriza her son is here."

"Aye, Milady."

"Sit down, my Lord Jarrett," Darrla said. "Frann, bring wine and honey cakes."

A short time later, Sherriza entered the room. "Jeri!" she exclaimed.

Jarrett rose to meet her. Hurrying across the room, Sherriza hugged him close, her eyes bright with tears of joy.

"Where is Leyla?" she asked.

"Rorke has her."

Sherriza sat down. "Is she well?"

"Last I heard." A muscle worked in

Jarrett's jaw as he took a seat beside his mother; his hands clenched and unclenched as he fought to control the anger coursing through him. "By Hadra, I swear Rorke will die an inch at a time if any harm has befallen her."

"Rorke will die an inch at a time at any rate," Darrla remarked, her eyes glittering fiercely. "At your hand, or mine, it matters not."

Jarrett met Darrla's gaze and nodded. He had seen that look of ferocious intent before, seen it in the eyes of warriors on the battlefield, in the faces of contestants in the arenas where he had fought for Keturah, but never in the eyes of a woman.

"Tell me of the Pavilion, my Lord Jarrett."

"I would rather not speak of it, madam."

"I cannot believe the Games were being played all this time, and we did not know of it."

" 'Tis true, nevertheless. All those who tried to stand in Rorke's way were sent to the Pavilion. When there was talk of war with Aldane, all the prisoners were executed."

Darrla sat forward on the throne. "Yet you remain."

"I was being saved for one last Game in the arena. With the help of my wife, I escaped."

"Why did you not come here? Surely you knew you would be heard."

"Rorke was here. I dared not risk it while

the King was away."

Darrla nodded. "My brother and I owe you a great deal, my Lord Jarrett."

"I want nothing, madam, save the return of Greyebridge lands that were forfeit to the crown, and the right to return to Gweneth."

Darrla bowed her head in a gesture of assent. "Consider it done."

"My heartfelt thanks, madam."

Rising from her throne, Darrla crossed the room. Pausing at one of the narrow windows, she gazed, unseeing, into the distance. She stood there for a long moment, unmoving as a statue.

Jarrett watched her, sympathy for Darrla rising within him. She was a proud woman, the King's sister, heir to the throne. She was a beautiful, accomplished woman. She had borne Rorke five children. He could scarce imagine the pain she must have felt upon learning that her husband was plotting against her, that he intended to take the throne and share it with another.

"Is there anything I can do, Milady?" Jarrett asked.

Darrla shook her head, her shoulders squaring, and Jarrett knew that she had put any affection she still felt for her husband out of her heart.

"All we can do now," she said, her voice brittle, "is wait."

Chapter Thirty-five

Jarrett stood at the window of the west tower, gazing down into the courtyard. The watch fires were burning and he could see the king's men patrolling the battlements. Others sat near the flames, warming their hands.

Jarrett stared past the fortress walls. Rorke was out there, marching toward the castle. He would arrive on the morrow, near dawn, Jarrett thought. Would he have Leyla and the babe with him, or had he left them somewhere en route?

Leaving the room, he wandered through the castle. No one else was about at this hour. The men were all outside; the serving girls and maids asleep long since.

He went up the stairs to the King's chamber, surprised that there were no guards outside the door. Apparently Tyrell had ordered everyone, even his personal guards, to man the catwalks.

He was turning away when something — a noise, a feeling, prompted him to enter the room.

Jarrett paused in the doorway, letting his

eyes grow accustomed to the darkness. By the light of the near moon streaming through the window, he could see Darrla, asleep in a big leather chair beside her brother's bed.

Finding nothing out of place, he started to back out of the room when, from the corner of his eye, he saw a dark shadow glide across the wall.

Jarrett whirled to the left, felt a rush of cool air whisper past his ear as the edge of a blade hissed past his head.

Instinctively, he dropped to the floor and rolled to the left, drawing his sword as he regained his feet.

"Who's there?" Darrla's voice, thick with sleep, cut across the darkness.

"Your husband, madam. Don't move. I'd hate to slit your pretty throat."

"Rorke!" Darrla exclaimed, her voice sharp. "How did you get in here?"

"You forget, madam, I am the Minister of War. I know every tunnel, escape route, and trap door within the castle."

"Rorke?" The King's voice came like an echo as he lit the candles at his bedside. "Put away your sword."

Rorke shook his head. He stood behind Darrla, his hand steady as he held the edge of his sword to Darrla's throat. But it was Jarrett who held his gaze. "Drop your weapon, traitor, or I will indeed slit her throat."

"Do it," Jarrett said dispassionately. "You

can kill her, here and now. You can kill the King, as well. But in the end you will still have to face me."

"Damne! I should have let them kill you long ago."

"Where's Leyla?"

"Safe enough, for now, but her life will surely be forfeit should I fail to return to my men."

"I don't believe you."

Rorke shrugged. "Believe what you will. Perhaps we can make a deal."

"No more deals, Rorke."

"Then die!"

Without warning, Rorke lunged forward, his blade driving toward Jarrett's chest.

Jarrett's blade swung up to parry the blow, and the fight was on.

Darrla scurried across the room to sit beside her brother, her heart pounding as she watched the two swordsmen. This was no ritual fight of honor, but a battle to the death.

"I will yet have all that I desire," Rorke vowed, his sword slicing through the air. "You will not stop me."

Jarrett paid no heed to Rorke's boast. Instead, he focused all his energy, all his attention, on his opponent, knowing that the slightest miscalculation, the merest distraction, would cost him his life.

Darrla shivered as the clang of steel

meeting steel echoed off the room's high stone walls. She bit down on her lower lip as Jarrett drew first blood, gasped as Rorke opened a nasty gash in Jarrett's shoulder.

Though only a few minutes had passed, it seemed as if the fight had gone on forever. Both blades were stained with blood now, both men were breathing hard as they maneuvered around the room, each one seeking an advantage. Their faces, set in hard, determined lines, were sheened with sweat and splattered with drops of blood, giving them both an eerie, demonic look. Rorke's eyes were filled with hatred; Jarrett's with savage intensity.

A cry of rage erupted from Rorke's throat as Jarrett's sword slashed across his chest, opening a long, shallow gash. He could feel himself weakening, feel the strength ebbing from his legs. A torrent of curses poured from his lips as Jarrett drove him backward. He was on the defense now, fighting for his very life.

He had to win. If he lost now, he would have nothing left. At best, he would be stripped of his holdings and exiled from the kingdom. At worst, he would be branded a traitor and publicly executed.

Knowing he could not win, Rorke grabbed one of the thick yellow candles from the bedside table and hurled it in Jarrett's face. At the same time, he lunged forward, his sword driving deep into Jarrett's chest.

With a triumphant cry, Rorke jerked the blade free.

The king uttered a soft oath.

Darrla screamed, her hand at her throat, as a bright crimson stain spread across Jarrett's shirt.

Jarrett staggered backward, then slowly sank to his knees.

As from far away, he heard Darrla's horrified cry.

Through a thick red haze, he saw Rorke turn and walk toward the bed, his sword raised.

Summoning the last of his strength, Jarrett gained his feet, swaying slightly. "Rorke!"

Rorke turned around, his eyes mirroring his disbelief as Jarrett's sword plunged into his heart.

For a moment, the two men stood facing each other and then, as if pulled by the same string, they both fell to the floor.

Darrla scrambled off the bed and ran across the room. Throwing open the door, she started to scream for help, but the words died in her throat.

Help was on the way. The castle was ablaze with light. A half-dozen men, led by Commander Haarkness, were running up the staircase, their swords drawn and ready. She could hear the sound of excited voices coming from below.

"It's all over, Milady," the commander declared, bowing. "We overtook Rorke's men and put them to flight."

"Jarrett! Where's Jarrett?" Pushing her way through the throng, Leyla hurried up the staircase, her face pale as she clutched her child to her breast.

A moment later, Sherriza stepped into the corridor. "What is it? What has happened?"

"There's no time to explain," Darrla replied, struggling to keep her voice calm. "Sherriza, take the child. Leyla, come with me."

"What has happened?" Leyla asked anxiously. "Where is Jarrett?"

"You haven't much time. I fear he may be dying."

"Dying!" Leyla shook her head. "No!" She thrust the baby into Sherriza's arms and followed Darrla into the King's chamber.

Tyrell was kneeling beside Jarrett, his expression somber as he covered the fallen warrior with a blanket.

"Jarrett!" Leyla rushed to her husband's side and took his hand in hers. "Jarrett, don't die," she sobbed, her voice filled with anguish. "Please don't die."

Jarrett's eyelids fluttered open at the sound of her voice. "Leyla?"

"I am here."

"What of . . . Rorke?"

Leyla glanced across the room to where

430

Rorke lay in a pool of blood. "He's dead."

"The . . . baby?"

"Thee has a son. I pray thee, do not leave us."

"Love . . . you."

Leyla nodded, hardly able to see his face through the tears that welled in her eyes. His voice was faint, his face as pale as death, and even as she watched, a sigh escaped his lips and the life went out of his eyes.

"No!" She threw herself across his body, her shoulders heaving with the force of her sobs. "No, please, no, no, no . . ."

Darkness, and then a light, brighter than the sun, and he was walking toward it. In the distance, he could see a tall figure clothed in a long white robe moving toward him, and he knew it was his father, long dead.

From far away he could hear a familiar voice sobbing, "No . . . no . . . no."

He paused and looked over his shoulder. His body was lying on the floor, and she was touching him, pressing her hands to his chest.

He felt a sudden heat flood his being, the touch of her hands upon his flesh, warm, loving hands that belonged to the voice that was calling him back, begging him not to go.

He looked back at his father. Shammah was smiling at him, one hand extended in welcome.

Jarrett hesitated, knowing that all he had to

do was step forward and take his father's hand and all earthly cares and sorrows would be forever behind him.

But her voice was calling his name, begging him not to go, whispering that she loved him, could not live without him. He felt the heat of her hands grow stronger, heard the anguish in her voice.

We need you. Please come back to me . . . to us. . . .

His eyelids fluttered open and he saw Leyla hovering over him, her face streaked with tears. Her hands were spread across his chest, and he felt again that sweet, all-encompassing warmth that had healed his body's wounds so many times in the past.

"Beloved?"

She lifted her gaze to his face and he watched as disbelief and joy played over her features, drying her tears, bringing a radiant smile to her lips.

"Jarrett! Oh, Jarrett."

He glanced past Leyla to see Tyrell, Darrla, and Sherriza gathered around him. His mother, too, had been weeping.

"Jarrett, I thought I had lost thee."

"Your touch brought me back."

"It could not. My power is gone."

He glanced down at his blood-stained shirt. There was no wound beneath the torn cloth, not even a scratch.

His gaze moved up to her face again.

"Then how do you explain this?"

Leyla shook her head. "I cannot."

He smiled at her as he sat up, his hand caressing the curve of her cheek.

"It was your love that brought me back. I heard your voice, felt your touch, and knew I could not leave you. Perhaps it was the power of your love that always healed me."

He gazed deep into her eyes, basking in the love he saw reflected there. "Perhaps love is the only true magic."

A soft cooing caught Jarrett's attention, and for the first time he noticed the small, blanket-wrapped bundle cradled in his mother's arms.

"My son?" he asked.

Sherriza smiled through her tears as she knelt and placed the baby in Jarrett's arms, then motioned for the others to leave the room.

Rising, Sherriza followed the others out of the room. She paused in the hallway and looked back, her heart welling with thankfulness and love as she watched Leyla and Jarrett exchange adoring glances over the head of her grandson. Then, with a smile, she closed the door.

Leyla stared at her husband as he gazed at their son's face, then examined his tiny fingers and toes, the soft down of his hair.

Seeing them together for the first time filled her heart with such tenderness that it was almost painful. It had been worth every moment of suffering to see the look of awe in Jarrett's eyes as he gazed at his child. The lad would grow up to be like his father, brave and strong and honest of heart. It had all been worth it, she mused — the months in the Pavilion, the loss of her gift, everything.

"Thee can go home now, my Lord Jarrett," Leyla murmured. "There is none to stop thee."

He looked up at her then, his beautiful green eyes so full of love it brought tears to her eyes.

"You are my home, beloved," he said, and drawing her to his side, he kissed her.

In the Mountains of the Blue Mist, or on the Isle of Gweneth, in the bowels of the Pavilion or the palace at Heth, time and place mattered not at all. What mattered most was that she was there beside him, that she would always be there beside him.

Epilogue

Jarrett stood on the balcony outside his bedroom at Greyebridge. Five years had passed since Rorke's death. Much had changed in that time.

Jarrett's lands and titles had been reinstated and Greyebridge Castle had been restored to its former state. The cottages on the hillsides rang with happy laughter once more. Black and white gentlesheep and fat brown cattle grazed on the thick, yellow-green grass.

Six months after Rorke's death, the King had passed away peacefully in his sleep, and Darrla had assumed the throne. Her first act as Queen had been to burn the Pavilion to the ground. In its place, she had erected a church with brilliant stained-glass windows and tall granite spires that reached like praying hands toward heaven.

Jarrett had journeyed to Heth to watch the destruction of the Pavilion, the sight of the flames burning the last of the bitterness from his heart.

Leyla had borne him three children — a son and two daughters. Father Lamaan had come to Greyebridge to bless their children, and he journeyed to the castle each Holy Day to preside at services in the chapel. Leyla's parents came to visit once each year, in the spring, bringing gifts for their grandchildren.

Fenduzia now ruled Aldane. When Darrla's son, Jerrain, came of age, he would ascend to the Aldanite throne. Until that time, Commander Haarkness ruled as High Lord of Aldane.

Jarrett gazed into the garden below the balcony, a smile on his face as he watched his three-year-old daughter, Dorrinda, pluck the petals from a midnight flower. Sherriza, sitting on a low stone bench in the shade of a yew tree, was telling a story to young Jarrett, who was now five years old, while Leyla held their infant daughter, Varrinia, to her breast.

To Leyla's delight, their two oldest children were already showing signs that they were gifted with the power of sight. It appeared that their son would possess the gift of healing, as well. Already, Leyla was teaching young Jarrett and Dorrinda the customs and beliefs of the Maje, pleased beyond words that her birthright would continue through their children.

She had high hopes that their youngest child would also be blessed with the gifts of the Maje.

To Jarrett's chagrin, his son also possessed

the ability to read his mind. He was proud of his children's gifts, happy, for Leyla's sake, that the blood of the Maje ran strong in their veins, though there were times when he wasn't sure it was such a blessing, having a son who knew what he was thinking. Slowly, though, Jarrett was learning how to shield his thoughts, how to erect mental barriers the boy couldn't breach.

Now, watching as his family walked down the narrow, flower-lined path that led into the castle, Jarrett was filled with a deep and abiding sense of peace.

The horrors of the Pavilion had faded. The nightmares that had once haunted his dreams troubled him no more, kept at bay by the love of a silver-haired woman whose gentle hands and warm smile had the power to banish all his ghosts. All he had ever wanted, all he would ever want, lived here, within the high gray stone walls of Greyebridge Castle.

He heard the sound of his daughter's voice in the hallway, begging Leyla to tell her the story of the goddess Judeau. He heard Leyla's gentle reply as she told Dorrinda to go along with her grandmother, promising to tell the story another time, and then Leyla entered their bedroom.

She had grown more lovely with the passing of each year, Jarrett thought. The blue of her gown deepened the color of her eyes. Her hair fell over her shoulders in waves of silver, shimmering like moonlight on a starlit sea.

"So, I have found thee at last," she said, closing the door behind her. "What is thee doing in here, all alone?"

His heart quickened at the sound of her voice. "Alone no longer." He glanced at the closed door, one black brow lifting in question.

"I was missing thee," she explained, moving into his arms. "Thy mother and Tannya have taken the children to the nursery." Her cheeks pinkened. "They promised to keep them entertained for an hour or two."

"I see." His palms slid down her arms, his thumbs lightly stroking the curve of her breasts before his hands settled around her waist. "Was there something you wanted?"

"Indeed." She tilted her head back, the better to see his face. "Varrinia Sudaan is near three months old."

Jarrett nodded. He was well aware of his daughter's age. The birth had not been easy on Leyla. The long weeks of abstinence had been difficult for them both.

"I thought . . ." Her flush deepened, and Jarrett grinned. Her shyness charmed him, the eager light in her eyes sparked his desire.

"Thought what?" he asked, feigning ignorance.

He was teasing her! With studied nonchalance, she moved toward the door. "Nothing. I've changed my mind."

A low growl erupted in Jarrett's throat. Heat flared in his eyes and his hands tightened on her waist as he drew her up against him, pressing her length to his so that she could feel the sudden pulsing need that pounded through him.

"It has been a long three months," he declared, his voice husky with desire. "But I would wait another three months rather than hurt you. Are you sure it's safe?"

She gazed deep into his eyes, her expression one of love and longing. "Quite sure, my Lord Jarrett."

"Leyla."

She felt her breath catch in her throat as he lowered his head, blocking everything from her sight, her mind, save the face of the man she loved above all else.

She kept her eyes open as he kissed her, wanting to see the fires of desire dance in his beautiful green eyes.

Without taking his lips from hers, Jarrett whispered her name, and then he was kissing her again, his tongue like molten flame as it found her own. Her legs seemed suddenly weak, and she clung to his broad shoulders as desire unfolded within her, layer upon layer, like the petals of a midnight flower opening to receive the kiss of the moon.

His hands were urgent as he undressed her,

his eyes like burning emeralds as his gaze swept over her. She tugged at his clothing, hungry for the touch of his flesh against her own, and then he was carrying her to the huge canopied bed, pressing her down upon the soft feather mattress.

And all the while he murmured her name, telling her that he loved her more than his next breath, and she knew she would ask no more of life than to live and die in his arms. He was everything to her: fierce warrior, loving father to her children, loyal protector. Husband.

His hands and lips caressed her until her world was filled with his touch, his scent, his magic. Loved and beloved, for this moment in time there was nothing in the world but the two of them, linked heart to heart and soul to soul.

Later, as he kissed her cheek and held her close, Leyla realized how blessed she had been that day when two strangers kidnapped her and carried her beyond the Mountains of the Blue Mist into a filthy dungeon to heal a proud Gweneth warrior with hair as dark as liquid ebony and eyes the color of new grass.

"My Lord Pirate," she murmured, a smile of utter contentment curving her lips. "My Lord Jarrett."

Lying there, with Leyla cradled in his arms, Jarrett listened to the sounds of happy laughter echoing from the nursery. In time, his son would rule Greyebridge, and his son's sons.

Bestowing a kiss on Leyla's cheek, he prayed that their children would find the same happiness within the sheltering stone walls of Greyebridge Castle that he had found.

Madeline Baker

I never intended to be a published author, so it's always a thrill to see one of my books on the shelf. When I started writing, it was for my own pleasure. Had it not been for a friend, I might still be writing in longhand and storing my manuscripts under the bed!

I've loved Indians forever. I think my first crush was Eddie Little Sky from Disneyland, whom I saw when I was twelve. As I grew older, I developed a deep admiration for Native American customs and beliefs. Crazy Horse and Cochise were my idols, so it seemed natural that my heroes would be warriors who were tall, dark, handsome, courageous, gentle and tender, strong and sexy.

I love when my readers ask if I'm Native American. For me, that's the highest compliment!